F
H86
a

Hubler, Richard G.
The soldier and the
sage.

F
H86
a

Hubler, Richard G.
The soldier and the sage.

Temple Israel

Library

Minneapolis, Minn.

RULES

1. Not more than one book may be drawn at one time on this card (unless special permission is given for more.)

2. Books may be kept two weeks unless otherwise indicated.

3. A fine of three cents a day will be charged on each book which is not returned according to the above rules.

4. Fines will be charged for damage to books or loss of same.

THE SOLDIER
AND THE SAGE

A NOVEL ABOUT AKIBA

OTHER BOOKS BY RICHARD G. HUBLER

Fiction:

I'VE GOT MINE
THE QUIET KINGDOM
THE BRASS GOD
THE CHASE
IN DARKEST CHILDHOOD
THE PASS
MAN IN THE SKY
THE SHATTERING OF THE IMAGE
TRUE LOVE, TRUE LOVE
THE BLUE-AND-GOLD MAN
THE WORLD'S SHORTEST STORIES (editor)
TRIAL & TRIUMPH (with Lester Morrison)
SOUTH OF THE MOON (verse)

Nonfiction:

LOU GEHRIG
I FLEW FOR CHINA (with Royal Leonard)
FLYING LEATHERNECKS (with John DeChant)
SAC: STRATEGIC AIR COMMAND
ST. LOUIS WOMAN (with Helen Traubel)
BIG EIGHT
STRAIGHT UP
WHERE'S THE REST OF ME? (with Ronald Reagan)
THE COLE PORTER STORY
THE CRISTIANIS

THE SOLDIER
AND THE SAGE

A NOVEL
ABOUT AKIBA

BY RICHARD G. HUBLER

CROWN PUBLISHERS, INC., NEW YORK

To Jane

THE SOLDIER
AND THE SAGE

A NOVEL ABOUT AKIBA

CHIEF CHARACTERS

AKIBA BEN JOSEPH, Jewish rabbi
ANNIUS VERUS, Roman centurion
ANTINOÜS, Bithynian youth
CURTIUS SACCUS, Roman centurion
DOMITIAN, Roman emperor
DOMITILLA, wife to Flavius Clemens
ELEAZAR BEN AZARIAH, Jewish rabbi
ELIEZER BEN HYRKANOS, Jewish rabbi
EPICTETUS, Greek philosopher
FICUS, Roman soldier
FLAVIUS CLEMENS, cousin-german to Domitian
FRONTINUS, Roman pro-consul
GAMALIEL BEN SIMEON, Jewish rabbi
GLAUCUS, Greek slave
HADRIAN, Roman emperor
HARPOCRAS, Greek-Egyptian physician
JOSEPHUS BEN MATTHIAS (JOSEPHUS FLAVIUS)
  Jewish historian
JOSHUA BEN HANANYA, Jewish rabbi
JULIUS SEVERUS, Roman general
LUCIUS NORBANUS, Roman general
LUSIUS QUIETUS, Moorish general
MARCELLUS, Roman governor
PAPPIAS, Jewish rabbi
PONTUS, Syrian slave
RACHEL, wife to Akiba
SARRA, Jewish girl
SEXTUS RUFUS TENEIUS, Roman tribune
SIMEON BAR COCHEBA, Jewish revolutionary
STEPHANUS, British slave
TRAJAN, Roman emperor

CHAPTER 1

I remember clearly that night forty years ago. It was just before the nones of the month which marked the vanity of the divine Augustus who stole a day from the second month, so that his share of the year might match that of his uncle, the equally divine Julius. It was the year which marked the eight hundred and forty-sixth anniversary of the founding of Rome.

On that night the mistress city of the world slept a perfumed sleep upon her seven bosoms of earth. Not a breath stirred the white pennons of the city guard stations, an extraordinary omen in this region of moving airs from the sea. In the towers of the wall, the torches had burned to resinous ash. Even the night lamps in the windows of the palace of Pompeius Atticus had guttered out. To the north, in the Umbrian hills, dry lightning played, filling the sky with ghosts of light.

I had no idea why I had been invited—commanded, if one likes—to come at midnight to the summer villa of Flavius Clemens outside Rome. I did not believe in the demons of the Jews and Christians (as I knew the wife of Flavius, superstitious Domitilla, did) but, if ever they stalked ravening abroad, it would have been at such a time as this, under the hot and motionless night sky with its spattering of stars. The messenger had come to me at the feast of a friend in a mansion near the Capitoline Hill. I had left with wreaths of violets still around my head, to the sound of drunken laughter at my compliance. Jolting out the Via Triumphalis in my litter, I arrived in a wretched temper. I dismissed my slaves to their guest quarters and entered the vestibulum of Flavius.

I was surprised to find no slave ianitor sitting dutifully under his carved motto, NOTHING EVIL MAY ENTER HERE, to cry "Dextro pede," right foot first for a lucky entrance. I pushed past the curtain into the atrium. To my further puz-

3

zlement, it was also dark—only the eternal coals glowing from the small lares altar. But I could see brilliance from beneath the broidered wool of the peristylium drape beyond. I made my way across the inner court, imagining the animals and god-figures wrought in the mosaic of the floor clutching at my sandals as I went.

Here, in the most private part of the villa of Flavius the Consul, lamps burned brightly at the head of a low bronze couch. At one side a censer smoked, sending out reeks of sandalwood that made my head ache. On the bolster, supported by rawhide weavings, lay a form concealed by a sheet of crimson silk.

Behind it stood the slight, emaciated figure of Flavius, with his slate-colored eyes and cadaverous face, dominated by a nose pulled thin enough to slit parchment. He passed a hand lightly over his head, back to front, a familiar gesture. Though he was only twenty-five, the same age as myself within a month, his forward-combed hair was already receding. He believed it an honor somehow connected with the well-known baldness of the Julian clan; he was proud of it.

Flavius had never been sure of himself nor his place in the Roman world. He owed his rank and honors simply to the fact that he was the cousin-german of the emperor Domitian and husband to his niece, Flavia Domitilla, thus bound with a double knot to the purple. But I had no right to be critical. I owed my rank of tribune in the Praetorian Guards and my position of his confidential drinking companion to the fact that we had been youthful friends in the portico of Epictetus and, indeed, to something more secret.

I blinked stupidly to find Flavius alone. He was clad in the robe of his rank of consul, a garment he shared solely with Domitian. Supposedly an office just below that of the emperor himself, it was an empty title yet it pleased his vanity. The broad stripe of purple ran from his neck to the golden hem of his full toga. His formal boots were tightly hook-laced, fastened with their crescent ivory buckles from Africa. I thought instantly, despite the pain of too much wine in my head, that this was a special occasion—but I had no idea of how shocking its purpose was to be.

Flavius raised his right hand in salute to me, I to him. "Tonight," he intoned gravely, "I have sacrificed seven perfect white cocks."

"Excellent," I replied, not knowing what else to say. The pillars of rosy marble cast colored shadows; the flowers shone

4

white around the fountain; the smell of herbs, crushed purposely by slaves at sunset, vied with the sandalwood smoke. I stared hard at the motionless figure under the red silk.

"I held the smoking entrails in my own hands. I was haruspex, I read them myself. I know that I must do what I must do."

I turned my head slightly, inquiring, waiting for him to speak again and enlighten me. Flavius advanced a step. "One of the cocks had a liver with a double lobe," he murmured solemnly, this ass of amateur augur-casters.

"Very good," I said.

"The time has come," he announced, throwing back his head and looking at the square of moonless sky overhead, "that the will of the gods shall be made known."

"Certainly," I assured him, "but can it be truly interpreted by mortals?"

As if in answer, Flavius stooped and seized a corner of the light silk covering. He gave it a jerk. It fluttered from the couch. I shut my teeth in a gasp of dismay.

On the couch, all ivory and rose, lay the magnificent, naked body of his wife, Domitilla.

"You would not sacrifice your own wife?" I asked. Despite myself, my voice shook. I was wholly sobered.

Flavius' lip curled in disgust. "She is necessary to the ceremony," he replied, "as you are necessary for a witness."

"This is shameful," I muttered.

"Nothing is shameful when it is done in obedience to the gods."

His tone struck me like the blow of a fist. At that moment I commenced to have suspicions about the sanity of Flavius. I could say no more but I saw Domitilla's face shift perceptibly. Her tight-closed eyes flickered. Her mouth twisted downward, whether in anger or disgust, I did not know. Her body, broad-hipped and full-breasted, turned slightly on the couch. Against the dull bronze of the headrest, her crown of dark braids shone. I noted the glint of red in her hair and guessed she had enhanced it by the Gallic soap she secretly imported.

"A marvelous woman, is she not?" demanded Flavius.

He sucked in his breath, slowly licking his lower lip. He surveyed her as if she were a woman he had never seen before, as if he had not held her countless times in his thin arms.

"Marvelous," I whispered.

"But who is more worthy than I to be husband to the blood of Domitian?"

5

"No one," I said.

"The servants are confined to their quarters under penalty of death," Flavius confided. "Only we know of this."

Suddenly he clapped his hands, flinging his arms outward in the gesture of a priest. He brought his palms softly together and reached into his bosom. He produced a bit of red ochre and stepped close to Domitilla. Upon her flesh, he traced an irregular circle, about the huge lump which disfigured her belly.

I commenced to understand: red was the color sacred to the safe delivery of a child.

I could not keep my eyes from the shadow of the fleece between her legs which would give the first caress to the baby as it was born. Without reason I felt a spasm of jealousy; I was startled to hear Flavius speak again.

"The auguries have promised me it will be a son," Flavius said unctuously, stepping back. He crushed the chalk in his hand as he glanced at me; I nodded. "Domitilla," Flavius said softly. "You know it means the same as the Greek *basilina,* Rufus?" I nodded again, hiding my irritation. Flavius knew very well that both of us had been blessed with the tuition of Epictetus the Lame, the finest teacher in the empire (now exiled by order of Domitian), and that of us both Flavius had neglected his studies.

"The little queen," Flavius murmured. "That is its meaning. She shall give birth to a prince."

Unexpectedly, quicker than my eye could follow, he whisked an object from behind one of the pillars. To my horror, I saw it was a wreath of laurel mounted upon a fillet of richly worked silk. It joined the old Roman insigne of a conqueror to the diadem sacred to the emperor.

Before I could speak or move, Flavius had placed this double crown upon the bare tumulus of birth within his wife, pressing it down so hard that the sharp edges of the laurel leaves bit into her body. Domitilla writhed, stifling a moan. I could have sworn I saw a movement from her unborn child.

"The stars have spoken," Flavius whispered thickly. "He will be emperor!"

"Stop!" I hissed.

I was paralyzed with terror. This was unmistakable madness: I had good reason to know that the spies of Domitian were everywhere. If they heard a syllable or even suspected this weird ceremony, neither my life nor that of Flavius—

6

nor, for that matter, the lives of Domitilla and her infant—would be worth an obol from a dead man's mouth.

"Kneel, Rufus," Flavius addressed me. "You shall be the first of his subjects to swear allegiance."

He saw my step backward, my shuddering instinctive reflex of refusal. His eyes glittered in the lamplight; his hands trembled. He waited. I shook my head slowly, pleadingly.

Flavius stepped close to me, drawing his short jeweled Egyptian knife free of his sash within his robe. "Kneel," he said savagely into my ear, "kneel and adore your sovereign-to-be!"

I felt the urgent pressure of the point digging into my back, pricking out the blood. I was unarmed; I was his guest. I had no choice but to acquiesce to this dreadful act. I am no coward, as is known to everyone, but sweat sprang out on my forehead. I sank to one knee only, reserving that much of my homage.

"Here is the hope of my house," Flavius said grandly, placing the blade of cold watered iron on Domitilla's deformed belly. She winced and shivered and I quivered in sympathy.

"Domitian Secundus and Vespasian have the emperor's favor," Flavius went on, "but the auguries are against them." He shook his head over the ill luck of his other two young sons, who had been named for rulers of Rome. He sheathed his knife. Over the body of his wife he flung another covering—this time one of purple silk, woven with flowers, one that should be used solely to robe a general in triumph. I averted my eyes from the sight.

"What disturbs you?" demanded Flavius in a tone of malice. I was about to speak when I saw in the shadows a very tall, stooped man. He stood dressed in a coarse yellow robe, holding his hands folded across his bosom like a peasant. The apparition startled me.

"You said the servants had been banished from the house," I accused Flavius. He gave his high whinnying laugh. "But this is no slave," he said, "this is a guest, the special guest, of Domitilla. He is her preceptor, a rabbi of the Jews called Akiba ben Joseph."

The figure in the half-light remained motionless. I stared at it with distaste, observing the skullcapped head as bald as an egg, the beard, the piercing dark eyes under shaggy brows. "Have no fear," Flavius said almost jeeringly. "You know I do nothing without surety. I have consulted his god and he agrees with ours."

7

"The mighty Domitian does not favor the Jews," I muttered.

"Neither does he curse them," Flavius responded promptly. "My beloved Domitilla even believes that such as this Akiba may be correct in what he says about religion. As for me, I have no objection: I make my peace with all divine beings."

"Does the god of the Jew, then, agree that your child shall be what you say?"

"He shall be a prince, the son of a star," Akiba said in an unexpectedly deep and sonorous voice.

"It is best to be sure," Flavius agreed. He turned and flung aside the curtain behind me. He went directly to the half-pillar of marble that supported a carved scroll at the farther end of the atrium, the lares altar. He knelt and poured a libation of wine and honey, scattering grains of incense, mouthing indistinguishable words.

On the couch, a corner of the purple robe was blown lightly aside. I gazed full into the beautiful face of Domitilla. Her great black eyes opened and fastened to mine. Neither of us spoke. Each of us felt the impact of the other's thoughts to the accompaniment of the soft splashing of the fountain.

In three months or less, nature and a midwife would deliver her of a child. If the auguries according to Flavius were correct, it would be a son. But, curiously enough, his fate would not be that predicted; it would be something resembling a Sybilline prophecy. In my head, it shaped itself into respectable form:

Not a bastard will he be, though
He will never father know.

It might have been Flavius who had impregnated Domitilla. It might, as easily, have been myself. Or, if such a thing is possible in this world, the fruit of her womb would be the son of us both.

I felt a burning stare upon me. I looked up: Akiba, the Jew, watched us impassively.

I wonder about these things, I, Sextus Rufus Teneius. I judge it right that matters of my own time so worthy of mention should not remain obscure forever, unknown, subject to the fancies of those who will write fables for the generations to come. I sit here, an old man, wasting away in my villa in Gaul. Since those days I have done and seen much: I have been soldier and administrator, attendant according to the

8

law at court and tortures, I have seen my friends die in fire and battle. But nothing has remained so deeply cut into my brain as the night, in the year that the Christians number as the ninety-fifth after the death of their prophet, in the peristylium of the summer villa of Flavius Clemens outside Rome. Now the story is ended. I write as I wish—in the old way, upon the black wax inlaid within these triple tablets of beechwood which may be sealed after my death. I may say what I know to be true about the greatest wars the Romans ever fought—both against the Jews—and the souls and bodies of those concerned in it. I may surmise with sincerity as to what the result must be. At sixty-five, I am too old, too harmless, to be persecuted for the truth. No one will read these records; even if they are seized, too few will believe what I say for my words to be a danger to great Hadrian, emperor of these times. My memoirs will be considered as the ravings of an ancient, to be treated with compassion rather than concern.

At least, so I trust, for I am not without honor. I have been prefect for provinces of the East. My counsels have been heard and heeded in the highest circles by the most mighty. I have fought the enemies of the empire within and without for nearly forty years. I have looked proudly into the empty eyes of death a dozen times and cried him salve. Twice was I offered the crown of empire for myself and, at the risk of my life, I refused. Not, I must admit, so much out of loyalty to the emperor but because I doubted if I could maintain myself in such a perilous place. By that time I was old enough and had seen enough to know it for a fate worse than death. Long ago, the greatest heart's desire of any Roman, to possess absolute power, went wholly out of me. I am satisfied. Though I am not a Christian, I know well enough what their Jesus meant when he declared that the meek should inherit the earth.

Sitting here, I look about me and I am content. My house in Gaul stands at the foot of a gently sloping hill, with broad porches to the north and south. A glen, flanked by two wooded hills, opens before the entrance hall to carry my weary eyes farther than vision will sustain. In a corner are my baths, built directly beneath a bluff from which the slaves can cut the timber and roll it over the edge, to fall directly into a pile for seasoning and use in the furnaces. Lead pipes from Greece carry the hot water along the walls into the bath apartments that are of gleaming marble with domed roofs and graceful columns executed by an artist from Ravenna.

In my piscina, through the carved heads of gorgons, the waters from an icy hillside stream rush continuously; tame fish caress the skin of the bather. I have made sure that the inscriptions on the walls are decent, taken from Horace. The sentiments are neither bad enough not to be read nor good enough to be read a second time, thus improving the possibilities of both conversation and bathing.

Next are the rooms for the baths for women and the spinning rooms of the slaves. Beyond is a long colonnade which looks over my own lake, lying on the eastern side of woods that are cool green in summer and flaming with color in the autumn. The gallery on the south contains the winter dining hall which has always a bright blaze in its fireplace. Up the broad staircase with its painted walls of Alexander's conquests, my visitors find themselves on a gallery overhanging the lake itself. One may fish or dive into the waters, or watch the sunset and the drying of the nets. Most often, I myself nap in my chamber here, screened from the southern heat, listening to the cicada on hot afternoons or the shepherd's piping in the morning; at evening, the nightingale and the silences between his song lull me to sleep.

Such a delightful spot, of course, is not immune to the raids of the wild tribes that often break through the borders in these unsettled times. I have learned to accept these forays as the price for such living. Upon being warned I leave for the south, in accordance with long-established plans. I take with me only my money, clothes, statuary, and my cartload of writing tablets. Not because my rude visitors can read but because they have, in the past, acquired the habit of using my precious beechwood blocks for firewood.

The only precaution I have taken in my house is to build everything as soundly and solidly as possible. Thus, when the barbarians arrive, they loot the buried food bins and sunken wine jars and gorge themselves: I call this my yearly "rent" and count myself fortunate when I escape it. But my impromptu tenants soon discover it would take too much work to destroy the villa—it is important that everything be made of stone, for fires delight their spirits—and, besides, the pictures and mosaics seem to enchant them. They stay a week or so, befoul the place unspeakably, then move on—either in restlessness or fleeing before the imperial troops. Thereupon I wait a week or so, then return with my slaves; I clean up and refresh the house and resume my old habits of leisure.

10

Such a good life gives me time to meditate and remember. This is needful, for I wish to write about one of the most remarkable men who ever lived. He was not a Roman citizen: he was one of the despised race of the Jews. From our first meeting in the house of Flavius Clemens, it seemed that our lives were destined to be intertwined, though he was learned and middle-aged and I was ignorant and half his years. It was the decree of fate that Akiba ben Joseph and I should be both friends and enemies and that our spirits should join out of our bodies like smoke rising from two fires and borne on the same wind.

Let me write first that Akiba was an extraordinary fool whom I loved. Not because of his virtues—which were many —but because of his faults, of which he had few but which made him human. I loved, too, his foster-son, Simeon of Gozeba, but for different reasons. This handsome youth might have become more wicked as he grew older, as most of us do, but he died at the age of thirty-seven, so we shall never know. The pressure of the unseen force which rules the world pinched Simeon between its monstrous thumb and forefinger like a melon seed and shot him into outer darkness.

Known to the world as Rufus the Prefect, yet I was the intimate of Akiba for nearly half his life. As the gods directed, I was in some degree the tutor of Simeon's youth, his unfortunate counselor, his foe in battle. Even much more was I to Simeon than this, but he never realized it nor has anyone else save Akiba—until the moment two days ago when I sat down and fitted this stylus to my hand.

I would not toss this tale of these two lives onto the heaps of malicious material which the envious and spiteful, Jew and Roman alike, have piled above their tombs if it were merely a matter of vindication. A Roman disdains to justify the deeds of himself or his friends. It is enough to act while others ponder and fret, to have faith that the travail of history will, in the end, produce offspring who will resemble the truth as it was. Akiba himself never minded the scurrilities; and Simeon caught the javelins of abuse flung against him and sped them back at his tormentors with more vigor than they were sent.

No: in any case, such a history, however true, would not be believed. We live in troubled times, when men turn away from old gods toward the new. We think differently, twisting words so that, if you like (according to the Christians), three gods become one—an economical procedure but hardly logical. We persecute each other for the pleasure of forcing someone to worship our own idols. I have slain many men for many reasons—chiefly for love of Rome—and with many weapons: most by the short spear, a few by arrows, more by the sword, two by crushing them beneath my shield. But I have never killed a man for the love of any god.

Therefore my telling of the lives of Akiba and Simeon is merely to demonstrate the sadness of the world where one may be good in a wretched age and perform wonders of valor and learning, only to perish and be cursed like the rest of us. Or the glory of the world where one can see the sight of one young man rising like Ajax in his old age to defy the thunder and cry to the gods, "You cannot kill me, I have paid my debts to you, I owe heaven nothing!"

Here I pause. I have searched inwardly for months, rummaging the corners of my brain to find an answer to the question which has pursued me like one of the furies for most of my life. Man must have a cause to justify his life: what has been that cause to which the Romans seek to dedicate themselves?

Land, I suppose. That is an old itch of the veterans returning from the wars, as Sulla discovered; and it has been an obsession with our rulers, too, such as Nero the Ahenobarbus. Gold, perhaps. Treasure of all sorts, as in the case of that pseudo-philosopher, Lucius Annaeus Seneca, who hoarded his five hundred ivory tables inlaid with rare citronwood. Command of men, possibly. It was this on which the first and greatest Julius prided himself and it was this which prompted him to write his paean of stolid self-praise, his commentary on the Gallic wars. Slaves, flattery, the bended knee, the yoked neck, the supple bodies of women or young boys: the list is interminable.

I have accused myself of an overpast desire for power and I grant that this may underlie all other desires. But I find myself denying this to be the image before which we worship when I think of great Trajan and Vespasian and Titus and their passion for the common citizen. And what of the legionary who dies cheerfully for his general (who may be a Frank or a Syrian), praying with his last breath to the image of Mithra who is not even his own god?

I have come to think that what we seek is a reflection of ourselves to outlast time itself—which may be the reason that so many of us, like the noble Livy, write histories. We feel we are doomed to fame. We seem to see the gigantic eidolon of Rome above all future history, dominating the thought and deed of people we now exclude from citizenship. We have seized art and treasure, territory and language, gods and grain from all the lands of the world. In exchange we have given nothing but law and order.

Our people, our colonies, even our enemies have seemed satisfied with no more. Is it possible that we Romans have found by accident the single most valued possession of mankind? Akiba once told me that his god was God because he brought order out of chaos. This is strange because it was Simeon who plunged all into chaos again.

The last time I went to visit Flavius Clemens at his summer villa was the afternoon before he planned to close it for the approaching winter. It was a day late in the eighth month when I stood in the great drafty atrium next to the ever-smoking altar and watched as Akiba himself solemnly carried out a bundle of purple-striped wool. He unrolled it carefully at the feet of Flavius, again clad in his ceremonial robes in his role of paterfamilias.

The coarse bindings undid themselves. Out tumbled a tiny red object, gasping and yelling, with gummed eyes, coughing up phlegm in its miniature passion and fear; hairless, groping with tiny fingers, its toes working like those of the emperor's ape—inhuman in all except for a shrill bawl, its tiny stomach clotted with blood from the cut cord. For a moment in the chill Flavius looked down at the babe. Then his sunken face convulsed with pleasure.

"Susceptio!" he cried loudly. "I accept him!"

Thus was I the official witness to the act of lifting up. Flavius swooped down upon the child. As he raised it in his arms, it squalled more loudly than ever but its cries were drowned by the applauding shouts of the slaves about us. The expression of Flavius changed. He looked with disgust at the squirming infant and his huge nose wrinkled. Promptly Akiba snatched the child from him and wrapped it up once more.

"My family will survive," Flavius remarked meaningfully to me, taking a wet cloth to wipe his hands.

"Forever," I said. "My felicitations, noble Flavius."

Flavius nodded, flinging his toga carelessly over his shoulder. "I am happy that it is over; now I can ignore the brat until he comes of age," he said.

"What will you call this third-born?" I asked.

Flavius hesitated, pulling at his lower lip in thought. "We

have the eight days of primordia before we give him a name,"
he said at last. "He is a lusty one. We need not worry about
the spirit of this pupus. He will fulfil his destiny." Taken with
a sudden resolution, Flavius leaned close to me, breathing his
sour breath into my ear.

"Do not tell another," he said, "the luck will be bad. I shall
call him Simeon Flavius Julius."

"Flavius? I understand."

"Certainly."

"Julius? That is not so clear."

Flavius snorted. "He is a distant cousin of the first Julius,"
he asserted. It was a claim which I knew to be false.

"You ensure the child's destiny," I said blandly.

"How so?"

"You give him a guard of emperors."

The face of Flavius twisted into a smile, but before he
could speak, I went on. "Simeon, that I do not understand,"
I said.

Flavius held up his hand, looking furtively about him.
"That old Jew Akiba has influenced her," he whispered. "She
insists it is a noble Jewish name, one that is lucky. I have
agreed to it—on the condition that Domitilla speak to her
uncle about—well, about family financial matters."

My contempt for this man surged up into my throat. I had
discovered his faults again and again, but this was incredible.
No true Roman would have been so weak as to allow one of
his sons to be named after his wife's whim unless he were
womanish himself. "I see," I said. "How is Domitilla? Is she
doing well?"

Without warning Flavius laughed his long high neigh. Instead of replying to me, he abruptly quoted:

> *Rhodo, I build you marble sarcophagi*
> *And joyfully I give the poor my purse;*
> *And if your shrewish shade demands me why,*
> *I say: "I ride to freedom on your hearse."*

Again he laughed and, struck with an inexplicable fear, I
made no comment. Flavius examined me closely, rubbing his
beardless chin, his eyes narrowed. "Did you appreciate that?"
he wondered. "I thought the Greek verse of Julianus delighted
you, Rufus, soldier-scholar that you are."

"Yes," I said. "It was delightful."

Flavius scanned me and nodded as if what he discovered

14

was satisfactory. "We have not had an occasion for drinking together for a long time," he said. "I have saved a cratera of old Capito, mellowed by a sea voyage, for just such an occasion as this. You will stay to dinner. Afterward we shall drink and, if you wish it, I shall allow Domitilla to attend us."

It was a tempting offer and I did not hesitate. "Susceptio!" I exclaimed. Flavius clapped me on the shoulder as we went in, though without chuckling at my joke.

Thus it was that we sat in the glimmering shades of the peristylium late that cold night in October, surrounded by four low braziers of glowing charcoal for warmth, and drank and drank again. When there is not much to be said between two such as we, drinking is the only social substitute. It could not have been much more than an hour after the meridian of the night that I felt I was drunk. I was certain of the condition of Flavius. He had become silly and sentimental by turns, heehawing at nothing, examining the ants creeping across the black marble of the tabletop as if it were an event of importance.

Nothing he said made sense. Yet I was convinced he had invited me to remain for a sensible reason: he wanted to offer some sort of challenge I felt I had to accept. I waited for the moment and drank the tarry Capito wine as a substitute for the revelation. It had been so long in coming that I had almost decided my anticipations were groundless. I settled myself down to sleep on my couch when Flavius leaned across the table and touched my bare arm. His chilled fingers made me jump.

"A charming serpent," he said, pointing to the band of gold about my right biceps, molded in the shape of an asp. "Where did you buy it?"

"It was a gift," I said.

"From a woman, eh, Rufus?" Flavius grinned widely. I felt a tremor of expectation: the moment was here. Domitilla had given it to me as a love-token, in the tradition of Caesar's Cleopatra, long ago. I braced myself on my elbow for the attack.

My determination to say nothing was not needed. Flavius did not wait for my answer, shifting to another subject. "It is altogether possible," he said, "that the Jews have a more powerful god than the Romans."

"Not at all," I replied in relief. "The divine Titus destroyed

15

their temple and chief city twenty-five years ago. The people are dispersed, their altars and priests destroyed."

"But they persist. What Vespasian and Titus did was no more than the act of the sower, scattering seed broadcast."

"Surely not. And, at any rate, politics is all and religion nothing."

"Not in what the Jews call the World-to-Come," Flavius said.

"You seem to be well acquainted with their thoughts," I replied cautiously.

"Who could help it, married to a madwoman like Domitilla?" Flavius said crossly. Then, again shifting: "You do not wish her to interrupt our drinking now, do you?"

"She is fortunate to have an understanding husband," I said. "No, Flavius, I do not wish her here."

I had gone too far and I knew it instantly. Flavius thrust out his lower lip, gnawing it between words. "I agree," he said, "she need not know how fortunate I have been to have you set as a guard over me all these years by her uncle Domitian."

I had a spasm of surprise. In wine there was more to be discovered than I had bargained for. Flavius slowly turned his favorite double-handled cup of Persian gold between his fingers, his rings rattling on the metal. "You have been close to me, Rufus," he said and sipped his wine. "Close, indeed," he added, baring his teeth as the liquor stung his palate.

"I have been honored," I said automatically.

"Closer than a twin brother."

"I thank you for a thousand favors."

Flavius gave one of his quick broken cries of laughter. Then, as if puzzled as to its source, he looked about him. "That was a strange sound," he said, swallowing another gulp of the snow-cooled wine.

"It was not meant to be," I told him, dreading my own revelations in this drowsy drunken dialogue.

"Is it not strange that we should be such boon companions?" insisted Flavius. "I know you are a handsome, courageous fellow with more than your share of scholarly sense; and I also know you are a liar and a thief."

I forced a laugh. I felt dizzy; the wine had gone at last to my own head. "I cannot be blamed for what you think you think, noble Flavius," I said bitingly.

The cloudy look vanished from his eyes as he peered at me.

16

His face drew itself down into a frown. "You have insulted me," he said, picking his way between the words.

"Never, not at all," I protested.

"You believe you have made a fool of Flavius," he said, his voice rising, "of your friend, of one who has protected and nursed you at his breast like a child."

"No, no, that is not so!"

"You contradict me again. Like a child, I tell you, I have nurtured you and you have made me a fool, you fool!"

I shook my head, partly in denial, partly to clear my thoughts. Flavius watched me owlishly. "Did you never imagine that I knew of you and Domitilla?" he asked softly.

I sprang from my couch, lost my balance, staggered, and sat down hard in a wooden curule chair. I beat the table twice with my fist and bowed my head, tears of shame springing to my eyes.

"You might have guessed that I knew," Flavius' voice went on, inexorably gentle. "We have been friends for so many years."

I raised my head, the hot tears coursing my cheeks. I gave him back stare for stare and, to my amazement, he commenced to blubber like myself. "So many years!" he gasped. "My poor wife! I weep for her as you weep for her!"

"You don't understand," I said indistinctly.

"What is there to understand?"

"I weep for *you!*" I shouted.

Flavius' jaw sagged. "Still less do I understand," he muttered. I shook my head helplessly. My thoughts were fleeing my brain; I could not think what to say.

Flavius clapped his hands. A beautiful slave youth, curled yellow hair and blue eyes like the sea, with a profile and white-togaed figure like that of Apollo, brought in another jar of wine. He looked at me coldly, then at Flavius. I could see the effeminate softening of his eyes, almost like that of a mistress seeing her beloved. He bowed and left the peristylium.

"Which of your slaves is that?" I asked.

"You are jealous of me," Flavius tittered, filling my cup with wine. "He is Stephanus, sent me a year or more ago from Britain. Only now has he been trained to serve at table." He glanced at me. "I think it fortunate that you did not serve in my legion in Britain, my friend, when Domitilla and I were there," he said with a snort. For no reason he burst into hilarity and I joined him. We rocked back and forth, roaring at each other, helpless in mirth. I dried his eyes with the hem of my toga and he wiped mine with his.

"You should have invited me," I said, wagging my head.

"And share Stephanus? That would have been unbearable—equally so with Domitilla."

"How so?"

"Stephanus would have remained childless. But Domitilla—I should have had two bastards instead of one."

The moment had come. My head cleared instantly of the purple mists of wine. I was glad of the ending to this long deceit. I stood up, in my veins feeling the same exaltation—the same cold fear, the same hot fury—that mingled in me just before battle. It had always served me well.

"Your sons have a father," I said. "You are he. They are your sons."

Flavius, enjoying himself, wagged his finger up at me. "Two of them, perhaps," he said, "though that may be doubted. But one, surely not."

Comprehension swept through me like a cleansing storm. Flavius was not as stupid as I supposed. All this mummery of the haruspices, the false ceremonies, this was to humiliate me and Domitilla. Rage shook me; Flavius saw it and coughed with glee. "She will die before her uncle can save her," he whispered. "I am consul and I have ordered it."

I seized him by the throat, lifting him up from his chair suspended between my hands. His eyes goggled at me like those of a fish. His hollow cheeks went in and out like the gills of an underseas creature. His hands dropped his precious goblet to the table and tore feebly at mine. He could not cry out nor struggle: I felt the strength flowing out of him into me as I gloried in the moment, in my revenge for Domitilla.

Suddenly my wrists were gripped by strong hands, torn away. I was thrust aside by the slave Stephanus as the limp figure of Flavius dropped back to his couch. The youth sprang at me as I dodged without thought; he would have dared to attack me if the curtain behind us had not been ripped aside. I sidestepped swiftly and wheeled to meet this new challenge. To my astonishment, I saw the unmistakable glint of Roman mail in the doorway. A centurion stood stiffly at attention. At either shoulder I glimpsed the cuirasses and the stiff brushes of horsehair that mark the helmets of soldiers on palace duty. It was a detachment from one of the cohorts of the Praetorian Guard.

"Ave," said the centurion curtly, as Stephanus vanished be-

18

hind a hanging, "I come on business of the most powerful emperor Titus Flavius Domitianus Augustus."

"Salve," I said, standing stiffly where I was.

"You are not the eminent consul, Flavius Clemens," he said, half on a note of interrogation.

"Who are you?" I demanded.

"Curtius Saccus, of the Second Scythians, assigned to Praetorian duty."

"You know me, Rufus Teneius, good Curtius?"

He flicked an eye at me disdainfully. "You have been long away from the barracks," he said.

"But I am still Rufus, tribune for the First Alauda and the Praetorians," I said softly. "Will you cross javelins with me?"

"Gladly," he returned carelessly, "but my will is not my own tonight. Forgive me, noble tribune." On this note of irony, he saluted me and I returned the salute. He looked at the reviving Flavius, then at me; I nodded.

Flavius saw what was happening and struggled to his feet. "Before you give me the message from my cousin," he croaked, "I order you to arrest this man!" He pointed at me. "Conduct him to the imperial palace!"

"My orders concern you," the officer said shortly.

"You have interrupted me!"

"Pardon, great consul," said Curtius, a sardonic touch to his voice. "We have no orders except for you."

"It is I who give the orders! My wife is niece to the emperor himself!"

"She is allowed to come with you, if you so desire. Is that your wish?"

Flavius paused uneasily. "No," he said in a subdued voice.

"Then I am instructed to say that she must appear with you. Also, that you shall have no fear. The emperor has taken an oath before the gods that all his kin, including yourself, shall be safe from any punishment."

Flavius frowned. "That is evil," he said finally. "Punishment? For what reason?"

"Consul, I do not know."

"What is the charge?"

"I am a soldier, not one of the court."

Flavius peered at him, his face screwed up as if one of the insects fluttering about the lamps had flown into his eye. "The children?" he inquired.

"They, too, must come with you."

A voice cried out from the rooms to the right: "They're

here, they shall stay here!" It was the voice of Stephanus. He appeared with stripling Vespasian and little Domitian Secundus beside him, luminous flesh in the gloom, calm and wondering in their short sleeping tunics.

For a moment, Curtius said nothing. He stared balefully at Stephanus from under the brass brow of his helmet. "Are you Stephanus?" he demanded.

The handsome young Briton bowed in well-trained silence. "You will attend your master," Curtius told him shortly. "The emperor has taken a fancy to you."

"And the newborn child?" asked Flavius dully.

The centurion shrugged. "There are orders for two only," he said.

"Allow me to take care of him," said the voice of Akiba. It startled me to see him appear again in the shadows, cradling the form of the infant. I saw the eyes of Curtius narrow and his face wrinkle in contempt: then I knew. The charge against Flavius and Domitilla must be that of becoming Jews. My brain shriveled. Akiba in the house was proof positive that Flavius admitted Jews to his household, that he must have listened to their counsel. It would avail nothing to him or his wife to deny they had adopted such a religion. Akiba was enough to condemn them in the mind of Domitian when his centurion, as he must, reported what he had seen. I, too, was in mortal danger.

Flavius nodded almost absently to Akiba, as if it were a matter he would take up later. He drew himself up as tall as he could and addressed Curtius. "When my sons and I return after audience with the emperor," he said, a caricature of threat in his voice, "I shall remember you."

Curtius nodded. "Remember me then," he said briefly, "as a soldier who obeyed his orders."

The mouth of Flavius twisted. "A most Roman soldier," he murmured.

"For you," Curtius said to me, as if he had not heard, "I have this, honored Rufus."

He extended a sealed imperial tablet. A cold chill took my breast: my glance flew aside to a bandy-legged little soldier directly behind Curtius. Between his two hands he twirled a shining cord, as thick as half a finger. He stretched it absently between his two hands, wrapped about his fists, tightening and loosening it alternately.

Flavius followed my gaze. His face became expressionless. He picked up his golden cup and looked at it closely. Around

20

its rim, embossed until they almost leaped from the metal, the slim nude figure of Diana and her hounds pursued Actaeon. Flavius dropped it to the mosaic floor. Deliberately he set his boot upon it, crushing the priceless workmanship to a shapeless mass of metal.

He beckoned the little soldier forward. The latter looked wonderingly at his centurion; Curtius nodded. The man advanced and Flavius took the cord. He held a deep breath. "Bring my cloak," he ordered Stephanus. Thoughtfully, he tautened the cord between his fingers.

"At least," he said, "it is silk."

The color of it was the true Tyrian—a bluish-red, shading toward brown, the color of half-dried blood.

"At least," Flavius repeated, "it is purple."

CHAPTER 2

Curtius and his cohort left the villa with Domitilla in a closed litter, Flavius walking with bowed head beside it. The two condemned children marched joyously along with Stephanus, imitating the quick short strides of the soldiers.

I sank down nervelessly between the smoke of the dying braziers in the peristylium. My body felt as if the strength had melted out of its bones. I despised myself. In other circumstances, perhaps, I might have snatched a sword and fought for my own, my mistress and my child. But to any Roman soldier there is a numbing awe about an order from the palace. It is an edict more holy than one from the gods— and more sure in its punishment and reward. Such a tablet as the one on my lap confronted me with all the accumulated might of Rome across the centuries. It struck me down as mercilessly as the blow of a pilum shaft across the bridge of the nose.

Tears crept out again at my humiliation. Shaking my head from side to side, flinging the salt drops from my eyes in order to read the scored wax, I slipped the thread attached to the red sigillum. I scanned the tablet rapidly. I felt the blood drain from my heart; I raised my head toward the stars in the square emptiness of the dawning sky above and howled like an animal. I was to report to the spot farthest in the world from the capital city. I was ordered to the infamous Colonia, the fort at the ends of the earth, in Upper Germany, in the most remote wilderness known.

"May all the gods damn the soul of Domitian!" I said—but it was not a shout, barely a whisper.

The discipline of my long training held me like an iron girdle. Young as I was, it seemed to me that the angular characters inscribed in the wax by some obscure court secretary were tiny furies fluttering about my body, carrying me from heaven to hell. I half wished for the cord around my own throat rather than this assignment, far from the delights of Rome. A sudden gust of wind shook the flowers in the garden. It shivered the drops of the fountain, bringing a sour smell from the kitchen. I grew sick; I rose to leave the doomed house of Flavius.

Again it was the Jew Akiba who forestalled me. His gaunt burning-eyed form stood before me, the same bundle of swaddling clothes in his arms. "The child," he said slowly, "you have forgotten the child of your friend."

"Curse the child!" I shrieked in a paroxysm of rage, glad enough to find someone to vent my fury on. "Dash out its brains, strangle it! What do I care for the bastard of Flavius?"

"I did not know it was a bastard," Akiba replied in his soft tones. He appeared to hug the child closer to his breast. I glared at him and choked back the bile that was rising in my throat. Grinding my heel into the mosaic, I strode from the place.

Gathering my gear, selecting a horse for the first post northward, selling my house-fittings and slaves—for henceforth soldier orderlies would serve me—I had time to think sombrely of how the gods assign a guardian spirit to each man when he is born. It is the duty of such a genius to accompany him through life, protecting him from accident or ill-fortune, except as the all-powerful fates decree. At the end, it rises with him to rejoin the company of heaven or it resides with him in the shadows of the underworld. The old Greek saying goes:

> *To every man, a genius is assigned*
> *At birth; his life and death are both designed.*

22

That night at the villa of Flavius I had thought my genius had abandoned me but I might have known better. I discovered that it was then that the genius of the Flavian family deserted them. The gossip in the streets of Rome next day had approved my surmise. The accusation against Flavius Clemens and his household was known to be the fact that they had turned away from the true gods and had become Jews—or Christians. Domitian did not know or care enough to make a difference.

I suppose there may have been good reasons for Flavius' death, but those given were so slight as to astound everyone. Domitian was enraged because the servants of Flavius, like Stephanus, dressed in white togas such as were worn by the emperor's household. He ground his teeth when he recalled that, when he and Flavius were announced as consuls, the nervous herald had proclaimed the name of Flavius first. These and like charges were enough for Domitian to give out that Flavius had attempted to assume the purple for himself and his fellow Jews. As for the treason I had seen with my own eyes a week before, this was never reported to the emperor, but undoubtedly Flavius had ambitions.

As for me, enmeshed in the same net, Domitian feared me for the very loathsomeness of the task to which I had been set by him. As his spy—I say it now with contempt for myself—I had certain knowledge of the many imperial crimes. Domitian feared that, if I were strangled or poisoned, what I knew might be scribbled by my friends across every monument in Rome. Thus, exile to Germany: it was much cleverer and, in its way, as terrible as the fate of Flavius. He and his two sons were never seen again. As far as rumor went, somewhere in the cool arched bowels of the dungeons below the Forum, they were strangled by the cord. It was not a bad death, I heard afterward; the little soldier-executioner was skillful enough to place the knot so as to attack the nerve beside the windpipe, twisting his fists hard behind the neck. Domitilla, who could not in any case succeed to the throne because of her sex, was spared the extreme penalty but exiled for life to the remote island of Pandataria. Long afterwards I saw her again but many years had passed. She was much changed.

I realized it was best for me to be off, to keep out of the way of Domitian as one might avoid a mad dog foaming at the mouth. I had my sword and javelins polished, my breastplate and greaves burnished, purchased (not without distaste) a pair of heavy hobnailed military boots and shook the dust from off my sagum, the military cloak. I sent presents and messages of farewell to my friends. I prepared to set out to the trackless regions of the north without delay—with despairing thoughts of the month-long ride through evil provinces and the rugged life I would be forced to endure despite my tribunal rank.

I completed what I had to do within a week. I knew from experience how easily the minds of emperors change. I had no desire to give Domitian the opportunity of countermanding my orders into a death sentence. My services to him in the household of the late Flavius might commend me to his mercy or his caution—but the latent frenzy I had seen in his cousin would be a thousand times more dreadful on the throne.

Thus it was that I stood alone in my stripped domus by the Tiber and listened to the susurration of the wind-driven waves behind the walls, ready to leave. It was the eighth night. As I looked about me, preparing to pass out into the street for the last time, a knock sounded on the pillar beyond. I drew back: such a visitor at such a time could mean only that I had delayed too long. I listened but heard nothing. My suspicions deepened into certainty. I determined to sell my life like a soldier rather than kneel to the cord. With a yell, I drew my sword. I flung back the curtain, at the same time thrusting with all my might at the figure which stood there.

To my utter astonishment, my visitor made a single swift motion. He moved his oak staff to the right. It deflected my point. It pinned the blade against the wall with such force that it numbed my arm. My sword fell ringing to the threshold. My late caller stooped, picked it up, and returned it to me. I saw, in the flickering torchlight from the street, that it was Akiba.

I recoiled. He looked down at me, shadows shifting on his face.

"What do you wish?" I demanded harshly.

"I have heard that you leave Rome," he said.

"Well?"

"Is it not the Roman custom, as it is with us, for friends to say farewell?"

"I had no notion we were friends," I said abruptly. "But if you wish it, Jew, farewell."

"Do you leave tonight?"

"Yes."

"Is there not one among your friends who will give you a last feast?" Akiba asked.

"It is the custom, perhaps," I said wryly, "but there is none among many who dares. I am under the displeasure of the emperor, as good as forgotten by any sensible Roman."

"But I am not a Roman and some think I am not very sensible."

"What do you mean?"

"I invite you."

I laughed shortly. "You yourself are a fool to remain in Rome," I told him. "It would be best for you to flee as well. Did not Curtius Saccus report your presence in the house of Flavius that foul night?"

"He saw only that I was a Jew; he did not inquire my name."

"It is fortunate for you that Flavius was not allowed audience with the emperor, that he was spared the torture," I said ironically. "Assuredly, your name would have passed his lips."

"I am merely a provincial, beneath his notice," Akiba returned imperturbably.

I shook my head. "You do not know the emperor," I said.

"I have a protector," Akiba told me. "I have come to invite you to dine with him, with us, before you leave Rome."

"A protector?" I frowned. "A citizen of Rome?"

Akiba nodded solemnly. "He is a prophet favored by Vespasian, the mighty father of the emperor."

"What has this great one foretold?" I sneered.

"He called Vespasian emperor while Nero was still seated in his palace. He foresaw that Domitian, disguised as a priest, would escape the wrath of Vitellius and ascend to the throne."

"This man is all-seeing, indeed," I said coldly. "You must ask him my fate, as well."

"I have," Akiba responded calmly. "He has told me that we shall both love and hate each other, that we shall both save and destroy each other."

His impudence left me without words; his assurance daunted me. I stared at him for a long moment, then Akiba turned slightly. "Come," he said.

I untied my horse's reins from the block and clambered into the wooden box of a saddle. I sighed: I knew it would chafe my thighs raw before I had spent three hours ahorseback. Akiba took the bridle and commenced to walk with his peculiarly long stride toward the west.

I confess that my unpremeditated acceptance surprised myself. A peculiar curiosity, not untinged with fear, worked in my liver. Dining with a Jew was abhorrent, yet the prospect

25

intrigued me. I was superstitious enough to want to meet his mysterious omniscient friend.

I had braced myself for an evening in the foul sty of the Suburra, the Jewish quarter—in one of the insulae with their warrens of flats which housed most of the pestilential populace of Rome. But to my surprise and relief Akiba turned again, this time to the south. He entered a respectable neighborhood, free of shops, filled with the domi of equites and freedmen. He stopped before the barred peephole of a pepperstone façade, then proceeded to the entrance with its columns of Travertine marble. Entering, he actually received a bow from the door-slave as I was dismounting. Akiba gravely turned and bowed to me: I caught myself just in time to prevent answering his courtesy in kind.

Inside, it was well lighted by lamps rather than torches, with the glint of pools and the glow of greenery; a moon-paring glimmered above the rectangular light-well. Here and there stood excellent bronze nymphs and tritons green-sporting in the fountains; huge vases of Carthaginian workmanship, Greek mosaics which were rich, if a little too restrained for my taste.

As I passed (right foot first) to one side of the pool, feeling out of place in my armor, the heavy blue wool curtains at the rear were swept back. A diminutive old man, clad in Roman garb, emerged briskly: thick eyebrows, heavy white hair, beardless, both dignity and assurance in his approach.

"Ave," he said to me in a firm, friendly voice.

"This is Josephus ben Matthias," Akiba said. "Josephus Flavius, historian to both Romans and Jews."

"Salve," I said. Despite myself, I was impressed. I knew—as who did not—of the reputation of Josephus. I had heard how highly valued he was as a friend by both Vespasian and Titus, of whom he had written so praisefully. Even though they were dead, yet Domitian himself feared to close his hand toward this Jew who also possessed citizenship. He was famous and rich and powerful; and his last history, that of the antiquities of his race, had in great measure restored him to the esteem of his fellow countrymen. Nor, I knew, had he always been merely a historian. He had also been a great general, first faithful to the Jews and leading them in their desperate defense of Jerusalem (two years before I was born), then, in the army of Titus, equally faithful to the Roman destiny.

I roused to hear Josephus reprove Akiba. "You make too much of my slight contributions to history," he scolded.

26

"We shall explain them to our guest," Akiba said. "It is needful that he know many things."

"You must be Rufus Teneius, the young soldier of whom Akiba has told so much," Josephus said with a bow.

"Only after you cast the augury of my future," I said boldly.

Josephus regarded me keenly. "I use another method," he said. "Not the flight of birds but the flight of time."

"As you wish," I returned. "I hope you did not derive it from what Akiba said of me." My probe for information fell short. "Oh, it was good, very good, it was the very highest praise he had for you," Josephus said, leading the way back into the second chamber.

Baffled, I followed him. The inner living-court amazed me. It was only a little less rich and ornate than the villa of Flavius. Thoroughly Roman, quite tasteful: I was enchanted by the red-veined pillars about the pool, by the fountains and rare flowers, by the dignified statues and the abundance of cushioned couches and chairs and tables. The ceilings twinkled with gold fretwork and every inch of the walls was covered with colorful encaustic paintings, though most of them of scenes I did not recognize.

About a long low citron-veneer table squatted three men, all of them more aged than Akiba but less than my host. It was Josephus who brought them forward, one by one.

"Gamaliel ben Simeon, Joshua ben Hananya, Eleazar ben Azariah," he said. "These are the chief sages of Israel, peace be unto them!"

"Peace, indeed, to all of us," I said, sitting quickly on a couch before they could resume their own seats, pouring myself a cup of wine from the ruby-glass pitcher. "But if you seek peace, you travelers should not have come to Rome—as you yourself know, good Josephus." Over the rim of my cup, inhaling the wine, I covertly observed their queer costumes of heavy robes and shawls, tiny caps, and silver neck ornaments.

"We come truly for peace, not a sword," intoned Gamaliel. His beard was longer and whiter, his look more venerable, the respect paid him more evident; I guessed he was the leader of this deputation. "Our people are disturbed and unhappy," he went on, "because of the decrees of great Domitian who, doubtless, does not know of our unrest. We have come to pray that he will allow our Nasi to rule upon the small things and to pray a dispensation from the emperor himself on great things."

27

"Build not your hopes upon air," I said. "Logic is a leaden sword with our ruler." I tasted the wine cautiously; to my further surprise, it was excellent.

"I must do what I can for these friends," Josephus said proudly. "Among our people, they are most holy men. They must not have come all this way from Judea to Rome for naught."

I finished my wine. "Your friendship is a shelter of merit," I admitted, "and Akiba made no idle boast when he declared he had a great friend. But the emperor has no emotions other than fear and hate. Those whom his father and brother loved, he hates—but he also fears and holds them sacred."

"I was the instrument of his hope, even under the cruel Vitellius," Josephus protested.

"I have heard that, too. But Domitian—as is no secret—hates the race of Jews and puts tax after tax upon them. He has standing orders to the courts to seize those like yourselves on any pretext and fine them heavily for the benefit of the state. He calls it 'healthy bloodletting.' As for the decrees you complain of, it is rare that the best of provinces receive remission; the Jews and their rebellion are still fresh in the memory of Rome."

"That was a generation gone," murmured Eleazar, a slim dandy of a man with a well-cut robe. "I have heard that Romans forgive, if their enemies surrender."

"But the Jews—have they ever surrendered?" I asked.

"For fifteen years," said Joshua heavily, a homely, misshapen man with thinning hair on face and cheeks, "Rome has been merciful to us. Now we endure such stringent regulations that the people begin to mutter again of rebellion. We ask what we do for the ultimate benefit of peace to Rome."

I laughed and filled my cup again with the wine. "How is it that so much wisdom is contained in so ugly a body?" I jeered. Joshua took no offense, wagging his head with a slight smile.

"That wine you drink," he said softly, "is it good?"

"Superb," I said.

"Where is it kept?"

"Where else but in jars of earthenware?"

"But why not in jars of gold and silver? Our friend Josephus is rich enough to afford it."

"Any idiot knows that the metal would spoil the wine," I cried impatiently.

Joshua shrugged and spread his hands. "You have answered your own question," he said.

"This is nothing for our young guest," Akiba said in his slow deep voice, covering both my discomfiture and my rudeness. "Let us have food, good Josephus, lest we starve in the midst of your luxury."

"At once," Josephus said.

The meal surpassed not only my expectations but my hopes. Simple, rich: served with grace and hospitality, it was a fitting feast by which to recall my last night in Rome. Delicious Picenian bread, enormous spiced olives, Apennine meats (of which none of my hosts partook), turbot and eel, cheeses, quince juice for the Jews and all the wine for myself without stint. Nothing of the ceremony of grand cena but an abundance of all that was good and fresh and impeccable service by what I guessed to be Greek slaves. At the end, I belched and belched again, even a third time. My companions at table sat about me and nodded, smiling approval. Only Akiba did not change the gravity of his face.

"Does this feast not appeal to you?" I asked him. "It has satisfied the depths of my soul and I offer Jews the thanks of a Roman."

"I find that I am most sober when I am most joyful," said Akiba, "and that I laugh when I am wretched."

"Come, that's better," I told him. "The Jews borrow from the Greeks. This is a true combining of merry Democritus and melancholy Heraclitus."

"Our friend Akiba is a tearless man," murmured Eleazar. "He will laugh at the most sober things."

"Aye," Gamaliel added, "when we passed our ruined Temple in Jerusalem and paused to pray for safety on our trip to Rome, he bowed his head but he chuckled."

"I should think that would be a Roman gesture," I said with amusement, "except for the bowed head."

"Not Roman but Jewish," Akiba broke in. "For when I saw the desolate Temple I remembered the verse."

"What verse?" asked Eleazar.

" 'The Mount of Zion is desolate, the foxes patter upon it.' I laughed because our Scriptures tell us, good Rufus, of the rebuilding of the Temple as well as its destruction. I looked into the future and I was happy."

"Do you believe this?" I asked him. In spite of myself, my lip crooked.

29

"Indeed, I do," Akiba said earnestly. "How may the good come until the evil is past?"

"Nay, I do not think his laughter is Roman," put in Gamaliel maliciously, "for Akiba laughed when he landed here and saw Rome."

I raised my brows and finished the good wine of Josephus in my glass. I threw a glance at him, nodding in his chair, and returned my gaze to Akiba. "I have heard of many emotions on the part of those who first saw Rome," I said slowly. "Awe and respect, wonder and fear, and many others. But I have never before heard of one who laughed at our glories."

"Again, it was no disrespect," Akiba returned. "Again, it was the future. I thought that if God is so good to those who either do not know or acknowledge Him, how much better will He treat His own when their days come."

"We Romans acknowledge all gods except those which would overturn the state," I said carelessly. "You remind me of what you said at the house of Flavius Clemens, that his son would be a prince."

"All the children of Israel are kings," Akiba said evasively.

I banged my cup once on the table irritably. "But he is a child of Rome, not of the Jews," I said.

"Let me give you some more of this wine," Josephus said, rousing suddenly at the crash of my cup, coming instantly to his duties as a host. "It is excellent wine, virgin wine, taken from grapes that were dry before the flies came."

"Our brother Akiba is fond of sharpening his tongue on the mind of someone else," Eleazar said apologetically. "He has never been to Rome before. He does not know the manners of the Romans."

"But Eleazar, Joshua, and myself have been here, as long ago as ten years," added Gamaliel, "to plead with your great emperor Titus to appoint a Nasi among us, a request he was pleased to grant."

"And I have been here for more than twenty-five years," murmured Josephus, "honored of Vespasian, of Titus and his brother Domitian as well." I pursed my lips, replenished my cup, and took a long swallow of fresh wine. I could hardly tell my host that I knew he had achieved eminence by being a Jewish turncoat and writing what the Romans had wanted to read; true enough, perhaps, in its way but wholly traitor.

"Nevertheless," I said, wiping my mouth with a rich linen napkin, "Akiba should have more respect."

"But he has little respect even for his elders such as we," interposed Eleazar hurriedly.

"Let us be philosophers, then," I said, "and let a Roman pit himself against five Jews—the odds are equal. Now, first, you claim that your Jupiter—forgive me, your god—is all-powerful?"

The three across the table nodded, a trifle anxiously it appeared to me; at my right, Akiba assented in a low voice. "Then," I continued, "if this is true and he wishes not only Jews but the whole world to worship him, why does he not destroy the thousands of visible images of other gods in the temples?"

"God does not seek worshippers but in spirit and in truth," Akiba said firmly before the others could reply. "If one wishes to come to His throne, He accepts the humble and contrite heart. He is the one God, unchanging."

"Why, then, is He so remarkably careless as not to blast the other false gods with his lightnings?"

"Hear this," Akiba said. "He may do all that He wishes and to Him there is no time but eternity. He regards your laughter with pity; it is for our minds to understand only a small part of His being. I may answer you thus: if the only idols worshipped were those of stone and brass, of gold and silver and wood, then He might destroy them. But you also worship the sun, the moon, the stars, putting them among the gods. Shall the true God destroy His world, that He loves, because of a few fools?"

"Because I have drunk your wine," I replied, as steadily as I could against the heating of the fumes in my head, "you may not insult me."

"Philosophers," Joshua said soothingly, with a warning look at his alarmed companions, "do not insult each other. We talk of the things which pertain only to ideas, is that not so, noble Rufus?"

"I suppose so," I said foggily. "But your hairsplitting and Jew bargaining cannot shake me, though it may have served its purpose for Domitilla." I stared at them and a sudden thought struck me. "Why," I said, "you are no different from those who worship idols, not in the least. You have your rituals, your altars, your priests, do you not?"

"No longer," Gamaliel said, his voice melancholy. His commanding presence appeared to droop under the vital responses of Akiba and, indeed, except for myself, they were all under the spell of this strange awkward man.

31

"No longer," I mimicked him. "No, the power of the Romans has put an end to all that. It has tumbled down your temple and sown its foundations with salt. Where was your god then, tell me that? Why did He not appear to avenge himself on Vespasian and Titus?"

"Our sins were many," Eleazar said strongly. "The Romans are the scourge ordained for our pride."

I choked on the wine. "Do you escape so?" I cried. "Do you perform such ridiculous rites as you have told me and expect me to believe that your god abandons you?"

"Our God is a jealous god," Akiba said.

"What nonsense!" I exclaimed. "Such doings would ruin the world. Because you are a small, mutinous sect, you are privileged; you live off the activities of others, as insects devour good grain. Pompey Magnus defeated you merely by working his troops on your sacred Sabbath. You keep holy and meditate at such a time but even your god does not do this!"

"How so?" asked Akiba calmly.

"The sun rises, the winds blow, the clouds cross the sky, the sea storms, the earth fructifies, the rivers run to the sea—all is at work, even on your Sabbath. Your god violates your own laws, does he not?"

Akiba shook his head. "No," he said sonorously. "It is our belief that within his own house a man may be holy and yet active on that day. And is the whole universe not the house of God?"

"Enough, enough!" I said violently. "I perceive nothing here but a quarrel. Let us not talk of gods but of Roman things: of war and peace. You, good Josephus, have seen much of these if the tales of your past are true."

"That is so," Akiba returned. "Both Josephus and myself have fought before, in the Jewish War."

"You, as well?" I said in astonishment. Akiba nodded; I remembered his use of the staff at my door and was convinced.

"But you," I said to Gamaliel and Eleazar, "were you not also fighting?" I looked at Joshua.

"Can one serve God and mammon?" asked Gamaliel haughtily.

I chuckled. "Not only can he," I said, "but it is often more profitable than otherwise. The Jew, the second Agrippa, served Tiberius, Caius, Claudius and himself and became your king a century before my birth. In the civil wars, many a Roman

32

became famous by shifting sides at the propitious times. They died rich and respected while those of unshaken loyalty went down to unmarked graves. A man may serve as many masters as he pleases if none knows he bows to the other."

"But God knows!" protested Gamaliel.

"Perhaps your god does," I said carelessly, "but not our gods, wrapped in the smoke and fury of war. Janus, the progenitor of all gods, is himself two-faced."

"It is true," Josephus said, stroking his chin, "that mine has not been a peaceful life. From the beginning, when I was the youngest and most vehement commander of the Jewish forces in Jerusalem, to the day when I came to Rome, my life has been tempestuous. I have been the victim of slander and jealousy and envy, because I have continued in the favor of the great, of many nations."

"You will confess, privately, that you deserved some of your tribulations," I remarked, loosening the points of my armor.

"Not only privately but publicly. I am not afraid: those who have attempted to take my life, here and in Judea, will testify to that. But the wonder of it! To rise from a struggle for a humble portion of my own land, the governorship of Galilee, to be the intimate of Augusti!"

"Worldly fame is not always to be desired," Akiba said.

"If it is used in the right cause," Josephus answered hotly. "Generations from now, those who come after will read of what happened and will bless me for having the knowledge and leisure to write."

"My son," interposed Gamaliel, "you have still too much pride."

Josephus considered: "You came here to me," he said at last in measured tones, "and you, sage of Israel, were among the four that rapped on my door. My servants opened, I came to greet you. I said: 'Welcome and peace to you, sages of Israel, and to Rabban Gamaliel ben Simeon above all.' I have given you hospitality and protection that even the most powerful Roman himself next to the emperor might not have afforded. I have housed and fed you, disputed with you, advised you. If I have any pride, it is not in my works but in that I have been allowed to serve you."

The conversation had become too personal for enjoyment. I endeavored to change the subject.

"If the Jews think to challenge the power of Rome," I said, "they must raise Romans, not Jews."

33

"I labored long to create a Jewish army," said Josephus, "but it was no use."

"You labored like a Roman," I said maliciously; "to your own advantage, fighting against your own people."

Josephus stiffened, looking at the others for aid. Their faces were stony except for a certain mildness on Akiba's countenance. "I did what I had to do to save what was left of Israel," Josephus said in a muffled voice. He looked me squarely in the face. "One day," he said, his voice trembling, "with the same knowledge that tells me that the lives of you and Akiba ben Joseph are one, you will find that the Jews will rise again with their own leader against the oppressors!"

"And will they win?" I asked mockingly.

Josephus' head sank on his breast. "That is hidden from me," he said at last.

"As the prophet Hosea truly says," murmured Akiba, " 'the children of Israel shall abide many days without a king, and without a prince, and without a sacrifice, and without an image, and without an ephod and without seraphim.' "

"Then who will you secure to lead this mighty force you propose?" I inquired."

Eleazar looked at Gamaliel and sighed; Gamaliel fiddled with the fringes of his shawl and looked at Joshua. Akiba said quietly: "He will rise; he will wait until the change comes and he will rise."

"Then he will have to be a Roman in body and spirit and a very Jew of Jews in cunning, truly the son of the mating of a lion and a fox!" I cried.

"Simeon ben Gamaliel, blessed be he, last of those who led our faith before the destruction of the Temple," said Akiba, "instructed us that we must be as cunning as brave; we are lions but also the sons of foxes."

I shrugged, and dismissed his enigmatical sayings. "You repeat me," I said. "It is very tiring." I thought briefly. "Simeon," I said lingeringly, with a covert glance at Akiba. "I have heard that name before."

"It is the name of the second son of Jacob," said Gamaliel. "It is my father's name."

"It is the name of a dispersed tribe," Eleazar added.

"It was Simeon and Levi," said Akiba quietly, "who destroyed all the males of the house of Shechem because the son had violated their sister, Dinah."

A peculiar shudder passed through me, seeing these old and worn faces, like so many sheets of parchment before me, writ-

34

ten on by wrinkles, blotted by dead passions, as if they had never been young and fair. I felt stifled by my company. "I see," I said.

"Simeon is the avenger," said Joshua, "and if Jacob cursed what he did by mouth he approved in his soul."

"This mythology is interesting," I said loftily, "but hardly informative to me. You understand that my own philosophical leanings are rather toward the Stoa and the doctrines of exiled Epictetus. I hold that these are the only noble teachings in existence, to show a man how he may live." I pointed upward with my forefinger. "The stars are our only true friends." I drank deeply.

Akiba lifted a swift glance, reckoning the time of the sky above. I saw him make a slight gesture to the others. They rose, bowed, gave me blessings for my journey, made their farewells, and left. My suspicions, lulled until now, rose into my gorge; the wine in my head subsided. I stood up and tightened my cuirass. "Where are you going?" Akiba asked.

"The others have gone; it is time I left for my journey."

"Stay a moment," Akiba said.

I leaned across the table to him. "Why did you bring me here, old man?" I demanded harshly. "It was not because you had compassion on my journey."

"No," Akiba admitted.

"What do you wish of me?"

"Eight nights ago, in the villa of Flavius Clemens, you bade me take his newborn child."

"I must have been drunk," I muttered cautiously.

"No more than you are now," Akiba said. I gave him a suspicious glare, but he was imperturbable. One never knew when this Jew was joking or serious.

"I am sober," I announced, slamming down my fist on the table. "Tell me what you want."

"Do you have the right to give me the child?"

"I gave you no child!" I cried.

"Is it yours? Is it a child of Flavius? Which?"

"What?" I mumbled. His rapid fire of questions confused me; I wanted time to get my wine-numbed brain to think. "What?" I said again. Akiba did not speak but I could hardly bear the searing glance he gave me.

"It is the child of Domitilla," I said at last. "Only she can surrender it."

"But she is gone and left young Simeon as if he were yours," Akiba said cunningly. I shook my head. He went on:

35

"She wanted me to take care of him. She knew I would be kind to him as if he were my own son."

"He is not a filthy Jew. He is of good Roman blood, of royal blood!"

Akiba's deepset eyes glowed in the lamplight. "Do you then give me permission to take the child back with us to Judea? Or will you take him with you?"

"I depart for the German frontier," I said loudly. "It is not recommended for babes."

Akiba made me a deep, slow bow as if he were immensely grateful for some gift. "You are good," he said. "My wife Rachel and I have had two daughters and a son but he—he died. The daughters are married now, our home is childless. Small Simeon will be as our own."

"Do what you will," I said doggedly, "he will be forever a Roman."

"Wait," Akiba said. He disappeared into a nearby chamber and emerged with the bundle that was the sleeping child. With a quick gesture, he shucked off its swaddling and thrust the small crotch almost into my face. I jerked back, blinking.

"See?" Akiba said, a note of eagerness in his voice. "Do you see, noble Rufus?"

I looked and gaped, not able to believe my eyes. To my stupefaction the small penis was circled with a scabbed angry red. "He has been circumcised!" I shouted, pushing myself upright.

Akiba nodded solemnly. "I held him on my own lap, I said the prayers before and after, according to our laws of Leviticus," he affirmed.

"He can never be a Roman now! How can he appear naked in the baths? How can he strip for the exercises on the Campus Martius? How can he—how can he—everyone will know!" Helpless, my sorrow was transformed into rage. I rasped out my sword from its sheath. I swung a backhanded blow at the Jew. At the last moment, for no reason at all, I turned the edge. The flat of the blade slapped hard against Akiba's jaw; it sent him staggering back into the table. But he held tight to the tiny body of Simeon, though his face turned white as a tunic and his breath came in ragged gasps.

"Then—then," he managed to say, "you love the child yourself!"

"I loved what he might have been before you disfigured him," I said coldly. The shock had made me truly sober; I had wholly regained my senses. I drove my sword back into its sheath and turned to go. As I did, small Simeon writhed in Akiba's arms. He had felt the cold; he commenced to cry in an eerie voice. Instantly Akiba rose and bundled him back under the coverings.

I knew some gesture from me was required, if only one of repudiation. "Very well," I said, my voice shaking. "The child is yours. But a time shall come when you will pay in full for this mutilation and sacrilege against Rome. Until that time, I charge you to keep him close."

I detached my purse from my belt and squeezed it in the middle, opening out its thongs. I strewed the floor with half my money. "There," I said, "that will pay for a few years."

Akiba shook his head. "His mother has already given me far more than enough," he said.

Fuming, I wheeled toward the door, all desire to remain in such a house vanishing. I cursed the hour when I had entered the place. Pulling open the door, I shouted at Akiba over my shoulder.

"Pick up the money! Give it to your friends! Become famous for charity!" I yelled bitterly.

Akiba raised his hand in farewell. I did not respond. But all the way to the gate of the Via Flaminia, I felt his eyes at my back.

CHAPTER 3

Nec lecturo fastidum ferat—not to weary the reader, I must tell a little of myself, as guide in this long narrative. I am a well-built man of considerably more than middle height, short-waisted and long-legged, with thick shoulders and thighs. My hair and beard are long and white, my belly slack. My legs tremble from a walk through my gardens, though my back and arms are still strong. No one would believe, to see me now, that Rufus Teneius was once able to march forty miles a day with full pack and furniture, with shield, pila, and sword. Nor that my beard was black and bristling as a wild boar's, my head shaved, my expression fierce, my cuirass ajingle with medals.

I took the oath of the Army at the age of fifteen. I had worked in the fields of north Italy since I was able to toddle and glean, my father an ex-slave from Sicily. When the recruiting officer came, I admired his brusque contempt of my farm master. His shining brass armor dazzled me. When, in the name of imperial Rome, he demanded a dozen stout field-workers for the ranks, his hoarse drillmaster's bark thrilled me.

I longed to spring forward but I dared not. It was my overseer who obsequiously suggested that some of the younger men like myself—not as experienced in the furrow as their elders or as faithful in harvests—might be available. I leaped at the chance. I was enlisted as an overgrown recruit in the I Alaudae of Lower Germania, the legion which wore larks' wings as their helmet insignia.

It was nearly six months before my pleasure died; before I realized I was trapped in the invisible fortress which was Rome's bulwark, the thirty legions of its power. I would be forced to spend twenty years or more in service. I could neither marry nor have children. My life would be at the disposal of a commander's whim, my skin subject to a sergeant.

At first I did not care too much. There was an old legion saying: "Fill the purses of the soldiers and let whoever wishes rule the world." This became my motto: it did not concern me who sat upon the throne as long as the leather sack at my belt chinked with coin. I knew that the strength of the legions —then and still—was everything to Rome. Even the worshipful Senate, which pretended to so much dignity, groveled in the dirt before us. We had discovered long ago what apparently those high-and-mighties had never known: a sword, a hand's-breadth in the belly, settled the longest discussion.

Our obedience was to the emperor and our officers and, sometimes, to ourselves alone. It was held together by money, by love for an individual leader, by comradeship—rarely by loyalty to the vague and distant glories of our country. If the Senate had dared to defy us, we would have instantly sacked the Curia with fire and blood and thought it a rollicking good deed. All of us knew the story of Decius, the soldier of Marius, who bought for $100 a confiscated estate worth $300,000. Each of us hoped this ancient campfire tale would again come true for him.

Born in the reign of the good Vespasian, I enlisted under the evil Domitian, served under Nerva and Trajan, and retired under the rule of Hadrian. Thus, in all (counting the noble Titus), I have been faithful to six rulers. My first training— I was as clumsy as a Pannonian cub bear—was to be put under the vinestock, the clump of tough twisted vine branches with which we were beaten when we were stupid or slow. No answers were allowed except "No," and "Yes," and "No excuse." A man's pelt might be torn from him in punishment, and even we would applaud. How drunk we could get on the chantings of Rome's traditions! How many times, even now, at night, do I dream of those thrashings and turn and groan under my eiderdown quilt!

Three things I learned better than my own pulsebeat: to obey orders instantly, to throw the pilum accurately, to use the point of the sword always. Very little else, believe me, is necessary to conquer any enemy, if you have good officers. One had to know maneuvers, of course: massing into the eight-rank phalanx to handle the clumsy lancea from the rear, the agmen quadratum that was a hollow square, the famous triplex acies of Caesar. There was the order of march, protected front and back by the alae of cavalry with the exploratores skirmishing ahead; the assigned tasks each night in building the forts of turf, wood, or stone. Finally, it was essential to remember to stay five feet apart in open battle order or, in charging a fort, to stay tight together to form the testudo, that pyramid of raised shields which both protects and enables one to storm a wall.

Secretly we laughed at the heavy lances, rattling slings, and unmanageable swords, the clumsy formations and disorderly crowds of barbarians we fought. But we never mentioned our amusement. We never expressed less than admiration for such weapons and tactics to the prisoners. If there was any one secret of our success, it was that we knew, in the end, that no battle is decided by a struggle between masses. It resolves itself at last into a man-to-man encounter, hundreds and thousands of them, on any field in the world. It is no more than a monstrous series of tavern brawls with edged weapons and, of course, a comrade or two to envelop a foe from the rear. That is why, I think, that the Roman legionary likes nothing better than a fight in an inn; he is merely practicing for his life.

Our breasts were scaled like a fish or hooped like barrels with ribs of brass and iron. We had helmets of solid brass with horsehair tufts like cockscombs, brow- and cheek-pieces (sometimes jeered as coward's accessories), occasionally a dainty nosepiece. Our oriflamme was the helmet. Our first duty, each night, was to polish it until our distorted features grinned back at us through the sand and water. Still do I have calluses on my breast where I carried it on many a weary march. My fingers could fit it on without thought, even as I bawled our *braha-brahaha-braha* war cry, preparing for an immediate attack.

Our weapons, best in the world, were the sword and the javelin. The cavalry had others, like slings; there were the bows and knives, the longer spears like the lancea, but the legion customarily used only these two. The pila were more than body-length. Four cubits of heavy wood for the butt with an iron shaft sunk deep into it, extending two cubits beyond, with a long head barbed and sharp enough to cut whiskers. I remember one of my fellow recruits, ordered to sharpen the pilum-head, asked why. "To cut your meat," said the centurion and brayed a laugh. The joke was apparent when the man learned the legion had no meat at all; even better, when he came under the vinestock.

Such a javelin could sink deep through armor and shield if thrown by a strong arm. I have seen men pinned through harness and body, the barb sunk four inches deep into a pine. Even if it did not kill, the pilum could knock down a man; the iron behind the point was purposely soft so that, if one kept hold of the shaft, it broke off—allowing the head to remain imbedded while one acquired a useful club.

The sword was forever with us, doubling the length of our arms, with a twin edge that cost a beating to use. The irrevocable law was to thrust. It was keener, quicker, easier, better, and no effort to withdraw—unless one turned the blade in the wound, which was occasionally useful. The flat was for riot or insurrection or camp punishment.

Next to this pair, our best friend was the shield, both as protector and weapon. Nearly as high as we, as wide as an arm, square in shape and rounded from side to side, it was made of tough bull's leather rimmed by iron. Its two handles behind allowed us to lock it on our left arm. Its uses were many. Its design was such that it shed all arrows or javelins barring those which struck full on. Except for overhead strokes, sword cuts could be deflected. More than that, the shield was an offensive weapon. We practiced with it alone for hours in camp: the sudden crushing advance which overset the enemy and slew him by the pointed boss in the center, the twist which disarmed, if an enemy weapon got stuck in the leather, a dozen other maneuvers (ever the left foot forward). My left arm remains large to this day from the muscles I created in heaving the shield into the face of the enemy, fending and lunging with it like a dancer in the Pyrrhic measures.

Fling the pila at short range, charge with the sword, get back a pilum if you can, flail shield with the left hand, thrust and thrust again with the other. Go for the throat or eyes with the free hand if you lose your shield but never cease the thrust and thrust like a lover into his bride. I can recall the excitement of those wonderful moments better than many nights of love.

All that is over. After forty-eight years as a soldier of Rome, I desire no more of an epitaph on my tomb than that of Similis. The prefect of Hadrian retired to the country for seven years after such service and desired his heirs to write: "Here lies Similis, who died an old man but who lived only seven years."

I was meant to be a scholar, not a soldier. My first enthusiasms gave way to sullenness, punished by extra duty and, once, being forced to eat barley bread for a month alone outside the camp. These, with my floggings, brought me to my senses. I commenced to realize dimly that the only way I might escape from the servitude of the legions was first to rise within the ranks; then to educate myself to be worthy to be chosen for higher posts. Even at that time I had sound practical instincts: since I could not beat the Army, I decided to join it with all my strength.

We trained forever. It was vital to become tough enough to march, swim, leap, sleep, work, and eat in armor until the brass and leather turned green and stank under the groin. Raw courage was not enough; indeed, it was a trap. We had to learn when to advance, when to hold ground, when to retreat to the armed camps in consonance to the bugle blasts of the tuben. Every man could handle his body under burden and armor as featly as if he had been naked. Three times a month the legion would march thirty miles at quickstep, each man taking with him his baggage, half a bushel of grain, stakes for the palisadoes, spade, axe, rope, and tools—a sixty-pound kit. We made and repaired roads and bridges, we made bricks for camps, we dug ditches and erected tents, we rebuilt temples—and, on occasion, we crushed locusts or rats for hour on hour with our spades to save the crops of our allies.

The food was nothing like that which my stomach requires

41

nowadays. It was rough coarse fare, but who draws back when appetite is ravenous and the flesh trembling for nourishment? We never cared for flesh or vegetables, complaining when there was too much beef and not enough wheat. We loved wheat gruel so much that the rare barley diet was condign punishment enough as to almost inspire mutiny. We drank it down with posca from the carts, cheap wine diluted with vinegar. We slept where we could, under what shelter we might improvise, relishing furs captured from the barbarians and envying the tents of the officers.

Impelled by ambition, it was not long before I got my first banderole for my spear of honor; an even shorter time before medals began to clink on my breastplate. I spent little of my 1,200 sesterces of yearly pay, putting most of it into the legion bank. Within nine months I was duplarius, a double-pay man, principales within the century. After that came, as might be expected, the duties of tesserarius, holder of the password, and signifer, bearer of the image of the goddess Victory for the century. At last I became optio, chosen deputy of the centurion himself, Annius Verus. But it was two years before I rose to be centurion of the eighth cohort on my own account.

Now came the turn of luck without which the fortunes of man are barren indeed. I had already acquired two civic crowns of oak leaves for rescuing comrades in battle, as well as two corona muralis of gold for being first in storming the log-and-clay German fortresses. One day, with the commanding tribune absent, I got news of a besieged outpost six miles to the north. Without instructions, I marshalled the men and led them to the rescue. Just in time it was, as the Marcomanni tribe had broken through and were busily cutting throats. We drove them off with the usual slaughter and the outpost commander, one Julius Severus, a youngster with a bleeding gash on his cheek, embraced me on the field. Clumsily kneeling, he plucked up twigs and grass to weave me a siege crown, a most unusual honor. This involuntary award was approved and, when at last the first centurion was killed in battle, I was duly promoted to his position. I won the post of primipilus, first javelin of the whole corps of centurions. So, in my third year, I was entitled to counsel with the tribunes over strategy, to address the legate of the legion himself, to wear fine armor, to defend the great golden eagle—and, above all, to be able to collect fees from my men and triple my pay.

A few months later, I was ordered to the headquarters of Lucius Maximus Norbanus, commander of all the forces of

Lower Germany. I stood at stiff attention before him as he examined me. Finally Lucius, a thin solemn officer with a look of eternal harassment, nodded to his tribune. "He will do," he said and waved me out.

I was given orders. Notice had come to the legions of a "great victory" by the emperor Domitian over the Dacians. He had been awarded a triumph by the Senate. I was to ride publicus cursus to Rome to represent the Roman legions in Germania in the procession. "You understand," Norbanus said, summoning me for a second time, before my departure, "that it is a mission of merit. I dare not leave my post for reasons I shall not tell you. Nor will Lucius Saturninus, commander of Upper Germany, send a representative; he has been harassed and insulted by the emperor, he believes, too many times. Your responsibility is great." He gave me a sealed tablet, enjoining me to protect it with my life.

I shall never forget the occasion of my entering white-and-gold Rome. It awed me beyond measure; its extent, its buildings and monuments seemed the very embodiment of eternal might through the ages. The endless procession of the triumph, winding to the temple of Jupiter Capitolinus, was terrifying to me. Piles of trophies and largesse in plate and coin; colored works of art; pontiffs, consuls, and pompous lictors that led; magistrates and handsome pictures of the cities conquered; gold, silver, and copper ingots; spoils and standards, robes and jewelled crowns given to the legions; downcast prisoners and battered arms, victims and lowing sacrifices; chariots and diadems, captured kings and their families; obscene mockers of the vanquished, dancers and players on flutes and lyres, triumphal arches. Finally, Domitian himself standing tall in a golden chariot, sprayed by perfumes and flowers, followed by the unhelmeted generals and their armies and crowds of cheering Roman citizens, who expected—and received—donatives of coin and bread. All this—noise, glitter, music and wonderful sights—transfixed me to my spot in the Forum of Augustus for hours.

When at last that evening I was allowed to approach the emperor's tablinium, his throne room, I was forced to conjure up all that was left of my courage to stand upright. Guarded at every point, plated with marble polished like mirrors, the lofty roof upheld by twenty-eight pillars of Corinthian craft, it held eight niches filled with colossal black basalt statues, the largest being those of Hercules and Bacchus. I stood between two immense pillars of yellow marble before the gilded dais where purple-robed Domitian sat on his ivory curule chair. From my knees, I stammered my memorized message to the tall, well-made emperor, much handsomer than had been his thick-necked, heavy-faced father and brother. As he indolently watched me, listening to my offer of homage from the legions of Germany, he blushed deeply: a sign, I learned later, of his being pleased. By the end of my short, stammered speech, he appeared restless, but he nodded affably in dismissal. He deigned to receive the sealed tablet of Norbanus with his own hand.

That night Pontus, one of his slaves, gorgeously dressed, more haughty than his master, waited on me in an apartment of the palace. "You have pleased his mightiness," he said disdainfully, "and he wishes you to remain in Rome and make use of your unworthy body and brain in his service. He wishes you to attend the school of the Greek dog Epictetus in the portico of the Forum. There, most especially, to woo the friendship of one Flavius Clemens." He swirled his tunic up about his shoulder as if to go. "You will, of course, give daily secret reports to me, Pontus, concerning Flavius. For this you will be promoted to the office of tribune in the Praetorian Guard."

Tribune! Praetorian Guard, the elite unit which guarded not only the emperor but all Rome! For such a dizzying reward I would have visited the underworld and strangled Cerberus, the three-headed watchdog, with my bare hands, I thought exultantly. I did not know then how true this presentiment of my fate was to become.

So it was that I turned into a palace soldier, lost my reputation in the field, and insensibly was changed into a miserable informer. I did not know at the time, but the tablets of Norbanus from Germany must have warned the emperor of the pending revolt which broke out later that same year. That and my height of six feet, perhaps the bloom of my eighteen-year-old cheeks, must have persuaded Domitian to my appointment—which I naïvely thought was due to my virtues as a soldier.

My world became the world of Rome. All other events than those which took place in its bustling streets seemed dreamlike and far away. Even when Saturninus revolted in Upper Germania, with his four legions and three German tribes upholding his treachery, it seemed no more than a ridiculous phantasm to defy such a city where the dignity of conscious power exuded from every marble pillar and toga fold. Only when Domitian erupted in rage and announced he would set out for the frontier himself in the depths of winter—when he forced the whole Senate, most of them old men, to march with him—did the danger strike home. I was commanded to stay in Rome with the rest of the Praetorians and the city troops to prevent any rebellion in the ever-discontented mobs, but Domitian summoned the VII Gemina from Spain headed by one Trajan, son of a sagacious old general and former consul.

We waited the news with some anxiety. Ever since the years of tumult with Vitellius, the year before I was born, which overset the throne time and again, Roman perverseness was ready to hail a new name. But this time the emperor had covered only a few leagues when the news met him: my old commander had marched north, attacked the rebel Saturninus (deprived of his tribal allies by an unseasonable flooding of the Rhine) and totally defeated him. Domitian sent back the Senate but continued on his journey. He exacted a terrible revenge: all the heads of the dead and captured were cut off. He packed them back to Rome to be set on spikes about the city wall, to rot in the sun and stifle the air.

It was this which gave me my first uneasiness. I began to believe the rumors that Domitian had really been defeated in Dacia, especially when the returning hero ordered the Senate to decree him another triumph and added Germanicus to the Dacicus in his name. My suspicions hardened when, within the next few years, Domitian voted himself an extraordinary twenty-two triumphs.

Events were to show that my convictions were correct. But here I must pause to explain myself to myself. If I was such a mighty warrior in the field and such a perceptive hireling in Rome, how was it that I remained a spy of Domitian's corps of informers in the household of his cousin?

Looking back down the corridor of years, I find so many doors then open are now closed. I can scarcely believe I was such a scoundrel. I make no apologies for my love of Domitilla: a man of force needs no more than desire, the beauty of a body, and the opportunity, to justify the act. But betraying the faith of a host is against all a good Roman holds virtuous.

I think it must have been an infection in the air of the times. Terror of the emperor's will, perhaps, dread of the endless reach of Rome. Nowhere, no matter how one might flee, was there a spot in the world where one might escape the vengeance of the throne. The dead eyes of traitors and miscreants—so they were called—stared down at us every day from their niches over the gates. Bodies were flung down the Capitoline cliffs, despoiled corpses littered the streets after nights of riot or plunder. It was a mad time in a mad world. I was young and weak, dazzled by the confidence placed in me, possibly half-crediting Domitian's own mania about being in constant danger of his life. This alone would have spurred me to commit private disloyalties; the emperor's person was the first concern of any citizen, most especially a soldier in the Praetorians.

I know now that I was a fool and a pawn in the inscrutable game played by the gods. That does not excuse what I did nor does it altogether explain it. I recall that in those times I felt an inexpugnable disgust at my occupation, a gnawing desire to relieve the womb of my conscience of the deadly growing tumor of sin it carried. What sustained me—what first gave me the knowledge that I was fitted for the ways of a student—was my attendance with Flavius Clemens at the school of Epictetus.

One occasion made me uncomfortably aware of my life and my unhappy place in the scheme of things. I was squatting alone in the shade of the old portico on a cool day, facing Epictetus, hearing high-humming conversations of those passing as if they were bees in summertime. I had asked him, as he sat nursing his lamed leg, the supreme question of my life. "How," I said, "may I live best?"

"Your body is not yours," he said, "only a clever mixture of clay. What Zeus gave you was a part of his divinity—the faculty of being able to act or not to act, of willing to do or not to do. If you realize this ability, you will never groan, you will blame no man, flatter no man. Does this seem a little thing?"

"No," I answered fervently, "by the gods, no!"

"Does it content you?"

"So surely as I hope for the gods' favor. But explain what you mean more fully."

"Think of this: your body is your property, brother and friend, child and slave—but it is not yourself. We must make the best of those things in our power and take the rest as nature gives it. Let us playact, a little, to show it better. Suppose you were condemned to be executed, what would you say?"

"I would say," I said slowly, "what a terrible thing! Am I to be beheaded, alone and friendless?"

"Why?" demanded Epictetus. "Would you have us all beheaded, as your consolation? Remember Lateranus, when Nero ordered his execution. He stretched out his neck and took the blow; and when the first proved too weak, he shrank a little then stretched it out again. I must die. Very well: but must I die groaning? I must be imprisoned. Must I whine about it? I must be exiled. If so, can I not go with a smile, with courage, and at peace?"

"Tell me the secret!" I cried.

Epictetus smiled, still pretending. "I refuse to tell you, for this is in my power."

"But I will chain you!" I cried with imperial rage.

"Chain me? My legs, my arms, perhaps, but not my will. Not even Zeus can do that."

"I will imprison you!"

"My little body, you mean," Epictetus responded.

"Very well," I said, "then I will behead you."

"Why not?" Epictetus replied. "Did I ever say that I was the only man in the world that could not be beheaded?"

I ceased. My thoughts spun wildly as a child's top. Epictetus watched me, then said gently: "Thrasea used to say, 'I had rather be killed today than exiled tomorrow,' and Rufus, you should reply to anyone like that, 'If you choose it as the harder, what is the meaning of such a foolish choice? If as the easier, who has given you the easier? Study to be content with what is given you.'"

I began to speak but Epictetus silenced me with his upheld hand and went on: "It was in this spirit that Agrippinus used to say: 'I will not stand in my own way!' News was brought to him, 'Your trial is going on at the Senate,' and he replied: 'Good, but it is the fifth hour, time for my bath and exercise.' At the baths, one came to him and announced: 'You are condemned.' He nodded: 'Exile or death?' They replied: 'Exile.' He asked: 'My property?' 'It is not confiscated.' 'Very well,' he said, 'let us go and dine.'"

"But such a man was a paragon of virtue!" I burst out.

Epictetus shook his head and rearranged his lame leg before him. "He was a good man only, one you may imitate," he said softly. "Say to yourself: 'I must die, must I? If at once, then I am dying. If soon, I will dine now, as it is time for dinner, and afterward I will die. And die how? As befits

47

one who gives back what is not his own, with thanks and smiles.' Now help me up; I am tired and dying to dine."

I took him by the arms and raised his thin body to escort him on his limping way home. He refused to say another word to me. But what he had already said (as he well knew, cunning fellow!) sang in my head. It echoes there still.

It may be believed that the innumerable posts back on the road to Germania were not unknown to me and that, for most of the trip, black thoughts like ravens perched upon my mind. Summary dismissal from the Praetorians—for this is what my transfer amounted to—after four years of service was ignominio missio, a discharge without honor. Worse than that was the seesaw of thought that vacillated in my brain between serving virtue as Epictetus had described it and fulfilling the duty I had been taught for the past ten years. Clad and hooded in my lacerna, my rough-weather cloak, I rode along the Via Flaminia to the northeast, past the landmark of half-mile-high Mount Soracte, in the dawning. I headed toward Fanum Fortunae on the coast where I would then turn northwest on the long straight Way of Aemilia which would lead to Bononia, Ariminium, and Placentia and, finally, to Mediolanum. From thence I would wind through the passes of the mountains and head straight for Lugdunum. This, the last jumping-off place for Colonia, would take me directly north along the Rhenus River to my ultimate station.

I was young and foolish, unable to meditate upon my fate in the future or what had happened in the past. I slowly shed my regrets and fears. My spirits rose after my lodging at Fanum Fortunae in one of the vile highway taverns. I was cheerful on the side of necessity. Like the crow in the Greek fable, I had tried awhile to dress in peacock's feathers; now things had fallen out so that I could return to the respectable task of fighting for the empire with the legions, I thought. My muscles were tauter, my eye quicker, my thighs had hardened to leather. My blood ran faster. I almost forgot the sewer-sink that was the great city I had left behind me.

My orders and Domitian's own seal were all the passport I needed for food and mounts. The horizon-straight roads were good, the bridges marvels of work; there were even tunnels through solid rock. Every dozen miles or so there was a posthouse where fresh horses could be hired. Milestone after carved milestone were my only friends. The thousand-odd

48

miles I traveled might have been covered by imperial riders in less than two weeks, but a soldier on public dole would have to take at least a week longer. I met few travelers, only one or two carts, not a single litter. Thus I beguiled the time by the sights and the simplicities of my hopes. I had been away from nature, sealed in the gilt-and-marble tomb of Rome too many years. The keen winds and bright colors of approaching autumn in the rising ridges of mountains made me sing some of the ditties of the legion. They gave me inspiration to recite aloud some of the verses I had learned from the tattered Greek tutors who inhabited the porticoes of Rome. Corrupt versions of Hellenic dialects were everywhere in that city; even the most ignorant could understand a sentence or two in the gabbling of the sermo plebis. I recited a mouthful of love lyrics, one called "The Raisin":

> *When you were sour-young,*
> *Your told me 'twould be waste;*
> *When you were sweetly hung,*
> *You still were rather chaste;*
> *But now you're wizened in the sun—*
> *Pray, let me have a taste.*

I thought it very funny and repeated it with appropriate gestures; it dredged up from my memory another, in an equally merry vein:

> *"Sweetest bed lamp, in the corner,"*
> *Heraclea swore, in oaths a spendthrift,*
> *"I'll be true unto thine owner!"*
> *And I had sent thee as a gift*
> *Without a doubt.*
> *Now I fear the hussy tricks me*
> *With another. If thou art kind,*
> *Do not let their sporting vex me.*
> *This I beg thee: strike them blind,*
> *Dear lamp! Go out!*

For some reason this rhyme from Meleager did not make me laugh. Unaccountably, my thoughts turned to more serious things. I suddenly recalled a bitter distich of Ammianus upon one forgotten Nearchus. I promptly changed the name:

> *Domitian, may the dust upon thy grave be light—*
> *The better for the dogs to drag you out at night.*

I chanted others aloud, all that I could think of. I had not spent my days with Epictetus for naught. I learned to read and write; I had acquired the taste for learning. It had driven me to scroll and codex, to papyrus and parchment and tablet, to hanging on the words of the reciters and rewarding them with a sesterce or two. I spoke defiantly aloud some of the scurrilous verse that the famous Martial had written secretly about the emperor. Then, without warning, I found myself thinking of that extraordinary Jewish rabbi Akiba ben Joseph, and my last feast in Rome. I sneered at the memory and improvised a verse of my own that was pure venom:

> *Whoever says Akiba's nose*
> *Is useless on the face of it,*
> *Lies. For what do you suppose*
> *That he could use in place of it?*
> *A tool for hoeing;*
> *A trumpet for blowing;*
> *A sickle for reaping;*
> *An anchor for keeping;*
> *A plow for the spring;*
> *A fishhook for fishing;*
> *A wishbone for wishing;*
> *A fork for his forking;*
> *A handle for working*
> *Or any old thing.*
> *How lucky can Akiba be!*
> *A nose for any emergency!*

Of course, all of it was malicious nonsense. Indeed, my own nose was larger and sharper than his, but—as in the case of Flavius Clemens—this had made me unduly mischievous about the noses of others. Again I fleered off into melancholy as I thought of Domitilla. I recited softly and romantically a verse I had heard from an unknown forum poet:

> *Would I were the windy west!*
> *Then, walking on the shore,*
> *You might clasp me to your breast*
> *And hold me close once more.*

It brought tears to my eyes, though I could recall thinking at the time that I considered the poet to be the "windy west" himself. I sighed thrice and was silent, hanging my head in time to the rise and fall of the horse's back. I kicked him impatiently with my heels. He looked back reproachfully but accelerated not at all.

At that moment I was passing through remote and mountainous regions on the road to Mediolanum. The hills were snow-capped, the roads icy. I might have been more cautious: I had been warned at the last post that these forest heights were infested with thieves and criminals—most of them deserters from the Army or runaway slaves—bands which none had ever attempted to root out. It would not have been worth a campaign; they were merely a nuisance. Such men were so few and miserable in the empire that one pitied their state rather than condemned it. However, those who passed through sometimes took their lives in their hands, and I was to be no exception.

In that late afternoon, riding along the slippery jut of a cliff, musing on my fate and vainly trying to remember a few more verses of a bawdy Praetorian drinking song—how did it go?—I started at a tumbling shower of rocks and earth before me. I pulled up short, jerking a look upward along the sheer of the mountainside. I glimpsed a body hurled down, the glint from the blade of a knife. I flung myself forward on the neck of my horse. The human projectile brushed by, his desperate lunge no more than ripping the far haunch. My mount squealed, skidded, and reared. I had all I could do to prevent being plunged into the chasm on the other side.

From the corner of my eye, however, I saw the ragged form of the attacker strike the side of the road in a cloud of snow. He slid over the slick edge. He vanished with a long echoing yell of hopelessness. He struck a ledge on arms and legs, pinwheeling like a mime dancer, whirling into the depths of the cold mists. I shivered, observed that the haunch cut was only a scratch, took a deep breath, and trotted on. Next moment I paused: a reflection on the road made me rein in and dismount. It was a knife, iron-bladed and horn-hafted, wellbalanced, if crudely wrought. I thrust it into my belt, remounted, wrapped my cloak more tightly, and went on with my spoils of the encounter: glad to have the knife as a weapon, no matter how unorthodox it might be in battle.

I arrived at the gates of Colonia at the eve of the twentyfourth day. It was an unexpected sight: a city larger than most of the provincial towns, as well built in brick and wood —even in marbles, with the temples and principal structures —as any I had passed through. If I had thought about it, I would have guessed the reason: this was the ancient site of the chief town of the German Ubii tribe, built by the Army after its capture forty-five years before by the emperor Claudius. Then it was called Colonia Agrippina (after his wife) and had gained many extraordinary rights such as Roman law and justice. Vitellius himself, as emperor before Vespasian had rebelled against his rule, had spent many months here.

The city lay in a semicircle as neat as one drawn in the sand atop a mathematician's table. Surrounded by ditches and walls, it was a great fortress, but it buzzed with commerce, peacefully besieged by harvest wagons and carts as well as those afoot and horseback like myself. None recognized me: though I had served in Germania, I had never marched this far north. I gave my name and showed my seal to the sentry; he summoned the centurion on duty who saluted and gave me instructions. To my surprise, I was ordered on, to report to the commander of all Upper Germany, the noble prefect Marcus Ulpius Trajanus and his personal VII Gemina legion.

I responded mechanically, repeating the order with whitened breath. I set out, according to directions, toward a secondary fort closer to the wide waters of the Rhenus. Trajan: I recalled one of such a name who had commanded the X Fretensis in the Jewish War when I was born, who had done great deeds in the east, become consul and a patrician, governor of Syria and proconsul of Asia—all despite the fact that he was a lowly native of Spain, born in the province of Baetica. My heart commenced to beat heavily and quickly; if such a man had risen so high, what might not be in store for myself, with Rome holding out the baton of command and responsibility even to the child of an ex-slave? But, I reasoned, this could not be the same man: it must be the son of the same name who had served as military tribune with his father for ten years, then as quaestor and praetor. I smacked my saddle pad; my horse jumped. "That's it!" I said. I recalled the rumor in Rome that this same Trajan had been appointed consul for his speed in coming to Domitian's help. Then, as a further favor, he had been given the post of governor of Upper Germania against those barbarians whom Domitian most hated and feared.

Whichever it was, the omens were good. I made speed to arrive. I came to the fort, snuggled in a wide bend of the river, just at twilight. It was a pretty vision: I have never been able to see anything in nature itself so charming as the regular lines of a Roman military camp, neat, organized against haphazard nature, holding out so many promises of refuge and renewal. This one, though larger, was no exception. The pioneers had leveled the ground exactly, outlining a perfect square of eight hundred yards to a side, enough to hold 20,000 soldiers easily. There were the familiar broad streets, the perfectly aligned tents, the twelve-foot-high ramparts with interwoven palisades, ditch as deep as the wall was high, sentries pacing along the parapet. On a plateau in the center shone the white tent of the commander, centered by the gleaming gold of the legion eagle that was as brilliant as a beacon in the rays of the dying sun. At the gate I was given immediate entrance and escorted to the tent of the commander. As I ascended the steps to his pavilion, I was puzzled to see only a single sentry posted at the entrance.

Trajan was alone—even more unusual—seated behind a small table on a folding curule chair, his cuirass and helmet laid aside. He looked up as his sentry escorted me in—piercing blue eyes under gray-flecked brown cropped hair in a lean, tanned face—and nodded in return to our salutes. I stood at attention to the left side as the sentry retired. Trajan bent his head again to his work: he was, I noted with inward amusement, writing laboriously in the wax, his tongue thrust into his cheek, his stylus making error after error. I longed to step forward and take it out of his hand, to write myself in the elegant style that my schooling in Rome had taught me, but I desisted. I waited, instead. The moments passed by on the golden motes of the last single sunbeam that came fading through the door, interrupted by the scissoring shadows of the sentry's feet as he strode back and forth. The sounds of the camp rose to me: rasps of steel, cries of the sutler, indistinguishable boasts and bursts of laughter, clank of war engines being moved, clink of shovels and thud of stakes being driven, even the trailing remnant of a rowdy song. I felt myself actually homesick to be among the soldiers, to sit around the crackle of the campfire, more brilliant than all the gilt of Rome, against the black background of the menacing pine forest on the opposite bank of the Rhenus. Moment after moment, I stood there immobile. My legs and back began to ache, but I had no thought of breaking my pose. The light in the tent grew dimmer, Trajan bent closer to his work, slowly shaking his head.

Now came the second gift of fortune in my life. As I stood waiting, I heard a scream outside, the sound of tearing canvas. Directly behind my new commander, the tent parted in a

53

ragged gap. A squat, wild-eyed half-dressed soldier, hair and beard flying, plunged in. He jerked back his arm, his fist clutching the blade of a pilum. He drove it directly at the back of Trajan.

I cannot recall thinking: what I did was reflex, born of my long training with the legion. As the soldier-assassin flung himself toward the general, my hand flashed to my side. I whipped out the knife I had acquired on my journey. Almost in the same motion, I swung around with a single step, put up my left arm, and drove hard with my right. If the barbarian had thrown the shaftless head, Trajan might have been dead. As it was, it pierced my forearm past the bone as my dagger drove deep into his midriff. He staggered and coughed, slowly crumpling.

As he collapsed, to my amazement, I looked straight into the stern countenance of Trajan himself. It took seconds for me to realize, as we stared at each other, what had happened. So quick had been the general's reaction to the sound of the ripped tent, I had not seen him act. He had whirled out of his chair, ducked under the javelin-barb, and come up behind the would-be killer. His own sword stood deep in the soldier's back.

The sentry rushed in. Trajan waved him off, smiling slightly. Streaming blood from my forearm, I laughed in exaltation at what had happened. Both of us stepped back, wrenching our weapons free from the slumped body between us.

"My general," I said, "that was a master stroke."

"Yours," he said, "was as good." With his foot, he turned the dead man over so that he could see his face. "This one was condemned at any rate," he said unemotionally, "for desertion. There are a few such, even in the legion: black cockroach madness, camp madness. His guard shall be punished." He beckoned to the sentry and nodded toward the corpse. The sentry seized an arm and started to drag it out, cursing angrily at the inert flesh as he did so. Trajan glanced at my arm and took my hand firmly in his. With his other hand, he withdrew the shaft. I felt a wave of dizziness, sweeping it back with an effort of will.

"You are wounded," he said shortly. "Get yourself tended, then report again to me." My giddiness did not return; a feeling of pride and expectation swept over me as I emerged from his tent and gave my first order to a soldier, sending him for the medico legionis. I knew that, although Trajan had saved himself, I had demonstrated my loyalty and ability. Of this—

54

rewards being as predictable as punishments in the Army—something was bound to come. Nor was I disappointed, though the result was hardly what I expected.

Back, saluting, before his table, almost as soon as the corpse of the soldier had been dragged out and fresh sand sprinkled to soak up the blood, I waited again. Trajan had resumed his writing. I stood silent until he finished. He slapped the tablets together and pushed them aside. He placed his elbows on the camp table and peered upward at me with calculating eyes.

"You are a good soldier," he said at last. "More compliment than that, I cannot pay you."

"I thank the general," I said, a trifle breathlessly. "You might post more sentries, noble Trajan."

"I trust my soldiers," he said, frowning.

I bent my head submissively; I was not used to such faith in men after my sojourn in Rome.

"I commanded that you appear before me on your arrival," Trajan went on, "because a message has arrived for you."

His expressionless voice, the impassive cast of his face began to frighten me. I did not know what to answer; I remained silent and intimidated. The sentry came in, bearing a lamp. He placed it on the table, and retired respectfully. Trajan continued to watch me through the flicker of the yellow light. At last he reached into the leather pocket below the desk and took out a small ivory tablet, tossing it to me on the table.

My face prickled with blood. I saw the seal but I did not recognize it. What I did see was that it was stamped with small Hebrew characters. It was an insult to any Roman: verily, Akiba had his revenge on me for my jesting verse.

"It came by imperial post from Rome," Trajan said in his soft voice. "I have kept it here because I imagined you might be an important person to receive such a message in such a way." The veiled contempt in his tone stung me. I did not move. "I do not allow my officers to have secrets that come from Rome," he continued, "and I intended to order you to open it and read it in my presence. But I see by its seal and by your face that it is not important at all. You are free to go."

My bowels seething within me, unable to answer, impotent to exhibit my rage, I turned away. I knew that the message must be from Akiba but I did not care if it brought news that I was emperor. It had humiliated me before the only man in the world who had jurisdiction over my life and my ambitions.

"Before you depart," came Trajan's gentle, inexorable voice. Once more I turned, at attention, holding my bandaged forearm a little advanced so that he might notice it.

"You may have saved my life," the handsome graying man said. "Neither of us will ever know. It gives you the right to ask a favor and I am known to be grateful. But I must tell you here that you shall expect nothing from me. You will never rise in my legion nor in my favor."

I stiffened so much that I gasped from the shooting pain in my arm. My hopes fell in shards about me, in a hideous silent clamor. "As you command, my general," I said, striving to keep my voice level.

"Your letter from Rome," Trajan said quietly, "you have forgotten it." He indicated the ivory tablet. I picked it up with cold fingers. My thoughts flashed back to the evening at the villa of Flavius Clemens; to the appearance of Akiba and that of the centurion Saccus; to my last night in Rome. I cursed myself inwardly for having been such a fool as to have dined with Akiba and his friends. I knew above all that Trajan must have seen and recognized the twisted Hebrew lettering on the seal.

"Am I condemned, sir, because you believe I consort with Jews?" I asked in a shaking voice.

To my utter amazement, Trajan shook his head. "No," he said. He seemed mildly amused; he became thoughtful. "The Jews interest me with their odd religion; they provoke my admiration by their devotion to their own. They are an ancient and noble people, inclined to superstition and madness but nonetheless powerful and terrible in war. I remember my father telling me that the war which the divine Vespasian and Titus waged against their nation lasted for three years. It was the most bloody of all the wars of the empire, the one the Romans came nearest to losing. No, it is not the Jews."

"Then," I said, "forgive me, I do not understand."

Trajan's tone sharpened. "It is yourself, Rufus Teneius. You are what I have always despised, what is beneath a Roman. I have good and trusted agents in Rome and they know you as a filthy informer. Go!"

I stumbled out of his tent into the darkness, shivering and mindless. A soldier led me to my quarters. As I stumbled after him and his torch, the wind shrieked and tore at my cloak. It seemed to me to be the veritable doom which Trajan had pronounced.

CHAPTER 4

"GREETINGS TO THE ILLUSTRIOUS SEXTUS RUFUS TENEIUS, TRIBUNE, VII GEMINA, FROM AKIBA BEN JOSEPH, the following:

"Even a short letter like this one, I hope, will be measured by the rule of affection rather than length. I write to say that my friends and I have become enchanted by Rome and the majesty of all-powerful Domitian, emperor and god of the world. We wish to stay here forever but, in the wisdom of the emperor, we may be forced to leave. Rome is our chosen city and we are no longer lonely for Jerusalem and our people; we have cast our lot with our many countrymen who live under the shade of Mount Janiculum.

"You must know that the most compassionate Domitian at last gave us audience after many gracious refusals. It was due to the fact that some enemy had spread the news that we, the leaders of the Jews, had come to Rome to await the coming of a Messiah who would conquer the earth. As you know, nothing of this sort could have frightened the ruler of the Romans, but it aroused his curiosity. He ordered us to be brought to his chambers. We fell on our knees, dazzled by the light from his face, and made our plea for his rescinding the decree which he had lately contemplated, that of expelling all Jews from the borders of the empire. Despite the foul rumors, he contemplated us with understanding and sympathy, unwilling to condemn us unjustly as conspirators against his majesty.

" 'I have heard that you await the coming of a mighty Messiah,' he said to me.

" 'That is true, great Domitian,' I replied.

"He smiled benignantly. 'I have heard also that his dominion is to be over all the earth,' he said in a most kindly fashion.

" 'But that is not true,' said Josephus quickly; he had accompanied us and, as you know, is held in high favor. 'The Messiah that these simple fellows expect, most renowned Domitian, expects to rule only in heaven, not on earth.'

57

"I stood motionless but Gamaliel, Joshua, and Eleazar nodded their heads like wooden dolls. There could be no doubt that they were sincere. Domitian, seeing the rumor was a malicious lie, broke into laughter, his court with him.

" 'You,' he said to us jestingly, 'are the three greatest idiots who have ever come before me. I have a mind to throw you to the lions in the Circus Maximus but you would prove too tough for their digestion.' Thereupon he dismissed us from his august presence.

"His magnanimity so impressed us all that we decided to stay in Rome for the rest of our lives, if that favor might be granted. But we are desolate lest he send us back to Judea and therefore implore your help in petitioning the throne to allow us to remain. Such aid would leave us greatly in your debt.

"I can add nothing except that the small one is well, happy, getting fatter every day and—unless my imagination deceives me—looks a great deal like yourself. I hope you will, as they say, be able to make your way through this Labyrinth of Porsena and help us. May your gods and our god protect you. Vale."

It was a curious letter, one I did not understand at all. It did not make sense for Akiba to write it. Nor did his description of Domitian ring true.

Akiba and his friends were far from fools. I was certain that to stay in Rome was the least of their wishes. The fulsome praise directed to the emperor puzzled me also, unlike his usual blunt way of speaking. In fact, I reflected, it seemed this communication—undoubtedly from his hand—said exactly the opposite of what he felt and thought.

I struck my forehead with my fist. The Labyrinth of Porsena! Of course, that was the answer! It was the maze beneath the ancient tombs of Rome: in which the beginning is the end and everything comes out the opposite of what is expected. Akiba and his fellow rabbis were anxious indeed to flee Rome; evidently their request had been refused. They were forced to remain. Akiba had taken a daring method of writing to me to ask for help, knowing full well it would be read by an imperial informer. It had deceived them so well that it had been forwarded by the fastest post, arriving even ahead of my more leisurely trip: and possibly was a trap to snare me.

Even so, the script had baffling information in it. Was Akiba's "affection" really hatred? Was Simeon truly healthy? Did he indeed look like me? I meditated upon what Akiba

58

had written and came to no conclusion except one. I could only hurt their purpose of leaving Rome by petitioning the emperor—and condemn myself. I could not write in return. But, on impulse, I sent off my whole purse for their use, not knowing quite the reason for my generosity.

All this had not come about directly after my first interview with Trajan. Indeed I had taken the tablet into my tent, torn off the Jewish seal and hurled it into the dirt of the floor, grinding my heel upon it. Next day my orderly found it and placed it on my camp table. I flung it down again; again he picked it up. Time and again this happened until the mellow white of the bruised ivory was like an accusing eye—like Akiba's eye—fixed upon me either from the ground or from the table, by night or by day.

At length I let it repose on the table during the three weeks it took to heal my arm. Luckily, the pilum head had gone lengthwise through the muscles, not severing a single one. I recovered quickly. Despite it, I had joined the exercises of the legion next day, though without a shield, gaining considerably more dexterity with the sword than I had before simply because of the helpless condition of my left arm.

Trajan noted this. He ordered all the legionaries to have their left hands tied in practice to improve their swordplay with their right hands. This mark of approval heartened me. Not long afterward, I discovered I could enter my tent and open the tablets of Akiba without rousing my spirit into a fit of rage. I read what he had said, pondered upon its solution and blamed myself: it was not the fault of the Jew, after all, that I had been a fool. There was more to fate than I could fathom. I determined to accept it. Thus my purse to Akiba in Rome was no more than a sacrificial offering to the gods. I found myself insensibly swayed to the opinion of vanished Flavius, that all gods were powerful, that it was best to placate as many as one knew. After all, the Jews seemed convinced, so there might be truth in their contention about one-godding. I determined to send—what was it, a tenth?—of my pay every month to Akiba. It would relieve my conscience about the child and it would pacify the unknown deities. I wondered whether or not his pride would accept it even in the name of Simeon. It was more than a year later that I found he had indeed done so.

We had nearly 13,000 men in the camp—a total of two legions—and there were more than 130 centurions alone, not noting the tribunes. So it was not strange that weeks passed before I met a familiar figure: Curtius Saccus, the brusque centurion who had arrested Flavius that fatal night outside Rome.

I saw him before he knew me. I stepped across his way. As he halted, I addressed him in ironic reply to his automatic salute: "Greetings, great Saccus! Have you left Rome for a vacation?"

He knew me. His face drew itself down into grim lines. "Greetings, noble Rufus," he said. "Have you returned to the wars?"

"They have transferred you?"

"From the Scythians to the II Augusta. And you, sir?"

"The emperor thought I knew too much," I replied, "and perhaps you knew too little. Yet this is an exile not without merit."

"We shall have our bellies full of war," Saccus said with almost a sigh. "Our general is fond of the clash of arms."

"So much the better," I answered promptly. "Are you still of a mind to curl your lip?"

Saccus' gaze broke, turning away from me. "A centurion cannot quarrel with a tribune," he muttered. "Both of us would be executed."

"There are places in the woods where none can see," I said, stepping aside. "Remember that. Perhaps our opportunity may come." He saluted again and went on without another word.

Winter passed into late spring. As the ice commenced to break up on the banks of the Rhenus, so the barbarians in the forest fastnesses became restless. But they restrained themselves until the beginning of high summer. One morning, as we were busy about rebuilding the south wall of one of the forts outside Colonia, just across the river from the black nodding forest, I heard the brass bray of the trumpets. I turned about only in time to see Trajan beckon to me. I followed him to a protected stone embrasure. We looked out and down upon what seemed to be a sea of barbarians, momently growing as they swarmed across the Rhenus in their skin coracles. It seemed an angry mass of skins and white limbs and long disheveled blond hair and beards. They did not approach the fosse or the wickedly pointed palisade but stayed beyond it in a stamping, heaving mass. From them rose a constant hoarse ululation of rage. They bore all sorts of weapons, antique, captured, or manufactured. Their low

60

angry shouting occasionally rose like a surf and then died away as an ebb might retreat from the shore.

"It has been a long while since you have seen Germans," Trajan said to me. He smiled. "What do you make of these?"

For a moment, I made no answer. I gazed at him and saw him as utterly without fear, as calm and composed as if he were watching dancing youths at a feast. I admired his composure, but I could not help thinking it might be attributable to lack of knowledge of the rending cruelty and savage bloodthirst of the Germans.

"Why do you stare at me?" Trajan inquired, his level brows knitting.

"Forgive me, my general," I muttered. I turned my eyes in the other direction, screwing up my face against the morning sun in order to see our impromptu besiegers. I commenced counting tens on my fingers, then gave up. "These are all Alemanni," I said. "They are the worst. There are chiefs among them, I am sure, but I recognize none of them."

"Do you think they seek battle or plunder—or what do they seek?" inquired Trajan.

"Each of these and all of them seek war, women, and hostages besides food and wine," I answered. "They love all violent actions. They believe life is not to be desired half as much as a glorious death." I peered over the wall once more. "They are as they always are on such occasions," I added, "drunk on their own wretched beer, blowing their horns and shouting until their cheeks flame and their eyes bulge. They are whipping themselves up into a battle rage."

"Like talking," Trajan said softly. "Much blowing and groaning makes a man foolish."

As if they were horses on display, some of the barbarians in front tossed their heads proudly, their hair floating behind them. The motion communicated itself to the whole host, like foam on a rocky beach driven up by winds.

Saccus came up to us and saluted with a bow. "Great general," he said. Trajan stopped his mouth with a look. "I am a soldier only," he said sternly, "at moments like these."

"Great soldier, sir," said the formal centurion, "I have ill news."

"Speak."

"One of the targeteers, one by the name of Rubrius, has deserted. He had committed the crime of stealing a thousand sesterces from a comrade and had been convicted by the camp court. He broke away, hurdled the ramparts, and ran into the arms of the barbarians."

"When was this?" asked Trajan coldly. He did not care for breaches of discipline.

"Last night. This morning our spies have reported that he has betrayed us. They know we have no more than 13,000 men in our army. That is the reason for the rising ferocity of the tribes and pleasure in the coming battle. They believe they outnumber us, ten men to one."

"Battle?" demanded Trajan incredulously. "Do they wish battle? You thought so, too, Rufus."

"These are madmen, not soldiers," I said.

"Rubrius even now runs among them, repeating our numbers, saying we are weak in courage and arms," Saccus insinuated. He pointed: indeed, we could see a small man in Roman dress moving as rapidly as a weaver's shuttle through the ranks of the Alemanni.

"They will send envoys and make demands before they fight," I said.

"You know them well enough," Trajan said abstractedly.

"That is their way. They have singular habits of war-making, of winning or losing or threatening. Always, this comes first."

Trajan gave his rare inimitable laugh. From such a sober leader, its merry sound was better than a trumpet. Those who heard it lifted their heads and smiled and went back to work with more spirit and confidence than ever. The soldiers loved him for this quality of mirth, even at the most fearsome moments, almost as much as they did his concern for their welfare and safety and his demands upon himself. "Well," said Trajan, still smiling, "we shall wait upon their sending."

I was not wrong. A little before the sun was overhead, a solemn delegation of German warriors, chewing moustaches, with horned helmets awry, advanced with unsteady pace. They were drunk and weaponless, their hands clutching air at their sides as if a part of their bodies had been abandoned when they left their spears and clubs behind. Trajan, and I with the other tribunes and his bodyguard—for no one knew what such madmen might do—stood forward to welcome them. We had no chance to say a word.

"Depart!" howled the first. "Leave the lands we have won with sword and valor! Depart, lest ye get what shall be yours!"

"If it is to be ours, in any case," Trajan said easily, "we shall stay and see what it is." He spoke through interpreters, of course; this transfer of tongues gave us time to see the result of his speech upon the delegation. Their faces turned purple, they shouted imprecations (which even our interpreter was powerless to understand) and foamed at the mouth. For an instant they seemed willing to throw themselves upon us and tear us flesh from limb—but they restrained themselves. Their rage was interrupted again by the snort of laughter from Trajan. He turned his back on them and made his way through the soldiers behind, paying no more attention to the Alemanni. The color receded from their faces at the insult; they stood stiff and bared their yellow fangs at his departure. Our guards prodded them with scabbards. They turned and marched out without another word. I watched Trajan as they left: to my surprise, he was not perturbed but seemed actually amused. He resumed his station at the coign of the wall and beckoned me to him: "Who is that?" he said, pointing.

I looked where he directed. I saw a tall man clad in bearskin and bearing a club plated with iron. He moved from group to group, speaking and gesticulating. We could not hear his words—even if we could have understood his language—but his gestures left no doubt of his intention. As he spoke, he exaggerated what he said with motions of his thick golden eyebrows, and I recognized him.

"That must be Rhodomarius himself; I have heard he is their king," I said.

Trajan nodded quietly. "We shall have time enough to deal with him," he said. "Let us finish our fortifications first."

I hardly felt as assured as Trajan seemed over the outcome of what promised to be a pitched battle some time within the next day or two. Certainly we were trapped in the castellum. Our foes outside were swollen with confidence and rash courage, their ranks growing; they were the sort that would take no account of those killed but press on until numbers alone overwhelmed us. Rhodomarius was one of those Alemanni who could speak with absolute knowledge of Roman arms: a few years before, he had met the previous commander of Upper Germania, Saturninus, with an army no larger than his and had utterly crushed him, overrunning the Roman settlements with fire and sword with complete freedom until a humiliating peace was made. Trajan, I knew, had sworn to put an end to this; I was with him in his will but, judging the outcome of what must follow, I did not know. Rhodomarius was far our superior in numbers and strength—and

63

they knew by experience that Romans were not invincible. Had they not bent Saturninus to his knees? Had they not joined him in a conspiracy only a few years before that threatened the whole of the empire?

Now the devices on our shields no longer inspired terror but contempt. For the Alemanni knew that we were no more than mortal, that our blood was as red as theirs and could flow as freely; that we could run as well as advance.

Such thoughts must have plagued Trajan as well. All that night he went from place to place on the banks of earth, making sure of the vigilance of the sentinels, heartening the men, perhaps hiding his anxiety and doubt over the coming day with his usual composure, keeping fires burning and seeing to it that weapons were sharpened and polished. Never once did he breathe anything but confidence and the desire to get to grips with the tribes of Germania.

Dawn came. With it, as the sun commenced to redden the sky, our legionaries donned their armor and moved into battle array. Blares from the trumpets sounded and sounded again. At their usual stride, thirty inches to a step, the infantry advanced toward the gates, Trajan at their head, myself and the other officers in ranks. Our heavy wooden portals swung back and we passed into the open field before the camp with squadrons of our cavalry maneuvering on our flanks: the light-armed as well, cuirassers with their heavy armor, clouds of auxiliary archers, testing their bowstrings, loosening their arrows from the quivers on their hips.

The main camp of the Alemanni was more than twenty miles away. No immediate clash was to be expected. Trajan sent messengers to recall all outriders and patrols before the fort. We waited for them at ease, in the cool dew of the morning, wondering what would happen. The usual jokes passed between the men and, as far as I could tell, their morale had never been as high. Trajan waited calmly, accompanied by his guard. When all had assembled by companies, the sun was over the treetops, bright enough to make blinding flashes out of the scoured armor and pila heads. Trajan ascended a little mound of earth and spoke to us.

"I shall not talk long," he said, in a tone almost like one of his intimate conversations but with words that carried clearly to every man in the stiff, silent ranks. "We have other business to perform. But our common safety and desire prompt me to speak not as your commander but as one of you, who shall be as bloody and sweaty as anyone before

64

the day is over. I beg you, fellow-soldiers, to remember your discipline and courage, and to choose the way of caution—not the foolish ideas of breaking ranks and dashing helter-skelter—to win personal glory. I do not mean that when we are in danger soldiers should not be energetic and daring; I mean only they should also be obedient and careful. Every life here is worth more than ten of the barbarians. I intend to make them even more valuable.

"Hear me say what my opinion is. Give me leave to declare what I have in my heart, and see if your own murk of red fury, controlled by your clear thoughts, does not agree. We shall march forward, not waiting for assault. They have declared for battle; we accept. By the time we reach the enemy's camp, it will be nearly noon. We will be weary from the march. We shall have advanced by steep and narrow paths and will be tired.

"If we reach them without mishap, what shall be our situation when the enemy's swarms, like angry bees, rush down to sting us with their spears? They will be rested, fed, full of activity. But we—what strength can we have when our limbs are feeble with hunger and toil? Shall we retire behind our walls and trenches once more?"

Trajan paused, as if expecting a reply. For a long moment there was silence. Trajan smiled, and raised one hand. "Well?" he asked in a loud ringing voice.

His words had astonished me. They seemed the speech of a coward, not a general; I had not realized how clever and stirring they were to the average soldier. My first intimation of their effect came with a universal shout of rage. The men would not allow him to finish. They ground their teeth, brandished their spears, beat them against their shields in a booming, deafening din.

"Lead us, lead us!" they shouted. "We will trust the favor of the gods, the favor of our own courage and discipline, the favor of our own might in arms! You are a lucky general, we are filled with fortune! Lead us, mighty Trajan!"

Trajan raised his hand again. Instantly the clamor ceased. He was still smiling, his quick, bright, boyish irresistible smile. His head shone, aureoled by the sun, brighter than all else. "Then onward with our triumphant eagles and our victorious standards!" he cried. The troops echoed him with a ringing shout. Centurions and tribunes, myself with them, shouted their orders in ecstasy as we moved into line. I commenced singing one of our rough Roman legion songs. Others joined

65

in, then all. We broke into delighted cheers to see Trajan chanting the same words in a robust shout.

As we stepped out, catching the rhythm of the drumbeat, I realized that Trajan's words had not been what they seemed: rash headlong judgment or mere eagerness to join battle. On the contrary, all the night before—between his pacing on the walls and his visits to the fires of the soldiers—he had been consulting in casual conversation with the experienced tribunes, including myself, in our roles as group leaders. We had judged that, though the effort was risky, it was worth taking. We might fight, we knew, while the savages were massed together. We might cut them down but, if they scattered, the hot temper of the legions would break our own ranks. Our men would be destroyed one by one by guerrilla bands or ambush. They had a tendency already to insubordination from their long inaction in winter camp.

What the plans of Trajan were, they neither knew nor cared. But in a council before the battle our commander had revealed that the Germans had been crossing the Rhenus for three days. They had abandoned their log barricades on the far side, determined to loot the fair fields across the water.

We marched in good order along the winding pathway that bordered the river, making sure our skirmishers and scouts were far out to prevent surprise. At last, about noon, we came upon a wide space filled with growing yellow grain, a gently sloped hill in the center. From atop this point, like the boss on a shield, we saw three scouts of the Germans ride off furiously to warn their comrades.

Seeing this, Trajan halted. He ascended the hill, planting the eagle at the very crest, surrounding its standard-bearer with his own guard. We formed the army in close wedge formation like a wall, backed by the spearmen and staff officers. Trajan ordered the cavalry to the right flank.

Now the enemy appeared in sullen mass and imitated us. They put their troops opposite us in every instance to overwhelm us by their onslaught. Among the cavalry they scattered their own scouts and light-armed infantry to creep about in case of a charge and gut the horse's belly so as to throw the rider. They also wormed their way into the dense forest on each side neighboring the plain, creating secret ambuscades. Spying out over the growing German host that massed before us, my heart sank. I put the number at no less than 30,000.

German trumpets began to blare, rousing their spirits for

66

their attack. Trajan changed his formation, opening out the ranks into fighting array, determined to hold his hill position. He himself went from group to group, encouraging and exhorting. To some I heard him say: "Now has come the time for real fighting which you and I have long desired and which we called for a few hours before. Be men and be Romans and the day is ours." To others, he declared: "This is the day when we wash out all of the disgrace suffered by our arms before and restore honor to the majesty of Rome. These savages are driven here by fate to fall to our swords."

As a climax, Trajan mounted on the shoulders of two officers and shouted his final instructions: "When we conquer, as we must, I command you not to stain the glory of the day by following the enemy too closely into ambush; nor do any of you, not one man, give way before these savages. As for me, I shall be with the foremost!"

At this point, hearing the wild and mournful yells of the Germans, drums beating and horns making a hideous tumult, he leaped down and took his post. As he did so, the Germans broke into a run toward our first ranks. Our auxiliary cavalry swung out, so as to encompass their left flank. They paid no heed. One could see the barbarians clearly, gnashing their long teeth, their hair flowing in the wind, a kind of madness shining in their eyes. They came on, brandishing their glittering spears, waving their clubs of skinned pine, uttering their horrible guttural war cries calculated to paralyze the enemy. Their huge white limbs gleamed everywhere, mixed inextricably with the furs of bear and panther. Slings hissed, missiles rattled. Their feet made a crackling sound on the crushed wheat like a multitude of tiny fires.

I looked down along the ranks of our legions. How pitifully small they seemed, even in their helmed armor! We waited, for no longer than a thud or two of the artery in my throat. Then, with a simultaneous shout, our whole line moved forward as one man. My throat swelled, my eyes dimmed with tears. Our curled trumpets snarled, our drums commenced a steady beat.

The Germans seemed to hesitate; I saw a few, no more than twenty yards away, look at each other in puzzlement. Then, quickly, we halted. Forward left foot and shields, back with the right arms! The heavy pila of the legion flew glittering, buzzing through the air, the sound of their passing piercing through all the din.

As if attacked by a horde of gigantic dragonflies, the Germans stumbled. Their front rank collapsed, falling and plucking at the spears in their throats and torsos, the upright shafts in their bodies sticking up like a palisade. The next rank could not help itself; it, too, tumbled—some of them being transfixed by accident. But their onrush came forward with redoubled fury.

So did that of the legion. The primopilis, bearing the golden eagle, stretched his arms upward and broke into a run down the hill toward the enemy. With a wild burst of enthusiasm, all of us charged after him. We seemed to me like a wedge of iron that drove straight into the midst of the disorganized crowd of Germans. Now, and now only, it was every man against every man. Here our lesser height and armor meant everything. It meant that Romans could distinguish friend from foe, that we could unleash the cold steel of our arm-length swords, the deadly edge of our shields with sharp-pointed bosses.

The battle lines melted together, like two tides forced into spume by contrary winds. I saw a score of our men actually tossed a dozen feet into the air, thrown up like corks, tumbled aside, still plying their swords like scythes while still off their feet, conscious of nothing but fury and blood. The white and the glitter and the shine—silver on one side, golden on the other—became obscured with the thick wet red of gore. Cries did not diminish but became intensified, with the low ululants of the wounded beneath the sounds in a horrid chorus.

Now the critical time poised over us. It came in every battle, sometimes more than once—that fierce moment of stasis when everything seemed sculptured in the mind but the breaking of which decides the day. For a moment, the two lines were inextricable and immovable, dealing out death, face to face. Then I saw our wedge was unbroken, the banners and eagle still erect in the heart of the German host and moving relentlessly forward. The day was ours! The sudden realization of it thrilled the hearts of every Roman legionary simultaneously. Trajan shouted an order. There came the second surge of might in our warriors; the rest of the legion, half of our reserves, joined combat. The crackling thunder of the hooves of the auxiliary cavalry reserve came from right and left, drumming of doom.

The Germans glanced wildly about them, men trapped. A few, only a few, broke ranks and fled. The rest grinned under their long blond moustaches and kept flailing ceaselessly, uselessly away like reapers at chaff. The metallic clang of helmets being beaten in came to me, but our legions were not falling; they were pushing ahead, VII Gemina and II Augusta, over the naked bodies as if leaping floating logs in a stream, slipping in the juices of battle, regaining footing, going ahead, going ahead.

Almost before I knew it, the battle had become a field clearing of men. The Germans everywhere doubled up, clasping the cold steel that was driven into their bellies. They fell backward, edges of our shields catching them under the chin and breaking the neck, bosses penetrating the leather straps across their breasts. Small as we Romans were, our strength gave us added leverage. Some of the Germans actually toppled over shoulders. We worked like woodsmen to cut down this human forest.

Trajan cried out again, both appeal and order. Few heard him, none understood him, but I knew what he feared. This was the last moment of a battle where, like the reflex of a dying snake, the enemy would make the last mighty effort that had so often won a fight seemingly hopelessly lost. We had to wait and brace for that. I glanced at the one last line of the legions held back, handling their pila with all the eagerness of hounds held in leash. They were thirsting to fight, but Trajan could not release them yet.

As Trajan anticipated, the Germans roused themselves to a last frenzy, roaring like wild beasts. For the first time, our forward advance was stopped. I saw the men in the front give back two steps. The banner wavered. Trajan lifted his hand and brought it down in a cutting gesture. "Now!" he shouted.

With a wild shriek, the final line of the legion flung their pila and bolted into the fight. They fought like demons coming to the aid of their comrades. Nothing stood in their way. They even vaulted over bodies, one using the wooden butt of a spear as a jumping pole, directly into a huddle of Germans, onto their shoulders, slashing them down. It was the Germans who gave way, wailing and weeping.

In a moment the retreat was on, fleeing back through the forest toward the river. Our men, unrecognizable in a shambles of blood and flesh, their faces so stained as to constitute a disguise, hoarse and triumphant, still making their tired way after them, moving as one, hacking and stabbing down to the slippery riverbank already filled with despairing Germans, the waters full of those drowning in the flood. The battle was over except for the necessary killing of the fugitives and the throat-cutting of the wounded.

To my astonishment, it was twilight. The battle, which had seemed to take no more than seconds, had lasted the whole of the afternoon.

Dusk came down as was its custom in those dark riverside woods, without courtesy of a warning. It swooped, as if it were a bird of gigantic dark wings that enfolded the earth. First, the long slanting yellow rays over the battle, then, tenebrous shade and, finally, darkness. Already these shadows filled the river valley. They were rising rapidly toward the grain field knoll when I staggered free of a knot of fighting men. I fell back a pace or two toward the cleared space. I had disposed of my man, a huge bearded warrior; I needed only to catch my wind a moment or two. I heard the sharp, shrill notes of the tuben, telling us by the blast on the circular trumpet that we were to fall back, re-form for withdrawal to the camp.

As I looked up, with renewed energy at the prospect of breaking off the fight, I saw beyond me, in the forest to my right, a fantastic sight. There seemed to stand a monstrous man, all in white, nodding and grinning at me. I recognized him. It was the figure of Akiba, out of all mortal height, beckoning to me in a sort of vague hithering, daring me to further deeds of valor. He seemed to hold the babe Simeon in white wrappings while his other hand waved me on. If I had been in my right senses, I might have known it was no more than a vision, so tall was the figure and so commanding its aspect— so different from the humble man I had known in Rome. But his lank figure, his drawn aspect, his capped bald head and beard seemed so real, in that frenzied moment, that I shouted in reply to his challenge through a sunbaked throat and charged once again into the melee. The energy of my thrust carried me crashing through the knot of fighters, across the waters of a small stream, into the black forest itself.

There I found what I had not expected to find. A large ambush of the ferocious Germans had surrounded nearly a century of Romans, separated from the rest. They were driving hard upon them, silent, like a pack upon the kill. As I came madly running, brandishing my sword in the last of the sun, it must have flickered like the lightning bolts of the gods. The Germans heard me slashing through the underbrush. They turned. The savagery in their eyes dulled into doubt, sprang alive again in fear. They gave way before me alone, thinking that behind such a daring Roman officer must follow troops of legionaries. In that moment, the harassed cutoff remnant of

70

our Army thought the same. They plunged forward with renewed cries of hope and salvation, hewing and hacking their way through the German circle, widening it with dead. I joined them as the barbarians gave back. I took command, and, step by step, we won across the stream and into the open. Sighted, a flying column came to our relief. The dogged tribesmen were plucked from our flanks by pilum and sword.

As the discomfited Germans were sent flying back to their fastnesses in the woods, the centurion of the group appeared before me with bowed head. Still with a gapped, flowing wound in his thigh, face hidden, he stooped and plucked grasses. I straightened with pride. It was to be my second corona cerialis. With an expression of haggard envy, he placed it on my forehead and I saw who he was: the centurion Curtius Saccus.

I lifted my eyes over his head to where I had seen my vision of Akiba. Lo, there was nothing there! Nothing but a tall tree covered with white blossoms in the full of summer bloom, nodding and smiling and bowing to me.

"This is our destined meeting in the forest," I said. Saccus nodded, but I knew he did not understand me.

That night, within the encampment, as we sang and rejoiced and cleaned our weapons, drinking our victory fill of posca, I received orders to report at once to the headquarters tent of the commander. I rubbed up my helmet and cuirass and marched proudly up the steps in response to the summons I had expected. Past the single sentry, Trajan sat alone and brooding behind his camp desk. He looked at me without expression.

"Are you satisfied with your actions today, Tribune Rufus?" inquired Trajan. "Dashing into the woods like a raw recruit?"

I lifted my chin. "Is my general dissatisfied?" I asked.

"Have you no tales to bear to me about the cowardice of your comrades?" asked Trajan grimly. "Is your valor otherwise in Germania than in Rome?"

I felt a trickle of blood down my chin; my teeth had met in my lower lip. It was the greatest effort of my life to restrain myself under this cruel amusement of Trajan. "I am a soldier of Rome, fighting in Germania," was all I trusted myself to say.

"You have done well," Trajan murmured, watching me. "But the award of the crown is disapproved. Such a second honor might make you eligible for legate of the legion. I prefer not to have such as you in high posts." He gave the negligent upward flip of his fingers that meant dismissal.

I kept my face hard and straight, marching blindly ahead until I gained my tent. I flung my helmet into a corner, sank on my couch, and took my head in my hands. Tears and chill sweat together squeezed through my fingers: evidence of hatred, of disgrace, of anguish. There was nothing to be done. I was a slave to Roman arms, to Roman discipline. I had done nothing but obey orders under Domitian; I had done nothing in Colonia but obey the orders of Trajan. Nevertheless, I was exiled by the one and damned by the other for doing no more than what I conceived to be my duty. I longed for death in battle, to rid myself of the burden of life. I wished I had the courage of the antique Cato or Cicero, to fall on my sword or stretch my throat for the cutting.

One of my old talks to Epictetus came flooding into my mind, his faint image bearing the same dry asperity of tone I remembered so well. I had gone to him on an occasion when my mental gout, my twinges of conscience about my being a spy, had afflicted me most sharply.

"Epictetus," I cried, "I can no longer bear to be bound by the chains of my body. Meat and drink, rest and purging are indifferent to me, as nothing. Is not death far from an evil? Am I not kinsman of the gods, can I not return to the place from which I have come? I see nothing here but robbers and thieves and law courts and so-called emperors who are accounted to have authority over us. Let me die and show them that they have authority over nothing!"

The rare compassionate smile of Epictetus lighted up his thin face: "Rufus, as you are, wait upon the gods. When the signal comes to release yourself from this service, then depart; but for the present be content to dwell in this country where they appointed you to dwell. Your offering to the gods will be pitiful indeed, if you cannot make them the gift of a noble spirit. What do they care for a corpse and a few quarts of blood, which is all you are, beyond such a spirit, eh?"

I became sullen. "But I came to Rome to rise in the world, to be educated in higher things." Epictetus nodded. "Such a man as you describe yourself, then, ought to strive to follow the gods in everything and be content with divine leading."

"But I want everything to happen as I think good."

"Are you insane? Merely to want one's desires realized is the most shameful of all things. Education is only learning to frame one's will in accordance with events. We should not

72

strive to change what happens but to change ourselves to be free under whatever conditions. The art of each man's living is his own life."

"That is not the soldier's oath I have been trained upon," I said rebelliously.

"You have taken a greater oath by being born," Epictetus said quietly. "Soldiers swear to uphold and protect the state. You must swear to protect and uphold the gods. This is your oath: Never to disobey the gods, never to accuse men, never to find fault with any of the gifts of the gods, never to let your will rebel. A soldier swears to respect no man above the emperor; but let us swear to respect ourselves first of all."

I dozed off to sleep that night with the cheers and singing of the victory celebration still in my ears. All night long, I was haunted by my dreams of Akiba's gigantic eidolon in the woods; it was still with me at waking. But my fears and disappointments withered at dawn. I thought with sour impatience when I woke, at what the Jew would have told me about the rigid Roman discipline. I knew he had come, with his three friends, all the way from Palestine to complain about nothing less than a threatened edict of Domitian. Such courage nonplussed my instincts. I would have faced a thousand barbarians alone rather than question a decree from the throne.

Walking through the camp in the early morning mists, I came upon an impromptu fustuarium. Two lines of soldiers stood in the gray morning, licking their hands and fondling fresh-cut cudgels. It was to be a punishment for the obvious culprit—a burly, squat, bowlegged legionary who stood sullenly by under guard. He would be forced to run the gauntlet between the files while they lashed out at him. I stood by to watch the fun.

The signal was given. The man was released. To my perplexity, the victim did not bother to run. Instead, he squared his shoulders and strode resolutely forward, disregarding the blows rained on him between neck and thighs. Before he had gone halfway, he was a mass of welts and bruises; blood began to pour from some of the spots where he had been repeatedly pounded. I heard a rib crack, the bone snapping. Yet his face remained placid and unchanged, as if the whacks were no more than raindrops.

I decided to stop the affair. Obviously this fellow, with such a high standard of courage and endurance, would be beaten to death before he got halfway down between the two files. I raised my hand and barked an order to halt the punish-

73

ment. Despite the growls of the other soldiers—most of them stinking still with fumes of wine and foreheads corroded with the signs of their hangover from the festivities the night before—I ordered the prisoner escorted to my tent.

When he arrived, I dismissed the guard and had the legion physician examine him. He rubbed him with olive oil, pointed out that although two ribs were broken, his arms were intact. I nodded and waved him out. I stared at the man's repulsive face and almost regretted I had come to his aid: his lumpy and misshapen features seemed like those of an old battered gladiator.

"What is your name, soldier?" I said sternly.

"Ficus."

"Ficus!" I started to laugh but smothered it with my hand. The squat legionary stared at me without animus.

"My name is Ficus," he repeated. He put his finger to his crushed nose. "Because of this. A cestus wrapped around the fist of one of the fools of the XXI Rapax smashed in my nose three years ago so that it looks, now and forever, like a dried fig." He hesitated. "Of course," he said in his grating tones, "it means something else, too, as you realize, but the man who dares to give it that meaning will be a corpse or a deserter before sundown." He stopped again. "I killed the man who did it, in fair fight, but now I regret it and honor the name. But I thrashed another last night who jeered me, hence my punishment."

"Have you no other name?" I inquired, more and more interested.

"Once I did," he replied. "I have forgotten what it was except for Marcus which, you will agree, is a patrician name—at the least, that of a knight. My mother gave it to me."

"Who was your mother?"

"She is nameless."

"Nameless?"

"She was a woman free with her rump, sir, a meretrix in the camps. It is my boast that there must be in my single body the seed of a dozen men, so many did she entertain before her belly swelled with me."

"But this is a decent ancestry for any soldier!"

"Yes, sir."

"Perhaps your father was someone named Marcus."

"Around the campfire," Ficus said seriously, "I often dream of who he might be."

I pursed my lips. "Now you are a soldier, a veteran, and you have no desire for any other kind of life."

"No, noble Rufus."

"Are you sure?"

"Sir, I am a soldier of the Seventh Legion, the luckiest and the fiercest of all legions. I am not boasting when I say that I, Ficus, am the best fighter in my century, even in my cohort. I do not doubt I could conquer—fair fight or foul—any of the six thousand men in the Seventh or, for that matter, any other legionary of the imperial Army."

"That is your opinion," I said, amused.

"Your pardon, sir, but it is not merely my opinion. It is agreed to among all my comrades, who would wager their last denarius on my ability."

I made a quick decision. "Very well, Ficus," I said, dismissing the subject. "I have brought you here to tell you that you are now my concern. Since I intervened, I am responsible. I shall dismiss my orderly and replace him with you."

"Me, sir?"

"No one else. You will be loyal to me to death, defend me, and follow my orders without question. I shall not force you to accept. I wish you to come with me freely since you will be my most constant companion in the future." The look of surprise on the twisted face commenced to turn to one of pure pleasure; he tried to produce a word of thanks. Only two large tears rolled down his cheeks.

"Come, man, come," I said hastily. "Do you wish to be my orderly?"

Ficus rolled his eyes around my tent and nodded silently. He hawked and spat sentimentally on the floor. I jumped. "The first thing to learn, then," I said severely, "is not to spit on the floor of your officer's tent."

"I thank you from my heart, noble Rufus," he said with an effort. "Why, this—this is like almost being a tribune myself."

"You are not to forget you are a soldier," I said.

Ficus licked his lips; his heavy eyes commenced to burn. He shuffled his caligae twice. "I understand," he said, "but, sir, this is like being with the gods!"

"Not quite," I told him. "You are not exempt from camp chores, nor from battle, nor from any of the duties of a soldier. This is merely extra duty, imposed instead of the punishment from which I rescued you."

Suddenly Ficus reached out his paws and took my hand between them. He knelt, placing my hand to his forehead in

75

pledge of fealty, rising and backing out as if in the presence of majesty.

That night he brought his gear to my tent and prepared his small corner. I was satisfied: somehow I felt myself an outlaw and an exile within the VII Gemina like Ficus. We were allied together against all the mysterious forces of the gods who would slay us like flies.

I expected a rebuke but no word came. I inquired discreetly and found that Trajan, indeed, knew of what I had done and approved it. His reason, he said, was that I had saved the hide of a good soldier who could still serve Rome, who deserved to die under the sword of the enemy rather than under the clubs of his comrades.

Summer passed. We came into the ides of Domitianus (as the emperor had officially re-named September). Finally came the eighth month (which he had decreed should be called Germanicus in his honor) and with it a sweat-streaming dust-covered messenger from the outside world to Colonia. He did not stop for the sentry's hail nor did he halt his quivering beast until it collapsed in front of Trajan's tent. He showed some all-conquering credentials to the sentry before the commander's pavilion. The soldier on duty snapped to rigid attention as he passed.

Seeing the arrival, as did many another, I waited in the growing murmuring crowd outside the tent. It was obvious that the messenger had been imperial publicus cursus, that he had ridden directly here from Rome. But what was the message he brought?

Almost immediately he reappeared. He sought refreshment and food as the others flocked about him. But he shook his head to all questions; I know he had taken an oath of silence. Nothing would be gained from him. I turned in the other direction, Ficus on my heels. Just then, the sentry called my name and motioned me into the commander's pavilion.

As the curtain dropped behind me, Trajan looked up at me from where he reposed on his couch, the tablets of the messenger in his hands. He threw them on the table with a hollow rattle. He looked more tired than I had ever seen him, even after battle. I stood awaiting orders while he slumped back on the couch, glancing from under his gray eyebrows in the odd habit he had. He fingered a small ball of ivory as he spoke.

"Tribune Teneius," he said in a low voice, "I want the troops assembled. I wish to address them."

"Very good, sir," I said. I had saluted and begun to turn on my heel when his voice halted me.

"Rufus," he said. His voice had changed subtly from a commander to almost the tone of a confidant. "I am weary," he said simply. "Much has changed in the world." He smiled, as if to himself. "That messenger was from Rome," he told me.

"Yes," I said: it was hardly confidential news.

"I shall tell you now what I shall announce to the troops. The divine emperor Titus Flavius Domitianus Dacicus Germanicus Augustus—" Trajan paused, putting a strange accent to the words, "—is dead. He was murdered by one Stephanus, the ex-slave of Flavius Clemens whom you knew. The venerable old fool Nerva is declared emperor by decree of the Senate and the power of the conspirators."

CHAPTER 5

As the gods know, all things end badly or in boredom. I no longer complain about this, though in those days in Germania I protested bitterly. I thought the news of Domitian's death was direct evidence of my favor with heaven. I rejoiced in the poetic irony which had made the British slave Stephanus an instrument of justice in the act of the gods in revenging Flavius and Domitilla and their two sons. It seemed to me the moment was propitious for my return to Rome and its delights. When other couriers arrived telling of the magnanimity of Marcus Cocceius Nerva in manumitting sins against the throne and destroying false informations laid against such noble men as Pliny, I was sure of it. Even Ficus, my orderly, rejoiced in having the same given name as the new emperor.

It was Ficus whom I instructed to quest about the camp to sound out the possibility of a transfer to Rome. He reported back sadly after a day or two that such an application as I intended would be a warrant of disgrace. He told me Curtius Saccus had put in his name to be sent south to the rich living and easy discipline of the Praetorians once more; he had not only been rebuffed, he had been reduced to the ranks as optio in his century.

Nor was Curtius the only one. It appeared that our commander had been instantly besieged with pleas for joining the garrison of that delectable city, the only happy spot for all true Romans (or so I thought), from which exile was tantamount to a living death. Reluctantly I gave up all thoughts of leaving Upper Germania. I applied myself to my duties.

Soon I became conscious that the death of Domitian had marked a change in the Roman world. The wild succession of Galba, Otho, and Vitellius still remained as a warning, despite the monument inscriptions: "This Is Guaranteed for All Eternity by the Roman Empire." As all men do, we Romans had discovered we were mortal; as we were mortal, so our institutions. It was only the firmness of the divine Vespasian, training his two sons in the Flavian succession, who had succeeded in restoring the ancient belief in Rome and its destiny. It was he who had said: "If not my sons after me, then no one!"

Now with Vespasian and Titus dead, Domitian had also vanished into the shades. Nearly forty-five when he was stabbed by Stephanus in his bedchamber, he had reigned fifteen years and five days. He had begun his reign auspiciously —refusing to listen to informers, upholding the old customs, purging the public morality, giving and building and bestowing. But after the revolt of Saturninus, he had become a man marked by fear. He studied cruelty by reading only the memoirs of Tiberius. He executed patricians such as Helvidius Priscus, Arulaenus Rusticus, and Herenius Senecio simply because they sought a return to republican rule. He buried vestals alive, called himself Lord and Master, demanded public worship, and marched with an outrageous twenty-four lictors instead of the traditional dozen. He indulged in vicious practical jokes such as running about at night, pricking people with poisoned needles.

I had seen much of his mania about persecution and assassination myself. The scum of the city were secretly commissioned to gather all gossip; they disguised themselves as strangers and travelers and pretended to be clients in the noble houses. Afterward a back door to the palace, such as mine to the slave, Pontus, was always open. Domitian listened with horror to their concoctions, rewarded them, and issued his decrees of death. Sometimes it happened that the head of a household whispered a rumor in the ear of his wife abed and next day was accused of it. Some were judged guilty by the mere shadow of suspicion, put to death without being able to open their lips. Others lost vast property to the throne and

78

were sent into exile; wealthy houses were burned by mobs, caprice was justice, revenge ravened the streets, the virtuous feared for their lives.

In all this, I say, I had taken a miserable part. But I never reported falsely nor accused a man unjustly; and none went to the torture or died because of me, not even Flavius Clemens. His arrest had been a complete surprise. Not that it cleansed my conscience but I know Domitian had not been altogether a tyrant and had indeed marched with the legions more than once. The soldiers loved him for raising their salaries from 300 to 400 denarii a year and eating their coarse food—as much as the cultured despised him for his crude vaunting poem about the Jewish War and his whimsical essay against baldness, "The Care of the Scalp." There had been great hopes of his reign but the terror of his last four years, crawling slimily through the streets of Rome, had demoralized all. I had known, in my bones I suppose, that either Domitian or the Roman people had to die.

However this had been, no one knew now what would happen. Nerva was agreed to be a gracious, learned old man, possibly destined not to become much older. Few had any faith in his ability to control the Praetorians, least of all myself, who knew their power in their immense fortress of a barracks and their devotion to the bribes of Domitian. It was no surprise when we heard that they had forced the old man to surrender the other conspirators, including Domitian's wife, for execution. The huge troubled pot that was Rome commenced to bubble again, brewing its black liquor of dissension.

Less than a month after we had received the news, I was commanded to report to Trajan's quarters in Colonia. I made my way there that night and entered, to find my commander deep in thought. He nodded to me and pointed to a chair. I sat, still at attention, and he said irritably: "At ease, at ease." I relaxed and he surveyed me curiously.

"Of all my officers, Rufus," Trajan said slowly, "I prefer to talk to you. Not because I trust you, because I do not. But because you are young, handsome, intelligent, cunning. Because you are a man whose head I carry in my hand. You are too wise to reveal confidences or to try to gain credit by gossip with others. With me, you dare to speak frankly, and I value your advice because I am ignorant. I am contemptuous of your virtue and envious of your learning."

I attempted to reply but I had no opportunity. "Come,"

Trajan said sardonically, "you are an excellent tribune, a better camp jester. You can recite Greek poetry, tell riddles, and lead troops to kill barbarians as well as having other talents. Well, tonight I am melancholy. Tell me something to dispel my gloom."

I was angered and greatly daring. "Do you ask me, sir, if you will be emperor?" I said.

Trajan's eyes glowed in the lamplight. "Perhaps," he murmured.

"There is a verse by Lucilius," I said.

"Recite it."

I drew a deep breath and began:

> *Athletic Onesimus asked a priest*
> *If he would win the Games: "Why, yes—at least*
> *Unless someone shall prove himself more fleet,*
> *Or knock you down or tangle up your feet,*
> *Or toss the discus farthermost—or cheat."*

Trajan nodded. He repeated the last line reflectively, then said: "But I am Trajan, not Onesimus."

"Epictetus in Rome once said something on the same subject to me," I told him respectfully. Trajan made a gesture for me to continue. I paused to recapture the memory:

"I asked him: 'Suppose I am promoted to the priesthood of Augustus?'

" 'Do not accept,' he said. 'You will spend a great deal of time in foolish ceremonies.'

" 'But those who draw up contracts will read my name!'

" 'Will you be there to read it?'

" 'My name will remain.'

" 'Scribble it on a stone and it will remain; but what will it mean? One man's name is as good or as bad as another's.'

" 'But I shall wear a golden crown.'

" 'My boy, if you really want a crown,' he said, 'take roses and weave yourself one. You will look much better.' "

Trajan's face became dark. "Domitian did right to drive him out," he said harshly. "The state must be upheld."

I said nothing, tight in my seat. After a moment, Trajan's face became placid. "All the same, he spoke much truth," he said softly. He waved to me to go and I stole silently out.

Weeks passed. The German frontier stayed quiet, as if the barbarians as well as the rest of the world were holding breath, waiting to see what would happen in our mighty capital. We went about our daily tasks, building the long line of wooden lookout towers and stone walls along the Rhenus, ditching and paving roads, now and then making a scouting foray across the river with our fleet to keep all assured of our readiness. It was a lonely task for me. The other five tribunes of our legion were young senators and knights, hardly weaned. I was forced to teach them what I had learned in my post as commander of the legion, as one of two leaders holding the command for two months on alternate days. I say "commander" but, of course, everyone who understands military matters knows that we ranked under Trajan as the legatus legionis, even beneath the prefect of cavalry. Nevertheless, it was our duty to lead the legion on all marches and to head them in battle.

The suspense ended finally in the next year, that of Rome 849. Before the ides of the eighth month, sentries on the walls of Colonia spied two far-off clouds of yellow dust behind two tiny couriers, much different from the low gray clouds raised by carts. He raised the news. Two hours later the first rider dashed through the gates and sprang off his foaming horse directly in front of the praetorium, that square one-story building with wooden pillars and courts which housed Trajan and his staff. He entered directly, to be closeted immediately with our commander. A half-hour afterward, the second rider—a tall dust-covered man with a grimace of disappointment on his face—also entered the town and won admittance to the praetorium.

As before, we surmised that the riders came from Rome. We knew, from the furious ride given, that this was no ordinary occasion. The horse of the second rider died before he could be stabled, drowned in his own blood and foam. Rumors commenced to circulate in the excited barracks of the legions. I felt the pressure of them but resisted all temptation to try to discover what was afoot. My patience was not rewarded until late that same storm-ridden evening when I was summoned alone to the chamber of my chief.

It was a small room, sparsely furnished according to Trajan's custom. Two other men were there before me, undoubtedly the two who had arrived that afternoon. They had bathed and assumed loose robes. The remains of food were scattered on the table. They were drinking their wine, savoring it slowly.

"Tribune Rufus Teneius," Trajan said shortly. He waved his

hand toward the other two. "My nephew, Publius Aelius Hadrian," he intoned, indicating the nearer of the two—a slightly plump, somewhat effeminate man with a dignified air. "This is my good friend, Lusius Quietus," he went on. The second was a tall Moor, one of the first I had seen in the service of the Army: dark of skin, with tight-curled hair and a hooked nose that overhung thin, cruel lips. His air was both moody and arrogant.

"I am indebted to Aelius for news," Trajan said. His voice held a curious weariness. "You know how ignorant we are of events in Rome. Lusius came a little later but he is no less honored." He paused, as if to give weight to his further utterance. "The emperor Nerva," he said deliberately, "has been kind enough to adopt me as his heir. I shall take his name."

My heart bounded as I bowed low. "This is remarkable news," I said, "and it rejoices my heart, great Trajan."

"There is more to it than that," Hadrian said indolently. He smiled into his wine cup like a cat with cream.

Trajan nodded. "From this moment forward," he said, dragging the words, "the keeping of the empire devolves upon me."

"You are emperor!" I burst out.

"Let us say that I am still young and that the venerable Nerva is an old man," murmured Trajan. I bent my knee to him and he said sharply: "Up, man, up! I am no more than I was."

I stood erect, my face burning. Trajan looked at the others and then at me with amusement. "Vae!" he said. "I think I am becoming a god." He was quoting the joking last words of Vespasian. He shook his head as if denying them and roused himself. "Good friends," he addressed the others, "you have done me a service and I thank you from my heart. But you have ridden far and should rest. As for me, I entreat you to leave me a little: things must be set in order, commands given, arrangements made."

With murmured protestations, Hadrian and Quietus rose and said their farewells, each studiously ignoring me. As they left the apartment, Trajan rose and commenced to pace back and forth, a species of perturbation I had never seen in him before. "My father told me once, friend that he was of Vespasian and Titus," he said half to himself, "that the purple robe is like the robe of Nessus the centaur which ate away the flesh of Hercules. In the end, the strongest man must be devoured by it."

"You have not sought it," I said, "though no one deserves it more."

Trajan shot me a quick, narrow glance. "It comes to me as the request of a man who is noble and wise and compassionate—but too aged to rule. He cannot hold peace without being willing to make war. The legions are not with him; without them, he is nothing."

"For a long time," I said respectfully, "the legions have known their power. They are faithful to you."

"They should be faithful to no man, only to Rome."

"That is impossible," I said.

Trajan ceased pacing and turned round, facing me directly. His expression gave no indication of his thoughts. "Sit," he ordered, pointing to the chair Hadrian had left. I bowed and obeyed. "I know you are courageous in body," Trajan continued, "for I have seen you in battle and you have never failed me. But you lack that honesty of spirit and simplicity of nature which marks a true soul. You still seek to find yourself, you are restless and probing of all. As for me, long ago, I learned that what I am I will be and I will be what I am. Nothing shall change me." He spoke as if he were taking an oath before the altar. He took his own chair again. There was silence for a long while. Distant thunder rolled and crashed.

"When do you travel to Rome?" I asked respectfully.

He did not appear to hear me: his fingers flipped in his characteristic gesture. I knew it was the signal for me to leave.

Outside, I huddled my sagum about me. The thick darkness was now laced with rain, beating down on the praetorium portico, dripping loudly from the edges. Ficus was nowhere in sight, and I cursed him. At the sound of my voice a figure detached itself from a nearby pillar and came toward me, pulling aside the hood from the face. To my surprise, it revealed the handsome features of Hadrian.

"Greetings, Rufus," he said carelessly.

"And to you, noble Hadrian," I said, mindful that he was a nephew of Trajan and, as such, a participator in his uncle's honors.

"You seem good friends with my most illustrious father's brother," Hadrian said, almost lisping.

"Hardly so much."

"Yet you stay late with him."

"He is pleased," I said, "to allow me to speak with him

83

familiarly because I have learned some Greek rhymes and can tell him of Rome."

"I am fond of amusement," Hadrian said obliquely, staring out into the black rain just beyond us. "Perhaps I could have told him better tales of Rome."

"I am entirely of the same opinion."

Negligently Hadrian paced closer. I could smell him, the imported attar of a dandy. "Tell me," he said, lowering his voice, "you know that both Lusius and myself raced as messengers from Rome and that I gained the laurel?"

"Indeed I know it," I responded, "and if I know your uncle, he will reward you handsomely for bringing such good tidings."

"I think so," Hadrian said casually. I began to detect all this nonchalance as no more than a shield for a gross ambition. I warned myself to watch my tongue.

"Tell me," he said, "is my uncle well?"

"Very well, indeed." I laughed. "So well, in fact, that if he were to die his soldiers, madmen that they are, would be sure he had been poisoned and would wreak bloody vengeance on anyone at hand."

Hadrian bit his lip. "I am sure he will be healthy for a long while," he said.

"He has no diseases, he is strong, he has learned to endure all misfortunes of mind and body," I told him. "You need have no fear, good Hadrian; there is no man in the empire better fitted for the high task laid upon him."

"Yes," muttered Hadrian abstractly. "That is why I inquire, of course." Suddenly he turned to me and smiled, a charming smile which transformed his plump face. "You are faithful to my uncle," he said. "And clever, too. I like people who are clever and faithful. If the time comes, be loyal and amusing to me, as well. I will be even more liberal with rewards." With that, he hooded himself abruptly and strode off into the downpour. I gaped after him until his footsteps died away on the stones that splashed constantly with the beating drops. For long moments I thought about the crooked vista of the future, then dismissed it. I bundled up my neck, pulled down my broad-brimmed paenula head covering, and prepared myself to depart.

As I did, the leaves of the door behind me opened and a tall figure emerged into the torchlight. He did not conceal his face. It was easy to see that it was Lusius Quietus, the sullen Moor. He saw me and nodded dourly. I approached him out of curiosity.

"We regret you have come to Germania in such weather," I said tentatively.

Quietus rolled his eyes in a scowl. "This forsaken underworld!" he snarled, his face writhing. "Freezing in winter, soaking in summer! I loathe it!"

"Then you have been here before?" I inquired.

Quietus nodded grimly, peering mordantly forth into the night before he replied. "More than once," he replied. "I led and fought with the cavalry for the good Domitian." He spoke the adjective as if it were a foul oath.

"You are a Roman citizen?"

Quietus gave a short cough of laughter. "I was prefect of the cavalry," he said slowly. "I led the charges against the enemy myself; my cuirass had more than thirty spear slashes across it. But I, like my good friend Agricola recalled from Britain, became too famous, and that ended everything. The emperor heard accusations that I plotted to gain the throne, and all was over."

I said nothing, my caution now overtaking my curiosity. But Lusius, as if I had uncorked some evil wine, continued to speak. "No," he said, "I am not a Roman citizen. I am a provincial, a Moor from Libya. I am accustomed to sand and sun, to winds that are furnace breaths, that bite and howl; I am used to thirst and privation and battle. Domitian called me too cruel, too impetuous, too ambitious. If so, the yellow fires of the desert, the only home I know, have made me cruel in order to survive, impetuous to seize any opportunity, ambitious to better myself." He looked at me disdainfully. "You foot soldiers have many chances to make mistakes and live. But we ahorseback have only one chance. We must make up our minds to it instantly or all is over."

"You are honored by the friendship of Trajan," I murmured.

"I have always been his friend," Lusius said proudly, "because he knows my prowess. This night he has offered me citizenship and the office of leading his cavalry. I am a brave man, he is a brave man: what greater bond can there be between men?"

"Virtue," I said, remembering Epictetus. Lusius rounded on me, his eyes glowing green like those of a cat in the reflected light. "Virtue?" he repeated softly. "Does any soldier know what that means except that he must live and another die?"

"Honor, then."

"Honor lies in obeying orders!"

"Courage."

"That," Lusius said deliberately, "means no more than being a fool and lucky at the same moment. If you fail, you are still a reckless idiot—whose luck has run out."

"Duty," I said.

"No more than fulfilling what is expected, a little persistence thrown in. It begins as ambition, settles into the lees of habit and ends by being thrown to the dogs." Quietus twitched his mantle about him. "I hate peace, I love war!" he cried vehemently. "I love the dry rattle of the spear-clouds; I love the clear ringing of the swords, the shouts, the smells, the sights; I love the sound and feeling of a good thrust into a living body! I love the pennons on the lances, the clatter of advancing feet, the smell of sweat and blood mixed, even the cold caress given to a dead enemy's face by the sole of the boot!"

His outburst stunned me. But before I could collect my wits, this strange man had thrown back his head and gone straight into the darkness without a farewell word. As he disappeared, I saw from the other direction an approaching sputter of orange light. It was, as I suspected, the rain-soaked Ficus. Before I could warn him with a reproof, the hangdog wretch declared in his stumbling patois: "I beg forgiveness, noble Rufus, I beg pardon: I was too intent upon maneuvers."

"Maneuvers?" I was amazed. "At this hour? In this weather?"

Ficus rolled his eyes drolly. "Romans must always be prepared for any eventuality," he said.

"I see," I said shortly. "What were these maneuvers?"

Ficus sighed. "A game of knucklebones," he admitted.

"As punishment," I said, as we stepped off, "I shall take all your winnings."

Ficus sighed again as if his heart would break. "I lost," he said.

As they were wont to do, the months passed over into winter. The last of the year approached. The Rhenus had frozen over in one of the bitterest seasons in many years. It offered a highway to the barbarians; our watch was keener than ever. But within the walls of Colonia we took time to celebrate the passing of the calends of January by exchanging the usual presents and paying official calls. Ficus touched my heart by presenting me with a writing tablet he had carved himself from oak, together with a dish of preserved sweetmeats—the while wearing the tall pointed pileus, the liberty cap. He choked with laughter, the rogue, when I sampled the sweets and nearly broke a tooth. They were only clever clay imitations under the sauce.

By far the most solemn ceremony of these holidays was the traditional gathering in honor of our commander. Trajan welcomed us with courtesy and kind words, but he seemed more abstracted than I had ever noted before. There was good wine and we ate a few cakes while self-consciously conversing; there was little laughter and the talk languished. Soon Trajan excused himself and passed into his inner chambers. Thereafter, one by one, we sought more congenial company of our own.

Our commander must have had one of those premonitions from the gods to which he confessed in later life. It was not long afterward that the great event in Rome must have happened. It came to us only in weeks. We knew it solely by the fact that another imperial courier had arrived who was immediately taken in to see Trajan and who was thereafter closeted with him for an hour. He was sworn to silence and taken to a special room in the praetorium to rest before his return. So much I learned from the closemouthed guards, no more. Yet I suspected the fact and what I felt was in the heart of everyone in Colonia. Nor was I summoned as before, to my disappointment, to the commander's chamber.

News has a strange way of traveling in a military encampment. There seems to be a special vibration about it which sets the whole quivering as one fork tuned to a special note will make a second vibrate. That evening we had a demonstration of this mysterious power. Somehow the troops received the same impression as the officer corps. It spread like a conflagration in a dry forest, tent to tent, bivouac to bivouac. Soon the camp was filled with leaping fires, illumining the hours just before morning, showing the veterans of the wars brandishing their spears and clashing their swords, hurling their pila up into the darkness and catching them dexterously as they came down. To an enemy, it would have been a fearsome sight unless he could have understood that mad joy possessed the hearts of the men. Their shouts, that could have been misinterpreted for battle cries, were really cries for Trajan to appear and be crowned first of all by his loyal legions.

The guarded pavilion of the commander remained dark and silent. No one issued forth. No signal was given. The men themselves continued to disport in front of the praetorium, booming their shields together, leaping and caracoling like horses, bandying insults and jeers. For hours it went on until, at last, just before dawn, tempers commenced to become ugly. The men turned on each other; their simple natures could not endure. They knew patience in waiting for battle but this was more than they could stand. They set up a mighty tumult, demanding that Trajan appear. If he did not, they swore despite death, to drag him out of his hiding.

Trajan did not respond at once. There were actually three fights begun with the sentries; others, in the outskirts of the mob, started to quarrel with arms. I saw one soldier dash a greaved forearm into the mouth of his comrade, bursting the face and lips: a common way of quarreling, one which indicates why legionaries prefer wheat gruel to meat: most of them have no teeth. Next moment, the whole seething situation might have exploded into riots—except, at that precise moment, without warning, Trajan stepped out of the praetorium and mounted the small stone tribunal where he was accustomed to speak. He flung up his hand angrily.

"Citizens!" he shouted. On that hated word, the crowd of soldiers fell silent, dumbfounded. Trajan went on, his voice filled with scorn: "Citizens, I call you, not soldiers! Soldiers know their duty; they allow their commander to sleep."

"We have heard the news!" shouted one irrepressible.

"Augustus, Augustus!" shouted the whole mass in a frenzy. They surged forward. Again Trajan lifted his hand. As the legionaries halted, the first beams of the rising sun struck his fine, open countenance. He smiled, the slow, lifting smile that was so reassuring. "Soldiers," he said, "let us not quarrel now. We have been comrades for so long, you cannot regard me otherwise. I am a soldier, too, not an emperor, though I take the robes of Rome upon my shoulders." He ceased. The shouts rose again: now they were almost reverent, as if they had seen the favor of the gods descend with the sunlight. A few of the foremost actually knelt as if in adoration.

But the rougher spirits prevailed. They swept around the tribunal and seized him with gentle hands, Trajan submitting with a resigned face to the manhandling. They brought a shield and placed him sitting on it, raising it high above their heads. Trajan caught my eye and smiled wryly. It was an undignified position for anyone, most of all an emperor of the world.

"Augustus, Augustus, Augustus!" they shouted again and

again. Cries rose for a diadem to be brought, for Trajan to produce a crown. He shook his head disdainfully, pulling his cloak about him. "I have never possessed a crown," he said clearly.

"We shall give you one!" cried the same voice that had started the tumult; I recognized it this time as that of Saccus. The centurion took off the chain which he wore as Carrier of the Dragon, the new standard of the cohorts, and—climbing upon the shoulders of his fellows—respectfully draped it over Trajan's head. Thus was the emperor crowned; not, as you may have heard, in Rome, but in Germany, in Colonia, at the first break of day.

The ordeal was not over. Late that morning, Trajan commanded an assembly. He appeared in state on a sod tribunal built for the occasion on the frosted plain outside the fort. I could see the tiny figures of curious Germans climbing trees across the Rhenus to spy out what was happening. Our commander appeared in greater splendor than usual and wore a single ribbon of purple about his neck, his white breath over it like a cloud.

"Brave and faithful defenders of myself and of the state," he commenced sonorously, "you who have often risked your lives for the provinces as well as Rome, the gift of fate has advanced me to the pinnacle of all human power. It is needless for me to review how many battles we have fought together, how often even in raw winter as here, we have upheld the shining eagle of our hosts against the barbarians. Your great and glorious exploits alone support my hopes of the future. If you defend with courage and resolution the man who has been honored by the Senate with the title of majesty, I cannot fail. The rewards of the brave and deserving men shall remain without corruption: I pledge that intrigues and plots shall vanish, that informers shall perish, that the honor of Rome shall be held as high as our eagle, that Rome shall grow greater and more noble than ever!"

As he finished, the men leaped into the air, mad with enthusiasm, clashing their spears against their shields. With one tremendous voice they acclaimed what Trajan had said. For his part, the new emperor gave the troops a solemn farewell salute, hastily turned, and was escorted by the troops once more into Colonia. The new reign had begun.

"Rufus," Trajan said to me that night, "do you know why I have come to trust you?"

"No, Sire," I said.

"Because you do not bore me, because you do not fret me as do the others. Ask the question that is on your mind."

"Sire," I said, "are you emperor in fact?"

Trajan nodded tiredly. The lamps in the room gave his shadow a certain majesty. "Yes," he said. "Good Nerva is no more. Three months ago, he gave me the duty. Now his death gives me the robes. He was old, provoked by his friend Regulus. He succumbed to the breaking of a vein in his head. The gods have him in their keeping!"

"Long live the emperor!" I cried. "When do we march for Rome?"

"You asked me that once before," Trajan said shortly. He eyed me, seeming to see my thoughts crowded with the pictured delights of the city. I struggled to erase them from my brain and bowed submissively.

"I shall not leave Germania for a year," Trajan said flatly. "Nor shall I accept the consulship. The safety of the empire depends upon these borders. Germania has not yet reached the state of true pacification. Until then my duty is here."

"But the triumph! The march through the city, the chariots and prisoners and trophies, the crowds of citizens, the honors of the Senate, Sire!" I gasped. "Think not of the barbarians and war but think of the disappointment of your fellows in not seeing and sharing the glory of your elevation!"

Trajan smiled slightly. "Elevation follows deeds, not parades or words," he said. "I have told you before that such as I am, I am determined to remain, no matter what post I hold."

I bowed my head to hide my disappointment. "As you command," I said. I had no idea why he had called me to him this time. This visit, which might have been so dazzling to me, had turned dull and dusty.

"Look at me," Trajan snapped. I raised my head. "You have courage and resource, strength and sense, Rufus Teneius. But you do not have the ability to remain yourself as the color of the emerald is the same, no matter where it lies."

I said nothing as his thought veered. "To many Romans," Trajan mused, "Domitian was an evil emperor. I hear they have torn down his statues and obliterated his inscriptions, even on the milestones. The people wish to wipe out his memory forever, but this is impossible. Much of what he did was good for the Roman state, regardless of his personal vices. Remember, Rufus, that for a short time he was chief of state in Rome until his father came home from his campaigns in

Palestine and Egypt. He had dreams of power, dreams of con-
quering the Germans. But he did not know how to lead men;
he lost their good will. He failed in everything. It became an
obsession with him to show his power. That is why he constantly wore the gorgeous robes of a triumphator."

Trajan looked at me inquiringly. "What sort of emperor
shall I be?" he asked. "Domitian turned into a tyrant, Nerva
was a well-meaning cipher."

"Remember Vespasian and Titus," I said, "and the divine
Augustus."

Trajan slowly shook his head. I hastened to rectify my
error. "Be what you wish," I said.

"I shall be Trajan," he told me. His eyes became clouded.
"For the near future," he said slowly, "the western approaches
will be secure. Agricola did his work well in Britain and, with
modesty, a year shall be enough here. The Dacians under
their chief Decabalus will not remain quiet forever: Domitian
within memory did not truly defeat them and lost the general
Sabinus and an eagle. I shall have to march against them in
the end.

"But the chief threat to Rome lies in the east, in Parthia
and Judea. Here there are peoples conscious of their heritage,
impatient with restrictions on their freedom. I understand and
respect this feeling; it is quite Roman. I also understand the
necessity to impose the yoke of Rome firmly upon them, for
their sake as well as ours. Here lies the region where the arms
of Rome may find most glory and the empire itself, despite
the wish of the divine Augustus, may be enlarged with honor."

He looked at me quizzically. "No doubt you still long to
go back to Rome," he said.

My heart leaped. "If it will aid the emperor," I said humbly.

"You will aid me better in another spot," Trajan returned
placidly. I shut my jaws so tightly that my teeth hurt.

"The weakest point of our borders," Trajan declared, "is
in the east. Here the Jews form the key to the whole. If they
are subdued, all will go well. If not, the world will dissolve
in blood."

"But Vespasian and Titus subdued them," I objected.

Trajan shook his head. "The messenger brought me rumors
of renewed secret revolt in Judea," he said. "This people has
an insane obstinacy about their nation. I wish you to travel
by the fastest post there to investigate and report to me. You
are already acquainted among the Jews. You should have no
trouble in learning their intentions."

91

I sought but found no sting of sarcasm in what he said: his blue eyes did not waver, his face was firm. I was to learn that Trajan was one of those extraordinary Romans who meant what he said—no more and no less.

"What shall be my post?" I asked.

"I shall attach you to X Fretensis but you will be my personal legate. You will be loyal because you have none higher to be loyal to."

"You do me too much honor," I said, "and too little."

"I speak exactly," Trajan said sharply. "You know the Jews and their leaders, you can associate with them, talk their queer philosophy, argue and discuss without disadvantage. They will come to trust you and you, in turn, shall keep me informed of plots against the empire. You shall send them to me directly and I shall act as seems fit and wise."

"You make me an informer again," I said bitterly.

Trajan considered me. "But not as a disgrace," he replied gravely. "This is necessary to the public safety. If I were a monster such as Nero, you might well kill yourself at such orders and do it with honor. But I wish for justice and tranquillity among my people, provincials no less than Roman citizens. What you do will be both for their benefit and mine."

"I am still a spy. Can I not be given a military post?"

"Perhaps you have deserved one but I cannot grant the request. You are a man of unique talents. I cannot waste them simply because you misused them in the past."

"Then, Sire, what will be my power?"

"You will not be proconsul, if that is what you mean. All that may be decided later." He flipped his fingers; I saluted and went out.

In my quarters, I flung myself down on my couch and clutched until the linen fabric tore. My face was hot, barren of tears. Perhaps I was trusted but only as far as a bear on a leash by his trainer. Perhaps I had power but I was powerless in myself. Orders to go to Judea, I felt, were orders that condemned me to a second exile.

I told Ficus next day of the transfer, and his battered face became concerned. "Is there food there?" he asked.

"Of course, you fool!"

"Drink?"

"Naturally."

"Women?"

"I suppose so. What are you talking about?"

"And I'll have fights wherever I go," Ficus said cheerfully. "Nothing is missing."

"What do you mean, you rascal?" I demanded.

He looked at me wisely. "We are soldiers, sir," he told me. "What else do soldiers need but a bit to eat, a mouthful to drink, a woman to love, and when it all gets tiresome, a first-class fight?"

"As long as there are clods like yourself," I said coldly, "Rome will never lack recruits." I turned away and left him staring after me, plucking his long, seamed underlip.

CHAPTER 6

Shortly before my departure for the east that spring—on the long journey to Syria and Judea—more news of what had passed in Rome came to our camp at Colonia. The battle against the German tribes in which I had gained my aborted decoration from Saccus was, it seemed, the turning point of Trajan's adoption. The high-handed seizure of the assassins of Domitian and their execution by the Praetorians (despite Nerva's pardon) had made it clear his reign could not endure. The backbone of Rome needed the stiffening of iron nerve and blade. Nerva himself realized it.

When he received the news of our victory under Trajan, he placed the customary wreath of laurel on the knees of the god in the temple of Jupiter Capitolinus. Then he turned to the assembled people and announced from the steps his adoption of our Spanish general as his heir.

This report delighted all of Trajan's command staff. It meant promotion and emolument, no less than magnified power. It was no less pleasing to me, despite its aftertaste, in my curious position of confidence. Not as pleasing, however, was the fact that the treasurer of the VII Gemina informed me—upon my application to withdraw my savings from the legion bank—that I had been deprived of some hundreds of denarii. He respectfully informed me it was a legion fine, voted against me by the men for having saved the life of Ficus under the clubs of the fustuarium. The money was to be shared with each man who had not had his couple of blows, in lieu of the pleasure of which I had deprived him. I yielded: not without grumbling and a secret resolution to extract the amount from the tough hide of Ficus at some later moment.

The manner of my leaving was routine. I received my official credentials from the hands of Trajan himself—passage of the first order, lodging of the second—but he did not favor me with any further talks. He gave me only a curt salute and vale. Weeks before, I had loaded most of my military gear upon an ox-drawn carpentum headed up the Rhenus, then down the long road to Moguntiacum and on to the port of Aquileia on the Mediterranean Sea. With Ficus as my orderly, I was detached from VII Gemina and reassigned to the X Fretensis, encamped outside Jerusalem. Attached but not under command, I served as the personal representative of the emperor. My orders stated that I was to report to both Julius Frontinus, the senatorial general in charge of the province, and the knight Sextus Marcellus, who was second in command as governor of Judea. Both had headquarters established at the capital, the coast city of Caesarea which had served Vespasian as his muster point in the old Jewish War.

Knowing I had a long sea voyage before me, I preferred—as before in traveling north to Colonia—to take the road rather than the dangerous river route. I did not choose to endure the long pull upstream by the legion barges, marking their progress toward the headwaters by obscene inscriptions chiseled in the cliffs. In common with most Romans, I have always hated water (except in wine). Aquarius is an unlucky sign for me; most of all, the sea. I looked forward to embarking from Aquileia with growing distaste.

Two distractions served to ease my mind. The first was my realization, dawning upon me long before I reached Argentoratum, that I no longer had to hang my head. Trajan, by his mission assigned to me, had rehabilitated my pride as he doubtless meant to do. In going to Syria and Judea, I was in truth no spy at all. On the contrary, I was a double-paper man, a diplomat. No disgrace but a considerable prestige attached to such an office. I was free to operate openly, to declare my allegiance to the emperor, to invite equal frankness from those I might use to gain information. Trajan himself had told me he despised informers and I saw, as with newly opened eyes, his object in using me. To govern well and justly, yet firmly, it was necessary to have what Nerva in his sixteen-month reign, had neglected: information of the most factual kind. This was my task, one of singular importance. The realization of the authority I carried in my sealed leather pouch gave me much comfort.

The second easement was, oddly, the presence of Ficus by my side. Traveling with him as my companion, I commenced to see the land through his eyes. A native-born Gaul, Ficus had never gone farther than Upper Germania. He was fascinated by the sights of increasing civilization that culminated, as I well knew, in the grandeur that was Rome. Ficus rejoiced openly, loudly, in his froglike voice; his wonder was heard at each successive place along the limes through which we passed.

It should be remembered that going from Germania to Judea represented the longest imperial journey then possible— with the exception of coming from fogbound Britain. It literally spanned the 2,000-mile width of the empire, half by land and half by sea. Our route took us through every conceivable climate—from the inhospitable north to the pleasant south, the hot deserts of the far east. To Ficus, the whole appeared like an adventure of the gods. Indeed, he said in awe that ours was a road through lands fresh from the molding hands of a capricious giant.

Ficus questioned me incessantly about the Jews who peopled the land where we had been sent. I told him what I knew of this strange race: what I had been informed of and what gossip declared. "There are many ideas about their origin," I said, as we jogged along. "One is that they were natives of Crete who settled on the coast of Africa, calling themselves Jews after Jupiter who was their god. Or it may have been Mount Ida which gave them their name of Judaei. Another is that they were Egyptians, led by one Judas, who emigrated to a neighboring country. A third is that they were part of an Assyrian horde, a fourth is that they were of the tribes of Solymi. Most believe they were lepers of Egypt expelled for their disease from that land, led by one Moyses by ignorance into the desert."

"Are they like us?" croaked Ficus, round-eyed.

"They are men," I said, "but Moyses gave them a form of worship different from all others. What is holy to them is common practice by other men. They worship the wild ass and sacrifice the ox and ram. They will not eat pork because they think the pig responsible for their leprosy. They fast frequently in memory of their days of starvation, they rest on the seventh day because it took a week for them to emerge from the wilderness."

"These are disgusting customs," observed Ficus with a corrugation of his forehead.

"But everyone admits," I told him, "that the Jews, although wealthy, are always honest. Though they hate the rest of mankind, they are always ready to show compassion." I thought of Simeon and Akiba and nodded. "They sit apart at meals, they refuse intercourse with the rest of us, they circumcise in order to be different. Those who join them are taught to despise all gods, to disown their country; in exchange, they actually believe that the souls of their dead are immortal. This belief makes them unusually courageous in battle. But queerest of all is their faith in one god."

"One god?" asked Ficus in amazement. "This is very dangerous. It will rouse the wrath of all the others."

"Worse than that," I answered. "Their god is simply imaginary. They merely think of him. They allow no images but worship empty space. Before my birth, when great Pompey first captured their temple, he entered into the holy of holies and found it empty. He was dumbfounded. 'Nothing here!' he shouted. 'Nothing at all!' "

Ficus sighed. "Tell me no more," he said, "my brain already whirls with these mad thoughts." I laughed and we clopped on our way, entering Moguntiacum to turn east on the road to Aquileia. We passed through the lofty defiles of the Rhenus and around the shores of a vast round lake called Brigantia, surrounded by bristling, gloomy forests. I showed Ficus the miracle of the river pouring through the sluggish brown of the lake in a thick blue line that rushes on to emerge farther on with its force undiminished. We marveled at the Alpes Cottiae and the tunnels driven by the engineers of Vespasian; at the rocks melted by Hannibal with fire and vinegar, seeing the stakes driven into the melting snowbanks to guide unwary travelers by the safest way. At last we left this region of snow and ice and came into the pleasant plain and the straight road to the port.

There we took ship, a vessel that seemed to me no more stable than the coracles of skin which the Germans used to cross the Rhenus. Built of overlapped wood with a lead-covered keel to keep it safe from sea worms, it was almost as broad as it was long. It possessed a bow like the snout of a dog on scent, close to the water (underlaid with a wooden ram) and a high stern to keep the waves from overwhelming the craft. We waited in port for two days for the proper winds, and set out.

Sailing on the sea is a miserable experience at best. What heartened me was the comparison between my own trip under orders and that taken by Akiba and his companions of their free will. That was the sort of courage and hardihood I did not possess; but its example made me set my jaws many times against the turbulence of my stomach.

I began the sea journey to Judea as a comparatively rich man in my own estimation. I had, besides my pay, the usual donatives from the emperor and the cullings from the men in the legion. All this I kept with me in the saddlebags as I rode. I transferred it into a chest on shipboard. Not thinking my money safe there, I had Ficus sew me a hollow leather belt into which I placed the coins. I wore it night and day. As events turned out, my wealth—which was not really so much after all—nearly cost me my life.

All went well in our bowl of a ship for nearly three weeks. We stopped at port after port on our way, seeing the coasts of Dalmatia and Greece, scudding across the open sea to hug the rocks of Cyprus, driven to the north by flaws in the changing wind. The shipmaster decided upon a perilous course. He steered directly southward in an effort to reach his destination.

On a morning early in the month, shortly after sunrise, the black clouds of the euryclydon filled the sky above our craft in a matter of minutes. The wind freshened. The gusts commenced to jerk back and forth uneasily. Darkness at meridian descended upon us. It lay so low and thick we could barely see the yard amidst the scudding clouds. The captain, a burly Phoenician, shouted for the crew to lower the sail immediately. He threw himself forward to help them. Too late: the wind veered about. It blew furiously, directly from the bow. The sail cracked backward. Its reversed belly knocked the seamen down like skittles. Our progress boiled to a stop. The stern, despite its height, disappeared under the huge waves.

I was standing there, in the landsman's hope that it might be the safest place. The rush of green water swept me overboard. Luckily for my life, Ficus—at my side as always—was carried over with me.

I sank like the lead weight on a water clock. Down and down until my bursting eyes saw the blue of the deep change to black. Struggling vainly in the depths, lungs aching with water, my last conscious thought was that the leather belt with my fortune in it was the terrible weight which was dragging me to death. My convulsive fingers must have loosened the buckle.

What happened next I shall never know. When I came back to my senses, I lay across a hatch cover from the vessel. Ficus was bruising my sides with his hearty and anxious pumping of my lungs. The cover swooped from wave to wave. As I rolled over, I could see nothing except darkness and the white face of my orderly above. I felt nothing but a cold that penetrated to my bones. My senses fled again. When I wakened I was bruised and crusted with salt but the sky had become bright. The squall was past, the sea moderating.

"Where are we?" I gasped.

"Hatch cover, sir," Ficus said, saluting on his knees.

"Where's the ship, you fool?"

"I don't know, sir. Down below is my guess."

Lifting myself painfully on my elbows, I saw we were adrift on a sea that extended to the horizon. Our vessel had indeed vanished. As was later reported, it went straight to the bottom with its cargo of dolomite granite. With it had gone my whole belt of Fortunatus.

A night and a day later, we were dashed ashore. Not ashore, precisely, but onto a jagged breakwater. At first, it seemed a parade line of gods to our dim eyes and thirst-fevered bodies. In reality it was the long dike of stone, decorated with immense statues, built into the sea by Herod in order to make the harbor of Caesarea. The inclement waves, smoking as they dashed against, up, and over the boulders—doubtless our cargo had been intended to reinforce them—carried us past the first jagged line. We were thrown contemptuously onto a second mussel-incrusted heap of rocks. Our raft was broken to bits. We crawled, limp and breathless, onto the higher masonry of the breakwater.

After a long interval, we managed to get to our feet. Ficus and I weaved our way to the lighthouse where our landing had not been observed. Holding me under one arm, Ficus hammered on the door. We were admitted, given drink and food, and set aside with suspicion. Escorted into the city by guards—hardly those of honor, since I could not find my pouch of papers—we were about to be placed in prison as interlopers when I spied a leather bag dangling from the waist of my orderly. I snatched it. My fingers fumbled in its sea-soaked contents. It contained my own credentials.

"Here!" I cried, holding it high. "Do you dare to take a

Roman citizen to prison without a hearing? Appello Augustum!"

"Absolutely," Ficus echoed, boldly enough but without the slightest knowledge of the ancient legal formula I had invoked.

The sergeant cringed. I produced soaked documents he could not read but which he recognized as official tablets. "What shall I do?" he whimpered. "What shall I do?"

"Take us to the general, the most noble Julius Frontinus," I told him grandly.

Thus my official arrival at Caesarea passed into a jest. It turned into the story of the legate from Germania who rose from the waves like Venus to call upon the name of the emperor. Frontinus, a spare, soldierly man with more humor for others than toward himself, insisted on my repeating the adventure at feast after feast. The question most often asked was: "How did this Ficus acquire your pouch?" To which I replied: "He says that he salvaged it from the sea and did not know what it was. Myself, I believe he stole it from me."

In truth, I never asked my orderly the question. I had no interest in it. He had demonstrated his devotion to me. He had undoubtedly saved my life from the savage sea. If he had believed me dead and had taken the pouch in the belief it contained something of value, he had a right to do so. I did inquire how he had learned to swim: "In the rivers of Gaul, very stimulating, sir," he said.

Under such circumstances, it took more than a week before I could bring Frontinus around to the point of discussing my mission there. Caesarea was a surprisingly beautiful city. Designed and built by Herod himself in gratitude for the Roman permission to rule Judea, it was filled with marble buildings, spacious warehouses, wide streets planted with trees, statues of surpassing workmanship, and large markets. There were circuses, theatres, baths: everything a Roman could wish for. The most impressive buildings were the barracks erected by Vespasian and Titus a generation before, large enough to hold nearly 70,000 troops and their auxiliaries, together with storehouses of military supplies and hundreds of siege engines I had never seen before. It was after a personally conducted tour of these facilities by Frontinus, as we were lounging in the steaming-hot room of the principal bath, that he at long last deigned to discuss the topic I wanted.

"Do you believe that the divine Vespasian and Titus quieted

99

the Jews for all time?" I asked, wriggling under the long strokes of the strigil-edge in the inexpert hands of Ficus.

"The Jews will never be quiet," Frontinus said in the short decisive fashion which usually accompanied orders and prejudices. "Their nature is divisive, not cooperative. They hate each other as easily as they hate those not of their race. Their worst enemies are the Samaritans who are near them in blood."

"Do you mean it is impossible to pacify them?"

"No," said Frontinus, smoothing his chin. "That is always possible. But only by extermination. A dead Jew is the only quiet Jew."

I decided to try another way. "Tell me," I said, "have you been able to identify the root of their ferment?"

The answer came promptly. "Their religion, good Rufus. They believe themselves specially chosen by their one god to conquer the earth. They are clever enough not to set the time. Every day a new messiah rises among them, proclaiming the moment. The Sadducees are wise enough to see through such nonsense, but the Pharisees are taken in or do it for national propaganda. The Sadducees work with us. Some have actually insisted on very painful operations to remove the scars of their circumcision, to show loyalty to Rome."

"Is that possible?" I asked eagerly, thinking of young Simeon.

Frontinus shook his head. "It rarely succeeds," he said. "But they pride themselves on being Romans." He commenced to laugh silently.

"If it is only religion," I said, discouraged, "why do they turn against each other?"

"They are crazy. The gods make them mad."

"But since the destruction of their temple by divine Titus, how do they worship?"

"They worship in memory and prepare in hope. They foster their teachings in every conceivable way, holding stubbornly to customs as old as the world, they say. They are entirely unfitted for modern conditions of empire; best to do away with them all."

"There is nothing to be done?"

"Nothing. Except—forgive me for saying it—but I believe the destruction of their Temple was a mistake. A military necessity, a political mistake."

"How so?"

Frontinus shrugged his lean shoulders. "It is merely a feel-

100

ing," he said. "If steam is enclosed in a pot, it blows off the top. The Temple was the place where these Jews could express their longings and forget about them for a time. Its salt-sown site is a bleak expression of their despair. Unlike other nations, this does not discourage them but fans their discontent. Even an unusual fool, such as their King Agrippa, was hailed as a model of a ruler simply because he participated in their heathen rites."

"If their temple were restored," I said cautiously, "do you think this might give the empire some peace?"

Frontinus shrugged again. "Who knows?" he asked. "Their own prophets cannot foretell the moods of these people. They kill them or idolize them without warning. It would be a symbol to salve some of the wounds they break open every day in our courts of Rome."

"It might be worth trying," I said thoughtfully.

Frontinus stared at me. "Who would allow it?" he asked incredulously. "Who would pay the costs?"

"There is one man in the empire who might," I responded.

The eyes of Frontinus narrowed. "The emperor would never do it," he said.

"Possibly not. Yet Trajan is a wise man. If I am not mistaken, he plans to disregard the advice of Augustus and extend the limits of empire. He would not want these rebellious tribes at his rear."

"We can deal with them at any time," Frontinus replied. I thrust Ficus away: my poor skin had suffered enough. I endured the oil rub and perfuming in silence, and rose to be enveloped in a fresh toga. Another line of questioning had occurred to me and I turned to Frontinus who sat on a marble bench with his eyes closed, inhaling voluptuously.

"What of this new sect of Nazarite Jews that call themselves Christians, noble Frontinus?" I inquired. Frontinus opened his eyes languidly.

"They are the greatest fools of all," he said scornfully. "They worship a criminal crucified years ago, pretending he returned to life. No man of sense takes them seriously."

"I hear they increase every day."

"Do not believe rumors of the marketplace. If they increase, it is by their so-called agape love-feasts which take in the lowest rabble of the country—Greek, Roman, Jewish—anyone at all. They are hated by all other religions, they are forced to meet underground, they lose members every day to the cross and to the prison."

101

"I have heard they claim the meek shall inherit the earth," I said.

Frontinus laughed noiselessly, mouth open, bending back and forth in glee. "Surely," he said ironically, "surely we know this is to be true. This is how Rome achieved its rule, is it not?"

I smiled in sympathy. Indeed it would be a strange world, I thought, where someone would conquer by ridicule and error, rather than by strength of arms. "Every hand is against them," Frontinus said, regaining his solemnity. "Thus they must support each other, because they have nowhere else to turn."

"Are they dangerous?"

"They are sheep to our wolves. Not like the Jews, who slaver for our blood. There is the real problem. We may ignore the others, but the Jews, the Jews! Gods! How often do I dream of an insurrection! They multiply like animals, they crowd the cities and villages, they endure torture and fire, they spit at us as we pass. They care nothing for the justice and benevolent rule of Rome; they prefer fire and sword to peace. If they cannot vent their passion against us, they vent it against each other."

"All this is most interesting," I said. Frontinus rose and we sauntered toward the door.

"I hope you will report to the mighty Trajan that I do my best," he said. His tone was arrogant enough to make his words a mere formality; he was very sure of himself, as senator and general descended from an ancient family.

"Without a doubt," I assured him. Frontinus smiled disdainfully. He was pleased enough to unbend further with some advice. "You might consult with Marcellus, the governor," he said. "He is of low birth and worthless as a fighting man but he was, I admit, posted here long before me. Doubtless he knows much about these Jews. I say this because I have never spoken to him myself except on formal occasions. He bores me."

Out of pure pique, I suppose, because I had not followed the prescribed protocol and called upon Frontinus first, Marcellus refused to see me for two days after I sent Ficus to his palace to announce my presence. Only when I intimated to his familiars that I might refer his actions to the emperor as touching the imperial dignity, did the gates swing wide. But even then Marcellus had his revenge. He welcomed me with a pre-festal entertainment which had as its principal attraction a concert of music which he had composed himself. I was his only guest, long before the other arrivals.

I thanked the gods I had sense enough to order Ficus to remain away. His bellows of laughter, even from the servants' quarters, would have obliged me to flay and quarter him if he had come. As it was, I managed to shut out most of the sounds of the dreadful serenade by munching nuts and relishes as long as possible, then drinking my wine loudly. Mindful of the toper I had been in Rome, I strictly limited my glass to as much as would leave my mind clear and my temper cool. I saw to it that water was added often.

As the final notes died away, Marcellus nodded judiciously to me. "That is the last of my compositions," he said. "What do you think of my pastime of music-writing, dear Rufus?"

I said cautiously: "But you will not be offended, Sextus?"

"Not at all," Marcellus said, frowning slightly. "I give you leave to speak your mind. You have heard music in Rome, you know the modes so well, I cannot take offense."

That was not true and he knew it. I had disliked his concert thoroughly but I was now put upon the pedestal of both connoisseur and tactician. "Well, then," I said, with an air of judgment, "the flutes. You have written their notes—or perhaps it is the fault of the players—a trifle stridently in their sweetness."

"Well said," Marcellus said thoughtfully. "I shall speak to the players tomorrow." He moved his overflowing flesh in his chair.

"You are a man of taste," I applauded him. "Others would not take criticism so well."

"I have trained myself to be impartial," Marcellus answered loftily. "I see my own faults as I see those of others. If I can find no fault in a man, I say so. If it is otherwise, I say so as well." His porcine face was complacent.

"Of course," I told him, sipping his wine, "such shrillness is the Jewish fashion. A haunting thing on some occasions but to Roman ears, accustomed to the bugles of battle, quite another."

"Just so," Marcellus said languidly, "but let us not talk of Jews tonight. I am sick of priests and rabble."

"I sympathize."

"Let us speak of Rome," Marcellus went on grandly, "rather than of Jerusalem or Judea."

"I have been long away from the courts of Rome," I apologized. "As a soldier in Germania, I have had little opportunity of late to collect the imperial gossip."

"My dear Rufus," exclaimed Marcellus, "I have been buried here so long, hidden in this barbarian outpost on the borders, that I have come to look at myself, in my bronze Greek mirror, as a stranger."

"Yet this land is important to Trajan Augustus," I said.

Marcellus stared at me. "It is?" he said.

"Else," I said mischievously, "you would not be here, noble Sextus."

He swelled visibly. "Yes," he admitted, "I had not thought of that."

"Trajan still thinks of you as the proper man to subdue these people to the will of Rome."

"Subdue?" demanded Marcellus. "Subdue this race of stiff-necks? This mob of zealots, fanatics, and madmen?"

"The arms of Rome will prevail," I said solemnly, "especially under the direction of one so ingenious and battlewise as yourself."

"I would sooner have a short sword stuck through my guts," cried Marcellus, "than listen to the ravings of a Pharisee or Sadducee again!"

"Who are they?" I asked innocently.

"They are the flint to the steel, the tinder to the torch. They inflame their people with false promises, of a world empire such as ours, of a land flowing with milk and honey, tales of lions lying down with lambs." He subsided: "Name it, my Rufus, and they have promised it. They can twist any word into any meaning they choose."

"They sound boring," I said tentatively.

"Boring? They drive one to distraction. Wine?"

"Thank you," I said, taking back my goblet.

"Water?"

"A little."

Marcellus tasted his own cup and sighed. "Like everything else in this vile land, the wine is bitter," he said. His face assumed a melancholy expression; his small eyes took on a faraway look.

"I have come to relish the bitter," I said.

"It will stick to my tongue the rest of my days," Marcellus said gloomily. "And the stale water from these cisterns! I tell you, I dream constantly of the cool fresh water of Rome, coursing through the aqueducts, running down the gutters!"

"Are there no compensations here, good Sextus?"

"My dear Rufus," Marcellus answered, "do you know why I have not yet asked the emperor for my release from this pesthole?"

I nodded wisely. "Because you have not yet made your fortune from the Jews," I told him.

He laughed, a high snicker. "How discerning you are! You are quite right. Until I milk them of every last sesterce, I am condemned to stay here. I watch my health like a miser and there will come days, years, in Rome to spend my treasure!"

"Will it be long, do you think?"

Marcellus leaned toward me confidentially. "I have some good chests hidden in my cellars," he said in a low voice. "But not nearly enough to support both a villa in Tuscany and a house in the city."

"You will find enough, I am sure," I said. "There must be something left of the vast golden store of the temple of the Jews which Pompey or Titus overlooked."

Marcellus shook his head. "Even if I knew the location of such money," he said gravely, "I could not touch it. I do not blind myself about that. These people think nothing of raising a sedition every day. This they have been doing for years."

"Really?"

"I swear by the gods. They always have some impossible prophet or other telling of doom, and the nations of power, such as ours, most often oblige them by fulfilment. Less than a century ago a ragged fellow came out of Nazareth—the more rags, the more they worship—and claimed to be their Messiah and king. He was properly crucified for sedition, but the tumult continued into the great war a generation ago. And his sect multiplies."

"Even in Rome," I told him.

The watery eyes of Marcellus bulged. "Even in Rome?" he repeated.

I nodded. "What was his name, do you recall, Sextus?" I inquired. "His sect calls themselves merely Christians."

Marcellus shrugged. "I cannot remember the name of all those who rise out of these gutters and return there," he said contemptuously.

"A strange man, to call himself king," I commented. "The Jews are a proud people. Was he of the proper lineage?"

"I know nothing about it," Marcellus said. "Only that the eagles of Rome hunt down these pigeons of prophets as a weekly exercise. One succeeds another; there is never a lack of them among these pestilential Jews."

"Is that your opinion of them?" I asked.

Marcellus glanced at me over the rim of his cup. His gaze narrowed shrewdly. "You are trying to influence my judgment," he accused me.

He was more wary than I had given him credit for. I hastened to rectify my error. "I would imagine everyone tries and no one succeeds, noble Sextus," I murmured. "I have no political opinions myself."

"No," he said sharply. "You have emotional opinions that are worse."

"You split hairs, I think."

"By the gods!" Marcellus cried angrily. "That is what I do every day in this forsaken spot. Every day I split countless hairs for these people."

"Speaking of hairs," I said quickly, "have you noticed the splendid hair of the Jewesses who dance in the dens of the city?"

Marcellus leered at me. "Nay," he said, "I have not noticed. But your hair, prickly as it is, would be divine if it were no more than a bit longer, sweet Rufus."

I suppressed my distaste. "You sound like the inscriptions that slaves scribble on the walls of the baths of Rome," I said coldly.

Marcellus recovered himself in a flight of pompous philosophy. "I have often thought it remarkable," he said loftily, "that we have organs adapted both to the act of ecstasy and the act of easing ourselves—either of which gives us the extreme pitch of human satisfaction."

"I see you have done scribbling of this sort yourself," I said, my fingers itching to close around his fat throat.

"Only on vellum," Marcellus said airily, "only on vellum." He chuckled again. "There is a moral there if you will only look for it," he said meaningfully.

I drank off my wine at a draft and shuddered. I decided to take a daring chance, like a plunge into the frigidarium. "Do you know a Jew named Akiba?" I asked deferentially.

The governor's head swerved around like that of a serpent ready to strike. "Akiba ben Joseph?"

"Yes," I said.

The governor pulled his cheek and regarded me with eyes that had turned obsidian. "He is the leader of the Jews," he said at length. "If anything comes to pass in this province, it will be his doing."

"Surely not," I protested. "I met him in Rome when he

106

waited upon the great Domitian. He seemed wholly a man of peace."

"He waited upon Domitian? So high, so high. You see, such a fellow will dare anything. From that one he got nothing but from Nerva, see this!" Marcellus tossed me a sesterce. I examined it closely. On one side it had the portrait of Nerva; on the other, a candlestick, obviously Jewish, with the legend: FISCI JUDAICI CALUMNIA SUBLATA. Marcellus grimaced as I read it aloud. "It was better when the coins of Vespasian and Titus read JUDAII CAPTA, the Jews raped," he said.

"What does this mean?" I asked.

"As you see, the emperor had the goodness to remit the Jewish taxes of two drachmae annually," explained the governor. "Thus he impoverished the treasury at Rome and enriched the empire's enemies."

"Akiba asked only to save the Jews from exile."

"That request also was granted. The late emperor was a very generous man—at our expense. Think of the Jewish goods and treasures we might have confiscated!"

Decidedly Marcellus was not an admirer of the Jews. "Does this Akiba live in Caesarea?" I asked. Marcellus snorted. "I would not allow him within its walls," he said. "He lives where he was born, in the hotbed of revolt and dissension, where the damned rabbis gather to argue."

"Where?"

"Where but in Lydda, to the south, not too far from the coast. Why do you ask?"

I rose, sweeping my toga about me with a calculated gesture. Marcellus fluttered his hands in agitation. "You cannot go!" he exclaimed. "The feast is almost set. I have invited guests; I have reserved the place next to me on my couch for you!"

"It is indeed an honor," I said.

The eyes of Marcellus squeezed inward in his face. We stared at each other, our hostility hardening in the chill evening. "Why do you leave?" he demanded softly.

It was time, I thought, to drive the dagger home to the soul of this pompous little man. "I must rise early to travel to Lydda," I said. "I go to call on my friend, Akiba the Jew." I saw Marcellus' mouth gape open and felt pleasure.

"According to the emperor's command," I added.

It was a small house, built of earth and straw with a roof of thatch, with a small green garden. Water shone in tiny irrigation ditches. It was specklessly clean with its white-washed walls and stone borders. It had two twisted fig trees and a huge vine with dusty clumps of greening grapes that clambered over a long trellis and made a cool arbor.

I stopped at the gate which opened hospitably inward from the road. I looked about me, hesitating, having a strange reluctance to enter the place. I had ordered Ficus and the litter-bearers to wait in town while I came here on foot like a pilgrim; now I halted as if it were a temple sanctuary.

It was a feeling I had never experienced, even at the threshold of the most luxurious palaces in Rome—where, as a tribune of the Praetorians, I had been welcome at any hour. Here I felt as if I might desecrate peace: on the thought, my irritation rose. I banged open the gate, going in with a deliberately heavy tread, up the walk toward the door.

Over my head, from a large hanging cote of woven branches, a dozen white doves fluttered out, cooing in indignation at having been disturbed. As if it were a signal, faces appeared and disappeared suddenly in the square holes of the house walls which served as windows. The next moment Akiba himself, exactly as I remembered him, changeless and benign, appeared at the doorway in a white robe. He seemed so tall under the low lintel that the sight involuntarily reminded me of my vision in the forest near Colonia. I stopped with a gasp. Akiba came down the path toward me, beaming with pleasure, arms outstretched.

I hardly knew what to do. I felt repugnance at being embraced by a Jew, even one old enough to have been my father. But there was nothing else for it: I comforted myself by thinking that the emperors of Rome had not thought it strange to embrace such people as Agrippa or Herod the Great. I flung out my own arms and advanced to clasp him.

As we hugged each other, a current of extraordinary emotion flowed between us. The strength and warmth of his greeting drove out the last vestige of my reserve. There was no standing against the goodness of Akiba ben Joseph, no denying the sincerity of his spirit. Folded to his bosom, I discovered what Vespasian had meant when he had dismissed a perfumed courtier, saying he would rather he had smelt of garlic. Akiba's healthy country smell was exhilarating.

"Is it really so bad?" he asked as he let me go, his eyes moist with the moment.

"Bad?" I stammered. "What is this latest Jewish labyrinth?"

Akiba smiled. "Embracing a Jew," he said. He nodded: "I

108

perceive you understood my letter to Colonia correctly." I took the moment to rearrange my defenses and to get air into my lungs, for, in truth, Akiba's arms were still ropes of muscle, despite his age.

"We are both men, you my elder," I said. "You showed me compassion and hospitality when my friends shunned me. No Roman forgets such as you."

"You are not ashamed of visiting me?"

"I am proud!"

"You need not be so vehement," Akiba said dryly. "Another Roman might be listening."

I looked about me instinctively, then glanced at him shamefacedly. "Nevertheless," I said, "confess that you were indiscreet in circumcising the child."

"You were certainly disturbed about it at our last meeting in Rome years ago," Akiba murmured.

"I was drunk."

"Then you forgive me?"

"What else can I do?"

"Do not think of it as a thing of religion but as one of health," Akiba said. "One of your soldierly Roman precepts is to shun sexual excess lest it drain off energy. Circumcised, young Simeon should retain more of his natural vigor."

"Perhaps that is true," I muttered.

"You might try it yourself," Akiba said.

"The gods forbid!" I said hastily. "What is done, is done. I was taught by Epictetus the doctrine of acceptance."

Akiba looked grave. "There is such a thing as circumcision of the spirit," he said enigmatically. "But enough: come into my poor house and welcome, son of my son."

"You still talk in riddles," I grumbled.

Akiba turned. "The prophet Isaiah, blessed be he," he said, with more than a twinkle in his eye, "has written that 'a little child shall lead them.'" He pointed to the doorway. From it came toddling a half-naked, wholly charming, curly-haired and rosy-faced boy. I sank to my knees, as I never had before the throne. I caught him to me.

"Simeon, Simeon!" I said, a catch in my throat. Akiba smiled over both of us and stretched out his arms again, this time in blessing.

CHAPTER 7

I have often asked myself what bound me so closely to Akiba ben Joseph. As Roman and Jew, he and I were poles apart—as far as from the tides of the Euphrates to the Straits of Hercules. Yet, just as the magicked bits of lodestone come together only at opposite ends, so it was within this invisible web of attraction.

Manifold were the threads. One was guilt: for I knew not if I were the real father of Simeon. Another was respect: Akiba was my senior, a man whose thought and life were most worthy of admiration. Still another was philosophy: though I abhorred the religion of the Jews, nevertheless I understood it to be even more ancient than that of my own nation, and it had many things (much like the worship of Mithra by the Persians) to recommend it. A fourth tie was faith: in Akiba I saw somehow my own image, as in a mirror, reversed in arms. Finally, he was, I think, my tutelary genius embodied, watching over me in my life and, when he died, he left his spirit behind to guard me. Akiba was a warrior of this world, for the Jews, even as I for the Romans; but he was also a soldier of the spirit, not uplifting a buckler of iron and bullhide but his soul, fighting against powers and principalities of darkness unknown—toward which I march daily and which he has already encountered.

What held us together in this life was the nexus of Simeon. We delighted to do him honor together. And, if it were known, no child ever had so curious an upbringing. During the years I spent in Judea, the child was trained in both Roman and Jewish ways, an almost equal admixture of each. For my part (though it was much too late), I gave him a naming ceremony in the old style, dies lustricus, dressed in a fresh white toga. Akiba joined me in giving him presents of joy—flowers, incense, toys, sweetmeats, anything except that which was foul or bloody, except for the sacrifice of a lamb on my own house-

110

hold altar in his youthful honor. Into his hands I placed a small leaden sword with a lucky halfmoon handle of amber. I watched with pleasure as his small fists curled about it.

From me he received his first string of crepundia, to wear about his neck to ward off evil—small spotted eggs, cocks' heads, and statuettes of clay, little toys and shells strung together, a plaque of brass with his name engraved on it. It was I who begged to give him his bulla, two hollow bits of gold that formed a locket with an amulet inside of a tiny green-stone beetle from Egypt. I presented him with mice and desert quail for pets. His first set of carved ivory letters was my gift. I taught him how to spin his top by lashing it with a whip. Akiba and I often blinded him with a rag and made him wander until he found one of us—and never once did we neglect to cry out in pretended surprise.

Akiba, of course, had his own ceremonies of nonsense, according to his belief. I noted them with puzzled amusement. He had told me how Simeon, as a babe, had been rubbed with salt to strengthen him—to pickle his skin, I suppose, as the gladiators do their fists for the arena—and had been given a wet-nurse in Judea until he was three. He was a stubborn and often contrary child. "It is usual to apply the rod to such as he," Akiba sighed to me once, "but I cannot find it in my heart to whip him." I shrugged: "What other way is there to penetrate to the brain except by a welt on the bottom?" I asked. Akiba smiled but I noted he never raised a hand to Simeon and was shocked when I struck him, even ever so gently.

The ways of the Jews young Simeon learned from the songs and dances of his playmates and the admonitions of Akiba. The elderly sage spent long hours with him, telling stories of his people, asking questions and expecting answers. "He who does not educate a child to knowledge," he said to me, "educates him to be an ignoramus," one of the twisted aphorisms Akiba loved. He recited the traditions and commands of the god of his tribe to the youngster and even I, listening skeptically, gained some information.

Simeon seemed to love best the knowledge he got while tagging along with the caravans, sitting in the palm shade of the wells, or listening to the women. At the village gate he heard the haggling of commerce and the judgment of lawsuits by the elders. Though my position constrained me from accompanying him, Simeon was proud enough to recite to us what he had discovered at the Jewish festive meals (it seemed as if they had nearly as many holidays as the Romans).

"A few years before the destruction of the Temple," said Akiba, "there was a law established by the high priest, Joshua ben Gimla, that all boys of six years should attend school—but that is gone with the old days."

"That is very well," I replied, "but the Romans have better ways of inculcating wisdom."

I proceeded to prove this by assigning Simeon his first pedagogus. Glaucus was his name, a fat, lazy Greek slave stinking of rancid olive oil who, nevertheless, spoke his language with pure Athenian accents and who knew Homer by heart. It often delighted my soul to sit in the purple evenings of Lydda, as the heavens wrapped us in royalty, and listen to the roll of that ancient battle verse. But I must confess Simeon was often restless. It was Glaucus who knew how to soothe him by a joke or a quip. He was an impudent, shameless fellow, presuming upon my favor. When I invited guests of name and rank to visit in the palace assigned me in Caesarea by Marcellus—a little grudgingly, perhaps—it was my pleasure to have Simeon stand by to be instructed in protocol and the manners of the mighty. More often than not Glaucus was there to whisper asides and make the handsome child giggle. Glaucus also taught him politics and affairs of state in a sly fashion, modeling his precepts after the life of the Greek renegade Alcibiades. Dancing was Simeon's delight, as were arithmetic and geometric figures drawn in the fine sand of the abacus table.

What pleased me most—and distressed Akiba—was the manner in which Simeon took to the ways of war. He excelled in wrestling and boxing and was best of all in riding and swimming. His exercises with lead-tipped spears were instructive to me as to his future character: he attacked with fury and yielded not at all, even when common sense dictated retreat. It became a fault imbedded in his being—always to advance, with an energy wonderful to behold.

Akiba watched such exercises with disapproval. He complained to me: "It would be better for Simeon to spend more time learning to read and write," he said.

"It will be useful," I admitted, remembering my own experience, "but, if he is a great man, he will need to learn only how to speak and dictate."

To my surprise Akiba's face took on a gaunt foreboding. His eyes slid past mine into the distance. " 'I shall see him but not now,' " he said softly, " 'I shall behold him but not nigh: there shall come a star out of Jacob and a sceptre shall rise out of Israel and shall smite the corners of Moab and destroy all the children of Sheth.' "

"Quit such nonsense!" I said roughly. "What has the boy to do with that?"

Akiba became conscious of my presence. "At least," he replied, "he shall be head of a family and, for such, reading and writing is necessary."

"A Roman or Jewish family?" I asked jocularly.

"Either," Akiba returned. "Or perhaps both." He was himself again. I later discovered he had been quoting out of his sacred books: the words of some epileptic idiot named Balaam who had been kicked in the head by his ass.

I felt it was my duty to take the boy for a dozen evenings, to have him accompany me step by step down the colonnaded atrium of my residence. Here I had placed the pedestaled busts of the Flavian family. I thought it best to lecture Simeon on the fame and greatness of Vespasian and his sons, without informing him that he came from the same blood. Akiba, on the other hand, took it on himself to spend even more time droning on about Moses and the prophets, such patriarchs as Abraham and Jacob, and kings like Saul and David. I drew the line at any recital about the deeds of the warlike Maccabees. I told him so the evening we celebrated Simeon's demi-duodecium birthday at Akiba's house in Lydda.

"Such a tale comes too close to the interests of Rome," I said. "These were rebels. They deserved to be crucified."

"They were patriots and deserve a shrine," Akiba said sturdily.

"Beware!" I broke in. "We shall quarrel, Akiba."

"Jews and Romans have always quarreled," Akiba said coolly. "You have been organized, we have been solitary. You with cool heads and discipline, we with hot heads and frenzy. You with practical sense, we with religious fervor. You together, we alone. You have always won, we have always lost."

"Not always," I said generously. "Remember Caius—Little Boots, our emperor—who tried to establish his worship here and how Petronius, his own governor, dissuaded him because of what he feared from your people."

"And Claudius appointed Agrippa, a Jew," nodded Akiba. "But these were not victories. They were sops tossed to those that the Romans thought dogs, to keep them from barking."

"Do Jews have teeth?" I wondered.

113

Akiba looked at Simeon, playing absorbedly with his tiny lead sword. "Perhaps," he said, "perhaps." There was a depth of sadness in his tone I could not understand.

He called Simeon to him, fondly ruffling his hair. "I wish you to tell your uncle Rufus what you have learned from me," he said. "Tell him the lament of King David over the deaths of Saul and Jonathan." To my surprise, the youngster nodded and struck a pose before me, spreading his sturdy young legs. Akiba held up his hand. "Recite it in Greek, so that Rufus may understand," Akiba instructed him. Without delay young Simeon launched into his declamation:

" 'Thy beauty, O Israel, upon thy high places is slain!

" 'How are the mighty fallen!

" 'Tell it not in Gath,

" 'Publish it not in the streets of Ashkelon:

" 'Lest the daughters of the Philistines rejoice,

" 'Lest the daughters of the uncircumcised triumph.

" 'Ye mountains of Gilboa,

" 'Let there be no dew nor rain upon you,

" 'Neither fields of choice fruits;

" 'For there the shield of the mighty was vilely cast away,

" 'The shield of Saul, not anointed with oil.

" 'From the blood of the slain, from the fat of the mighty,

" 'The bow of Jonathan turned not back,

" 'And the sword of Saul returned not empty.

" 'Saul and Jonathan, the lovely and the pleasant

" 'In their lives, even in their death they were not divided;

" 'They were swifter than eagles,

" 'They were stronger than lions.

" 'Ye daughters of Israel, weep over Saul,

" 'Who clothed you in scarlet, with other delights,

" 'Who put ornaments of gold upon your apparel.

" 'How are the mighty fallen in the midst of battle!

" 'Jonathan upon thy high places is slain!

" 'I am distressed for thee, my brother Jonathan;

" 'Wonderful was thy love to me,

" 'Passing the love of women.

" 'How are the mighty fallen,

" 'And the weapons of war perished!' "

I clapped my hands in approval. "Very well done," I said to Simeon and the gratified Akiba. I was very courteous. "We of the Romans, since we are not a subject people, have no need to mourn. Our heroes like Trajan are still alive and mighty. Thus we have time to think of other things than war

114

and bloodshed." I beckoned to Simeon who came to me willingly. "Recite for Akiba," I told him, "what Cyrus, king of Persia, said as he lay dying, Speak in Latin," I said cruelly, "so that Akiba may understand."

" 'Never imagine,' " piped young Simeon instantly, " 'that when I have departed from you, I shall exist nowhere nor cease to be: for while I was with you, you never saw my soul; though you concluded from the actions I performed that it was in this body. Believe, therefore, that it still exists, though you will see nothing of it. Nor, in truth, would the honors of famous men continue after death, if their own spirits did not make us preserve a longer remembrance. I could never be persuaded that souls, while in mortal bodies, lived and when they had quitted them, perished; nor that the soul became senseless when it escaped from a senseless body; but that it became wise when freed from every bodily mixture, that it became pure and genuine.

" 'Besides, when the constitution of man is broken up by death, it is clear whither each of its other parts depart; for they all return to the source from whence they sprang; whereas the soul alone neither shows itself when it is with us nor when it departs. You see there is nothing so like death as sleep. Yet the souls of those asleep especially manifest their divine nature; when they are disengaged and free, they foresee many future events.

" 'From all this I conclude what we shall be when we shall have altogether released ourselves from the chains of the body. If this is the case, regard me as immortal; but if the soul is destined to perish with the body, you, reverencing the gods who control all the universe, will affectionately preserve my memory.' "

Simeon stopped, breathless; I bent and caressed him. "It was very good," I said. "Glaucus has not taught you in vain."

"Can I go and play now?" he asked. I nodded and he raced away. I smiled at Akiba. "Which do you prefer, putting aside all prejudice of race?" I questioned. "I have not asked you to listen to a really Roman discourse, such as that of Cicero. Such is even more beautiful."

"What is beautiful is not always true," Akiba said. "But Cyrus spoke truth."

"Is it not strange the Jews should always speak of war and bloodshed and mourning when we Romans speak calmly of life after death and peace in philosophy?" I inquired mischievously.

115

Akiba's eyes flashed. "What else are we allowed to think of?" he demanded.

"I have described you as a man of peace," I said.

Akiba nodded. "So I am," he admitted. He gave his slow, charming smile. "But it is often a temptation, noble Rufus, to be a man of battle."

"Simeon!" I called. The boy came back again, a trifle resentful at being called; he felt he had done his duty in recitation. I took a small silver stylus out of my pocket and handed it to him. "Here is a present," I said, "for your use, whether you write Latin, Greek, or Hebrew."

"Thank you, thank you!" he cried, clutching it eagerly.

"Now I shall recite my own verse to you with the present," I said with deliberate pompousness. I declaimed:

> *"Simeon, as your birthday debtor,*
> *I give you a pen to write a letter—*
> *Hoping you'll learn to scribble better."*

I dismissed him. Simeon scampered off as Akiba laughed. I shook my head in mock dismay. "Do not laugh, Akiba," I said. "I have a present for you as well."

I pointed to one of his fig trees at the end of the arbor under which we were sitting. "I have ordered that the spring on the hill be piped to that spot and a marble fountain erected," I said. Akiba frowned deeply. I hastened to go on before he could interrupt.

"You will not deny the gift of a friend?" I said. "You have made Simeon very happy."

"It is your contribution which has given us this house," Akiba said simply. "You have already made me a wealthy man in the eyes of my neighbors. They think I must have made a rich convert to the Jews in Rome; that this is a gratitude-offering."

"Domitilla gave much more to you," I said, embarrassed.

"Yes."

"You will not refuse the fountain," I exclaimed and stood up. "I have a poem for you, also." I held up my hands in the manner of a priest and said solemnly:

> *"Stranger, in the fig-tree shading,*
> *See the gentle ripples playing*
> *On the fountain-water cool—*
> *Refreshing both the sage and fool."*

116

I paused, abashed. "It is doggerel," I muttered, "but I am not a poet."

I was astounded to see Akiba's eyes filled with tears. He nodded. "I shall accept your gift, good Rufus," he said huskily. He cleared his throat. "I shall also engrave your verse upon the fountain," he told me. "In Hebrew."

One could never get the better of these Jews.

Indeed, sentiment was the only luxury permitted the Jews in devastated Judea. Wrapped in the great province of Syria, in Palestine, the province comprised much of the settled portion of that area. It had been dealt a series of blows by Roman power which would have obliterated any nation less tenacious. Many armies had swept over it before. Pompey Magnus had crushed it with an iron fist; after him, Vespasian and Titus in the three-year Jewish War. Rome had never trusted the Jews. Now it hated and despised them wholly and paraded its feelings to the world. The equites procurator that used to rule the land—such as Marcellus—had been placed second in command to the senatorial legate—such as Frontinus— who exercised absolute power. One legion—the X Fretensis —was permanently stationed near Jerusalem.

Colonia Prima Flavia Augusta Caesarensis, as it was still known, was given over to imperial domain. Not only had the Temple been destroyed, the city of Jerusalem was laid level with the earth, its ravines choked with debris and sown with salt. The land about for thirty miles had been shorn bare of trees and grass. The Jews themselves had been dispossessed of land and treasure, forbidden even to visit (except on the day of the great Roman triumph) the ruins of their former place of worship. Those who had fought us had been slain or sold into slavery. Those who had been quiescent had been exiled or made fugitives. With the exception of sparing some of the elderly leaders, such as Akiba, only those Jews who could prove their fervor for Rome were allowed their holdings.

The high justice court of seventy-one, the Sanhedrin, had vanished with the great priesthood. The veterans of the legions plowed the lands about Jerusalem; they had received them as donatives from the throne. Bitterest of all (until the time of Nerva), each Jew had been forced to pay two drachmae a year to the temple of Jupiter Capitolinus—the same tax they had rendered to their own god.

However, in this desolate region, there were still many green and fertile areas. Trade flourished and people crowded

117

the villages and cities: truly this area was the jostling street of the world, where every man met every other. Three cities —two in Judea and Rome itself—occupied my attention. Jerusalem, whatever sanctity the Jews themselves ascribed to it, had utterly vanished. Caesarea and Lydda were rival capitals of the country: one for the Roman government, the other for the secret Jewish cabals.

The palace where I lived—and Ficus strutted as major-domo—was shown to me by Frontinus less than a week after my coming to Caesarea. His craggy face unillumined by humor, he said: "I have requested Marcellus to offer you this as your residence in Caesarea."

"Requested?"

"Commanded, perhaps. Do you think it will be suitable?"

I looked about me and nodded. "It will be the most magnificent home I have ever lived in," I said truthfully. And indeed I was to come to cherish this as I have no other residence except my villa in Gaul.

"I have chosen this spot for a reason," Frontinus said, pacing away from me with long strides, returning. "There is an old rabbi here, a Jewish leader. He claims that one day a Roman proconsul will be cast up on the beach and rescued. He claims that such will be both savior and damnator to the Jews."

I felt astounded. "What has this to do with me?"

"You were shipwrecked. You are rescued. You landed here, in the harbor. The rumor had already been put about. Therefore I have selected this spot on the shore to emphasize it."

"I am no proconsul, as you realize."

"You will do until one comes along in the same fashion," Frontinus said equably. "The point is, this is a crude acknowledgment of the power of Rome. It may be useful. At the same time, in justice, I must point out it has its hazards."

"What are they?"

"Savior and damnator," Frontinus repeated softly. "Some of the Jews do not want to be saved with the rest. They prefer salvation with us. Others fear the second part of the prophecy. By any chance, do you know this same Akiba?"

"Yes," I said. "I knew him in Rome. Is he the one who has said this?"

Frontinus nodded. "Too bad," he said in his clipped speech. "You are already selected by one of the quarreling elements of the Jews, cursed by the other. It is quite confusing."

"Especially to me," I said, my head whirling. I wondered

118

what was in store for me, and Frontinus, observing my pre-occupation, nodded sympathetically. "Cave canem," he said sardonically. "The Jews snarl but the whelp may be Roman as well. Do not trust Marcellus."

"He is Roman!"

"In politics, all men are the same. Gods! If life could be nothing more than simple war, command and obedience, how wonderful it would be! But this intrigue and restlessness and desire to be free—for what, from what? It wears out the soul of man."

Abruptly Frontinus asked me if he might do me any further courtesies. When I expressed my thanks for what he had already done and refused his further services, he nodded and strode out, leaving me in the midst of what was to prove a most pleasant place for a miserable dozen of years.

Abandoned, the Roman stiffening of spirit rose in me—as it has always done in our breed. I called in Ficus to explore the residence with me. I found—now that we were truly in domo—that it was a pleasant home indeed. It offered every luxury, complete with slaves. It faced west upon the harbor, thus protected from the sledge of the morning sun, terrible in Judea. Down to the sea, before the spacious pillared portico, fell a series of grassy slopes hedged with all sort of growing plants, especially those with colored, sweet-smelling flowers. The portico gave onto a grand atrium with folding doors, opening to a view of the hills behind. To one side was a small apartment with a garden shaded by four plane trees, a double fountain in their midst; next to it was an enclosed study encrusted with marble painted with birds and foliage, another small fountain feathering coolly in the corner.

On the far side was a spacious chamber which had views of the sea with another garden noteworthy particularly because of a cascade constantly falling into a marble basin, a great rarity in this dry country. This room was always warm in the winter. From it one might pass into a pleasant undressing room next to a stone-bordered indoor pool. It was filled with cold water but a marble basin of warmer water rose in the middle. Over this was the games court where one might exercise, descending to the plunge. Leading from the baths was a staircase ascending to the gallery. Here were three apartments, each with its own view like a picture framed in windows. On the side of the gallery was another portico and intimate dining room, served by a slaves' staircase. At the rear a part of the house enclosed four chambers, so arranged

119

as to greet the rising sun, surrounding a beautiful little hippodrome that had never seen horses. It was heavily planted, entirely open. Terebinth, wreathed with ivy, hedged it about, and statues, cypress, and marble walks and benches were everywhere.

This was the spot I loved. Roses and greenery, pomegranates and olives, alternation of sun and shade, little meadows, almond trees, box greens cut into different shapes, obelisks and fruit trees, acanthus and rock gardens imitating nature abounded. My favorite resting place was a semicircular bench of Carystian marble, shaded by a flowering vine supported by four small pillars. Behind this bench was a cool fountain falling into a stone cistern; from thence silently it overflowed into a marble basin. Here I often ate with the dishes (in the form of waterfowl) floating about, enjoying the sound and sight of a second fountain continually bubbling to my right. On the left, a chamber of polished marble opened into a green enclosure furnished with a luxurious couch. I could lie under a second spreading perfumed vine and imagine myself in pristine woods. Through all this ran a small rill, murmuring over grooves and obstacles cut into its channel.

It was my custom to rise with the sun but to keep the shutters of my bedchamber closed. I wished to meditate and compose my thoughts, in considering the work of the day. When I opened the shutters, I called my secretary and dictated my dispatches and thoughts to him for transcribing. Then breakfast and, late in the morning, retirement to my little hippodrome to escape the heat of the day and enjoy nature. After exercise and bathing, I would again retire for repose and, late in the afternoon, take my chariot to pay calls or receive my visitors. Afterward I bathed and was massaged by Ficus. At dinner and in my favorite spot, I would entertain close friends. We either discussed events of the times or heard the reading of classics. Afterward, there were sometimes games such as chess but more often music or a small drama. I often walked late in the gardens, in the moonlight or torchlight, retiring at midnight.

One of my most welcome visitors, though not as often as I would have liked, was Akiba. He confessed himself ill at ease in such surroundings; he argued that I should come more frequently to Lydda. So I did: but I was satisfied when the business of the Jews brought him to Caesarea.

One evening, after a simple meal together—at least I ate, Akiba's religion preventing him from enjoying most Roman

120

fare—we strolled together in the tiny hippodrome. I mentioned that I had been preparing a message to Trajan on the occasion of his birthday.

"What does one say to an emperor?" inquired Akiba.

"It is quite easy, once you have the knack of it," I assured him. "You must say the same thing each year, year after year, exactly like a ritual. I can recite it from memory: 'May this and many more birthdays of yours be attended with happiness, illustrious Sire; may you enjoy continued health and prosperity and add even greater luster to that immortal glory which your virtues justly merit.' "

"That is a great deal to wish one man," Akiba said solemnly.

"It is hardly enough for an emperor," I told him.

"What does he reply?"

"Always the same thing: 'Your wishes for my enjoyment of many birthdays and the glory and prosperity of the republic are extremely agreeable to me.' "

"Do the Romans think he is a good emperor?"

"One of the best, certainly, perhaps the best."

We sat down on my marble bench in the moonlight. I continued: "Let me say that at least the Jews will never have another like him."

"Tell me about Trajan," Akiba murmured. "You must know that I am as much a spy upon the Romans as you are a spy upon the Jews."

In the darkness I flushed with anger but I calmed myself. I knew Akiba did not speak with malice, only as a statement of what he felt to be the truth—and, after all, he had classed himself with me. I began to relate what had come to me by courier in the way of news from Rome.

That summer night in my garden with Akiba marked the third year I had sojourned in Judea. It was the eight hundred and fifty-second year by our reckoning and the hundred-and-first of what the Christians claimed to be their new order. Trajan was known to be campaigning in the north beyond the Danubis River, in Dacia, against an arrogant barbarian chief called Decebalus. Though far from Rome, his two years spent in the city had left an ineradicable impress of love and respect on the Romans. They had given him a new title, fresh from their hearts: Optimus, the Best.

That last battle in which I shared seemed to have broken the spirit of the wild German tribes, at least for the moment.

121

Although the Rhenus froze over that winter, none crossed; nor did Trajan allow his troops to invade. As a result the Germans gave hostages and signed a treaty of peace. Only then, a year after my departure—in the first year of his reign and the second of his consulship—did Trajan descend to Rome.

From the first, his acts were extraordinary—those of a plain, simple, honest man. He published the expenses of the emperor every week in the forum for all to read. He cut the wages of the legions by half but gave full dole to all the poor, not only in Rome but in all Italy. The customary gifts, offered on his accession, he sent back to the cities and provinces. He exempted many from all taxes. He moderated the twentieth penny of inheritances due the emperor.

Most winning to the hearts of the Romans was the faith that Trajan placed in the people. Licinius Sura was his friend, one who had helped persuade Nerva to adopt him; but rumors flew that he wished to assassinate the emperor. Trajan went directly to dine with him, sent away his guards, had Sura's surgeon wash out his eyes and Sura's barber shave him. Next day, meeting some of the calumniators, he said quietly: "If Sura wanted to kill me, he would have done it last night." When he gave Saburanus the post of Praetorian Prefect, in command of all the city's troops, he declared: "Receive this sword and use it to defend me if I govern well but against me if I govern badly." He himself was reported to have said that he would act toward his subjects as he would have the emperor act if he were a subject himself. In a letter to me, he observed that "the emperor is to the state what the spleen is to the body; he cannot increase without wasting the other members." His final act, which raised him to the highest esteem, was to herd all the known informers of Rome into the Circus Maximus and have them stand in the arena for a day to be jeered at by the populace—then to have them transported to the same desert islands where their falsehood-mongering had placed many others.

So much I told the attentive Akiba and much more, ending with the observation that I had no idea if such a virtuous man could long survive in such a high place.

"You speak as if he had no vices," Akiba returned. "Is he really such a peerless person?"

"I have heard that he has an unnatural love for boys," I said uncomfortably, "and that he drinks good wine to excess, to such a point that he forbids his slaves to serve him after he is drunk."

122

"Perhaps he has the greater fault of loving war too much," Akiba ventured.

I was astonished. "Of course he loves war!" I exclaimed. "What red-blooded Roman does not love it?"

"It is not the best of loves," Akiba responded.

"It seems to me that once upon a time the Jews worshipped war," I said shrewdly, "until they were defeated." Akiba bowed his head and did not reply.

"Come," I said. "The moon rises and the evening is young. I have told you about the Romans and Trajan, about myself. What is the story—the truth, mind you—about Akiba the Jew?"

Akiba lifted his head, his deepset eyes glowing in the moonlight. "You must understand what sort of man I am, Rufus," he said softly.

"I comprehend. If I understand you, Akiba, you mean I shall understand all Jews."

"No, no, not at all. You will understand one man, one Jew, and that imperfectly, in the nature of our life. Just as I, if I understand you, would understand only one Roman, not the whole empire."

"That is reasonable."

"You must know that for the first forty years of my life, I was nothing."

This astounded me. I could scarcely believe it, and I said so. "For a man who has attained your eminence and learning," I said, "though you are of a small tribe, circumscribed in knowledge, it is impossible that you should be nothing for the first forty years of your life. Look at me: I was only twenty-five when we met. I was already tribune in the Praetorian Guards—and my father had been a slave."

Akiba smiled faintly. "Ah," he said, "but that was in the military. There, promotion comes more quickly than it does in wisdom."

"You would not say that if you had come under the vine-stock," I retorted.

"If you had endured the lash of the rabbinate every day for years," said Akiba, "you would believe me. The whip of the vine branches lays open the skin but, I assure you, the logic quotations of the sages lay bare the soul."

"There are some things we shall never agree upon," I confessed. "Perhaps this is one of them."

"For forty years," Akiba resumed, "I was an am ha-arez. Do you know what that means?"

I frowned. "No," I said.

"In this land it means you are a peasant, a worker upon the land; worse, you are a slave. A slave without the chance to be free, hating everyone and everything, living from dawn until sunset, hoping each day will be the last."

"You did not die."

"No. I was not guilty of the sin of slaying myself, even in prayers. I simply believed nothing, loved nothing, saw nothing good in the world."

"What happened to you, my friend?"

"I went to school," Akiba said simply.

I laughed despite myself. "This is strange," I said. "One of the miracles that you Jews make so much of, no doubt?"

"In a sense," Akiba said serenely. "I had fallen in love."

"With a woman or with—what is it you call your sacred book?"

"The Torah."

"Yes. Was it the Torah you fell in love with?"

"I hated it. I often said: 'I wish I were a donkey and got one of these scholars between my teeth; I would grind him to death.'"

"But this is very warlike, Akiba," I said, amused. "It is also inefficient: no soldier should hate his foe, it blinds him to the most expeditious way to kill him."

"I did not say that I was ever a paragon among men. War is only loss and shame, no matter who conquers. But I have fought."

I struck my forehead. "Ah, yes!" I cried. "I remember, that night in Rome years ago, you told me you had been a soldier, is that not so?"

Akiba nodded. "But that was when I was young and hot-blooded like you. I soon despaired of it as a solution to any problem."

"You took up warring with words?"

"If you like."

"Your own scriptures say these are deadlier than serpents' teeth or swords themselves."

"There are many things in philosophy which must be explained to you," Akbia said levelly. I laughed and continued. "Very well, let us go on then: did you serve in the Jewish War?"

"Yes."

"Tell me of it," I urged. "It was before my time. I have

124

heard that it was a mighty war, one in which the Romans themselves—more than once—feared defeat."

"The Romans never told us that," Akiba said with a flash of his usual humor. "What defeated our people, we think, was not so much the power of the Romans as it was our lack of arms, lack of organization—lack of everything except valor and desperation."

"And, I have heard," I said, "your own hatred and slaughter of each other."

"That is so," Akiba returned mournfully.

"Why did it all begin?" I pressed him. I had already studied the writings of Titus and Vespasian upon the subject but I was anxious to have the Jewish viewpoint.

Akiba smiled in the light of the moon, looking upward as if in reminiscence, caressing his beard. "It was a holy war for us," he said slowly, "but one that was little more at first than a political disturbance for you. How it started is painful to tell."

"Why?"

"Because such a war should begin only with noble deeds. This one commenced with the merely ridiculous."

"What was that?"

"It began," Akiba said, "when a Roman soldier farted at the Jews."

CHAPTER 8

Astounded by this revelation—not knowing whether to laugh or commiserate—I was rescued by the entrance of Ficus. He approached and whispered in my ear. I smiled, looked at Akiba and nodded. "Bring them in immediately," I said.

A moment later, escorted by my orderly and the discordant orange blaze of a pinewood torch, three dignified Jewish rabbis came into the silver coolness of my garden. They were the same I had met years before at the house of Josephus in Rome. I had never glimpsed them until this moment in Judea. They bowed to me. I returned their salutation.

"Gamaliel, Eleazar, and Joshua," I said amusedly to Akiba.

"They have come to pay their respects. I am sure you remember them."

"Very well do I remember them," Akiba said. "The last time you and I met them together, they beat a retreat from a single drunken Roman tribune."

I grinned shamefacedly. "I have not seen them in your company before tonight," I said. "This seems strange."

"Not so strange," declared Akiba. "Since your arrival here, I have been called 'the Jew of Rome' and worse. I have been suspected of being an informer against my people, even as some Romans must think of you as informing against them to the Jews."

Through my mind flashed the suspicious faces of Marcellus and Frontinus. "I had no idea of it but you may be right," I admitted.

"We believe we have been wrong," Gamaliel announced sonorously. "We have come here to ask the forgiveness of our colleague."

"To prove our sincerity," Eleazar nodded, "we have come alone to the house of a Roman at night."

"It is a poor compliment," I said, "but accept my hospitality."

"You see," Akiba said to me, "they keep good watch on my comings and goings."

"Akiba is justified of his bitter tongue," Gamaliel said, assuming the right of spokesman. "We have sinned against him in thought and deed."

"I grant forgiveness freely," Akiba said.

"But I cannot grant it," I broke in wickedly, "until Akiba fulfils his pledge to me. This very night he was commencing to be an informer."

The trio of rabbis looked startled. "Our friend Rufus is joking," Akiba said hastily, "but he is also right. It is fortunate you have come here. You may help me."

The looks of alarm increased; plainly they feared a trap. "We shall do what we may in conscience," Joshua faltered.

"We spy back upon the past," Akiba explained. "Rufus Teneius was born the year that the Temple was destroyed. He wishes to hear about the Jewish War."

Our visitors appeared immensely relieved. "It is a sorrowful story," Gamaliel said doubtfully. "Will it not rouse the wrath of Rome again?"

"Let us forget the past," Joshua said earnestly, "and live in peace."

126

"Not until you cease to talk like priests and talk like soldiers, such as I and Akiba were," I told them. "There is no harm in recalling old campaigns; the javelin has been cast, it rots away. You may not understand, not being soldiers."

"All of us fought in that war," Eleazar said proudly, "and all of us lost friends and relatives in Jerusalem." After that, there was no dissent. They even appeared eager to have the story retold.

Akiba was about to begin when Gamaliel raised his hand. "We bring news from those past times," he said solemnly. "Our old friend Josephus died three months ago in Rome."

Without more words, all of them bowed their heads in my pillared arbor, remembering and praying for the dead. I felt no shame in bowing mine with them. At last I said: "He was a great general for your people."

"He was a restless, turbulent soul," Akiba murmured, "who saw too well the things to come and tried to persuade the rest of us. We cursed him when he turned to the Romans, yet he redeemed himself. He was right. It was he who kept our religion undefiled."

"Is that the story of the war?" I asked.

"As it always is: man's beliefs against the realities."

I recollected what Akiba had said earlier. "You told me you witnessed an—an incident which set off the holocaust?"

"It was one of many incidents," Akiba said, "but that I remembered best. I was no more than ten years old; my father in the crowd held me on his shoulders and told me to keep the day in memory."

"You could not have enlisted at such an age," I said wryly.

"The war itself did not come until sixteen years later," Akiba declared. "My friends here know as much of it as I do: its story is graven in every Jewish heart."

I disposed my toga under me, padding the hard cold marble. I glanced at the loose expectant faces of the old men squatting on their heels before me. "Tell me," I urged them. "Rome needs to understand these things if justice is to be done." And, I added silently, if I am to understand the Jews.

A burning drop of resin fell past my shoulder. I looked up to find Ficus leaning over me, his mouth gaping. "Put out that dripping torch," I said irritably. "Tales like this are better by starlight. And bring me an amphora of wine."

"Sir, may I listen?" Ficus asked hesitantly. I glanced at the four Jews. "My servant, a soldier himself, is anxious to hear,"

I said. "He can be trusted to hold his tongue if you are concerned about that."

Their eyes turned to Akiba who nodded permission. My orderly instantly stamped out his torch (ruining the young grass) and came back with the wine jar and goblet, to sit down as eager as a child. "Get up!" I ordered. "If you tire, lean against a pillar." With a resigned expression, visible even in the gloom, Ficus rose and crossed his arms. I dipped my cup into the untempered wine and drank deep.

"Proceed," I said to Akiba, and drank again.

"The great war was more Jew against Jew than Roman against Jew," Akiba said surprisingly. "King Agrippa, John of Gischala, Simon, Eleazar—all at one another's throats, all Jews. Vespasian himself delayed his attacks more than once—in one instance for a year—simply to let Jews kill more Jews in Jerusalem."

"A great tactician," I said thoughtlessly.

"It must be admitted," Akiba said sadly, "that we Jews have an intensity of spirit which often overwhelms us. We feel so keenly, we often turn against our brothers. We love and hate with rage. Religion, to Rome only a plaything, is very blood of our blood. So when this soldier, on a holy day, standing on the portico roof of the Temple, turned round and pulled up his robe as he bent over, it enraged the huge crowd. There was a riot; more than thirty thousand were killed. My father and I barely escaped."

"That was in the days of Cumanus," sighed Gamaliel. "He was the Roman-in-chief in Judea."

"Worse followed. A Roman soldier found a copy of the Torah and ripped it up to wipe himself."

"I see," I said.

"More riots, more bloodshed. The Galileans and the Samaritans, Jews who have always hated each other, turned to fighting. Villages were looted and burned. Robber bands rose to rape, steal, ravish: Jews against Jews. The Romans quelled the war and executed the leaders."

"Then," said Eleazar, "a band of secret assassins, the sicarii —called thus because of the curved knives they carried in their sleeves—sprang up. Despite all attempts to stamp them out, they exist to this day."

"Madmen came here from Egypt," Joshua said mournfully, "and, with hordes of deceived followers, each claimed to be the Messiah. In this very city, the Jews and Greeks fought, one to claim authority over the other."

"The Romans themselves became victims of what they had previously condemned," Akiba added. "Festus, after Cumanus, stole, taxed, and seized. Lucceius Albinus, following him, robbed on a larger scale and even opened the prisons in return for ransoms supplied by the families of the criminals. Worst of all was the next, Gessius Florus, who paraded his vices openly, stripping whole cities and ruining the citizens. Many Jews fled the country in fear of the end of the world."

"Rome has not always been happy in the choice of governors," I said, "but this must not be attributed to the emperor."

Akiba darted a look at me, and I knew he was thinking of Nero and his crimes but he said nothing. It was Gamaliel who took up the story. "What came to pass," he said, "was so evil that Gessius had no choice but to incite the Jews to revolt to cover his own misdoings from justice."

"He stole seventeen talents from the Temple."

"We mocked him futilely by begging coppers in his name."

"But because of our ridicule he sent armies into Jerusalem and slaughtered at will, killing even the priests and destroying the holy sacraments."

"He dared to seize and torture Jews who were Roman citizens," Akiba said shrewdly. I stiffened: "That was a crime indeed," I said angrily.

"Near the sea Asphaltites, which some call the Dead Sea," Gamaliel declared slowly, "the Jews tricked the garrison of a fort called Masada. It was the first to be captured by our people and one of the last to fall. But that was not the real beginning of the war."

"What was it?"

"Eleazar, son of Ananias, the high priest, knew that every day a sacrifice was offered to the emperor in the Temple," said Akiba. "He persuaded the priests to refuse this."

"That was an act of war, indeed," I remarked. "Was not this Ananias the son of the high priest who condemned the Jesus of the Christians?"

"Possibly," Joshua said, "but it is not important. What happened was that the chief men of Jerusalem, the priests, the lovers of peace, took the upper city, trying to gain the Temple and prevent the vengeance they knew would come from Rome. The rebels, in possession of the lower city and

129

the Temple, rushed to slaughter them. The fight lasted for seven days."

"And the rebels won?" I inquired.

"Yes," Akiba replied sombrely. "That was the last opportunity we had to save the house of God from defilement and destruction. God himself willed that it should perish for our sins."

"What happened?" I asked, my interest whetted.

"An unpardonable sin was committed. On the Sabbath, in the Holy of Holies, the rebel Jews murdered Jonathan, the high priest."

Since it had been so long ago, I had not expected to be impressed by the narrative, but now a shudder passed through my flesh. "This is horror indeed," I said in a low voice. I refilled my goblet.

"When I saw him in his robes of glory, outstretched across the altar of unhewn stones," said Akiba in almost a whisper, "the sword stood out of his back. His blood bubbled slowly into the grooves prepared for the blood of the sacrifices. My heart ceased to beat. I turned and fled from the spot as if demons haunted it—as indeed they did, since God had abandoned it."

"The Temple, that took eighty years to rebuild after the destruction of the temple of Zerubbabel, was doomed," Gamaliel murmured.

"It was God, it was the hand of God that doomed them!" exclaimed Akiba. "It was He who stiffened their necks and gave them pride in their destruction! We had fought with those who had wanted to cleanse the land of the Romans but our own comrades betrayed us! There was nothing left for us to do but flee."

"Where did you flee?" I asked, finding the words thickening on my tongue.

"Back to Lydda," Akiba said. "My father wished me to marry at eighteen, but I had no home to which to take my wife. I had only my blanket, my goats and sheep to tend, when I went to Jerusalem to fight. There I met Rachel, soul of my soul, daughter of Ben Kalba Sabua. She came to my arms like a bird alighting, bringing her own tiny marriage portion. When I escaped through the nine gates of the Temple—in a fashion which perhaps I shall tell you one day—she was waiting for me outside the walls. We took the road for Lydda together."

"You and your friends were no better than rebels!" I said

and hiccoughed. "I suspect the hand of the Roman army had more to do with your flight than your god. And who was this Rachel that meant so much?"

"All I have achieved, all that I hope to achieve, is because of her faith in me," said Akiba.

I wagged my head back and forth. The scene before me, in the light of the rising moon, seemed blurred and giddy. I drank the rest of the wine and threw the cup ringing into the marble basin of the fountain. "It surprises me that you are married, old man," I said loudly.

"You knew, noble Rufus, that I had children."

"Oh," I said roughly, "as for that, it is quite possible to achieve such without a wife." I laughed and wiped my mouth. "As the poet, Ovid the Long Nose, says, 'any woman may be won who is well tempted.' "

Before me, as at a great distance, I saw Akiba's eyes commence to glow. I might have taken warning from the slight gestures of alarm from his friends, but the wine was warm in my belly, its fumes swirling darkly in my head.

"We Romans have a new writer, one Juvenal," I continued, "a practical fellow who asks why a man should marry when he can go insane or leap from a high window or jump from the Aemilian Bridge—any one of them better than submitting to a she-tyrant."

"We do not believe that," Akiba said in a strangled voice.

"Come, come! I know you Jews consider your wives as ba'al, as property: you the master, she the slave. But most often it is the reverse with these vampires."

"Then I shall say that *I* do not believe it."

"Very well," I said, stubborn in my intoxication, "we Romans are the same by law as you are by custom. But we know our wives make us slaves. Have one for appearance' sake, if you like: but bury her, as soon as you may, with the grand old epitaph: 'She counseled well, she managed well, she spun wool.' "

"Romans and Jews are different," Akiba said slowly.

"We are all men, we have the same handle for women," I said. The wine made his figure dim; I bent forward to leer into his face. "You are old but vigorous," I said. "I could swear you have more than one young girl for your own pleasure in some hut in Lydda."

Akiba sprang to his feet. He grasped either side of my toga and jerked me upright. I flicked my arms upward, flinging him back. His fingers tore the fabric. I saw Ficus, sword

131

drawn, the point touching the breast of the defiant and unmoving Akiba, awaiting my permission to thrust.

"No, no," I said dazedly. "Let the old fool go."

I sank back to my seat, already cursing inwardly the treachery of the wine I had taken. The procession of the four rabbis rustled past me, haughtier than I should have allowed to any Jews leaving my residence. But I resented even more the grim expression of Ficus and the clang as he thrust his short sword back into its sheath. Obviously he thought I had been weak. He was right. For the second time, wine had betrayed me with Akiba.

The consequence of that unfortunate evening was that I did not see Akiba again for many months. My pride rebelled against it. So too, I imagine, did his peculiar Jewish mores. Yet the incident had both good and evil effects: it removed forever the supposition of his fellows that he was a spy. It lost me, for the time being, my best hope of understanding his queer people.

Too late I learned why Akiba held his wife in such high regard. Rachel had been a beautiful heiress, an only child, of one of the richest Jewish families. She had renounced her family's wealth and social caste to marry a peasant much older than she, a man apparently without the possibility of rising in the world. It must have been one of those rarest of matches, an expression of pure love. Rachel had slaved with Akiba on the land, watched the herds with him, shared his damp cave and moldy straw pallet. At last she had persuaded this stubborn man to go to school. He failed miserably. Undaunted—perhaps with a secret purpose—she had borne him a child whom she sent to school, and Akiba went and sat with him to learn the mysteries of the twenty-two letters of the Hebrew alphabet: "Aleph, bet, gimmel. . . ."

All this came to me by way of Glaucus, the gossiping Greek slave of my household, who had instructed Simeon when he stayed with me. He told me that Akiba had followed the studies of the priest-established schools, reading first of all the dicult laws of Leviticus with their intricate barbaric rituals. "No one but a Jew could memorize such things," Glaucus told me with contempt. "Who knows what are burnt offerings, peace offerings, sin offerings, guilt offerings? Such a student must learn how to be pure, how to tell diseases, how to enact services, whom to marry and whom to avoid. Even such rules are given as what kind of animals sacrificed where, what yellow hair on a leper means, a thousand other things. It is not true learning; it is a game of idiots!"

"What brought Akiba to turn to be educated?" I asked. "Merely the birth of his child?"

"The story is that he saw an ever-running spring which had cut a deep groove into rock," Glaucus explained. "He is supposed to have realized that what water had done to stone, so could the flow of learning cut into his stupid brain."

"When did he choose to become a master of his people?"

"When he was no less than forty years old. It was then he entered the rabbinical school at the Vineyard of Jabneh."

Suddenly the thought of young Simeon stabbed me like a blade between the ribs. Rage assailed me. "And what do you do here, filling your fat gut, greasing your body?" I yelled at Glaucus. "Do you feed upon my purse, in my household, while your pupil is far away, being taught this poisonous Jewish nonsense, this heathen blasphemy? Why are you here? Tell me!" I seized the wretched slave by his scant oily hair, bringing him to his knees with the blast of my fury. He stared up at me, astonished, wide-eyed. "I—I had no thought of it," he confessed. "Never have you spoken of it before."

"I speak of it now," I said, calming myself, shaking his head to and fro for emphasis. "You shall go to Lydda and lodge at the house of Akiba at my command, at my expense. You shall teach young Simeon the great works of the Greeks and Egyptians, the antidotes for these rituals of the Jews!"

Glaucus stumbled quivering from my presence. He left for the south at the next dawn. Though the fates hid it from me, it was the last time I was to see him as a Greek, though for months—according to my parting instructions—he sent me regular reports of the progress of his young pupil.

The years passed as rapidly as dreamless afternoon naps under the green shade of the terebinths. The drone of the locusts and the plashing of the fountains seemed to devour time. Trajan returned victorious from his first campaign against the Dacians and their chief Decebalus. He threw himself with unexampled energy into the administration of the empire.

But in less than three years, Decebalus broke his pledges with fire and sword, ravaging the Roman garrisons. Trajan was forced to march once more to the north and east with his legions. This second expedition was one to the death. Merciful when suppliants deserved it, the emperor never forgave a shattered treaty: if one province could break faith, all might follow suit.

With him went many of the legions from the army of Rome. Trajan had made no secret that he was determined to settle the Dacian question once and for all. In marathon marches he avoided the ambushes of Decebalus, penetrating the rugged country by the passes of the Iron Gate and the Red Tower—using his great mile-long bridge of stone and wood across the Danubis (built by Apollodorus, the famous builder who was later to create the gigantic Forum of Trajan for his master). He crushed Decebalus in late summer the next year. The capital, Sarmizegethusa, fell. A short guerrilla war ensued before all was peaceful, and fifty thousand prisoners marched to Rome, chained together as slaves. The giant Decebalus, fearless to the last, concealed his treasures under a river, slew his kin, and flung himself from a cliff. Returning to Rome, Trajan did not say what Augustus had advised, "Spare the conquered," but what Domitian had said of the Nasamones tribe: "They have ceased to exist."

I rejoiced when I heard of his triumphal entry into Rome in the eight hundred and fifty-seventh year from its founding, the year the Christians called the one hundred and sixth from the birth of their prophet. But my joy turned to melancholy when I received a mocking message from the throne: "Kill yourself, good Rufus! You were not with us when we exterminated the Dacians!"

It was not only this which plunged me into gloom. Cornelius Palma, the new governor of Syria, had already been ordered out with the VI Ferrata legion to annex Felix Arabia. Others were marching to conquests, but I, during all these years, had never once been allowed to cross the borders of the province. Much of my effort, as I look back at it now, was of no consequence. Weary days and weeks of travel and negotiation, of argument and delay. I was powerless to execute any decisions of my own. Even the most minute details were passed by publicus cursus to Rome—a journey of fifty days out and fifty days more in return—more than three months' delay before necessary action could be taken. I was forced to act as mediator between Frontinus and Marcellus. Each accounted the other a boor and disgrace to Roman-kind. Only I, out of all the swarm of officials in Judea, was able to keep liaison between them.

Trajan's message and his assignments to other lieutenants filled me with an extraordinary restlessness. Indeed, I knew in my soul that I had been too long away from the camps and battlefields. My blood stirred with anger. A sort of impotent humiliation took me when I looked about my luxurious residence in Caesarea. I determined to go elsewhere, to rid myself of this incubus. For no reasons I could fathom, my mind fixed upon Akiba and his humble house in Lydda. I wanted to see Simeon again; that rascal Glaucus had not reported to me for nearly six months. It was time I patched up my pride and discovered what I could on the spot.

I ordered Ficus to load a pack-train with gifts and supplies and to prepare litters without delay. "None of your Marius mules," I warned him. Ficus grinned and shook his head as he saluted. He knew what the term meant as well as I: the pilum-shaft over the shoulder with a bag made of the military sagum, filled with the soldier's goods, dangling at its end.

"Come, Simeon," I said wheedlingly, "you are old enough for me to test your thought. At age thirteen, you should be able to answer some riddles. Come: since we Romans are the vanished children of Troy, let me put it as did Homer. There were seven hearths of furious fire, fifty spits on each fire, fifty smoking joints on each spit, and about each spit were nine hundred hungry Greeks. How many were in their army?"

The child figured for a moment on his fingers. He brightened, and said: "Three hundred and fifteen thousand, Uncle Rufus."

"Good!" I told him. "Now for another. I am the black child of a red father; a wingless bird but I fly to heaven; I make those weep that created me; and, as soon as I am seen, I vanish into thin air."

Simeon clapped his hands and cried: "Smoke! Smoke!"

"You are better than I thought," I acknowledged. "You have done very well. Here is a third: What is one wind, two ships, ten sailors rowing, one steersman directing both?"

Simeon hesitated. He said doubtfully: "Can it be the double flute, played with both hands?"

"Nothing less," I responded. I pondered. "Two more, young sir, if you please," I said. "Speak and you speak my name; speak not and you speak my name."

"Silence, is that it?"

"Oh, best of boys! Here is the second and it will bring you a silver sesterce if you answer correctly: I have nothing inside me but everything inside me and I grant my favors without charge to anyone except that I do the reverse of what is shown me."

Simeon rubbed his dark mop of hair. His attention was wandering. I snapped my fingers and he shook his head. "I don't know," he said pettishly.

"Foolish boy, a mirror, of course!"

"Is that not enough riddles, Uncle?"

"One more," I said hastily. "Democritus lived a fourth of his whole life as a boy, for a fifth as a young man, for a third as a man, and when he reached old age he lived thirteen years more. How many did he live?"

Numbers intrigued young Simeon. His lips moved as he stared unseeing past me, then he smiled in victory: "Sixty years. Fifteen as a boy, twelve as a young man, twenty as a man, and the thirteen."

Before I could utter praise and dismiss him, he lifted his impish smile to me: "May I ask you one, Uncle Rufus?"

"Of course."

"No one sees me when he sees but he sees me when he sees not; he who speaks in me speaks not, he who runs in me runs not; but though I am untruthful, I tell all truth."

I scowled and cudgeled my brain for minutes, not wanting to show my ignorance in front of the child. At last, with an effort, I laughed and said: "You try to trick me, young Simeon. That riddle is nonsense."

"No," he said brightly. "I swear it is not. Don't you know the answer?"

"I'll let you tell me," I said grandly.

"It is a dream," he said. "May I go now?"

"Yes," I sighed. I reached out to touch his tousled head, but his bare brown legs raced down the path of Akiba's garden toward his impatient friends waiting outside the gate. I watched him vanish down the dusty road and sighed again.

"Are you grieving, noble Rufus?" came Akiba's deep slow voice from behind me.

I got up from the warm stone where I was sitting and turned to meet his calm gaze. "There was no one here," I said, "except Simeon, and he did not know me. I had to tell him who I was."

"The women are at market in the town and I was meditating on the hill," Akiba said.

"Glaucus?"

"Six months ago, he vanished. I fear our food and room were not what he was used to."

"Run away?" I was aghast. I recovered. "Well," I said grimly, "he will be found. A man without a master in Judea is soon hunted down."

Akiba motioned behind him. "You see that the arbor and the fountain are finished according to your orders," he said.

"Not exactly," I said.

Akiba gave a short embarrassed laugh. "The nude marble statue of a nymph," he said, "was not exactly right for the garden of a supposed sage. Besides, it displeased my wife, Rachel."

"I have never seen her," I said. "Bring her to me."

Akiba shook his head. "She says the time is not yet right for you to meet her," he told me. "Indulge me in this whim."

Somewhat put out, I managed to laugh. "We Romans know how to yield to a woman," I said. "Let us rest in the shade."

I followed him. We took seats in the arbor across from each other, a small table of rough gray stone between us. Akiba looked at my toga. "You have a new robe," he said. "I owe you for that."

I shrugged. "As Epictetus told me, if you are angry with a man, it is useless to tear his flesh; it is better merely to tear a toga. You were unwise but I was to blame." The water trickled in counterpoint to our words. The sunlight shimmered through the golden green of the broad grape leaves. Akiba did not respond. Awkwardly I attempted another attack.

"Simeon is very well," I said. "He seems to enjoy play more than work."

"That is not unusual in a child."

"Is he good at throwing the ball?"

"He is never the donkey and never suffers forfeits," Akiba answered. "He is by far the best, the leader."

"The leader, eh?" I smiled with satisfaction. "And arms? Does he practice yet with the sword and javelin?"

Akiba nodded regretfully. "Too much, too often," he said. "He pays little attention to either Jewish scripture or Greek writings. Perhaps that was why Glaucus left: in despair."

"Why do you resent the child's love of things military?" I inquired.

Akiba shook his head. "I am of the persuasion of Johanan ben Zakkai, the great rabbi who led the peace party of Jerusalem," he said. "For eighteen years he struggled in Galilee to maintain peace and spread learning. He believed in this world as much as in the World-to-Come. 'If you are about to plant a tree,' he said, 'and someone comes to tell you the Messiah is here, finish your planting and then go forth to meet him!' "

"That is very Roman," I said in approval.

"He told the people of Galilee that because they hated the study of the Torah they would be overcome by the Romans. He was right."

"A wise Jew," I commented. "Did he survive the famous War—the telling of which I interrupted unseasonably long ago in Caesarea?"

Akiba smiled faintly. "Your head is not made to hold wine," he said. "Yes, though Johanan was an old man when it came. He saw the doom of Jerusalem and the Temple. All he could do was to save the sacred Torah. He decided to pretend illness, then death; to have his disciples carry him outside the wall for burial. Ben Betiah, his nephew, and two close friends —Eliezer ben Hyrkanos and one whom you know, Joshua ben Hananya—and I were to carry the bier of poles. We were young in those days."

Word by word, as a tower is built brick by brick, Akiba's tale re-created that terrible time. Johanan knew that he—and his followers—would be instantly slain if their ruse were discovered. He rehearsed the rigidity of his body for days, to keep eyelids and lips from fluttering. A corset of wood beneath his cerements of white covered his breathing. His face was waxed with tallow. His hands were plunged into cold water for hours, just before the attempt.

Yet everything had to be done slowly. In my imagination I saw the crowded, fetid streets of that vanished magnificent Jerusalem, the awed crowds, the insolent rebels—and the tiny solemn procession of mourners. At the gate the guards halted them. They disputed among themselves about permission. Two bent over and sniffed. Their noses curled: Johanan had put a piece of rotting meat between his legs.

"Let us stab him to be sure," one said.

Akiba deterred him. "If you do," he told him, "the world will spit on you for having stabbed the corpse of Johanan."

"At least, we should push him," the man complained.

"They will say you pushed the holy dead."

"So you fled Jerusalem," I commented. Akiba went on without answering: "Led by Johanan we went directly to the tent of the emperor-to-be, great Vespasian. We asked only that a school to teach the Torah might be established at Jabneh, only a little way from here."

"Many of the rebels, I have heard, came from Lydda."

"That is true but we had surrendered among the first. Those who saw the light came there to live. By the time the war was finished, Jabneh was the center where gathered all true Jews. The Vineyard of Jabneh was the rebirth of our people and their religion."

"Not the true Sanhedrin that used to meet for centuries in the Chamber of Hewn Stones," I pointed out.

Akiba chuckled. "Johanan was a wise man. He achieved that also. Our New Year's fell on a Sabbath. Johanan ordered the shofar sounded, the blast from the ram's horn. The others objected and he refused to discuss it. 'First let us sound the shofar and then discuss the law,' he said. So it was done."

"And then?"

"After the services he told them: 'There is no further use in discussion. The shofar has been sounded, the precedent is set.' "

"A Jewish trick," I said.

"One which all Jews understood," retorted Akiba. "It was necessary to reconcile the old with the new. Johanan would never have been able to do it except that all recognized his leadership. With us, cleverness is useless unless it has the authority of God."

"If your god still exists," I said delicately. "You are still under Roman rule."

"We shall rise again from the dust of our sins."

"Indeed? How may this be accomplished?" I asked.

"Come to Jabneh, to the Vineyard, and see," said Akiba, his lambent gaze catching mine.

"I shall," I said, standing up as a sign of dismissal. "By all the gods, I shall!"

Two figures came into the arbor. One, he who was lagging behind, I recognized through his dust and sweat as Simeon. The other seemed to be no more than a boy pulling him along until they stumbled in front of me, clad in torn garments, disarrayed, filthy from play.

"This is Sarra," Simeon said sullenly, not looking up at me. "I told her you were a real live Roman officer. She didn't believe me. She dragged me here to see you."

The other urchin looked up at me wide-eyed, with the bright twinkling curiosity of a squirrel, hands behind her back. I smiled at her. "Like a rare animal in the arena at Rome, I presume?" I said amusedly. My mood changed. I drew a sharp breath. This was an unusual child here before me—not more than a dozen years old—her manner respectful

139

but shy, fearless, and mischievous. What disturbed me was not her well-formed body shown so clearly by her sweat-dampened garments nor the sweet animal odor of her in my nostrils. But her serious face—its tanned skin, its full lips stained with red, her cheeks in blush, her enormous dark eyes that seemed to swallow up my gaze in their bold survey—took me by surprise. Above all, her hair—so heavy, I thought it must be tiring to carry. It fell in a flood to her waist, jet-black, with crimson glints put there by the sun. My memory flashed back to Domitilla, how she must have appeared when she was young. I found myself trembling as I reached out to touch this girl's hair; she shook her head and jumped back like a pet that dislikes to have its master caress it.

"She is very much of a woman," I said, controlling my unanticipated emotion.

"Yes," Akiba replied, watching me. "Sarra is the daughter of my brother, Samuel ben Joseph. Both he and his wife were killed six years ago by the plague. I have taken Sarra for my own."

"How is it I have not seen her before?"

Akiba's tone was amused. "Do you not remember how you told me of women and Romans?" he inquired. "I did not wish to bother you."

"I'm finished looking at him," Sarra announced. "Come on, Simeon."

Simeon stayed a moment longer, his face solemn. "I apologize," he said. "Uncle Rufus, she does not have good manners but she will learn. She is only a girl." With that, he marched away after her.

"Only a girl," I said to Akiba. "For such a one, that is quite sufficient."

"Simeon is very fond of her," Akiba said with a heightened inflection.

"Are they sweethearts?" I inquired, suddenly finding my tongue heavy.

"Perhaps they are too close in relationship to become married by our law," Akiba responded. "They are only friends, playmates." I raised my brows at this but said nothing. There the affair ended, but the image of Sarra, so reminiscent of that of Domitilla, lingered in my mind. It roused in me, for the first time for many years, a desire to see the one I had loved so long ago. I left Akiba with only the crumbs of farewell: that night I tossed in dreams I had not experienced for a long time.

Jabneh, as I found when I journeyed there the next day, was in the richest part of Judea. It was thronged with Jews, patrolled by indolent soldiers from the Roman garrison: mobs wearing bright colors, high-pitched chatter, explosions of gestures and sound, carts and horses, gay garments, sulfurous smells, a whirlpool of life. Passing through into the country, I breathed deep in the fresh air; I enjoyed the silences with thanksgiving. My litter passed long lines of sombre pilgrims, undoubtedly bound for my own destination: the famous Vineyard of Jabneh.

This lay along a gentle hillside covered with vines and heavy purple-dusted clusters, as far as the eye could stretch. In the middle was a broad arbor, surrounded by Jews in unbroken quiet except for an occasional buzz of excitement at what went on within the arbor. I could hear resonant tones of speech, never more than one man. Impelled by curiosity— the Jews being pushed out of my way by Ficus—I walked close to have a better view.

There were no guards. No one hindered anyone else from coming or going. There was no ceremony: the people stood or sat upon stones. Nor did they pluck a single grape. Wherefore I, to show the difference between this tribe and a Roman, plucked and ate a juicy bunch in deliberate defiance. I wiped my mouth and peered into the arbor.

This was a sophocracy, Akiba had said, what the Greeks called "government by wise men." Well, I would see. I was amazed to observe nothing but rows upon rows of backs turned to me: students and disciples, heads bent, meditating upon what they heard, attempting to memorize argument and authority. In a wide semicircle, facing the younger men and the audience, was a group of sages—most bearded, a few clean-shaved, all with keen aquiline features. Each wore a strange large blank cube on their foreheads and was wrapped in an enormous striped cloak with blue-and-white fringes. Among them I recognized Joshua and Eleazar; in the center sat Gamaliel. Akiba was on his feet, speaking in an outlandish dialect which I recognized as Hebrew.

What he said, I do not know to this day. I waited until he had finished and there was a general hiss of approbation and nodding of heads. I glanced at Ficus. He was supremely bored. I gestured to him that we were to leave; I had no taste for this droning mummery of another people. I had expected too much from Akiba's enthusiasm.

As I turned, pressed against those behind me in order to

141

thrust through the mass of people, the air seemed to become sultry, the way it does just before one of the terrible Syrian thunderstorms. The little man next to me drew back, as if from contamination. Ficus, directly behind me, saw the gleam of dull iron before I caught it from the corner of my eye. Before I could twist away, he acted. His scarred fist shot out in a chopping motion. His knuckles bunched like a hammer against the side of the man's arm above the elbow. I heard a loud snap. The bone under the muscle moved at a crazy angle. I saw the useless sinew, deprived of leverage, wriggle under the skin. The knife dropped to the ground. Ficus put his foot on it, watching the fellow, waiting instructions from me. The would-be assassin shrank back, unable to escape in the packed crowd.

I saw the curved blade on the ground. I understood that this was one of the feared sicarii. I stared at him and he gave me look for look, raging in spite of his pain. "Give him back his knife," I said in a low tone.

"In his throat, sir?"

"No. But mark him so that all may know what he is."

Ficus snatched up the knife. He seized the man by the nape of his neck. Next moment the man shrieked. The crowd scattered in alarm. My assailant clapped his left hand to his forehead—where Ficus had carved a rude S—and ran, his own blood staining his garments. Ficus threw the knife after him.

I saw Akiba coming, pushing his way through the crowd, his lean face anxious. He thrust his way to me and passed his hands over my torso quickly, as if to reassure himself. "What has happened?" he asked.

"A man dropped his knife and Ficus picked it up," I said.

Akiba was horrified. "None should carry weapons here," he said.

"Perhaps his meat was tough," I said. Ficus suppressed a guffaw. "Tougher than he knew," he muttered under his breath.

Akiba looked at Ficus and back to me again. His face was grave. Behind him, the meeting of the Sanhedrin was breaking up in confusion and dismay, despite the commands of their patriarch Gamaliel.

"I see that Romans are a disruptive influence," I said to Akiba. "Ficus and I will go."

Akiba was not deceived. The anger in his expression was formidable but it was not directed against me. "Thank you

142

for your forbearance," he said huskily. "I cannot believe it was a Jew."

"It is hard to believe otherwise," I said. I bade him a curt farewell.

"Wait," Akiba said. He followed us clear of the throng of lowering Jews. I halted. He spoke quickly.

"There is a new generation who did not endure the destruction of the Temple," he said softly. "They are young and fierce. The Romans, to them, are enemies. They speak already of a fresh revolt. I was wrong to have you come here: for your own safety, noble Rufus, do not come again until they are calm."

"I am safe enough," I said proudly.

"For the good of Rome, then, for the empire. For whatever reasons at all. We must not see each other."

I made no promises. With a nod, I entered my litter and drew the curtain. On the jogging journey that night back to Caesarea, however, my doze did not bring me visions of Akiba's anxious face nor of Simeon's earnest one, nor even of the mad agony in the features of the sicarius. Only the pert mischievous face of Sarra appeared in my thoughts.

CHAPTER 9

Nunc appositum est (ut existimo) dicere quod quinquennium contiguus—it is fitting to say here (as I think) that nearly five years passed before the lives of Akiba and myself again became intertwined. True, I occasionally saw him on his rare visits to Caesarea but I did not return to Lydda. His warning had been honest: there was hate abroad, festering and ugly. It was simply not a wise matter for an administrator who valued his hide to stir too far from the barracks of the principal city. Frontinus might march with a cohort; Marcellus was too indolent and cowardly. I moved without guard except for Ficus but I had learned well my lesson at Lydda.

Akiba, for his part, seemed occupied with his own curious travails in Jewish theology. From time to time he sent Simeon to Caesarea to see me but the boy appeared uncomfortable in my residence. I could see he was always glad to set out on his return journey; he thought of Lydda as home. I did not disabuse him. It is the Roman custom to pay little attention to youngsters growing up. That is the duty of women and slaves until the child is of an age to understand politics and battles. I was kindly, even affectionate, but Ficus spent much more time than I with him, reciting tales of war, chanting songs hideously out of key, initiating him into the advanced secrets of sword and javelin and fist, describing life on the German frontier. The pair grew inseparable, a comradeship of which I approved.

As for me, I was occupied with an increasing number of confidential errands for Rome: it seemed that never a ship came to port or a caravan to market but it had a special missive for me. In Rome, Trajan triumphant had undertaken the task of remaking the empire. Hercules was his favorite god in the pantheon and a veritable Hercules he proved himself.

It is an old Roman saying that the great emperors are those who "review armies, subdue provinces, found cities, bridge rivers, and build roads." To this one must add that he must also have courage, justice, and mercy. Trajan possessed all of these and more. Rome—as I was to discover later—was becoming transformed in manners and monuments. The Circus Maximus was rebuilt and enlarged; the temples were repaired and made magnificent; the spring-roaring Tiber was tamed by canals; aqueducts were built to bring better water within its walls. Trajan built three huge public baths—Oppian, Aqua Trajan, and Naumachian—and even some small theatres (though he never liked actors and pantomimes). His grandest achievement was the gleaming Forum of Trajan. Bright-colored marble everywhere, it was five times as big as the Forum of Augustus, gleaming white with pillars, filled libraries, gigantic statues, and stately halls, centered by the famous column which told the story of his Dacian conquest in sculptures.

To the Romans Trajan gave free wine and bread, more than ever before. He delighted the souls of the populace—pampering them almost to their destruction, as I believe—by offering 123 days of public games each year, using 25,000 performers and thousands of wild beasts. Nor did Trajan neglect the provinces. Everywhere he relieved the burden of taxes, forced the rich to aid the poor, built massive networks of roads, dug out harbors, drained swamps, and rebuilt sewers for the betterment of his people. Nothing seemed to escape

144

his notice. He forced all those about him to work as hard as he.

It was a golden time, in truth, one of which we shall never see the like again. During it, above all, Trajan prided himself on his clemency to his people. He had compassion for all except rebels and the wild beasts which he was accustomed to slay in his daily hunting forays—and for himself. The madness with which he consumed wine was monstrous. It was a vice I could understand; which, perhaps, I had cultivated too much myself.

But I go too far at a thrust. Let me return to my own isolation which, however luxurious, was still no more than an exile from all I loved best. Alas! Had I known I was to spend five years in the unforgiving duties of my office, I might have imitated the slave Glaucus and fled into limbo. As it was, my time came to be shared between Jerusalem and Caesarea, with trips into Mesopotamia and Egypt, to Cyrenaeica, and even to newly won Arabia. Numberless were the hours I reclined in a jogging mule litter, seeing nothing through the leather curtains but the thick legs of my marching escort and the endlessly monotonous silhouettes of the desert landscapes.

I longed to escape from Judea to some foreign land, even to misty Britain. Most of all, I dreamed of Rome. My pettiness commenced to show itself in my dispatches. I did not neglect my tasks, but my highly respectful queries to the emperor did not spare a single detail. Perhaps it may be said I annoyed the throne too much with small matters, but my boredom was lightened by such trivial bureaucratic revenge.

The province was in considerable disorder between the sternness of Frontinus and the secret lootings of Marcellus—and the latent malignity of the Jews. I had no desire to take steps which might expose me to blame. Trajan was a military man above anything else. I knew he felt that all but the most serious questions should be handled by those to whom he had delegated power: but what real power had I other than persuasion on the spot or appeal to the throne? As one of the first correctores civitatium liberarum, I was uncertain of my duties. I protested that I wished to be instructed. Of only one thing was I sure: that the powers in the heavens must pay homage to those on earth. The authority of the Army came first; then, that of the state; and, last of all, that of religion (though with the Jews, of course, it was quite different).

I recall a few of the endless messages I sent to the worthy Trajan. They are scraps in my memory, decorated with the ceremonious phrases that had to be used in addressing the emperor. Partially erased by the reversed stylus of time, snatches of their phrasing recur to me:

"By your gracious indulgence, Sire, the provincials have come to me to ask that my influence be used to appoint their judges by lot rather than by the governor." It was granted, a blow to the bribe-taking of Marcellus.

"Having been attacked by a severe and dangerous illness this year and only lately recovered, Sire, I employed a physician whose care and diligence I cannot sufficiently reward without your eminent favor. Though he is the freedman of an alien, he begs to be made a citizen of Rome." The man's name was Harpocras. He treated me for a lingering fever. Trajan granted my request, but I later discovered that Harpocras was originally an Egyptian, citizen of Alexandria. I was forced to plead that he be given the freedom of that city also. It was allowed but, I must admit, with a bad grace from the emperor.

"Your late sacred father, Sire, encouraged the public to acts of munificence. I have the honor to make the request that you will allow me to adorn the forum of Caesarea with your statue at my expense." This, too, was allowed, though with some imperial demur at my flattery. The statue, of bronze, was an inexpensive though passable likeness.

"Allow me, Sire, to congratulate you and the republic upon the great and glorious victory you have obtained over the Dacians, so fitting to the heroism of the ancient Romans." To which Trajan replied that he welcomed my sentiments. He promptly assigned me another task, that of looking into the tax receipts of all the Judean towns. It was the beginning of a series of events which left me alienated from everyone important in the province.

"I am at present," I wrote, after two years of laborious questionings and occasional floggings, "engaged in examining the public finances of the towns and villages—their payments, revenues, and credits. Several large sums due to Rome from private persons are missing. It appears that the public funds are unwarrantably used for other purposes. May I suggest remedial procedures to your governor, the honorable Marcellus." Trajan read the real meaning of my message and gave me full authority. What I suggested was hardly calculated to make Marcellus a friend, but it at least spared me attendance upon his wretched amateur concerts.

"I am distressed, Sire, that the province has no skillful

surveyors. I am of the mind that substantial sums of money for the public works might be recovered, if such an officer might be sent to affirm the metes and boundaries about Jerusalem." This did not endear me to Frontinus but he was a soldier. He harbored no real civilian resentment against the revised allotments which deprived some of his veterans of their land.

"I plead for your determination, Sire, in a doubtful point. Should public slaves be placed as sentinels about the Jewish prisoners of the province or should soldiers be used?" Trajan replied that only soldiers should be employed. This again left Frontinus disgruntled and, more than ever, my critic. To a degree, I could understand. Frontinus and his fortunes had changed. His father, who had served with consular dignity under Nerva and was accorded a high post with Trajan, had died in Rome of the fullness of years. Though Frontinus himself had virtues, this had nevertheless removed one of the strongest props of his position in Syria and Judea.

"Gabius Bassus," I wrote, "the visiting prefect from the Pontic shore, declares that my assignment of ten soldiers, two horse guards, and a centurion is not sufficient to maintain his dignity. Is it your will that I request more troops from Frontinus?" Trajan returned a firm negative which pleased Frontinus mightily. It also made the pompous Bassus my enemy.

"Sire, the inhabitants of Caesarea in the south have an ancient and rundown bath which they desire to restore at their own expense. Is it your desire that permission should be given?" To which Trajan assented, thus putting Marcellus into a rage. He had destined their funds for his own personal loot.

"Ficus, my orderly, Sire, has discovered that two slaves are among the Roman army recruits sent here. As you know, death is the penalty for such deception; I have deferred their punishment until I know your will." Trajan ordered that if they had acted in knowledge of the law, they should be executed; if not, imprisoned. Again Frontinus felt aggrieved.

I confess I was blind to how far events had gone, long before Trajan was to set out on his last campaign. I was a marked man, not only by the Jews (who resented my investigations into their affairs) but also by the Romans—who should have supported me—in the highest places. I had offended the cupidity of Marcellus and the disciplined instincts of Frontinus. What I had to fear from the latter was breast forward and open; from the former, however, I learned much of intrigue.

On one of my occasional and unavoidable visits on business to Marcellus, the enmity between us was sealed by a strange event. Couched in the fine audience hall of red Scythian marble, we talked and jested in our usual guarded fashion. I was alone and unarmed. As we sucked at some of the many and magnificent fruits of Judea, a servant hurried in. He whispered a few words into the ear of Marcellus. The governor nodded and waved him away; but as the slave went, he glanced at me with an expression of hatred. In that instant, I noted he wore, as did many of the slaves, a decorative curlicue of black beauty spots—but on his forehead. As he scrambled out of the room, I fancied that he also had a lamed right arm.

"Who is that fellow?" I asked Marcellus languidly.

"What do you mean?"

"The slave who attended you a moment ago."

Marcellus chuckled, his drooping belly jiggling. "That one? He is a Samaritan Jew, very useful as a spy and as a provocateur among his people. He hates the Judeans. He would do anything to ruin them."

"I seemed to recognize him," I said casually.

Marcellus cast me a quick look, then veiled his eyes behind the cushions of fat in his cheeks. "Perhaps," he said. "You must have seen him often in my palace."

"No," I said, "I do not remember seeing him here before. But I seem to recollect him in another place years ago."

"Another place?"

"My imagination, undoubtedly," I said, "but I thought it was Lydda."

"That seat of Jewish sedition?" demanded Marcellus incredulously. "Impossible. You should be careful of your visits there. People talk: Frontinus is not above spreading rumors about you."

"As you say," I replied evasively. We went on to discuss other things, most of them unsatisfactory. I wished to press the point no further. That evening as I gained my own residence, I beckoned to Ficus. "Do you recall that Samaritan Jew in Lydda?" I asked.

"The one who tried to carve you up, years back?"

"The same; the one we thought the Jews of the town had encouraged."

"The gods blight them!" replied Ficus. "I do indeed recall him."

"His face?"

"I never forget what a dog looks like."

"He is in the service of Marcellus."

Ficus whistled softly; his eyes grew round and bulging. "It is a lesson to us not to blame the Jews too quickly," I said. "But I do not wish to be bothered by this slave again."

Ficus nodded, saluted, and tramped heavily away. Two days later he came to me with a smirk on his face. "You will not be concerned again by that animal," he said satisfiedly. "Not unless he can walk out of the city rubbish heap with his throat cut."

"Very well," I said.

"I met him in the marketplace yesterday at twilight," Ficus went on, ignoring my frown. "I raised my fist at him and he scuttled, I tell you, direct for the gates of Marcellus' palace. But one of the governor's guard is a friend of mine. He hates all Jews equally; he was waiting for him with his knife."

"I don't wish to hear about it," I said irritably. "Stop that cursed saluting."

Ficus looked hurt. "I came to inform you of something else," he mumbled. "Young Simeon is here."

"What!" I cried in pleasure. "Bring him to me this instant!"

"With his companion?"

"Akiba is always welcome in my house," I said.

"This is not Akiba," Ficus replied mournfully.

"Who is it?"

"A girl," Ficus said simply. I felt stunned. I considered a moment, knowing very well who it must be, overwhelmed with suddenly returned memories of that piquant young face which had haunted my dreams. "Do not bring her to me," I said at last. "Give her the best room, but bring Simeon alone."

A few moments later, Ficus led Simeon into the atrium and then retreated, clanging the bronze doors behind him. I embraced the youth. I held him at arm's length, observing him with pride. He was a stalwart one past eighteen, shaking a stallion mane of black hair. He was muscular and confident, even a little brash. I reckoned it was no more than due to one of his background and birth. "Come, Simeon," I said, "sit next to me. Tell me the news of Lydda and of Akiba."

Simeon did not respond. He looked about the room as if

149

he had never seen it before. I arranged my toga and leaned back in my chair. "What is the matter, Simeon?" I asked.

"Nothing," he said.

"Come," I told him impatiently, "you may confess your pranks to me as your uncle—even as I sometimes confess my sins to Akiba. He is a vigorous sixty-eight and a sage; I am a vigorous forty-three and a soldier. You are a fierce and flaming eighteen and son to both of us. We are of an age to confess, each to each. Come."

"I think this is the last time I shall come here," Simeon announced.

"Why?"

"Unless I can find an answer to my question."

"What is your question?"

Simeon fixed me with eyes that startled me: black, direct, uncompromising. It might have been my own gaze reflected from a mirror.

"Who is my father?" he demanded.

I drew a deep breath. Here it was at last, the moment which I had expected for so long. "I do not know," I said truthfully.

"Is Akiba ben Joseph my father?"

"You might have asked him before you came."

"He sent me to you."

The sly Jew! The question of all questions, and he had evaded it!

"Why did he do that?"

"He said you would be the only one who could tell me."

"He has been your father for many years," I said, evasive in my turn.

"Am I flesh of his flesh?"

I considered. "Do you feel that you are?"

Simeon rose restlessly from his bench, pacing the chamber, a magnificent young man. "I feel many things," he said passionately. "I am drawn to him, to Rachel. I love them. But I do not altogether love the things they believe. I cannot stand the study of the Torah; I feel the impulse to do things with my hands, not my head. I dream of vague glories, of conquests."

I thrilled to hear him speak like this. "Have you told Akiba?"

"Many times. He says it is only because I am young. But I am no longer young, and the dreams are more powerful than ever."

"You sound like a Roman, not a Jew," I said.

150

"The glory of the Jews is older than that of the Romans," he flashed.

"When did a Jew rule the world?" I asked gently.

"That time will come."

"When the heavens open and their god conquers by miraculous powers, perhaps," I answered. "But not in the course of man by himself." It was the least I could say.

It did not satisfy Simeon. "Who was my mother?" he asked. "What blood is it in my veins that makes me so restless?"

"Is it not Rachel?" I asked cunningly.

Simeon shook his head. "They are very gentle, very kind, both Akiba and she," he replied, his tone changing. "But I find myself rejoicing in battle and strength, in—in the powers you rejoice in."

Ah! He had come very close, perhaps close enough. My pride in him rose within me like a flame, but I managed to control my features. I was within an instant of answering him with what I hoped and believed: that he was truly my own love-son. But I wanted to ask one more question.

"Why do you want to know all this?" I said softly.

"Because," cried Simeon, "I wish to marry Sarra, and Akiba tells me I cannot! He will not tell me whether or not I am his son and a Jew. If it is true, the law prevents it. If it is not, I am free!"

My thoughts grew dark. Upon them, projected as if by some art of the brain, I saw the fancied image of Sarra coming up the steps of my palace, hand in hand with him. My mind twisted.

"Think no more of it," I said, slowly and harshly, the words coming almost against my will. "You are a Jew. A Jew of Jews. Be satisfied with what you are."

Simeon stared into my face, his expression rigid as iron, searching, piercing.

"You swear it?" he asked in a whisper.

"A Roman does not swear an oath," I said. "His word is enough."

Simeon reached inside his tunic, gave a jerk, and flung something down before me: it was his gold bulla, sprung open, the little green-stone beetle from Egypt seeming almost alive as it tumbled out. I stooped to pick it up as he turned to leave.

"Wait," I said. Simeon paused at the door. "You are quite right to discard the bulla," I said. "You are nearly old enough and nearly man enough. Accept this as a gift instead from me." I reached to my left arm and unwound the golden asp which Domitilla had given me many years before and which I had worn ever since. I handed it to Simeon, who took it as if he did so in a dream, mechanically putting it about his own arm. "Let it remind us both of what we are to each other."

Simeon's lips curled into a half-bitter smile. "I shall make my own glory. I shall not borrow that of the empire," he said abruptly. He turned to go. Three paces off, at the door, he hesitated and turned. "The word of a Jew is not equal to that of a Roman," he said wryly, "but I could have sworn an oath on Jahveh that there was more kinship between us than you allow."

The next moment he was gone, leaving me throttled with my own lie. I think now, that if he had remained no more than a moment longer, I would have confessed that I had told him a monstrous untruth. But I know as well that my pride in what I had spoken would have kept me silent. So the time passed that I might have redeemed myself; and Simeon went on his way to become more glorious than he could know— one who nearly overturned the empire itself.

Possibly these things are done because of fate, but at that moment it was because of my longing for Sarra. I thought no more of the stripling Simeon, only of her. My resolution hardened and became reckless. I sent orders that she should come to me that evening at the tenth hour.

In my best robe, perfumed and massaged by Ficus, I sat by myself in the pale darkness of the small atrium, by the fountain, waiting for Sarra. I felt myself trembling like any callow lover at his first assignation. Why Sarra had appeared out of my past without warning, why I had reacted in such a mad manner, I had no true idea. What I had done all this day, three days removed from the fateful ides of the month, I could not tell. I prided myself on my logic and straightforwardness: now, in a matter of hours, all this pretense had been stripped from me. I was as scheming and unscrupulous as any man. Yet I felt no shame.

The atrium was filled with the scent of flowers, expanding after the heat of the day. Through the wide windows, the dark sky was overlaid with the brilliant stars of Judea. Behind me, the fountain flowed and gurgled in the corner. Half in the body, half out of it in expectation, I sat on a five-legged cedar stool inlaid with ivory, my toga perfectly draped. A large lamp burned, unwavering and golden. A breeze passed fitfully through the chamber.

By the brass water clock in the corner, Sarra was late. My heart sank in impatience and disappointment, tinged with a growing anger. I rose from the stool, intending to go into the corridor to summon a slave. I heard the faint tinkle of tiny bells. Hastily I sprang back to the stool, rearranged my robe, and composed myself.

It was Ficus who brought her in, presented her without a word, saluted, and turned about-face with a wooden visage. He closed the folding doors behind him with exaggerated care. All was silence, only the fall of the fountain timed to the throbbing of my heart.

This Sarra was no girl: she was a woman, though barely eighteen. I held out my hand. She slipped the long dark cloak from her shoulders and gave it to me. I tossed it aside and moistened my dry lips, admiring what stood before me.

She was clad in a simple white gown, fringed with red, adorned with small bells. Her figure was as erect as that of a soldier; her thick black hair flowed down her back like water at evening. Her skin was white, glowing in the lamplight; her high bosom heaved quickly with emotion. I saw the shining of tiny perspiration beads upon her high cheeks. Her fists seemed to be clenched. But my attention became riveted upon her swollen red lips and the enormous eyes that drew me as if I looked into an abyss.

"Will you sit?" I asked her, my voice harsher than I meant. She shook her head. I shrugged and stood up. "Do you remember me?" I asked needlessly.

"Yes," she said.

"It was a long time ago," I murmured.

"I have never forgotten you," Sarra whispered, as if it were a confession.

I looked down. "Your name is Sarra," I said, in an attempt to restore my calm. "You are the niece of the Jew Akiba, is that not so?"

"Yes."

"It is not usual for a Roman official to take notice of a Jewess," I said. I had no idea why my tone was so stilted.

"There was the emperor Titus and the Jewess Berenice," Sarra said.

I started. "Why do you say that?" I asked. She made no response. "How did you come here?" I persisted.

"There is a road from Lydda to Caesarea," she replied with

153

a hint of laughter. The recurring breeze tinkled the bells on her skirt.

"Why do you wear such a dress?" I demanded.

"It is the custom of my people on a happy occasion," she returned.

My heart increased its beat. "It was very dangerous to travel here," I said, clearing my throat.

Sarra shook her head. "Not with Simeon," she answered. "He has a great name already among my people. There are food and help, no matter where we might go in Syria."

"But the Romans, Sarra!"

"To them he speaks like a man accustomed to command, one who must be obeyed—and they obey, not altogether knowing who he is."

I grew fretful. My blood prickled in my flesh. "But why did you come to see me with him?"

"Because you did not return to Lydda to see me."

The simple answer stung and rejoiced me. "You have changed much since those far-off days," I told her.

"I have become a woman," she said. To my surprise, she turned slowly around, then faced me again. "I am different, am I not, noble Rufus?"

"Yes," I said with difficulty. "I had already noticed. You have grown up, Sarra."

"I have dreamed about you," she said slowly, "and this is what I dreamed of. Have you dreamed of me?"

"No," I said. Evidently it was destined that this day was to be black in my calendar, filled with lies.

"It is usual for women to have more dreams than men," Sarra said, unperturbed. Her voice suddenly became so deep and musical that it startled me. Involuntarily I took a step toward her, then restrained myself.

"Come here, Sarra," I said.

Moving as jerkily as a sleepwalker, she moved toward me. I did not stir, though my arms ached to reach out and crush her to me. I wet my lips. "Closer," I said hoarsely. She shook her head, keeping her eyes on mine. I turned away from her gaze to regain my self-control.

"What do you want of me?" she said calmly.

"Everything," I found myself saying. "Everything, nothing."

"I can give you neither," she replied. At that, words burst from me, babbling. I took a stride forward, almost touching her.

"Have you no pity on me?" I asked of this provincial Jewess, pleading like any rustic lover.

"You are my lord and master," she said, her eyes downcast.

"Speak," I said. "Why do you think of me as such?"

"Are not all Romans, any Roman, lord and master of all the Jews?"

I shook my head. "Man to man, perhaps," I told her, "but Roman men are not master or lord to Jewish girls."

"Can you not take what you desire?" Her voice fell lower.

I thought I scented victory. I advanced a step closer. "Romans do not seize merely for the sake of closing their fist," I said. "We wish to take hostages. To have them live better, happier; to make a province a rich and flowering land." They were the words of a maundering sannio.

"Would a true Roman, like yourself, take up from the flowers the serpent that stings his heel?"

She was thoroughly exasperating. I took her by her bare warm shoulders and bent her back. Her lustrous eyes opened full into mine. "Let us have no more of this nonsense," I said huskily.

"What would you have?" she asked, not struggling. More than a little of her weight hung on my arms.

"I would have you treat me as a man, even as I would treat you as a woman. Let there be no more chatter about Roman and Jew."

She drooped unresisting and languorous in my grasp. "Do you mean," she asked guilelessly, "that I am to be free to do as I please, to choose or not to choose?"

"You are as free as a dove," I said from my dry throat, inexplicably filled with hope.

Slowly she freed herself. She stood erect. I thought I had never seen anyone so graceful. "Do you give me your word?" she said quickly, her bosom rising and falling.

"The word and honor of a Roman!" I cried, exultant, ready to crush her to me.

I encircled her with eager arms. In that instant, Sarra jerked free. She struck me a stinging blow on the cheek, with as much strength as if she had flung a discus.

From the unexpectedness of it—not the force—I staggered back three paces. Caught off balance, I tripped over my stool. I sat down abruptly. There was an overwhelming splash, an icy shock to my rear. I had sat down in the basin of the fountain: its outraging trickle played down my neck.

Sarra had not waited to see what happened. She whirled,

155

forced open the doors, and ran out furiously, head down. But she was not to gain her freedom yet. She hurtled full into one just entering. She bounded off, regained her footing—and found herself gripped by the arm. "What has he done to you?" exclaimed Simeon, springing into the room.

Shocked into reality, disgruntled and once more in full control of my senses, I stood up and shook myself. The breeze was comfortably cool about my soaked thighs. "Nothing," I said bluntly. "Worse luck, nothing."

Simeon advanced, his face filled with fury, his fists clenched. I felt a thrill to see him so and, for the moment, I was glad that neither of us was armed. "You tried to seduce her," Simeon grated.

"Naturally," I said. "What did a Jew expect of a Roman?"

"I shall kill you!"

"Don't be ridiculous," Sarra's voice said scornfully. "You think you're so strong and righteous, Simeon. I can take care of myself and Rufus, too."

Both of us stared at her in utter astonishment. I was the first to regain my poise. "She has done very well," I acknowledged ironically. I indicated my condition.

Without warning, Simeon sprang at me. Sarra screamed, a light sound composed partly of pleasure, partly fear. As the boy leaped, however, his sandals slipped on the wet floor. I caught him by both arms and heaved him backward. He reeled to the wall. "Some day you will be able to fulfill your threats," I said. "Until that time, you would do better to keep your mouth closed."

I turned, plucking my dripping toga carefully away from my skin. Out of the corner of my eye I saw Simeon crouching again. I wheeled to meet a new attack. My own footing gave way and I sprawled again in the basin. I am sure Simeon would have pounced upon me, even so, except that Ficus loomed up in the doorway with a shouted warning. Simeon stopped and drew himself up proudly. Sarra turned to run, caromed off Ficus as she had Simeon, managed to duck free, and disappeared into the hall, fleeing like a gazelle pursued on the desert by ravening hounds—or, at least, that is how Ficus described her exit to me afterward.

Ficus grunted. "A soft one, she is," he growled, thrusting out his growing paunch. Simeon marched toward him. Ficus thrust out his arm, as thick as a beam. "Wait," he warned him. He looked at me. "What is your wish, sir?" Good Ficus: despite his affection for Simeon, his duty toward me was always foremost in his mind. I got up with care, not wishing for a third inundation. "Let him do as he pleases," I said, "and bring me a fresh robe."

Ficus dropped his arm. Simeon left silently. Ficus watched me with an expression I could not understand. I carefully began to wring out my garment. "What are you waiting for?" I demanded in exasperation. "Begone!"

"Did you—did you—" Ficus stammered. He swallowed his words. His eyes bulged, his big cheeks grew red. His crushed nose purpled in his vast face as he endeavored to check his emotions. He thrust out his paw, holding a sealed set of tablets. "Here, noble Rufus," he mumbled, "here. By special messenger."

Next moment he had clapped a hand over his mouth and rushed out again, faster than he had come in. As he vanished, the sense of my own ludicrous position struck me. I commenced to laugh helplessly, doubling over with mirth.

Still chuckling, I picked up the tablet where I had dropped it. Its seal proved that it was no common missive. Nor was it one that could be disregarded. It came from Rome. It bore the emperor's personal insigne.

It was from Trajan himself. It informed me that he was about to set out on a new campaign against the enemies of Rome. This time he was embarking within the next month for the East, against the ever-threatening Parthians.

I was to join him in the north. I was to meet the imperial entourage at the city of Antioch. My assignment was as tribune to the I Adiutrix.

Somewhere in the bowels of the palace that I was soon to leave, I could hear Ficus bellowing with laughter. And, I suspected, though I could not be sure, I heard also the clear giggles of Sarra. But I did not hear the laughter of Simeon.

From deep within me a quick tide of rejoicing arose. I was freed from the bonds of this life. I was given the chance to leave all temptation and administrative nonsense behind. I was to fight once more in the simple, uncomplicated manner of sword and javelin, to partake again of the comradeship of posca and wheat, sweat and blood, glory and conquest—no more of trickery, plots, love, and futile bargaining or sterile arguments with Jews like Akiba.

I caught a flirt of light at the left. I turned my head. Through the window, I saw a bright falling star outside, flashing downward toward the north. "A night of omens, in very truth," I muttered to myself. It could mean only that the gods

157

were displeased with kings, not with me; on my left, it was favorable to my future. But even if it concerned me as Trajan's legate to Judea, it might well be fortunate for me as a soldier again.

I strode to the door and flung it wide. I listened but not for the merriment of others; the roaring of anticipation for the future filled my ears. I cared no more about my shivering body, warmed by the heat of imagined struggles to come. I flung my soaked toga aside and stood naked in my loincloth.

"Ficus!" I shouted. "Ficus, you old war horse! Prepare the packs and burnish your weapons! We march!"

CHAPTER 10

A litter on a long journey is an excellent inducement to fits of slumber and meditation. The swaying of the poles, accompanied by the grunts and curses of the mule drivers; the sense of being apart from the dust and grime of the trip behind the leather curtains, brings peace of mind. My trip north to Antioch to meet Trajan was broken only by stops for food and rest at the way taverns that lined the long road built by Domitian from the north boundaries of Syria down to the Red Sea. These stations were cleverly spaced a dozen miles or so apart to correspond to the need for relief mules and for emptying the bladder. They were greatly appreciated. Between them, enclosed in my litter like a pupus, I had the chance to reorder my thoughts—chiefly those disarranged by the unexpected visit of Simeon and Sarra.

As I have said, like most true soldiers—like Trajan himself—I have always been addicted to the joys of wine and war. Dionysius sprang from the thigh of Jupiter as the god of war and madness, to be the lover of Venus. They are well matched. War is a passion like love. Death on the battlefield is as much a fulfilment as the orgasm in bed. Dulce et decorum est, certainly, as the poet Horace wrote, but not at all for his reasons.

Thinking of Sarra, I knew how fitting it was to have Dionysius-Mars as the lover of Love, with the connivance of all-powerful Jupiter. It reflected the deepest instincts of our soul: love is the war of man against woman, plots against force, intrigue against tactic. Both are the strategy of the gods to bend man to their will.

Nor are the terms of love and war much different. The stiff pilum, the sweet ambush, the steady thrust until exhausted, the rallyings and whispered curses that are endearments of the fray. Nor are the symbols alien: the bosses of the shields are bosoms urged against us, the hoops of brass on our cuirasses are embraces, our erect crests are phalli erecti. We tread the dead with our caligae as a cock treads his hens, we experience the same melting of sweat and emotion when the battle is done, the same depth of sleep and rejoicing revival. The rising pulse, the hammer of nerves knocking at our skull like a mace, the rhythms of attack and retreat, the final forcing of the barriers, the taste of blood— in what respect is love apart from war? Is the thrill of a steel kiss less than that of warm lips, the pain less than the pleasure? Only in this: in war, man fights man (except for the one-breasted Amazons who mutilate themselves to draw their bows better) and may call him friend afterward. In love, man fights woman who is his eternal enemy, impossible to be reconciled, except in the depths of the hatred that is infatuation.

These were the musings—as I recollect them now—that occupied my time during the three-day journey. We entered at noon by the massive west gate into Antioch which I had visited before but which never ceased to astonish me. It was one of the principal cities of the empire, next to Rome and Alexandria. Orientis apex pulcher, it was overflowing with rabble, rich and poor, from every corner of the world— Romans, Greeks, Jews, Syrians, Egyptians, a hundred races —each man in pursuit of riches and fame, having no thought except for luxury, pleasure, and impudence.

Four cities in one—not including the wondrous suburb of Daphne, where every delight known to man had its price— it shared the magnificence of order and arrangement which was the glory of the Greek founders. A free city, it had been given its rights by the first Julius himself, a generation before I was born. So much pride did the citizens have in their fame that they themselves contributed as much again in gifts to adorn the place as they paid in taxes. (I have heard since, on good authority, that Antioch burns torches for streetlights all night long, but this I find hard to credit.)

The whole city was an immense irregular rectangle with

parallel streets, crossed by others at right angles. One broad avenue ran east to west, from gate to gate: it was thirty-six stades long, paved with polished marble and mosaic furnished by kings such as Herod. Colonnades on each side, with ornately carved roofs, gave the people and markets protection from sun and rain. Arched arcades offered access to cross streets. On all of the stately avenues, four-sided monuments, decorated with statues, bestowed upon the whole an air of incredible grandeur.

Public buildings—round, square, oblong—rose everywhere. There were temples (such as the fantastically gilded one dedicated to Dionysius), baths, theatres, basilicas, gymnasia, stadia, and exedrae. Many-colored glass mosaics—a few actually worked in gems and gold and silver, guarded at all hours—completely covered the plain concrete-brick walls. Under the streets were buried double conduits carrying water under pressure from the famous aqueduct high above the city walls, even as high as three storeys. The toilets had running water and bags of goosefeathers to wipe one's behind.

We had arrived at the end of the year, during the Brumalian festival. I knew that the people of Antioch were great lovers of feasts and celebrations, but this took my breath away. The noonday streets were awash with people, floods of humanity: the poor in loincloths and fleeces mingling with the wealthy dressed in cloth of bright colors, embroidered with gold, their limbs weighed down with gems and bracelets. The air was heavy with oil and perfume. Wine was broached in the streets, the wax seals of the jars agape for dipping. Song and music resounded everywhere, shops and homes were open to anyone who desired to enter. Tumblers, rope-walkers, jugglers—all manner of entertainers—went about their occupations as if they expected a rain of coins from the sky.

I watched in fascination, hearing only dimly the bull-roar of Ficus as he pushed his way through the flushed, laughing throng. They jeered him: a mime alongside exactly panto-mimed his actions. I flung the man a coin, and he ducked, caught it in his mouth, made an obscene gesture, and danced away tiptoe into the crowd. At last, by dint of force and luck, we made our way to the palace of the city where a handful of Roman soldiers stood guard.

As I sprang out, I looked eagerly for familiar faces. I saw not one. Nor did a single legionary recognize me. But I was accorded the respectful salutes demanded by my insignia. The

160

emperor had ordered me to report to him upon arrival, and I was admitted immediately into the great atrium. Striding down between the long rows of ebony pillars and white imperial sculptures, past the fountains, into the inner chambers, I was seized by the conviction that this was a strange world gone awry. I followed my guide to the right and into a room surrounding a silver-basined impluvium. The golden afternoon sun poured full onto a richly broidered couch.

I halted and saluted. The fat reclining figure on the purple silk responded languidly. Suddenly, in the shadows to either side, I saw two familiar faces. One was that of Lusius Quietus, now gray, with an indefinable air of command I had not remembered; the other was a tense, handsome face with thinning hair above—the changed face of Hadrian.

"Salve, Rufus Teneius," said the figure on the couch.

It was a voice whose crispness recalled all the past. I sank to one knee: it was the voice of the emperor Trajan.

"Ave, mighty Trajan," I mumbled.

I knew at that moment what was wrong. Everything had changed: I had forgotten it was fourteen years since I had seen my old comrades-in-arms. We were young no longer. And Trajan was old.

"Do you remember," Trajan asked lazily, "that you used to amuse me, in those far-off days at Colonia, by reciting rhymes to me from the Greek?"

"Yes, Sire," I said.

"I have been amusing myself in your long absence," Trajan said, and hiccoughed. He took a drink from the jeweled cup in his hand. He wiped his mouth, spilling a little. "Tell me what you think of this, my own composition."

"Yes, Sire," I said.

Trajan rolled his eyes upward, as if looking for inspiration. He intoned:

> *"Conon is two cubits tall;*
> *His wife is more than four;*
> *In bed, their feet all even—*
> *His nose is at her door."*

The emperor burst into a bellow of laughter and winked at Quietus. I dutifully applauded. "It shows remarkable talent, Sire, in versification," I said. "If you did not wish to be an emperor, you might be a poet."

The shaggy-fleshed face came round to survey me. "Who has said I did not wish to be emperor?" Trajan demanded.

"I meant only that your genius is not confined to government," I said hastily.

"The noble Trajan is the best of emperors," Hadrian broke in obsequiously.

"Silence!" Trajan grunted abruptly. He turned to Quietus. "What do you think?" he demanded.

"I think that we have stayed too long in Antioch," Quietus said firmly.

Trajan laughed again, this time with something of the old ironic ring I remembered. He deliberately poured the rest of his wine back into the deep ivory bowl next to him.

"Enough," he said. He stared at me. "You have changed, Rufus," he growled.

"You are the same, Sire," I said. "I remember your promise to that effect."

" 'As I am, I shall ever be,' " he quoted. He nodded. "Yes, I have not changed. But the world has changed. You have changed. Hadrian, my sniveling relative, has changed. Plotina, my wife—well, who knows a woman? Lusius and I, we are immortal, we only remain the same."

Trajan closed his eyes. He let his head sink back to the gilt headrest of the couch. The three of us—pale Hadrian, lowering Quietus, and myself—stood silent and waiting. I could not believe great Trajan to be the shapeless mass of flesh that lay before me: thick veined arms, jowled, fleshy face, distorted features, bald head. This satyr on the couch could not be the same as the alert youthful commander I had last seen in Upper Germania.

Trajan stirred. He looked at me from under flickering eyelids. "Tell me the gossip of Judea," he said. "You have an ear for such things."

"I know none, Sire," I faltered, my thoughts fluttering wildly.

Trajan frowned. "You are not entertaining," he said severely, lifting his head. "You are merely an idiot. Why do you suppose I sent for you? To frighten the Parthians? Beware, beware, ye Parthians, Rufus Teneius is coming!" He sank back. "The campaign may begin—now that you are here," he said bitingly.

Tears of humiliation stung my eyes. Trajan went on, talking half to himself: "Why have I ordered him here, a man who can fight but cannot command, who has to ask me to let down his breeches?" Almost without thought, I stretched out to him my left arm. On the sun-dark skin, the long scar of the wound I had suffered for him in Germania shone white. Trajan saw and instantly understood. He tightened his flaccid lips and nodded. "Yes," he said slowly, "you are loyal, Rufus. That is much in these times." The look he cast at the others I could not interpret. Neither Quietus nor Hadrian moved a muscle in the shadows of the lengthening afternoon. Sounds of singing and merriment came from outside, verses satiric and laudatory addressed to the emperor. Trajan turned abruptly on his side. He dipped up another cup of the red wine. He flicked the drops from his fingers at me in dismissal. "Tomorrow," he said, "tomorrow."

I saluted and made my way out of the room in a swimming daze, barely noting that both Quietus and Hadrian moved as if to follow. Trajan waved them back. I walked slowly through the long echoing halls of marble toward the tumult that indicated the door. I passed through the beaten copper leaves of the portal and halted halfway down the flight of broad marble. A figure slipped toward me, bobbing in obeisance.

"Tribune Rufus," he lisped, "a word, grant me a word!"

I stopped and looked at him uncomprehendingly. "Do you not know me?" he asked. He was a thin, stooped man with long white hair. His hands bobbed nervously before him. "I have never seen you before in my life," I said.

"Do you not remember the court of Domitian in Rome? The small cypress door at the rear of the emperor's chambers? Do you not remember me?"

"By the gods!" I exclaimed. "Pontus! The slave Pontus!"

He nodded eagerly, this withered old replica of the pompous functionary that had commanded me as one of his corps of informers in Rome so long ago. "How have you survived?" I demanded, relishing the moment but almost pitying the shell of a man.

"It is the business of such as myself to survive," Pontus whispered. "Sacrifices, yes, but at least we remain alive. A secret which is nothing but lies and flattery, lies and flattery, it is quite enough to know that. I am of the following of the noble Lusius Quietus, good Rufus."

"I have seen him today by the side of the emperor," I said.

"Did he speak to you?"

"He had no opportunity."

163

"Ah," Pontus said softly, "then it is my mission to ask you to meet him."

I blinked, puzzled. "To meet him?"

"As soon as you may, just outside the city. I will show you the spot. He wishes to demonstrate the legions' new engines of war."

I felt startled. "But I have only just arrived!"

Pontus shrugged and waved his claws. His face became expressionless. "I know no more than that I was to intercept you and give the message, if he found it impossible," he told me. "Forgive a slave who cannot tell you more. The noble Quietus has reserved that for himself."

Ficus approached, saluting me and ignoring Pontus. "I have the assignment to quarters, noble Rufus," he said, "and your litter is waiting."

"I cannot come," I told Pontus.

The old look of prideful threat I remembered came over his face. "It is not wise to refuse," he said. I was astounded: it was the voice of Trajan to the life!

"You spoke with the tones of the emperor!" I exclaimed. Pontus shrugged. "A trick, imitating voices," he said. "I learned it from the mimes about Domitian."

I felt a chill of anxiety. I turned to Ficus. "Wait for me," I said. "I go to an appointment."

"This," Lusius said, "is the ballista."

He indicated a polished iron trough with narrow grooves, supported by a wheeled scaffolding. A thick cord lay across it, attached to springs of twisted rawhide. "It can fire five arrows at the same moment," Lusius said, "cocked by the sergeant as the men wind up the springs. Those hit by the shafts a half mile away are dead before they hear the whistle of its passage. Its force is enough to kill three men before it is stopped."

"We had nothing like this in Germania," I said.

"The forts there were small, of wood and earth," Lusius agreed. "We did not need them. And the emperor was younger and more active in leading the legions."

I glanced at his face, but he gave no hint of what he was thinking. He moved on into the weapon yard outside the walls of Antioch, into the depths of the vast collection of towers and sheds. "This is the new sort of battering ram, adapted from the Parthians, that uses a brass ram's head," Lusius continued, pointing to the massive mountain ash timber with its handholds and counterweights. "It is easy to swing: the weight and rhythms are irresistible. Sooner or later, the strongest gate must give way, the strongest wall collapse in ruins."

"I can believe it," I said.

"Just as men must at last surrender to the battering of their years," added Lusius. Again the subtle change of tone in his voice took me by surprise. Before I could answer, Lusius moved once more and pointed. "The testudo," he said, before a strongly built hutch of wood and iron, mounted on wheels and containing a lighter ram. "We no longer use our shields for such an assault, except when we mount the walls. No one can be successful if they are unprotected—not even an emperor, eh?"

"No," I said. I was beginning to be troubled, to wish I had not come with him to the weapon yard. The palisadoed camp with its guards outside seemed gloomy and threatening in the dusk.

"The scorpion," Lusius said briefly. Before us was a great oak framework bolted together. A long heavy pole tilted up at an angle, hooks and a leather sling at one end. It was mounted on a heavy bronze spring and there was a cross-beam to stop it short with a cushion of hair and straw. "Pulled back by the cables," Lusius said, "this trigger lets it fly when it is loaded with stones or lumps of iron. It can cause stones of three hundred pounds to fly like birds for a quarter of a mile."

"Extraordinary," I said. "A scorpion, because of its upraised sting?"

"Precisely. It crushes the enemy when it is least expected. But a soldier or a commander must expect anything at any moment, do you not agree?"

"It cannot be otherwise," I said doubtfully.

"The helepolis," Lusius said after a few more paces. I saw a huge wooden tortoise-shed fastened with iron and covered with green hides. Sharp heavy tridents protruded from the front, their management made easy by counterweights.

"The 'city-taker,' you call it," I murmured.

"It works very well but it takes a long time. But time conquers all at length, even the most mighty of men."

"Yes," I said.

Lusius led me even farther into the yard and stopped before a wheeled tower that shot its scaffolding fifty cubits or more up into the air and had its front boarded with iron and hide. At three levels there were doors for soldiers to thrust open and storm a fort. "We push it against the walls and the other weapons cover the advance," Lusius explained.

"And these?" I asked, picking up one of a sheaf of reeds, pierced with holes and bound with rope—much like an arrow without head or feathers. "That is a fire dart," Lusius responded. "It is filled with oil and oozings from the lake of asphalt and lighted. Shot from a loose bow, it breaks against buildings or dives in thatch. It sticks and burns for hours. There is a formula, I have heard, whereby the fire burns fiercer when water is poured on it—the only way to extinguish the blaze is by piling dust upon it."

"Very interesting," I assured him.

For the first time Lusius looked directly at me. "If the first man to mount the helepolis is killed," he said darkly, "another must take his place. The fires set by another must be put out. The battle must be carried on, no matter who falls."

"Of course," I said hastily, "that is essential. It has been a most interesting tour, noble Quietus; now let us return to the city."

Quietus held me by the arm. "You understand what we have been talking about?" he inquired in a low voice.

"Your description of the weapons has been perfect," I said.

"The battle for the might of Rome over all nations must be fought," Quietus said intensely, "no matter who sits upon the imperial throne."

"The gods preserve Trajan," I said piously.

"But if Trajan is not there," Quietus said grimly, his voice even lower, "who will be in his place?"

"I trust he will be immortal," I said.

"He is divine but not immortal," Quietus replied. His voice held an indescribable accent. "All of us must die."

"Whenever the gods choose," I answered.

"Perhaps you are right," Quietus said enigmatically. "And at that time, all of us will have to make a choice."

"Let us return," I said.

Quietus relaxed his grip on my arm, so tight that he had bruised my flesh. "By all means," he said, and commenced to walk so rapidly I was hard put to it to keep up. I said nothing about having seen all those siege exhibits long before in the arsenal at Caesarea.

Hadrian lounged against the wall of my comfortable Antiochan apartment in the barracks of the south city. He surveyed me with a calculating look, a slight smile on his lips. I tossed my few pieces of gear aside. I offered him wine. He took it with a condescending nod, as became the nephew of the emperor. "Let us drink to the good health of Trajan," I said. Hadrian half-bowed mockingly. But he drained his cup.

"You spent much time this evening with Quietus," Hadrian remarked. "You see, we both have our spies."

"He acted under the instructions of your great uncle, noble Hadrian," I said. "He showed me the marvelous new engines of this campaign."

"We have much to learn yet from the East," Hadrian said. He glanced at me as if calculating the chances of a roll of knucklebones. "What do you think of this new expedition of the emperor?"

"It is a way to gain much glory," I said evasively. "It extends the bounds of the empire."

"Yet it was the advice of Augustus not to do so," returned Hadrian. "As generals get older, they become bolder, eh? For others, I mean."

I did not trust myself on the current of conversation that he unloosed. I was unable to see his purpose. "If they have the gods on their side, as most certainly the mighty Trajan does," I said, "boldness is a requisite for victory, not a detriment."

"Everyone talks about the gods," Hadrian sighed with a smile. "You have been too long among the Jews." His expression changed. "Though you have not seen my uncle for these many years," he murmured, "you still enjoy his confidence. Tell me, has he said who will succeed to the throne?"

"Never," I said.

"Not a word?"

"Never to me."

"Strange," Hadrian said thoughtfully. "The report comes to me that he is considering the succession."

"He has not deigned to give me his confidence."

Hadrian went on: "At a feast, it is said, he declared that there were nine men to whom he would equally bequeath his power. Lusius Quietus was one of those he mentioned."

"And yourself, noble Hadrian?"

Hadrian darted me an enigmatic look. He shook his head. "I was not mentioned," he said.

I must have showed my astonishment. Hadrian laughed softly. "It is amazing, is it not?" he asked. "I have devoted my life to his care and his commands—as Plotina, may the gods bless her, well knows. Yet—he does not mention me."

"I am sure you were in his thoughts," I responded.

"Perhaps, perhaps. He looks very well, does he not?"

"He seems as strong and virile as ever," I said hesitatingly.

"May he live forever!" Hadrian replied. He turned to leave but halted. "If I were his heir, Rufus Teneius," he asked me quickly, "would you take the oath to me as readily as to him?"

"Whoever is chosen emperor is lord of me as he is of Rome," I replied.

Hadrian nodded. With an abrupt wave—I noted with inner amusement how he imitated his august uncle—he vanished from my tent. His departure left me to puzzle, not without suspicion, about his feelings, as I had puzzled over the cryptic words of Quietus. There was a heavy feeling in the air: one of plots and mischief. My quarters commenced to stifle me.

I paced the room restlessly for a few moments, then plunged out into the brisk night air. On the broad parade grounds that centered the barracks of Antioch, there roared a blazing fire. The soldiers gathered about it, chatting and drinking, roasting fruit and nuts over the crackling coals. I approached it to counteract the sudden chill that afflicted me, to rid myself of my thoughts.

Spreading my fingers at the flames, I soon made acquaintance with most of the officers nearby. None of them, I discovered, was an old comrade-in-arms, but I reflected that the legions, like the human body, changed every seven years. I asked about some of my old friends. They knew of Curtius Saccus. "He drew his pay from the bank, received his bronze tablets of discharge, and disappeared," one told me. "He had been transferred to the X Fretensis when his time ran out."

"He did not reenlist," I observed. "I know the officers of that legion at Jerusalem."

The other shrugged and moved off. Another, approached by me, knew of my old commander, Annius Verus. "He finished his time long ago. He took a small house in Rome," he said. "He keeps hospitality for old comrades and welcomes them on all but holy days."

"That is bad news," I said. "For I shall probably never see wonderful Rome again."

"Most of us have never seen that city yet," he answered, grinning. "Tell us of its wonders."

"You will see it in the triumph for the emperor," I assured him, tacitly evading the invitation.

His reply was interrupted by a hail from the guard. He responded, nodded to me, and strode out of the circle of firelight. I remained behind, warming my hands gratefully against the chill wind that drove in from the river. I had only a moment's respite. The centurion with whom I had been chatting returned with a scowl on his face. "Sir, you are Tribune Rufus Teneius, are you not?"

"Yes," I said, instantly alert.

"Here is a man asking entrance. He says he will be recognized by you." The centurion beckoned. The guards came up with a lean, familiar form between them.

"Akiba!" I cried. "What are you doing here?"

"At the moment," he said, "I am being detained by the Romans."

"Let him go," I ordered the soldiers. They fell back, and I took Akiba firmly by the elbow. "I will be responsible," I said. The soldiers vanished; the centurion followed, discreetly. The others drew back as if in fear of contamination.

"Come," I said to Akiba through my teeth, "I have been questioned by others all day. We shall go to my rooms. There I shall question you."

"My first answer to the first question you will ask me," Akiba said blandly, "is that I am going to Parthia by way of Antioch."

"Must you wear that filthy black skullcap?" I asked him as we settled down in the lamplight on opposite couches.

The gaunt old man nodded and smiled. "I saw Ficus in the city streets, trying to embrace a girl," he said. "I knew you must be here."

"Why are you going to Parthia with the Romans?"

"Not with the Romans," Akiba corrected me. "I must stay as far away as possible from your army."

"That is no answer."

"I go to Parthia to decide on our holy days, to arrange our calendar."

"What?" I demanded incredulously. "Is this some jest?"

"No," Akiba said. "If you knew the Jewish calendar, you would realize it is no jest. But even if you knew, you would have no idea of what I am talking about. The Julian calendar, your calendar, is quite different—and few Jews know whereof I speak."

169

"But how can this bring you to Parthia?" I inquired.

"There is unrest in Syria, between Jew and Jew," he said. "I was sent by the council to determine by star-sight in another country the correct dates, to perform ceremonies. It is a sacred mission, one that cannot be undertaken lightly."

"Tell me of it," I urged him. "We date our days from the founding of Rome, our years by the sun, our months by the moon. Can the Jews do better?"

"Our year is dated from the beginning of creation," Akiba said proudly.

"This is the eight hundred and sixty-sixth year," I said.

"It is the three thousand, eight hundred and seventy-fourth," Akiba responded.

Thereafter Akiba explained. The calendar of his people was not yet an accurate one. The priests still announced the beginnings of the months and the years. It was their duty to add a month once every third year because (as I guessed) they worshipped the moon more than the sun and judged it by the former's revolutions. This made them as much as eleven days short each true year.

"We cannot neglect this duty overlong," Akiba pointed out. "Otherwise our spring feast of Passover would come in winter and the harvest festival of Sukkoth in summer—and all the rest would be in confusion."

"Simply announce it," I said.

"No, no," Akiba protested. "It must be done with public and holy ceremonies that are part of our religion."

"Perform them," I said impatiently. "Such quibbling is beyond me."

"They were forbidden under Vespasian," Akiba said sombrely, "and the ban has not been lifted."

I shrugged. "Then forget about it," I told him.

Akiba looked at me pityingly. "What was decided—after much argument—was that the ceremonies would have to be transferred to another country, outside Rome's boundaries," he said.

"In Parthia?"

"There the Magi understand the needs of the Jews. They will not persecute us. I go to Nehardea to undertake the calculations and the necessary rites."

I made a mock bow of permission. "I have no objection," I declared. "A bit of mummery here and there is always amusing—if it is not against the law. But why do you come to Antioch first?"

170

Akiba considered. "Because," he answered gravely, "I have a much more important request to make of the emperor."

I raised my brows. "More important than the arranging of the calendar?"

"Yes. All Judea knows Trajan is here. With you here also, I may be able to gain an audience."

"I am not in favor," I said hastily, not without a pang of resentment.

"You are forbidden his presence?"

I shook my head. "I have been dismissed and ordered to return tomorrow."

Akiba smiled widely. "I shall come with you," he said.

"Akiba," I said sternly, "I shall not allow it. You have no business with the emperor."

"My business is that of the Jews," he said simply. "It is in the interest of Rome that he should hear me. All is not well with us, with our young people. You yourself have had experience of this."

"I cannot take it upon myself," I said stubbornly.

"I shall be on the palace steps tomorrow at dawn," Akiba said to me.

"I shall give orders not to admit you," I replied shortly.

"A Jew? Why should I grant a hearing to a Jew?"

"He is a leader among his people, all-powerful Trajan," I said humbly. "He says he should be heard in the interests of Rome."

"What is a Jew," grumbled Trajan, "that he should be listened to at all?"

"The slave Epictetus once told me," I said, "that 'when we see a man trimming between two faiths, we can say he is no Jew but a playactor. But when he has the attitude of one who is circumcised and has made that choice, then he is a Jew indeed.' This one has his faith and his duty."

"For that bit of stale wisdom you have given him entrance," Trajan said half-approvingly. "This is like your old self. My only faith is that of Rome eternal, but I appreciate that of others. Where is this old man?"

Akiba was waiting outside. I led him in, murmuring instruction on how he was to conduct himself. He paid no attention but made a deep genuflection before Trajan, who regarded him with curiosity. The usual morning mists of Antioch were clearing. The sun struck through the pierced roof,

171

filtering through the smoke of the braziers, making pale the lamps. "What do you want?" Trajan said brusquely.

"I come as an old soldier," Akiba said surprisingly. "I beg your indulgence, noble master of the Romans."

"A soldier? A Jew? In what war?"

"The Jewish War."

"Ah," Trajan said. His countenance became animated. "My father fought in that war."

"Indeed, mighty Trajan," said Akiba, "he was a hero. Josephus and I used to talk of your father."

"You were a friend of Josephus?"

"I fought with him. We remembered how your father led the X Fretensis against Japho with its ring of double walls. The inhabitants came out to fight, and he charged them—he drove them back and burst through the first enclosure in pursuit. Our own people closed the gates of the second wall, and twelve thousand of those who could not enter were slain. It was Trajan then who sent for young Titus to give him the credit for the conquest. He came and took the city in six hours, slaughtering fifteen thousand more."

"My father was always wise, cunning in the ways of rulers," Trajan murmured. "That is why I have made him divine and given him an altar in the temples. All that you say is true: I was there with him. I know well how true it is. Those were the excellent days, the old days!"

He shook his head at Akiba. "You were a Jewish soldier?" he said doubtfully.

"I left their ranks to save our religion. It pleased the great Vespasian to grant our request."

"I see."

"I am here to ask you to be as merciful."

"The emperor's clemency is well known," I said, striving to break off the conversation. Trajan glanced at me. "Let him alone," he said. He got up with an effort and led us into a small garden nearby, fresh with the dew and odors liberated by the rising sun. He sank down heavily into a creaking chair of withes. Akiba knelt before him in an attitude of prayer.

"Rise," Trajan said curtly. "I am none of your Eastern potentates. I am a Roman."

"May I speak?"

"Speak."

Akiba took a long deep breath and rose erect. "I come to you, most illustrious and powerful emperor," he said, "to ask

172

for mercy and understanding. Our scriptures enjoin us to do justly and walk humbly: I come in that spirit."

"What do you want?" Trajan asked coldly. "All who come before me require something."

"The all-powerful Vespasian and his great son destroyed our temple," Akiba said.

"The guiding spirit of your tribe is fanaticism," Trajan said bluntly. "It is the policy of the Romans to strike for the heart."

"Rome has its own temples, a thousand, to a thousand different gods," protested Akiba.

Trajan nodded. "And we worship impartially," he said. "We interfere with no man's beliefs unless they threaten the structure of the empire. The sect of Christians is an instance. In their obscene rites, they worship a mortal man. Therefore we have judged this to be a crime."

"But these are only Christians," Akiba said almost in reproof.

"You are only Jews," Trajan said. "Each thinks its god is the only one."

"Sire," Akiba said cautiously, "if the gods asked you to destroy Rome, would you do so?"

"That is a strange question." Trajan's voice became brittle. "Rome is founded by the gods, dedicated to them, upheld by them. If it is destroyed, the gods are destroyed."

"I ask it in all humbleness."

Clearly attempting to maintain an equable attitude, Trajan frowned and reflected. "We cannot answer," he said with finality. "If the gods will it, Rome shall fall. The gods willed that the Jews should be brought low and you stand before me."

"I do not blame the Romans for our plight," Akiba said surprisingly. "Our own sins, our own misdoings, brought a just catastrophe upon us."

Trajan's grim face relaxed. "Nor do I blame the Jews for their religion," he said graciously. "Worshipping as a man pleases in his right—as long as it does not constitute rebellion. Did not Vespasian give his consent for you to continue worship humbly at Jabneh?"

"It is true," Akiba said, "and we are grateful. But it is also true that the Temple is a symbol to our people, as the temple of Jupiter is to the Romans."

"I understand. Do you not have other symbols?"

"Our golden candlestick, the shewbread table, the ark, were carried to Rome in the triumphal procession of Titus."

"It seems to me these trophies were merely symbols of pride," Trajan said judiciously. "Do not the Jews exalt humility?"

"It is just to say that our pride has been overweening," Akiba confessed. "Yet now we feel set apart from the empire, even exiled from our lands, without Jerusalem and our Temple."

"Those were the very centers of rebellion, the souls of the uprising," declared Trajan.

"Sire," said Akiba, straightening to his extraordinary height, his deep eyes burning with audacity, "if we might again inhabit Jerusalem, if we might rebuild the Temple, it would be an act of mercy by the throne which would resound through the world. The Jews would praise the name of Trajan for untold ages. It would be the heart of peace, the soul of obedience." Akiba's eloquence seemed to shine in the air as he spoke, so intense was his feeling.

Trajan put his chin on his palm and regarded Akiba curiously. He seemed to sink into thought. At last, he roused.

"I have heard Jews have a gift for healing," Trajan said. He indicated his gross body with a flick of contempt. "What do you say to this?"

Akiba advanced solemnly, felt his wrist, his forehead, peered into his eyes. "Do you sometimes feel dizzy?" he asked.

"Yes."

"And your body drags you down?"

"Naturally."

"Your pulse beats slowly and heavily, your thoughts are giddy, your mind tires easily?"

"All these."

Akiba indicated the cup on the jar by his side. "You are fond of wine and food," he said.

"The physicians say it is good for me," Trajan returned. "Do you say otherwise?"

"I can say only that men must take care of their bodies as their most valuable possession," Akiba said solemnly. "You would not abuse an expensive slave, nor yet a favorite horse. Your body is your most faithful servant."

"Can I not drink when I am thirsty?"

"One must be sure. Sometimes thirst deceives."

"Wine is good," insisted Trajan.

174

"In small amounts," Akiba said. "It bothers the nerves, it decays the mind if used too often."

"You are older than I but your body is thin and hard," Trajan said. "What do you advise?"

Akiba paused, deliberately choosing his words. "Your food should be simple and rough, you must sleep well, you must force yourself to exercise. Above all, you must not fret."

Trajan jerked with silent laughter. "You ask for what the gods themselves cannot do," he said.

"The blood grows heavy and foul with rich food and too much wine," Akiba told him solemnly. "It will place too much pressure on your veins and burst them, if you are not careful."

Trajan silenced him with a gesture. "Enough," he said. "I shall live as I decree."

Akiba retreated a deferential step. "Will you consider my request, great Trajan?" he asked.

Trajan stroked his wattled face and turned toward me. "What says your sponsor, Rufus Teneius?" he challenged.

"Akiba ben Joseph is known as an honest man, a sincere man," I said evasively.

Trajan shook his head. "Such is not in dispute," he told me. "I wish to make sure that no insurrection has its source in this religion, just as I would not tolerate a rebellion from the devotees of Isis and Serapis in Rome."

I determined to be bold. "Perhaps the question of what will come to pass without the Temple should be thought upon," I said. "Is it not true, mighty Trajan, that a madman's vision is more inspiring than the real world? Will not these people, their chief place of worship taken away, be more inclined to be sullen and to revolt—than if the princeps of all the Romans, chief of the world, were to grant them their heart's desire? It seems to me they would praise the mercy and wisdom of their ruler and be less restive under the yoke."

"That may be true," Trajan murmured. Again he considered: later, I realized, that what had been in his mind was a military consideration, the pacification of the barbarians behind him as he struck deep into the unknown lands to the east.

"You have shown mercy to the chiefs of the German tribes, to those in Dacia as long as they kept faith," Akiba said urgently. "You have promised clemency to those who yielded. I would see my people at peace, even as the great emperor of the Romans would want them."

175

"Does your god want peace?" asked Trajan sharply.

"I believe our God wishes us to accept the rule of the Romans," Akiba returned slowly. "I am not a prophet, alas! The gift of understanding beyond men has not been given to me. Nor am I a Christian, but I agree with what their Jesus has said: 'Render unto Caesar what is Caesar's.' "

"Would you be willing to pledge yourself—your name and your life—that the Jews will remain quiescent if their temple is restored?" demanded Trajan.

Akiba bowed his head for a long moment. "Yes," he said, almost inaudibly. "As long as we may practice our beliefs in peace."

"Nothing is granted for nothing," Trajan said keenly. "You do not seem sure of your answer." Again he turned to me. "Do you believe that such a grant from the throne would have such an effect?"

"I do not know," I said honestly. "The Jews are a restless, violent people, full of schism and argument—but they are devoted to their god, and Akiba has great influence with them."

Trajan raised his finger. In response, it seemed, from nowhere, an old priest in a purple-bordered robe, carrying his curved-top staff, approached. "What do the auguries say?" inquired Trajan.

I was surprised at this, since such fortunetelling was long ago disbelieved and out of fashion; then I recalled that Trajan was attempting to bring back the ancient glories and customs of Rome. I watched fascinated as the augur drew a cross from north to south and east to west in the dust; he looked at sky and sun, raised a wet finger to the wind and nodded; then he sat down on a stool at the exact center of the cross and waited. Akiba slowly retreated to the edge of the terrace.

Suddenly, beyond the wall, swooping and rising on wings of silver, came a whole flock of white doves. They circled the throne with fluttering, filling the space with their soft cries. At last they came to rest, strutting in the dust, two on Akiba's lap and another on my shoulder. Trajan's face relaxed in pleasure at the sight. The augur raised his hands and staff as he stood. "Aves admittunt," he said. "The birds allow it."

I hardly heard what he said. I stared into the pink eyes of the dove on my shoulder. A horrid suspicion took shape, hardening in my brain. Dimly I heard the words of Trajan: "Very well," he said, raising his hand in his well-known gesture of dismissal, "we shall think upon this."

Outside the imperial palace, well beyond earshot of the

176

guards, I wheeled to confront Akiba. "Tell me, my friend," I said with harsh alarm, "have I not seen these birds before?"

"I do not understand," Akiba said loftily.

"You know what I mean. You could be executed for this! I would suffer the same fate!"

"Then we shall be silent," Akiba said.

"Tell me!"

"Yes," Akiba said in a lowered voice. "They are from my own cote in Lydda."

"Indeed! And they have flown this far, for such an important occasion, at this precise moment?"

"Let me say that a friend of mine assisted them a little, with a cage and signals."

"You had them released outside at the proper time?" I demanded incredulously.

Akiba gave me an enigmatic smile. "Even under the lash, I would admit no such thing," he said. "As you have often pointed out to me, to the Romans such miracles are common."

CHAPTER 11

Trajan made no immediate decision concerning the appeal of Akiba about the rebuilding of the Jewish Temple. He was far too experienced to be hasty in the subtle war of men's minds that is politics. He wished to consider all the possible effects of such a far-reaching edict. But, in order that the Jews might not be restive in his absence, Trajan allowed rumors to issue from the imperial residence that he was viewing such a restoration favorably.

The precaution was useful, for Trajan had decided to set out for Parthia earlier than planned that spring. It was supposed by most of us that he had meant to spend the winter in Antioch. It might have been wiser had he done so. But the emperor appeared to grow tired of the incessant clamor and merrymaking, of the bickerings and rowdy spirit of the city. Almost every day he was forced to sit on the portable ivory-and-gold sella curulis, the chair on the tribunal from which he dispensed judgment on disputes. More than once he ordered the mordant wit of those who came to be stilled by the cold flat of a spear placed across their lips. "In most of these things," he said once to me tiredly, "it is merely caput or navis. Heads or tails, tossing a coin in the air."

After the mad ceremonies of the first of the year were over, he commanded us to make ready to march. He commenced to order the affairs of Syria in preparation for his departure. One of his most important acts was to appoint a new governor. This was necessary because burly, laconic Palma, lately returned from his successes in Felix Arabia, was ordered to march with us.

Frontinus in Judea, who might reasonably have aspired to such a post, had indeed fallen from favor with the death of his relative in Rome. He was passed over (Marcellus was never considered) in favor of one Marcius Turbo, recommended by Quietus. He was a squat, obsequious fellow from Libya, hot-tempered and cruel. But he had proved himself an efficient and loyal administrator in Africa, who tolerated no rebellious nonsense—which Trajan was particularly anxious to avoid during our campaign.

I was one of those attending the emperor on the morning of the appointment. As Turbo left, with less than the usual magniloquent assurances, Trajan heaved a sigh that made his hulk of flesh tremble. "We must build with the timbers that are at hand," he said. "I am not at all sure this man is best for Syria, but he is the best available."

"I am sure, Sire, he will do very well," Quietus said austerely.

"If he does not allow his temper to rule his head," Hadrian murmured, standing negligently at the other side of the throne.

"Power most often chastens a man," Trajan responded.

"If it does not drive him mad," Hadrian replied. Suddenly he laughed. "Look at me, Sire! Look at me. Am I not proud, even without power?"

"These avaricious and rebellious Antiochans need a tyrant," Quietus snapped wrathfully. "Some day we shall assign them one, to their pain."

" 'We'?" Hadrian mocked him. The single word struck home. Trajan looked sharply up at Quietus; then his face relaxed and he turned to me.

"Here, good Rufus," he said with his old raillery. "These two of mine have plagued me with questions as to why you attend me so closely, one of my speculatores, my intimates."

"I am happy merely to supply my presence," I said quickly.

178

Trajan laughed and clapped his hands, nodding. "Well said," he declared approvingly. "You are enough of a diplomat to be emperor in my place."

I saw Hadrian's face grow pale; Quietus' fingers sought his dagger. "I am more than satisfied with your favors," I said.

Trajan nodded again. "I know," he said. He fumbled for his ever-present cup of wine and drank. "I know," he repeated and wiped his mouth free of the red drops. "You could never rule even a province," he said brutally. "It takes a man and more than a man, nearly a god. You are, Rufus, after all, only a clever informer in my service." He laughed loudly. I saw both Hadrian and Quietus smile thin smiles. I was never so pleased at an insult.

"I am at your disposal, Sire," I said.

Trajan looked at the others and scowled, rolling his eyes around the room. "Besides," he ejaculated, "there are others who are capable of taking the rule of Rome and the empire. But I shall not name my successor—which must be done, as did the divine Augustus—until my last breath. Wine, wine!"

It was useless to stay longer. The emperor was more and more given to his fits of solitary drinking when anyone about him could expect nothing but disfavor. He would be sodden in a few hours and be put to bed by the slaves. One by one we excused ourselves and retreated. We left the shapeless white glimmer lonely behind us in the dim vastness of the room.

As a result of what Trajan had said, I expected visitors that night in the mysterious duel that was being waged around the throne. I confess that the one who came was the last I expected. It was Akiba.

He was dressed for traveling in a thick undyed woolen robe and hood, bearing a pack, staff in hand. He put down his burdens, pushed back his hood, and stretched his hands over the brazier in my room with a suspiration of satisfaction.

"You are prepared for travel," I said from my couch.

Akiba nodded. "I go before you Romans set out next month," he told me.

"How do you know of our orders?" I demanded.

Akiba shrugged. "Does it matter? I tell you, noble Rufus, I had not hoped to succeed with the emperor."

"Perhaps your request has been denied," I suggested.

"Perhaps," Akiba said. "I do not think so. I must go to Lydda and Jabneh and tell them; I must send messengers to all the Jewish colonies—at Rome, Alexandria, in Cyprus, across the empire. We must gather funds for the rebuilding of the Temple."

"You don't seem to be as merry about it as I expected," I observed, "if you are right in your belief."

Akiba smiled. "I am old, and my heart melts inside me when I think of seeing the Temple as it once was, glorious and rich. But I have learned not to dance in the streets and riot in the alleys. My gratitude is in my prayers."

"To Trajan?" I inquired. Akiba ignored my jibe and went on: "Being old I see the work which lies before us—and I am wretched because I shall not live to see it finished."

"You will not rouse your people with false hopes?"

"Indeed not. I shall prepare their minds and wait the answer of Rome. The arrangement of our calendar can be delayed a few months."

"Where will you go?"

"South, to Pumbedita in Nehardea where live some of the wisest sages of our people. There at the tomb of Bostanai, the Nasi of the Captivity, I shall make the necessary calculations and perform the ceremonies."

"You will be safe," I said, "the Parthians will not suspect. We do not march that way."

"I know," Akiba returned mildly. I stifled my irritation and said nothing. Akiba continued to warm his hands, then abruptly turned to me.

"Is it possible for a Jew to trust a Roman?" he demanded.

"Is it possible for a Roman to trust a Jew?" I parried.

"I am wholly serious, good Rufus. I must speak to you before I go, on a matter that—if interpreted wickedly—would mean my death."

"You always talk of death," I said. I took a nut from a wooden bowl and wrenched it open. "I prefer life. Say what you will, we are friends. As long as it is not seditious, my lips are sealed."

"Precisely," Akiba replied.

I felt a stir of surprise. "Precisely what?"

Akiba shook his head. "That is why I cannot speak."

"Because it is seditious?" I asked, amazed.

"Because what I must say will be thought so."

It was too much for me, too solemn and mysterious. "I don't know what you are talking about," I told him. "The emperor may have granted you your heart's desire, yet you speak like this. You ought to be executed for that alone."

180

"You do not trust me?" he asked.

I considered. "Do you swear by your god that you have no thoughts against the throne?"

"By Abraham, Isaac, and Jacob, I do!" Akiba said fervently. "It is important you should know."

His oath cleared my mind. I knew he would not swear by his Jahveh, but what he had said was a mighty enough vow.

"Very well," I said. "Under those conditions, I shall be silent."

"And understanding?"

"Of course."

Akiba shot a glance about the empty room as if he were a conspirator. Again I felt troubled. He moved a step nearer.

"The noble and most powerful emperor Trajan is going to die," he said quietly.

I jumped to my feet. "What is it you say?"

"I told you that you might misunderstand," Akiba said calmly. "It is not what you think."

I heaved a sigh of relief. "You don't mean assassination, then?"

Akiba was as nearly indignant as I had ever seen him. "Never!" he said emphatically. "He is the best of all emperors to the Jews, as you have said. I would as soon destroy my own life as his."

"Well, then?"

"He may fall in battle on this campaign."

"You are an old fool," I said comfortably. "That is a hazard all Roman soldiers take in stride."

"Nor is it what I refer to," Akiba said. "The Assassin of us all may slay him before."

"Your god?" I asked incredulously.

"Or your gods," Akiba returned. "It needs nothing of magic or religion. One or two years, perhaps less—and he cannot help die of his disease of dropsy, of the falling sickness in his head. Forgive me, noble Rufus, but this great man is like a bladder of water and blood, ready to burst at any moment."

"He is not himself," I said thoughtfully.

"I have never seen him before this. What I learned from watching and touching him—that is enough."

"How do you conclude this?" I asked suspiciously. "Are you a prophet such as Josephus?"

"No," he responded. "Among my people, we rabbis are taught healing and the arts of herbs. I have seen others like great Trajan."

181

"You are sure?"

"I am sure. If you have plans to make, make them with this knowledge." Akiba's voice fell lower. "As you care for my people, do what you can to seat another emperor who will be as compassionate."

He picked up his pack and staff. He was about to turn to the door, when a figure plucked the hanging aside and entered without warning. It was Lusius Quietus. He glanced at Akiba, then at me.

"Has Trajan's favorite Jew been converted to Rome?" he asked. His thick lips twisted in derision.

"He is here to bid me farewell," I said coldly. I resented the intrusion, regardless of Quietus' high position.

"Then he is leaving?"

"He goes to—"

"I go to perform some ceremonies for my people in a distant village," Akiba broke in with a warning look at me.

"Yes," I said rapidly. "He will consult the stars."

The sneer of Quietus gave way to puzzlement. "A soldier turned priest turned astrologer," he said. "I can foretell the future of this one without stargazing."

"We despise astrology more than any Roman," Akiba said. "I go to determine the true calendar for the Jews."

"It is a religious matter," I put in.

Quietus shrugged. The subject had lost interest for him. He surveyed Akiba's height. "You were wise to leave off your soldiering," he said. "Not all Jews are unlucky enough to be so tall. The missile that would fly over the rest would take off your head."

"Those who ride high horses take more chances," Akiba murmured. Quietus reddened. "We have already had reports of Jews that take such chances," he said roughly. "There is rumor of revolts in Mesopotamia."

"Only the foolish or the ignorant try to overturn Roman rule," returned Akiba.

"The wise and brave will suffer with them," Quietus said. "The emperor will take the field. I have myself offered to take my cavalry and ride down such animals without mercy."

"Has the emperor given his consent?" I interposed.

"Not yet. He will: he will. If you resist Rome, remember Dacia," he said to Akiba. "Only ghosts now inhabit their lands."

"The Jews know their blessings," Akiba responded.

"That may please the emperor but not myself," Quietus

said with the savage expression that so often disfigured his face. "My men need exercise. There is none better than Jew-sticking."

I noted with alarm that Akiba, in turn, had become flushed. But he restrained himself. He bowed ceremoniously to both of us and left without a word, the curtain whispering behind him.

"You did not visit me to talk about Jews," I said, in an effort to relax the tension.

"That one will cause trouble," Quietus said. "However, we have things of more moment."

He looked at me with the insolent half-closed eyes of a cat: both calculating and questioning. "The princeps," he said, meaning the emperor, "has ordered that Hadrian remain here as head of the army of Syria—in Antioch with Marcius Turbo."

"He does not march with us?" I said, astonished.

"Evidently his valor in the field and his endurance on a campaign are wanting. He stays behind with the women—with Plotina, the emperor's wife, and his mother-in-law, Matidia." He laughed in harsh contempt.

"I cannot understand," I returned, understanding only too well.

Quietus masked his impatience. "The great Trajan has an affection for you," he told me. "He listens to your words. You have his ear, as witness the success of that old Jew only now departed. Would you plead for me in the same fashion?"

"Whatever the emperor decides is what I wish," I said.

Quietus' green cat-eyes burned. "I have spoken to others, and I shall speak to more in this campaign."

"Concerning what?"

"The emperor's wisdom is all-knowing, of course," he said impatiently. "What if he is ill or his mind is clouded by age?"

"What do you mean?"

"I mean," cried Quietus, "that Trajan may not select the one best fitted to rule after him! That will be decided by his intimates, those in the circle of his friends!"

"Is this his wish?" I wondered.

Quietus drew a long breath. His face became impassive. "I speak only of the shifts of fate. I have consulted Cornelius Palma, Publilius Celsus; I have had tablets from Julius Ursus Servianus and Avidius Nigrinus in Achaea. We are all in agreement."

183

"I congratulate you," I said mildly, "but I do not perceive what you agree upon."

Quietus smiled at me without mirth, in control of himself. "It is no matter," he said calmly. "But I should wish this conversation private: otherwise, I shall deny all, and I have great credit with Trajan. Those who betray me will suffer." He strode to the entrance and paused. "As in battle," he flung back at me, "there will come a time when a choice must be made."

His exit left me as thoughtful and gloomy as he must have intended. My suspicions were justified: the approaching dissolution of Trajan had spawned plots about the throne. The factions were clear: those joined with Quietus and those with Hadrian, struggling for tremendous stakes. If the personages the prefect of cavalry had mentioned were on his side, he was strong. But there remained others that had Trajan's ear such as Attianus, head of the Praetorian Guard, a bustling sprightly old man who had been Hadrian's tutor and was even now in Antioch, apparently as an aide to Hadrian. Trajan, it was rumored, had bestowed upon him the honorary office of ornamenta consularis. And Plotina favored Hadrian—for unsavory reasons, some hinted—but how far could a woman sway a Roman? Yet why had Hadrian been ordered to stay in Antioch?

Confused and troubled, I sought refuge in sleep. But it was nearly dawn before my eyes closed. I could not explain to myself my queer reluctance to join the forces of Quietus. Into my mind unbidden came some old advice. Once I had asked Epictetus about ambition when I had aspired to an office in the empire. "What," I inquired, "if I want to sit where the senators sit?"

"Then," Epictetus said, "you must endure the crush of the theatre."

"What if I cannot get a good view of the show otherwise?"

"Man," he said testily, "do not go to the theatre and you will not be crushed. Why trouble yourself about an exhibition of this kind? Or wait a little and, when the show is done, sit down in the seats of the senators and sun yourself and watch the greatest spectacle, that of nature."

Smiling a little in comfort, I fell asleep: I had decided to wait a little.

Nevertheless, as I marched out of the barracks of Antioch two weeks later at the head of my troops, the hints of Quietus

184

filled my thoughts. It was dawn but already the day was warm. The banderoles snapped above me in the dry wind. I could hear the jingling of medals and the creaking of cuirasses. Somewhere far in the rear a rough voice commenced to chant. Soon each soldier in the ranks at my heels was bawling the chorus, squabbling over a chance to compose a stanza to "gay Lucrece." I alone of all the hosts of Trajan seemed to be silent.

At the gates of Antioch a surprise awaited us: a howling crowd of all conditions of men and women appeared and escorted us outside the walls. They had no intention of joining the troops; in fact, this appeared to be some sort of rousting farewell. There were pleas and jeers, praises in hopes of rewards and cursings when no response was given; the holding-up of children for donations, the women exhibiting themselves lewdly. From his litter Trajan looked about him and waved. Instantly, their hopes rising, the mob burst out with shouts, wishing him an easy march, a successful campaign, a glorious return. The emperor halted his bearers at a signal. He stood erect with apparently no effort.

"I shall come back," Trajan cried in his clear ringing voice. Then, with the smile I remembered from Germania: "I shall bring you the kingdom of the Parthians!"

There was a roaring cheer. He sat down again; his litter was taken up into the march. For a moment, in my eyes, he had shed his unseemly flesh. He was once more the general I had known. I could not believe that what Akiba had told me was true. Nor that what the twin vultures of Quietus and Hadrian expected would come to be.

That spring campaign was one of mild and perfect weather —and of surprising inactivity. In truth it was more like a triumphal procession. We went out with only the lightest of siege engines and marched more rapidly than usual. I rejoiced, for it gave me an opportunity to regain once more the firmness of muscle and dauntlessness of spirit prized by all Romans. Moreover I had an opportunity to see the workings of imperial diplomacy: Trajan held enough conferences with vassal kings and booby governors to keep us away for seven months.

During that time we covered more than 1,200 miles. Our route was a great circle which ran north and east, then south around the dark waters of vast Lake Van and west. Much of our route was easy and level. This was the reason for its lack

185

of incident: the Parthians refused to join battle on the plain. They contented themselves with reconnoitering along our flanks, with occasional bravado skirmishes against the cavalry of Quietus. In the mountain defiles, however, it became more hazardous. The native mountaineers, bred on these slopes, bounded over the rocks like goats, attacking our columns with missiles and arrows, attempting to terrify us by night raids and savage howlings.

As first we sped a few centuries in pursuit, but they returned breathless and empty-handed. They told of being forced to scale lofty hillsides, again and again managing to save their lives only by clutching at underbrush to keep from slipping to their deaths. Not being able to get a firm footing or assume the battle order, they were at a disadvantage. The agile Parthians, running about above them, flung down huge masses of rock and triggered landslides in which more than a few men were crushed. I myself, in one such expedition, managed to catch a mountaineer by his covering of animal skins, but he wriggled out of it, showing only his sun-blackened bare bottom as he vanished around a crag.

We gave up such useless forays. We allowed the enemy peace, hoping they might offer to oppose us where we could slaughter them like sheep. But this they naturally declined. Much of our journey thereafter was punctuated with sporadic outbursts of guerrilla raids—but in time even this ceased, owing to the remarkable abilities of our slingers. Trajan had recruited a corps of fustibala, slingers carrying four-foot staves with long leather thongs. The slingers whirled their cudgels and released acorn-shaped lead pellets that flew accurately to amazing distances. I noted, too, how effective Syrian archers were. In Germania we had drawn our bows back only to the chest. Here they used a recurved rawhide-enforced weapon—difficult even to string—and pulled it to the ear. At fifty yards, their ironheaded arrows penetrated the best Parthian armor. Even the pila were given extraordinary range by being slung with a loop of cord wound round the shaft, one end held in the hand.

We made many camps and tribunals. The satraps and petty monarchs did us homage, but Chosroes, grand king of all the Parthians, did not appear: he had commenced sending endless envoys (even before Antioch, as far back as Athens in Greece) protesting his loyalty, but Trajan dismissed them without audience.

At length, at our camp near a town called Elegia, the royal

brother of Chosroes, Parthamasiris, appeared. We detained his bodyguards as Roman subjects but allowed the young man—tall, dark-skinned, flashing-eyed, as are most nobles of this race and with long hair and floating robes—to approach the tribunal. He wore a crown of gold and rough rubies. This he doffed and placed before the feet of Trajan.

"I am the brother of Chosroes, king of kings, cousin to the sun and moon, partner of the stars. I bring his greetings to you, O Trajan."

Before he deigned to answer, Trajan signaled me to remove the crown to safekeeping. Then, to the discomfited Parthamasiris (who doubtless expected to be recrowned), he said coldly: "I am merely a Roman, but we are always glad to receive the homage of heavenly bodies. What do you wish?"

"I have not been conquered by you," retorted the indignant Parthian, "nor am I your prisoner. I came here to be treated as my birth warrants, to receive the rule of this land from your hands as Tiridates did from Nero."

"This land belongs to no man but the Roman people," Trajan said sternly. "It was no part of the treaty with divine Nero that you should trample upon the just rights of the Romans."

"I have brought you my crown!"

"You have brought me a limb lopped from a body and pretend it is whole and healthy."

Parthamasiris looked about him like a man trapped. "I request the favor of a private hearing," he said in a shaken voice.

Trajan granted what he desired. They entered the imperial tent together. After a half hour, Parthamasiris emerged, his face veiled, backing away in the Oriental fashion. He was given his mount; but his escort was detained and his crown held. As he departed, Trajan flicked his hand toward Quietus. The Moor nodded saturninely and, a moment later, whirled out of the camp on the trail of the unfortunate prince. It was the last we saw of him.

After this, the spirit of resistance to our march was broken. Trajan replaced the king of the Albani who had not obeyed a summons to Satala. He sent Quietus with a mounted column down the Araxes Valley to force the Mardi tribes to submit. Abgar, Sporaces, Mebarsapes, and Manisarus were dealt with according to their deserts as vassal kings, the test being solely loyalty to Rome. Trajan ordered coins struck and inscribed: ARMENIA AND MESOPOTAMIA ARE BROUGHT UNDER THE POWER

187

OF THE ROMAN PEOPLE. At Singara, the main force of our army rejoined the flying column of Quietus. We advanced to Edessa and came back to Antioch early in the eighth month.

Most pleasing to all of us, Trajan appeared to have regained health and spirits. During the campaign, he had forbidden his retainers to bring him wine. After a few days of lethargy in his litter, he emerged to take personal charge of the expedition. He marched at the head of his troops—an hour or so at first, then all day. He went before the standards, inspiring by his example; he forded rivers, rounded up stragglers, and even, on occasion, ordered false alarms to be sounded in order to maintain proper vigilance. His health improved almost visibly day to day. His red-splotched countenance cleared, his flesh tightened on his bones, his face became tanned and firm. His stride was easy and, eating the rough soldier fare, he became again the very image of the all-conquering emperor.

Our hearts were gladdened by the reception we received once back in Antioch—especially by the large population of Jews. We learned that in our absence the edict of Trajan had been issued. It ordered that the Temple be replaced with funds from his own purse. It permitted the restoration of the sacrificial services in Jerusalem. It placed Akiba himself in charge of the plans for reconstruction.

I had been sure that Akiba, despite his trick, had lost his petition. I was wrong. The news brought me new insight into the political genius of Trajan. His decision was owing partly, no doubt, to his passion for building in imitation of Augustus. But it was also a penetrating instinct for popular support which had caused him to have his decision announced on the twelfth day of Adar, the sixth Jewish month. This placed the good news just before the feasts which celebrated the victory of the Maccabee Hammers over the Syrian general Nicanor, more than two centuries before, as well as the deliverance of the Jewish nation from the throttling grip of the tyrant king Haman.

As a result, it was instantly decided that the anniversary should be a three-day holiday in future. The first day would be known as Trajan's Day. At the urging of Akiba (by messenger from Pumbedita) a new prayer was added to the Jewish grace after meat, another to the Passover ceremonies, a third to the recitation of the Shema—all in praise of Roman magnanimity, and spilling blessings upon the emperor.

The posting of the edict itself had set the whole population

188

of Jews capering for joy in the streets and on the housetops. For weeks after we came back, the celebrations continued. Hosannahs in the name of Trajan resounded in the narrow alleys of the Jewish villages and in the square, beamed rooms of their synagogues. The hopes of the Jews rose to their highest pitch in nearly a century. Dissension with the Romans seemed to be a thing forgotten.

All this was eminently pleasing to people and troops alike (we mourned only the lack of a single good battle). We did not know that the fates had prepared a warning to issue from the depths of the earth itself. It was to come at the most unpropitious time, an admonition that good fortune must always be shadowed by the opposite.

I remember with horror the ides of January that year of Rome 865. The first of the year passed in the usual two weeks of revels. The city became as if dead. The celebrants—except for the soldiers bidden on guard—lay in the streets like corpses, unconscious, grinning where they fell. Doors swung open to the wind, houses and public places were vacant—so exhausted were the inhabitants and visitors of Antioch in that holiday season. Sated were slave and master with lust and gaming, with food and drink, dance and folly—all possible pleasures of the body. All was prepared for the wrath of the gods.

The dawn never came. If the sun rose, no one saw it, least of all myself. Assigned to the rounds of the sentinel posts of the city, I had returned to barracks early that morning. I was still awake at what I supposed to be the coming of a new day. From my window I saw ranks of solid black clouds marching across the heavens breast to breast, roiling just above the city's tallest buildings. Tongues of lightning flickered in their bosoms. A wind rose near the sea, blustering up the winding banks of the Orontes River toward Antioch. I cowered as I watched, pierced by the quick, bitter cold. A stinking mist rose from the waters, as from rotting bodies under the flood. It swept over the city and my eyes streamed tears.

Suddenly, as if the whole pantheon of gods conspired for our destruction, the winds of heaven whirled down together. I saw their invisible forces wrestling with pillar and portico, with the very blocks of stone in the buildings. They twisted off roofs and sent them crashing into the streets. At the same time, thunder skirled along the sky and roused all with a deafening clap. Whether by sound or by force, the marbles broke like mirrors, the granite ashlar showed yawning cracks.

189

Ornaments and jewels from the walls fell tinkling to the pavements. None heeded them in his fright.

The winds took shape with burdens of dust and debris. Paralyzed, I stared out at the monstrous funneled pillars of heaven which changed shape every second: bowing like courtiers, straightening like soldiers, turning with awesome solemnity, devouring what was touched at the base. With them rose sighs and shrieks of unseen demons; howlings like that of souls in Erebus; roars such as prides of lions might loose. The earth wavered. I flung myself outside and halted: the wind plucked at my garments, tearing at my hair and cloak.

I ran down into the streets, avoiding this hideous advance of the air giants. I perceived them moving among the stricken people with casual destruction, snatching up one and another, dashing them down. Only pulps of flesh remained, as they passed as reapers moving in a field of grain.

Up the river, terrible sight! I saw a waterspout coming in a stately dance, like a conjurer's serpent, swaying from side to side. It scooped up the water as it came, down to the thick yellow mud of the Orontes. It hurled shacks and boats to one side. Without warning, the ground commenced to heave yet again in rhythm as if the world had turned liquid, as if the waves of some gigantic sea underneath swept below the crust of earth. Tall siege engines toppled. Fires broke out in the armory. Buildings shifted and collapsed, a few feet away from their foundations. Houses and temples commenced to slide down toward me from their pinnacles on the hills, like children at play. Vast roars of destruction resounded everywhere.

Without realizing it, I found myself racing to the center of the city, toward the imperial residence. I had to reach what had become an obsession: the chamber of Trajan.

I dashed up the shuddering marble steps. The guard was there, no longer alive and upright: crushed under the fall of the pillars, the rubble of the roof. Entrance was impossible. I turned, dashing around the corner to the rear where I knew the bedroom of Trajan to be. Fire hissed at me with a dozen tongues. I felt the pain of burning, the sharp pangs of exhaustion. Hell clamored for the inhabitants of Antioch, and all shared an equal doom.

I sprang under the window of the emperor's chamber. I halted, astonished, seeing the sixty-three-year-old Trajan in his night-tunic leap upon the sill from within. He smiled at me. "Lend me your shoulder, good Rufus!" he cried. I leaned against the quivering wall. He sprang down to my back, vaulted to the ground, and we hurried away. I was amazed at the lightness of foot that Trajan exhibited, at his fearlessness. I had only to follow him, for both of us knew our destination: the wide spaces of the barracks hippodrome.

We gained it without mishap. Trajan stopped. He stripped the heavy sagum from a soldier struck down by a stone and flung it around himself. I secured another. Together, silent, we stood in the middle of the amphitheatre and looked at devastation raging about us. Part of the hippodrome wall collapsed, the stones tumbling almost to our feet, but Trajan did not stir. I noticed a thickening bruise on his left shoulder.

The tumult of nature subsided. We could hear the echoing screams of those seeking wives and children and kinfolk and the hoarse angry bawls of soldiery trying to restore order.

Almost as abruptly as it had come, the whole affair ceased. The earth quivered a moment, jelly-like, then became solid. The murk above our heads cleared, letting sunlight through, columns of dust and smoke; now only cries, the crackling of fire, and the rumble of still-falling rocks came to us.

"Tell me," Trajan said calmly, "if you know, about these phenomena of nature, Rufus."

"I believe the earth flows beneath us like a molten ocean, that it has tides and waves. Sometimes it rolls, sometimes it shifts—or gapes like a whirlpool."

"The subterranean fires?"

"Spray and spume bursting through."

"The roaring and rumbling?"

"Even so, Sire, the sea roars upon the beaches, crashing and bellowing, grumbling and retiring."

"It appears within reason," Trajan said thoughtfully and looked around us at the lightening landscape. I followed his example. His divine equanimity had restored my courage. But when I turned again to him, I found his piercing blue eyes gazing at me speculatively. I felt uneasy, though he said nothing.

Then, wholly unexpectedly, he asked me a question which I answered the only way I could—but one which has haunted me. To this day I do not know what else I could have replied —and it was the most important query of my life.

The emperor, stately and dignified despite the faded cloak he wore as toga, held up his left hand to me. "Rufus Teneius," he said in a curious tone, "what would you do if I gave you this ring?"

My senses stumbled. I felt as if we were surrounded by a

191

crowd of onlookers, though we stood alone in the midst of the rocks and field. I stared at the interwoven iron and gold, at the deep seal of the emperor in the black onyx.

"I—I—would return it," I stammered.

"Do you know what such a free gift, for you to have and to hold, would mean?"

"It would mean," I said in a dazed fashion, "that great Trajan was pleased to jest with a lowly tribune."

"You remember how this ring came to me in Colonia," Trajan said, his voice sharpening. "Then, as you are now, I was unprepared to receive it. But I nerved my spirit up to the glory and the duty."

He paused. I commenced to tremble. "If I gave it to you, fitted it to your hand," he said in a clear tight voice, "and told you to hold it—if tomorrow I stood beside you on the tribunal and laid my hand on your shoulder and told the army to hail you as emperor—would you take the ring?"

I shook under the lash of his voice as if I were being scourged. My mind surged and receded, my mouth went dry; spots of color flared in my eyes. Despite all my efforts to think clearly, I did not know what to say. I thought only that the wreck of Antioch might have driven the elderly Trajan mad.

"If I said I were weary of all the secret plotting and scheming which hides behind the throne," he went on, his eyes now flinty and becoming remote, "would you help me get rid of it once and for all?"

"You are my emperor," I faltered.

"Why do you suppose I march to the ends of the empire?" he cried. "Because, at my age, I love the long miles, the hazards of battle, the discomforts of camp, the hypocrisies of kings? No, Rufus: I march to get far from the intrigues of Rome, to breathe fresh air and to think simple thoughts again. But this does not persuade you, I know. Come: if I command you, will you take this ring and be emperor of all the Romans?"

Gasping, I fell to my knees. "Mighty Trajan," I mumbled indistinctly, "anything but this! Command me to die, throw me to the beasts of the arena, give me over to the torturers! Not this!"

Trajan did not look at me. He took the ring from his thumb and regarded it musingly. "So small a symbol for such great power," he murmured to himself. He seemed to see me kneeling, my face upstretched, for the first time.

"Get up, get up," he said contemptuously. "Why do you kneel, man? If you had accepted a moment ago, I would have stood by my word. Tomorrow you would have been master of the world! But I was right long since when I told you that you could never rise in my service. I am unchangeable Trajan, and you—you are simply Rufus Teneius, brave in body, cowardly in mind, wretched in soul—thirsting after fame but ever unable to find it!"

I shrank from the searing jeers in his words. I rose and felt impelled to step back in his presence as his lips lifted in a thin smile. "You may rule in that magical World-to-Come that your persuasive Jew Akiba talks of—but in this world you are destined to follow!" They were prophetic words; I have never forgotten them.

I heard the rattle of hooves and looked up. A filthy disheveled man, unrecognizable in soot and dust, flung himself prostrate from a rearing horse before Trajan. He cried out, perhaps in joy—perhaps in surprise.

"Thank the gods you are safe!" he exclaimed.

"Why are you here, nephew Hadrian?" said Trajan coolly.

"To make sure of your safety!"

"I am safe, thanks to Rufus Teneius. Where is Lusius Quietus?"

"He organizes the troops in the city to rescue those buried, to put out the fires. He is ignorant of your fate."

"You should be by his side," Trajan said bluntly. "It is for people of lesser responsibility to come to my aid. Your place, as evidently Quietus understands better, is to aid the people of stricken Antioch!"

Hadrian said nothing. He rose, retreated, and threw himself on his mount. In the moment before he wheeled off at a gallop, he cast me a stare of poisonous hatred. To my surprise, I lifted my head and gave him back look for look. Next moment he was gone but I felt a dark exulting in my soul: now that I had refused the power and the glory, I longed to seize it.

A squat form sprinted across the grass, slid to a stop, saluted, and threw up. It was Ficus. "Praise the gods!" he cried, sour drool dripping from the sides of his mouth. "Praise the gods! Here you are!"

"You have found me," I admitted.

"Hurrah, sir!"

"Have you no word for your emperor, soldier?" demanded

Trajan. At the words, Ficus dropped to his knees. He hung his head in the manner of one expecting decapitation.

Trajan looked at me. His face curved upward; he burst into uproarious laughter. A moment later, I joined him. A few seconds afterward, from his knees, Ficus laughed with us.

CHAPTER 12

Tremendous was the catastrophe to proud Antioch, third greatest city in the empire. Fully half was thrown down in ruins. Fire burned over much of the remainder for nearly two days, ravaging more before it could be quenched by our soldiers under the tireless direction of Quietus with Hadrian and Turbo as his lieutenants.

The destruction was so extensive that it affected even Trajan, inflexible as he was in his decisions. He had long planned an early second campaign into the southern part of Parthia. Now he delayed and, finally, hit upon the artifice of sending a cautious inquiry to the oracle of Apollo at Daphne.

Aside from the lore of the Egyptian priests, this was the most revered spot in the East. Here sprang the Castalian fountain, noted for its ability to tell the future of those who dipped a laurel leaf in its waters. Nearby rose a great stone stadium, centuries old, wherein sacred games were held. Between was a village built of marble, decorated with every sensuous inscription and representation, populated with enough diviners and devotees to be a city. A thick-leaved grove of laurels and cypresses, ten miles across, was watered by underground springs that kept the trees green and fragrant. Millions of sesterces were contributed yearly by all Syria to the public pleasures here.

It was to the Daphne priests, renowned as soothsayers, that Trajan sent his sealed message. The emperor was no fool. His first missive contained nothing but blank vellum. The priests were equal to his ruse. They returned the message, seal unbroken, but with a different sheet inside, blank as his own. Impressed, Trajan sent back a genuine query about the success of his campaign.

He opened the reply in the presence of the Army council. It contained only a broken vine branch. Trajan smiled wryly and held it up.

"What do you think this means?" he asked us.

No one ventured to answer until I spoke. "It means that unless we march, the vinestock will be broken over our backs," I said.

There was a roar of laughter. Trajan joined in approvingly. Quietus and Hadrian frowned. A certain ambition commenced to stir once more in my bosom as the emperor familiarly clapped my shoulder. The next day orders were issued. The following week we departed.

Our march, I might add, was a necessity of state—not merely the result of an oracle, a jest, or the intransigence of our leader. Chosroes was consumed with flames of vengeance for the death of his brother Parthamasiris. He was straining every resource to bring the eighteen great provinces of his rebellious empire under control, to invade Roman Syria.

It was the end of the second month, a stormy gusty day, when we set out. Hadrian had begged to go with us. Trajan had refused: he had chosen Turbo instead, admonishing Hadrian to assume command of the remaining troops and the duties of governor (with the help of Attianus) without complaint—and to watch over Plotina and Matidia as his most precious possessions. Hadrian accepted his orders with his usual pale composure; and I am sure Quietus rejoiced. But, as it turned out, it might have been far better had Hadrian accompanied the army.

No crowds went with us to the gates. There were no harps or timbrels, no cries of praise or satire, to harass our columns. The citizens, busy about clearing and rebuilding, watched us pass with sullen frowns. With the exception of the Jews, who still blessed Trajan for his edict concerning the Temple, we left in black silence.

This sombre farewell and the weather were evil omens. The days continued dark and cold, threatening in the extreme, during the whole week that we marched toward Batnae on the shores of the Euphrates. There, we crossed the river on a bridge of inflated bladders and planks, halting outside the city. Trajan had taken care to make our advance as secret as possible. He posted sentinel horsemen on all flanks to intercept spies or scouts, to prevent acts of treachery by the inhabitants. Nor did he enter the city.

But he could not deny the sense of ill-fate pursuing us. I

was sure within myself that calamity could not be far off. As we approached the ancient town of Carrae, my forebodings became as painful as labor to a woman. This was the spot where the Crassi—Marcus and his son, Publius—had been slain by the Parthians nearly a century before. The weathered piles of rocks, with the sacred battered ensigns of the troops thrust into them as memorials, were mute harbingers of disaster.

Trajan ordered a halt at this spot. He wished to consider which way he might go, faced with the forking of the royal Parthian highway. One road ran through Adiabene and over the Tigris. The other went through Assyria.

This halt did not indicate any indecision in our leader. He wished to find out if the auguries were favorable. He performed the necessary sacrifices and the gods gave him their blessing. He advanced directly toward Adiabene.

Our forces marched ahead for weeks in a leisurely manner. The pack trains and green infantry were enclosed in two veteran columns as a precaution against surprise. Thus far there had been no resistance from the Parthians—not even an indication that they knew we had invaded their country. We passed through groves and rich fields and blooming orchards. Each one had its own pleasure villa—painted in every room with pictures representing kings and nobles. Nothing else was depicted but the slaughter of men or beasts, war or the hunt —for this was their work and play.

Now from time to time we captured Parthian scouts on our flanks. These prisoners, I noted, were so much alike that they might have been cut from the same pattern of flesh. Slender, olive-complexioned, pale, eyebrows joined and curved in a half-circle, with eyes as grim as a goat's, they wore clipped beards and long shaggy hair. Most often they rode in flowing robes; occasionally they had plates of armor on face and body.

We came in sight of the west bank of the red-and-yellow flood of the Tigris one late afternoon. At a discreet distance from the earth cliffs that marked the borders of the river, Trajan called a halt. We set about constructing a camp with a double palisade. Plainly the emperor expected battle.

Before he allowed a single tent to be pitched, he ordered me to have an earth tribunal built. The blowing of the tubens summoned the soldiers to his feet. His officers, myself among them, surrounded the tribunal facing outward as Trajan spoke to the congregated legions, his crisp voice carrying far in the open air.

196

"Seeing your bravery and confidence, my soldiers," he said, "I have resolved to speak to you about the battle which surely lies ahead. This is not the first time, as many of you know, that this land has felt the heavy tread of Roman caligae. Lucullus and Pompey Magnus broke into the Parthian empire. So, too, did Ventidius and others. Remember, all of these were victorious. They retired heaped with spoils and trophies. We come for the same reason as they: to make ourselves equal to past greatness, to strengthen Rome and secure the eastern empire, to give future generations the stuff for glorious song. With the help of the gods, I shall be with you everywhere—as emperor, leader, and fellow soldier.

"We must destroy a most wicked people, on whose swords the blood of our comrades is not yet dry. Thus it has ever been with Romans, to annihilate anyone who threatens us. So shall it be with the Parthians!

"It remains for each soldier to put aside the desire to stray for early plunder, to keep up with the army on its march, to join battle eagerly under his own standard, to obey, to give the last measure of strength. I have ordered that, if a soldier flees or falls behind, he is to be hamstrung and left on the field.

"Rouse yourselves! Our cause is just! The gods themselves await the power of Roman arms!"

As the emperor stepped down, to the customary cheers and acclamations, he signaled me in the midst of the tumult. "I wish a careful guard kept tonight," he said. "See to it, Rufus. Wake me before dawn to ascend the hill yonder to spy out the intentions of the enemy."

I saluted, thrilled at his confidence. I could not help but mark that he passed by Quietus without a sign. Nor did I mistake the glance the latter exchanged with me, like that of an enemy considering a truce. I confess I strutted past him, blood singing in my head, almost daring Quietus to attempt an overt act. I had sounded the officers of my cohort. They were loyal to me and sure of the fidelity of their centuries: I was prepared for that occasion. But not for the next day.

I was at the side of Trajan at dawn on the small hill outside the encampment, striving to peer through the morning mists, when a water-carrier raced through the gates below. He shouted that the enemy was massing on the other side of the Tigris. Trajan immediately descended. He issued the orders for our attack to be mounted. A courier galloped upstream to

197

notify the auxiliaries when to release the boats for the bridging of the river.

Such boats were built specially, flat-bottomed and very wide. Fastened upstream, they were let loose by signal, one by one, to fall down the river with the current and be poled into the spot where it was proposed to make the crossing. Each was successively anchored to its brother by cables and baskets of stones, then lashed together. They were ballasted with more rocks and bridged by planks, in a great bending crescent toward the farther shore.

The bridging began and finally the last boat—a massive affair with plated mantlets and a drawbridge, flanked by four siege engines (two on either side) drifted into place. It instantly swarmed with men eager for the final assault on the far bank. I burned for the fight. I pushed into the foremost ranks of my cohort just as we came within enemy range. The Parthians commenced to fire their ballista.

The sun shone directly in our eyes. It blinded me. Then, as I squinted through the rays, I saw coming the doom of my life. It was a jagged block of flung red stone.

I saw the mass distinctly. Its sharp edges glowed in the sun. It turned slowly. I swear I heard its breath as it came through the air, the vicious hiss of passing.

The world stopped. All about me held position, like a tableau in a theatre. All but the stone. I saw it deliberately approach. It struck as I stood paralyzed in my place, hitting my shoulder. My right shoulder that guided the hand that swung the sword and pilum.

I saw it touch my harness, dent the flesh. A rending pain shot from my shoulder into my brain. The sky dissolved into yelling darkness. The world spun once more, this time in so frenzied an orbit that I tumbled backward in intolerable agony. I was scarcely conscious of the wet welcome of the Tigris as I toppled into its depths.

For an endless time, I moved amidst the horrors of clamorous night, with merciless sweeps of cold and heat, of ceaseless torture. What seemed an eternity of sightless groping in the abyss ended when I opened my gummed eyes wearily, tearing my eyelids apart with an effort, not caring to survive. The first object I saw above me, apparently hanging in space, was the soft rosy face of an old woman. Gray-haired, watchful, her deep dark eyes seemed to shine with compassion.

"You are awake," she said, as softly as if she did not want

to disturb me with the slightest vibration of air. "You are alive, you will grow better. For a long while, I have not desired to see you. But this is the time arranged by God for our meeting."

"Who am I?" I croaked vacantly.

"You are Rufus Teneius, the Roman tribune."

"Who are you?"

"I am Rachel, the Jewess," she replied simply, "the wife of Akiba."

Re hoc modo finita, the affair ended this way as far as I was concerned: I met myself again, with the kindness of Rachel. One of the worlds granted to me had vanished; another was preparing.

Now the reader knows the truth I have tried to conceal so long in so much writing. I am a cripple, shorn of my right arm, no longer able to wield a weapon or to stand in high places.

For the stone of the Parthians did more than endanger my life and tear off my arm. It took from me what chances I had for further advancement, most of all to the mighty post of which Trajan had spoken at Antioch. For, as all the world knows, no man who is not whole can be head of the Roman empire. He cannot even reside close to the throne. Such ailments are infectious in the ways of fortune: one man's ill-luck may affect the destiny of others.

That is the reason, of course, that I write on tablets instead of scrolls. Tablets may be fastened to a scrintum by clamps and remain under my hand—unlike a slippery scroll, which shifts with the motion of my single arm. But in those days of pain I did not think of this, only that I would never again be able to march and fight with the legions. I drifted off into sleep. Rachel's face still hovered above me, indescribable balm to my wretchedness.

When I woke again, my eyes were clearer. My senses sharpened. I found no one in the room that held only my couch. I managed a wavering cry. Almost instantly, three persons entered. I felt no surprise that they were Akiba, Rachel, and Ficus.

It was Akiba who came and knelt by my side, touching my wrist, passing his hand over my forehead. "Your heart is strong," he said at last, "but your fever remains."

"Wine," I croaked.

"Water," Akiba corrected me. He beckoned to Ficus. He brought me a jar and placed its cool clay lip to my own. I drank thirstily. Never had wine, however ancient and renowned, tasted so delicious. I nodded my thanks.

"Your soldier saved your life," Akiba said, indicating Ficus with his thumb.

Instantly the idiot snapped stiff and saluted. He began to babble. "It was not I," he rattled off, "but the emperor himself, noble Rufus. It is true that I saw you struck, driven into the river. I dived in and towed you to shore, unaccustomed as I am for many years to swimming. But it was the magnificent Trajan who examined you, who shook his head many times. He ordered me to send you to the rear. You were bleeding like a gutted sacrifice. The medico legionis could do nothing except stop the flow of blood. I took it on myself, forgive me, to say that the emperor had ordered you sent back to Nehardea."

"That might have killed him," Akiba observed.

"I knew that this admirable Jew Akiba was here, it was not far," recited Ficus. "I knew all Jews have magical powers of healing. So I was not wrong, was I?"

I deigned no answer at first but he waited, his face growing stricken. "You have saved my life once more, you rascal," I managed to say. A flood of relief relaxed his features.

"It was she," Ficus said in a loud confidential tone, pointing at Rachel. "And he," he added, pointing at Akiba. "But in some part, me," he added proudly.

I rolled my eyes to Akiba, asking a mute question. "Where I go, Rachel goes," he said, "like Ruth of old. She is a master of herbs and healing. Give Ficus credit for your rescue, Rachel credit for your nursing and medicines."

"And you?" I whispered.

Akiba's wise old eyes crinkled. "Credit me with the prayers," he said.

For a week after that, I saw Rachel daily. She refused to speak, finger at her lips, busy about the small white room with its slow-moving square of sunlight on the floor, tending my wound, changing bandages. Day by day my strength increased. Akiba visited me occasionally. After perhaps ten days, I was allowed to walk. At the end of two weeks, we left the small, learned, holy, and odorous town of Pumbedita.

Akiba somehow had hired a camel litter. He persuaded me to use it. We struck straight across the desert, five hundred miles of searing sand, heading for old Palmyra in Syria. We plodded for twenty days on the barely distinguishable camel

200

trails, hiding from the white cudgels of the sun at noon under the palms of the oases, traveling by night. I felt a growing amazement at the endurance and strength of the old man who insisted on walking most of the time. The last few days, I forced myself to get out of the litter and walk beside him for an hour or so to regain some of the strength in my wasted legs. Ficus, of course, was not with us: he had been recalled to the I Adiutrix for the final assault upon Ctesiphon. But Rachel, as well, had not come. I inquired about her. Akiba told me he had left her behind, to set out later with a caravan over the longer, less arduous northern route.

"You said she was always with you," I accused him.

"When I was offered the position of overseer of the poor in the community of Israel," Akiba said, "I went to Rachel to consult about it. She said to me: 'Take it, knowing you will be cursed and despised.' She has said the same to me now: I cannot satisfy all, I must satisfy God. He demands that I satisfy him who is in greatest need. That one is you, Rufus."

Even as he said so, my head reeled. I felt faint. "Help me, help me," I murmured. Akiba's ropy arms embraced me and lifted me back into the litter. His face showed no expression, but I knew he felt satisfied that my weakness had proved Rachel right.

At other times he walked beside the litter, answering my many questions about what had happened. He described what he knew. Evidently Ficus had hauled me out, my arm torn from its socket and floating the gods knew where downstream, my profuse bleeding stanched somewhat by the cold flood of the Tigris. The medico legionis had wanted to plunge my shoulder in boiling pitch to cauterize it, but Ficus and his queasy stomach had balked at this. Instead he persuaded the fellow to fill the wound with linen pads soaked in myrrh and frankincense and similar balsams, leaving room for laudable pus to accumulate and discharge. Soon after, Ficus was struck with his recollection of Akiba in Pumbedita no more than a couple score of miles off. He had hauled me there in a soldier's quick-cart and located Akiba, well known as he was, almost instantly.

For a time I lay ill with fever and chills, fed by Rachel and watched by Ficus. And—as Akiba claimed—I was looked upon with favor enough by his god to have my temperature and infection subside. It was Rachel who nipped off festered flesh, who opened pockets of infection, who blew upon the wound to dry it. The rest I knew but could hardly believe: indeed, the time I was wounded had passed like a dream. I still thought I could experience the feelings of my hand and arm on the right side though the limb was gone forever.

I inquired of Akiba what had passed in Judea during the long months I had been absent on the campaign. He sighed and averted his face.

"The wise old ones are all dead," Akiba said. "Most of those you saw sitting in the high seats in the vineyard at Jabneh have passed to the World-to-Come."

"Sometimes you tempt me to be a Jew," I said, smiling.

Akiba looked at me out of the corner of his eye. "You are not strong enough," he said.

"Not now," I admitted, "but once you would not have dared say that."

"No Roman is strong enough," Akiba went on. "Your military exercises are nothing compared to those of the synagogue. Sorrow and repentance are exercise to the body, as well as to the soul. Praying with others, I may be brief; but praying alone, my prostrations and genuflections and kneelings will take me from one side of the synagogue to the other and back again in an afternoon."

"Our gods do not demand as much," I said. "Is your calendar now determined?"

Akiba nodded. "I bring the news with me to Lydda and Jabneh," he said.

As my strength returned, I laid plans. The hot air of the desert cleansed the suppuration and hastened the drawing-together of my gaping wound. My talks with Akiba at dawn and at evening in the midst of the encircling blue horizon—like men caught under the palm of the gods—gave me no sense of loneliness, rather one of being in tune with choirs of silence. Akiba and I indulged in our only possible pleasure in those days: talking to each other with increasing frankness, as men do who are stranded in infinity.

"Why did you take such care of me?" I asked him. "Why did Rachel heal me?"

"Because man or woman who does not tend the sick," Akiba told me, "is as guilty as if he had shed blood."

"This is a new thought."

"It is as old as the world."

"Akiba," I said after a moment's bafflement, "you Jews appear to be an inexplicable mixture of bloodthirstiness and compassion. How did you come to be the contradictory self you are?"

"I see nothing that contradicts," Akiba retorted in his deep voice. "If you wish to know how I was taught, it was by Nahum of Gimzo, blessed be his patience! He showed me how holy was the mercy of the Torah—with every word and even every letter having a sacred significance."

"Cannot every man find such meanings to his own satisfaction?"

"Not unless his thought is adorned with prayer, careful of tradition, and obedient to the word of his elders. I studied for twenty-two years with Nahum, traveling from Jabneh to his village when he was ill, to hear his words of wisdom. Before him to show me the way was Joshua ben Hananya and then Tarfon and, even today, Eliezer ben Hyrkanos—who is my friend as a man and my enemy in thought."

"But you study with him," I said incredulously.

Akiba nodded. "Well," I said, "we Romans have always learned from our enemies. There is no reason why others should not. But why is he against you?"

Akiba smiled slightly. "The Romans hand down decrees from the gods or the emperor," he said. "And so it continues down to the lowest Roman. Not so with the Jews. Every rabbi makes up his own mind, guided by the Holy Scriptures, and he often is the foe of another in discussion and argument. What we finally decide is not the rule of one man but the decision of most of us."

"It sounds very much like the Senate of Rome."

"What is the Senate but the tool of the emperor? We, too, are tools, but our master is God."

I swallowed this somewhat prejudiced distinction and went on: "Do you all equally represent the Jews?"

"There are the workers on the land, the am ha-arez, of which I was one, the landowners, the rich and scholarly Pharisees, and the poor people of the city. Some of us incline to agree with the ideas of one class more than another—not because of personal profit but because we believe their ideas are right."

"And you?"

"For a long time the poor of the cities had no voice. Although I am from the country, now I find that I speak for them. It was for their cause that I have quarreled with Eliezer."

"I have heard of that from others," I said. "It brought you great fame among the Jews. What was the debate?"

I expected Akiba to give me an account of stirring oratory or some towering affair of state, but he simply said: "It was about the appointed season for sharpening knives for the sacrifices."

I could not restrain a snort of laughter. "Is this sufficient to give a man like yourself a reputation?"

"You do not understand. A small hinge can swing a mighty door. It was a point around which revolved the great tradition of our race, that of purification. Eliezer wished to confine work done—but I wished to set our people free from the old bonds. He declared that even knives must not be whetted on the Sabbath. I refuted him and became a Master of the Law."

"He must hate you," I commented, "whether he shows it or not."

"No, no!" Akiba remonstrated, showing an unexpected emphasis in his reply. "He is a good man, a great man. But it is possible to disagree about the details of goodness, is it not?"

"Perhaps," I said. "That is clearly a Jewish function. In our world we do not fret as much as that about it. Tell me, Akiba: I have heard it rumored that you are so holy that you can perform miracles. Is it true?"

"Like the miracle I performed for Trajan?" Akiba asked.

"That edict of Trajan you maneuvered represents a good omen for the Jews," I said, smiling.

Akiba halted. He looked at me with an indescribable expression. For a moment, I expected him to deliver himself of one of his interminable theological assertions. But his face changed and darkened. He shook his head without a word and started off again, at a pace so increased I had to beg him to go more slowly.

As we came nearer to our destination, I experienced the feeling that we were being accompanied. Night and day, I became conscious of an unseen bodyguard. I suspected that I was delirious. Our path seemed pillared with enormous invisible beings. Yet urgency became instilled into me; I told Akiba so. "I must go on as far as Lydda before I rest," I told him. Akiba nodded, returning my pleading with an enigmatic answer. "It is good to be alert to these days," he returned. "On Passover Eve, I give the children nuts and parched corn to keep them awake."

Thus it was we trudged toward Judea. Again and again we passed gangs of road workers, most of them Arab with

Roman overseers. They worked ceaselessly, carefully fitting the five-sided basalt blocks into new highways, leveling and ditching, erecting the milestones with Trajan's inscription. Each time we halted, the officials examined our credentials and respectfully sent us on our way. So it was with new and joyous hearts that Akiba and I saw the familiar blue juts of the Palestine landscape, stayed in Palmyra only a night, then pushed on. We skirted the desolation of Jerusalem (though Akiba paused to pray), and set out through the barren hills and angular valleys pocked with green fields. I began to feel a happiness I could not comprehend. We came to Akiba's lonely house, took down the poles that barred the door and windows, set the water running in the parched furrows, ate and slept like dead men.

But the next day, Akiba expressed his intention of leaving. He said he must go first to Jabneh to report on his journey to Nehardea, then on to the capital and Antioch. "If you will only wait a day or two," I protested, "I shall go with you," attempting to conceal my exhaustion.

"Rest," Akiba replied in an odd tone. "I may have more need of your help in the future than you have so far had of mine."

"What do you mean?" I said dully.

"Do not think that I returned so hastily to Judea with you in your weak condition only to tell of the calendar," Akiba said in a heightened voice. "Julianus and Pappus are dead."

"Dead?" I felt bewildered. I knew only that they were two of the most prominent rabbis in Judea.

"The day before we left, a messenger brought the news. Dead. Executed by order of Hadrian."

"Executed! What happened?"

Akiba gripped his hands before him, intertwining his fingers with emotion. "Like all Jews, they heard of Trajan's order to rebuild the Temple. They set up tables from Antioch to Acre to supply the needs of those Jews returning from exile. The Samaritans complained that they did not pay tax or tribute. Hadrian ordered, in the emperor's name, that the Temple sanctuary should be then built in another place or in other dimensions than those which are sacred. His command roused the Jews. They gathered into the valley of Rimmon and cried out for revolt. Not even Joshua ben Hananya could quiet them, though he told them of the lion's mouth they had entered."

205

"What happened?" I demanded, though I could guess too well.

"The people, a few of them, shouted against the government. Julianus and Pappus fled to Laodicea. The governor there captured them and jeered them, telling them to get our God to save their lives."

"But he did not?"

"They said they were unworthy of a miracle, and he was unworthy to see it. And they added that God would demand their blood at his hands. Angered, he broke their heads with axes and they died on the spot."

"This is terrible news," I said sombrely.

"Trajan's Day has been abolished with curses," Akiba said evenly, "and Julianus and Pappus have been declared martyrs."

"What will be the end of this, Akiba?" I asked slowly. "Will you, too, demand that your people rise against the Romans? If so, you must sever our friendship forever. I must fight with my own people—and you will be destroyed."

"No," Akiba said, "perhaps I see farther than you, Rufus. I see my duty still to persuade to peace rather than to incite to war against the Romans. Joshua and Eliezer ben Hyrkanos, I have heard, preach the same. The moment is not yet come for us Jews to be free of our bonds. Our penance is not done."

"Have any others of your leaders been taken? Perhaps all this may yet be remedied."

Akiba shook his head. "Gamaliel has been sought, but he has been warned and is in hiding. I am not suspect since I was in Nehardea and could have had no part in it."

"I shall go with you," I said with reviving energy. "Give me only until tonight to rest, and we shall travel together and appear before Hadrian together."

Akiba regarded me keenly and shook his head. "No," he said. "Now you must rest whether you will or not. I shall see that you have company here to take care of your wound until Rachel returns. There are signs that the Jews are ready to overflow the banks of their resentment against Rome; you are safer here for a time."

Nonetheless I would have gone with him—except that he stole away silently that evening, without a word of farewell. I heard the tinkle of camel bells and, after a few moments, became suspicious. I hurriedly rose to follow him but, outside in the dusk, I halted. I saw a visitor I had not suspected. The sight blurred my eyes with tears.

206

"I am here to see that you remain and get well," she said. I passed my hand over my forehead and brought it away wet with perspiration. An odd shiver took my body. I tried to smile. "Come in," I said. She followed me into the rushlighted interior.

CHAPTER 13

"Well, sweetest Sarra, we meet again," I said with the utmost banality.

"Yes," she replied. She watched me out of her dark-shining eyes. I felt embarrassed. I flapped my remaining arm against my side. "This time, I am helpless," I told her.

She smiled slightly. "You always told me I was free," she said, "and you kept your word. You are free, too, of many more things than you believe."

"With one arm?" I asked disgustedly. "I am only half a man." I raised my left arm and let it drop as if it were made of lead.

"You may slap me with it," Sarra said.

I could not help laughing, though it hurt my side. And, perhaps, from that moment dated the beginning of my recovery of real strength and vigor. Sarra came each day, taking up the duties which Rachel had bequeathed her, caring for my wound, cleaning the room. My eyes feasted on the sight of her. My nostrils were filled with her fragrance, my ears enchanted by the soft sound of her passing. More than once my vanished right arm lifted toward her. I cursed again and again the whitening hollow of my shoulder, the huge scar filling with dead tissue, thickening my shoulder over to my neck as if I were half hunchbacked.

After another month, mostly indoors—my desire to leave had evaporated—I was able to remain night and day outside in the arbor by the fountain. There, under the vine-leaf pattern of the sunlight, I felt comforted and rested. Healing seeped into my veins from the warmth and dry air, peace from the intimate chuckle of the flowing water. There, in one of the gorgeous brief twilights that seem to come only in

207

Judea, I beckoned Sarra to sit down opposite me. It was the first time she had consented to stay at evening; she sank down slowly, as if she were constrained.

"You need have no fear," I said. "I am no longer the bold seducer."

"Nor am I the wild, untamed girl," she answered.

"Let us talk," I said.

"I know nothing that would interest you."

"On the contrary, you know all I need to know," I replied, wanting to touch the gleaming of the dying sun on her hair. "Tell me, Sarra, where is Simeon?"

"Has not Akiba told you?"

"No. He was silent or evaded the question. Is Simeon here in Lydda?"

"No," Sarra said soberly, "he is gone. The slave Glaucus returned. They went away together."

"Glaucus!" I was dumbfounded. "What has he to do with Simeon after all these years?"

"The Greek has become a Jew," Sarra said.

My jaw dropped. "Become a Jew!"

"He has undergone circumcision. He keeps all our holy days, even more strictly than my uncle. He is as fiery as any about the necessity of the freedom of our people."

"And you, Sarra? Are you anxious to escape the yoke of Rome?"

She bent her head. "I do not know."

"You fret about Simeon."

"Yes."

"So do I."

"I have heard," she said, "that he and Glaucus have traveled to Goziba. He is known as Simeon of Goziba now."

"Simeon of Goziba," I repeated. "Where is that?"

"It is a desolate place, filled with caves. There many people go to meditate, to have visions, to become closer to God; become holy."

"You Jews are difficult to understand," I said.

Sarra looked at me steadily. "Am I?"

"I don't mean that," I complained. "You turn everything inward, toward yourself. Like a Roman suicide and his sword."

"Then you understand me?"

"No, no," I said hastily. "I don't mean that."

"You Romans are difficult to understand."

I sighed. "What do you think of me?" I inquired.

"I have sometimes one opinion, sometimes another."

208

"I see."

"I am with you so much these days, it is difficult to think of anything else."

"I am a thing," I commented ironically. "Is that what you say?"

I was so intent on her answer, on her lovely flushed face, that I did not hear footsteps approaching. Sarra stood up lightly, looked down the aisle of the arbor, and became tensed, ready to run. "Here is a friend," she said. She disappeared with a rustle of leaves. Annoyed, I turned in my seat—then flung out my single arm in glad welcome.

"Ficus!" I cried.

Thinner, more worn-looking than I remembered him, Ficus was relieved when I allowed him to sit down opposite me. "Speak," I invited him. "Tell me of the campaign."

"I come from Antioch," he said and licked his lips. "It is a long road—a dusty road."

"Drink your fill from the fountain," I said hospitably.

Ficus made a face. I laughed. "Cooling in the fountain is a jar of wine," I said.

Ficus sprang to get the jar, and upended it to his mouth, sucking noisily. I smiled at his eagerness, then became bemused. I had lost my own yearning for wine, somehow: his drinking did not rouse any longer the urge in me to taste liquor. I rapped his bare shin with my knuckles.

"Come, come," I said irritably. "Tell me of the campaign. If you have arrived from Antioch, it must be concluded."

Ficus put down the amphora with a reluctant gurgle and patted his belly. "Concluded," he nodded. "Gloriously concluded. Ctesiphon is taken. Chosroes is in flight to his highlands. The golden throne of the Parthians has entered the gates of Antioch."

"And great Trajan?"

"He is alive, noble Rufus, but—I think—he feels his years most heavily."

"So do all of us."

"He is older."

"He is tough—as tough as Akiba."

Ficus shook his head. "No," he said. "He has taken to wine-bibbing again, night and day."

"By himself, as of old?"

"No. Hadrian, his nephew, makes nightly feasts for him in celebration of the victory."

"Hadrian!" I cried hoarsely. Slowly I nodded. "At the suggestion perhaps of Attianus," I said grimly. "And the connivance of Quietus."

Ficus nodded in return. "The Moor has risen greatly in favor," he said. "But I come for more than that. You are needed in Caesarea, by order of Trajan."

"What has happened?"

"Frontinus and Marcellus are dead."

"Dead!" Another shock. I considered. "Why, then I am king of Caesarea!"

"The business is being carried on pro tempore by the sublegates," Ficus said.

My thoughts returned to Hadrian and lighted on another puzzle. "But what is this about Quietus?" I demanded of Ficus. "Higher in favor, you say?"

Ficus avoided my eye. "He is busy raising an army on another matter," he said.

"You shall tell me more about that another time," I said, dismissing my curiosity for what I believed to be immediate business. "We leave for Caesarea tomorrow morning."

Ficus stood upright and saluted with what was almost relief. Later, much later, I was to damn myself for not having asked more about the assignment of Lusius Quietus. I had thought it must be connected with the final mopping-up of the Parthian campaign. I was wrong.

The unexpected news had driven all else out of my head. Thus, when Ficus and the litters that were to carry our kit and ourselves to the capital came to the door in the blackness just before dawn, I was dismayed to find Sarra, pale and waiting by the threshold. I raised my lamp high, staring at her as if at a ghost, without words to say. Mutely she stared back.

"Are you well enough, Rufus, to take the journey?"

"Well enough to do my duty," I said.

"You will not forget Sarra?"

The lamp trembled in my grip, throwing the light over her like a dance-shower of gold. All that she had done, all that Sarra had meant to me returned to my mind with her husky words. Tears glimmered in my eyes as in hers.

"No," I said. "Rufus does not forget his friends."

"I am still a friend, then?" Sarra said painfully.

I fumbled for words. "My gratitude to you," I said clumsily. "To Akiba and to Rachel, for saving my life. If I were not a one-armed soldier, I should embrace you for all of them."

210

"But if you embraced me," Sarra said, "you would drop the lamp."

"Yes."

"And that would put us in darkness."

"Yes," I said, not comprehending what she meant. Sarra sighed and said nothing more. Words crowded to my tongue but it seemed I could utter none of them. At that moment Ficus poked his helmeted head through the door.

"All is ready, sir," he said significantly. "The sun is coming."

"I am coming as well," I told him. "Goodbye, Sarra," I said brusquely and plunged outside into the coolness. I set down the flickering lamp on the stone by the gate and clambered into the litter. Ficus gave commands; it rose and lurched away as he marched beside it.

I thrust my head through the curtains and looked back. In the distance I could see the tiny flame of the lamp shaking in the immense darkness and a white shimmering beside it that might have been Sarra. Next moment, it went out. I relaxed against the cushions of the swaying litter in thought. I might, I said to myself, have put down the lamp inside; or I might have handed it to her, Sarra having two arms unlike myself. There were a dozen ways to embrace her but I had thought of none of them.

After a time, as the sun came up slowly behind us, Ficus thawed out and commenced to talk in his hoarse monosyllables. All that morning on our way to Caesarea, he regaled me with gossip and what had happened to Frontinus and Marcellus. It seemed long ago that I had bade them goodbye before my departure for Antioch to welcome the arrival of the emperor, the last time I was ever to see them.

Frontinus had hoped to regain favor, to rise in the esteem of Trajan and in power in the empire when the Parthian war broke out. He had readied the X Fretensis for service. In fact, it was called into service with the Syrian legions and with veteran cohorts from the Dacian frontier. But he was removed from his post of command and his legion given to Turbo.

It was then, in the depths of his bitterness, before anyone knew of his disgrace, that Marcellus had come to him. The fat little man had obtained the news by his own spies and bustled down to Jerusalem both to gloat and to use his information. He saw it as a lever by which Frontinus might be enveigled into supporting his request that he be allowed to resign his position and take ship for Rome. Frontinus knew of his plunderings in Judea, and refused—whether out of pique or hope that he could bring him to justice, I could never discover.

Whatever the cause, Frontinus and Marcellus fell into a wrangle. Harsh words passed between them. Frontinus drew his sword and thrust it into the side of Marcellus; he died in less than an hour. That night, in hopeless disgust with himself (and, perhaps, for fear of the trial he would have to face), Frontinus took the same sword, wedged it into the crack between his stone curule seat and the tribunal, and fell upon it. Many times since, I myself have sat in judgment above the same limestone block with the black ineradicable splotch of his blood.

To my relief, Caesarea was much the same; to my delight, my residence had been well maintained by the slaves. I was welcomed back and, in celebration of my return, I ordered from my favorite goldsmith a hollow plate to cover the scar of my shoulder, connected to a fancifully engraved neck collar to keep it in place. As for the business of government, it was plentiful. I came back to it with almost a relish. The sublegates abandoned their desks with suspicious alacrity and I soon found out why: the Jews.

To the end of my days I shall never know what mad impulse it was that made the Jews of the eastern empire break out when they did—just at the time when they might have received all the desires of their souls. But since history enjoins us to guess at what we cannot affirm, I venture to say there were many reasons which, to the Jewish mind, were sufficient to induce them to such a disastrous course. It had been three years since Akiba had been promised the new Temple. By this time the Jews may have been convinced he had been tricked by the emperor. There had been a bitter wave of disappointment in all the colonies of Jews that were more widely dispersed throughout the empire than those of any other people. Moreover, the moment seemed opportune. Many of the legions—including those such as the X Fretensis of Jerusalem, to the Jews the symbol of the conqueror of their holy spot—had been remanded to Parthia for the war.

Still I think the Jewish revolt came about by accident, rising out of the ancient Greek-Jew rivalries, such as had obtained in Caesarea. Each race demanded supremacy. The riots spread from city to city and, at length, burst into outright hostilities against all authority. In the Christian year of 115 they infected Cyrene in Africa. Led by a fanatic called Andrew or "Lucuas"—of whom we shall hear more—the same conflicts sprang up in Egypt and Cyprus. Buildings and roads, bridges, monuments, aqueducts, public buildings—anything with the stamp of Rome upon it was burned or razed. All non-Jews who did not flee were mercilessly tortured and executed.

Such at least were the reports that came to me. They were emphatically denied by Akiba, who paid me a visit at the middle of the following year. Sitting in my private atrium, he spoke feelingly of the foolishness of his people but also of their sufferings. "My people cannot wait for the promised deliverance," Akiba said. "They are tired of taxes and tyranny; they no longer believe in the prophets."

"Have the Romans been tyrants?" I asked reasonably.

Akiba sucked his long lower lip. "Any ruler except our own is a tyrant," he answered.

"On Cyprus, so it has been reported by travelers, the Jews wiped out all except their own. They sacked and burned the capital of Salamis, killing above two hundred and forty thousand; in Cyrene, the number was set at two hundred thousand."

"Do you believe such figures?" Akiba asked me scornfully.

"I was not aware that so many who were not Jews lived in these places," I admitted.

"There are rumors of Jews torturing by tearing out entrails, by sawing people lengthwise—of sending non-Jews to the arena to be devoured by wild beasts, forcing citizens to fight as gladiators."

"That is quite possible," I said.

"For the Romans," Akiba said.

"Akiba," I said, "you have done much for me. I swear we are friends. Do not strain our friendship."

"They say," Akiba went on heedlessly, "that they eat the flesh of those slain, that they use their heads to decorate their houses; that they rub their own bodies with blood as if it were perfumed oil, rejoicing in the odor of the dead; that they cover their nakedness with human skins flayed from the living bodies of those who are not Jews. Can you credit this monstrous nonsense?"

"I know Jews do not eat the flesh of pigs," I said cautiously. "And it appears you decorate your houses otherwise. It does take a certain amount of time to tan even a human hide, and rubbing oneself with blood is hardly practical as a beauty treatment."

Akiba glared at me, his nature roused. "All such things are against our religion!" he cried. "No Jew would do such unthinkable acts!"

"Akiba," I said calmly, "in war men always accuse the enemy of atrocities. You know that yourself. The Romans have always suffered this way. As for me, I believe none of these idle tales. But others may."

"Others?"

"What if Trajan believes them?" I inquired quietly.

Akiba shook his head and was silent. I meditated, having heard Trajan's wrath quoted to me by Ficus: "The stinking and rebellious Jews disgust me!" he had cried. "I know of the unruliness of the Marcomanni, of the Quadi and the Dacians, but I am certain that the Jews are the most riotous and inexplicable people on earth!"

Since I could not repeat this to Akiba, I decided to try to change the subject. I felt sure Trajan would not contravene his edict about the Temple; its reconstruction might even be a master stroke of policy.

"How proceeds the building of your Temple?" I asked Akiba, no more than to fill the silence.

Akiba raised his bony head and gazed at me. "You penetrate my thoughts," he said in his deep voice. "I think of nothing but that."

"Then it goes well?"

Akiba slowly shook his head. "It does not go at all," he said. "Not a penny has been raised, not a block moved, not a grain of dust swept away from the holy places."

I experienced a feeling of astonishment. "But it has only been delayed by the order of Hadrian you spoke of in the desert!" I exclaimed. "Trajan himself will countermand it. You have only to appeal to him. He will remove all obstacles."

Akiba shook his head a second time. "It is too late," he said.

"It is never too late for Rome!" I cried.

Akiba put his hand gently on my sound shoulder. "Rufus, my friend," he said, "the Jews do not love each other. Those of Judea and Galilee rejoiced at the edict. Those of Samaria ground their teeth. They fear and deride the rise of the Temple again. They cried out against the benevolence of the Romans because they wished dissension."

"A cohort into the country will silence them," I asserted scornfully.

"They are our ancient foes, but there are also newer ones.

The Christian sect has demonstrated against the generosity of Rome. Their leader in Antioch, one Ignatius, who listened to a crucified charlatan from Tarsus named Saul, a renegade rabbi, for one—their leader, James, in Jerusalem for another —were sent to Rome during our absence by Hadrian for protesting. They have been torn to bits by the beasts in the Circus Maximus for disobedience. They are believed by the Christians to be martyrs."

"At least you approve of this."

"I never approve of bloodshed. A Sanhedrin that condemns a man to death should not eat the rest of the day—its mouth is full of blood."

"Well," I said, "it is only a matter of patience, after all. Trajan will confirm his original edict in good time."

For the third time, Akiba shook his head. "You do not understand," he replied slowly, "and perhaps I do not understand myself. One fatal flaw was in the rescript."

"What was that?"

"There was no date set for the restoration of the Temple," Akiba said flatly.

"What do you mean?" I demanded, almost angry at the insinuation.

"It may be an oversight, a subtle caution, or something more. It has not been explained."

An involuntary shudder sent a twinge into my right shoulder. I winced. "That is a foolish thing to say," I retorted. "Nothing is too late for the power of Trajan to set right. I myself, as an old crippled soldier"—I shut my eyes in pain as I spoke—"will plead your case for you."

For the last time Akiba shook his head. "It is too late," he repeated. "I have told you before that my people have not learned patience. The Jews in Mesopotamia and Armenia have now threatened to break out into rebellion."

I stared at him in dread. "So soon?"

"They refused to delay. They think the Romans are deceiving them."

"What has happened?" I asked fearfully, remembering how ruthlessly Trajan had put down the Dacian revolt.

"Your emperor," Akiba said, "has sent his best general, Lusius Quietus, to quiet the provinces."

His terrible punning understatement collapsed my lungs as if a weight had been dropped on my chest. For a moment I could not breathe. Then I managed to move my lips.

"Yes," I said. "Yes, in truth, it is too late."

215

It appeared, not long after, that Ficus and Akiba had known what I had not. Trajan had detached two considerable armies from his host of legions. He sent one, under Turbo, to Egypt where the prefect, Marcus Rutilius Lupus, had lost his head and surrendered the country to marauding Jews, shutting himself up in Alexandria and murdering the remaining ones of that race at his leisure. With Turbo went also a fleet of ships from Caesarea. The second army, under Quietus, was dispatched to Mesopotamia. Here no open revolts had yet occurred, but Trajan feared that the large Jewish population might be infected with the idea. The riots increased everywhere. The repressive measures grew stronger. On Cyprus, for example, all Jews were forever forbidden to live. Even those who were cast ashore by accident or shipwreck were seized and killed—and the law endures to this day.

The most significant result of all came in the spring of the next year. I was informed that Trajan planned a third expedition deep into Parthia. I hoped against hope to be ordered back to duty. But what I received instead was an unexpected visitor. He brought with him the largest retinue yet to visit Caesarea on official business.

But he was not a Roman official nor a highly placed Jew. Nor was his following sedate and dignified, intent on honoring their leader. This man proved to be a fugitive, followed by a rabble determined to put him to death.

I came upon him almost by accident. That day I had spent —as I did much of my time—mediating between the Greeks and the Jews of Caesarea who, undaunted by what such feuds in other provinces had cost in lives and treasure, still boiled with hostility. It was only a matter of time before actual war might break forth. I had sent urgent missives to Antioch asking for at least three additional cohorts to garrison the city and keep order.

Meanwhile, hatred and violence took their own ways out. Strangers were suspect; criminals lurked in the streets by night; buildings were defaced, homes invaded. Anyone alone and unfriended was liable to rough handling in such spots as the marketplaces—and it was at the small one near my residence where Ficus and I heard the uproar.

We had no bodyguard, but we did not hesitate to turn toward the source of the hideous sound of a mob at work. The grim visage of Ficus, his muscular frame, and the sight of my golden shoulder had a curious intimidating effect on the bold-

216

est. All knew that the power of Rome stood like a fortress at my elbow. As we rounded into the square, the loiterers gave back. We advanced toward the surging, compact crowd. It was screaming with rage, tearing up paving blocks, hurling them at an invisible object in the center. The wild ululation reminded me of the German savages outside Colonia—except that I understood some of the mouthed epithets.

Ficus and I halted on the outskirts. He looked at me inquiringly, wrapping his iron-studded leather belt around his fist. I nodded.

Instantly Ficus sprang into the midst of the crowd. His bowlegs moved like battering-rams. He used his knees, his fists, his boots in a continuous flailing action, his face set and grinning. In truth, Ficus did not care whom he hit or where or how, as long as it was action. People shrieked and tumbled over one another to get away from him. One burly fellow, balancing a huge boulder over his head, Ficus tripped neatly. The stone fell heavily on the man's outstretched sandal. He sprang upward with a scream, then fell over in agony, his foot crushed. Ficus kicked him out of the way and continued on his relentless progress around the circle. In moments, the mob had dispersed in fluttering filthy garments. They ran like animals, in all directions, mouthing curses and obscenities at the indignity of being robbed of the object of their wrath.

Ficus, as a final gesture, picked up a few of their stones and hurled them after the retreating figures. I approached the silent bowed object of their fury. Mounting the heap of rocks already about him, I put my arm around the bruised and bleeding shoulders and lifted him up. The man was unconscious. His head fell back. I gazed into his face with amazement.

"Order executed, sir," Ficus said, coming up panting beside me.

"Look!" I exclaimed.

Ficus studied the dirty bloody countenance. "Well," he said unemotionally, "there's something to pay for this."

"No," I said slowly. "They would not have dared stone him thus—unless he were a Christian." The face was the face of Curtius Saccus, former centurion in the legions of the emperor Trajan.

"In that case," Ficus said indifferently, "let him die."

"No," I said. "I wish to talk to him. And he will be of interest to Akiba."

217

In point of fact, Akiba waited for me in the palace. He was almost a daily visitor during these days of growing uncertainty. He rarely smiled, and a frown of perpetual worry had etched itself into his forehead. We dined together in the cool evening in the garden (Ficus by this time had acquired a stock of food from which Akiba deigned to partake) and exchanged information. At last I told him of what had happened on the way home.

"If the Christians have come down to Caesarea from Antioch," Akiba said, knotting his brows, "it makes the maintenance of peace triply difficult."

"Let us question Saccus," I rejoined.

In a few moments Ficus had brought him to us and, though covered with bruises, he managed to tell his story. He was indeed proselyting in Caesarea but had just arrived. He knew nothing of any others of his sect, but he explained that he had been converted in Antioch after his discharge from the X Fretensis. "The world is soon coming to an end," he mumbled. "We will be rid of both Rome and the Jews."

"By war?" I inquired idly, amused.

"Jesus brought the sword of love," Saccus replied.

"For one who is accustomed to fighting," I said, "and quarreled with me constantly in the old days of Germania, you seem a changed man."

"The holy Christ has changed me," said Saccus through his thickened lips. "As he would change you."

"I can hardly agree," I said. "I have studied the stories of the Messiah of the Christians. Your Jesus, far from being a holy man, seems both irritable and childlike."

Saccus tossed back his battered head, wincing with pain. "You speak like a Roman," he articulated. "A Roman who has not had the mystic experience, noble Rufus."

I snorted. "What else am I to speak for except Rome?" I inquired. "Tell me: did not this Jesus of yours curse a fig tree? It seemed unnecessary; to say the least."

"It bore no fruit."

"Come, come, it was not the season," I told him. "He was unreasonable in all things. He hated his own race, calling them snakes and vipers."

"You must know," said Saccus painfully, "that the truth is not a condemnation. He spoke the truth."

I pursed my lips. "He was hardly persuasive," I said. "His sense of courtesy, for such a great man, was wanting. What of his damning of a man without a wedding gown?"

"You speak of mere parables as if they were fact."

"How can we separate one from the other?" I protested. "Speaking of the talents hidden in the ground, did he not praise usury in the man who increased his and curse the good sense of him who buried it for safekeeping?"

"I have no desire to argue with you," Saccus told me. "If you have eyes and see not, you are as good as blind."

"You are quoting your Christ," I said severely. "He seems to me not much more than a young man with a temper, seriously wanting to reform the world and becoming angry when he could not do so. He had some strange visions, you must admit, calling himself a god."

"He is the living God."

"There you go again," I said patiently. "I know only that many Jews consider him a bastard child. They claim he was born of a Roman centurion named Pantheras of the X Fretensis, in illicit union with a Jewish woman."

"That is blasphemy!" cried Saccus, rising as if to strike me, groaning and falling back.

I shook my head. "Restrain your religious frenzy," I warned him, "or I shall have to have you confined. This is a discussion of logic and philosophy." Saccus eased his position, but his angry eyes remained on my face.

"You will admit he seemed rather sensitive about adultery," I went on. "How do you reconcile this with his injunction to love your neighbor as yourself?"

"That is obscene!" the other said.

"And his rejection of his mother?"

Saccus said nothing, but I felt the heat from his burning body, as if his very resentment would consume him. I went on: "His miracles I believe in, for there are many miracles in the history of Rome similar to his. But his short temper and his convictions of divinity remind me of some of our own emperors."

"You will burn in Gehenna for such words," Saccus told me fearsomely.

"That is the old refuse place behind Jerusalem, I think," I said calmly. "You are not dealing with an ignorant man. Understand, I respect the force and wisdom of your Messiah but I cannot agree with his claims. Can you convince me?"

Saccus seemed to swell up in one last outburst. "I only know your pride and power will not last another week!" he cried, licking the dried blood on his lips.

"How do you know that?" I asked. I waited for long moments for him to respond, but Saccus merely closed his eyes and did not move. I waved my hand. "Take him away," I commanded Ficus. "This is an impossible discussion."

As Saccus was escorted back to prison, I turned to Akiba, who had sat silently next to me on the marble bench during the questioning. Akiba shook his head disapprovingly. "You must not tell me that you have become a Christian," I said in mock alarm.

"No," Akiba said seriously, "but after all, this man was a Roman, one of your own. You were merciless to him."

"Should I have had pity because he was a Roman?"

"You were trying to humiliate him, not discuss the question."

"You are as foolish as he," I said angrily. "If we cannot talk of the gods of different kinds in a sensible manner, how may we arrive at any decent conclusion?"

"You must experience God," Akiba said, "as Saccus told you. Only then are you won over, by the soul's rising to the surface and becoming all."

"Like a carp taking bait?"

"Like an angel ascending, noble Rufus. Since the soul and God are above nature, they cannot be proved by natural means. You seek too little with the wrong purpose; your track turns upon itself."

"The only difference, it seems to me," I said, "is that we and others, such as the Persians and Egyptians, have gods for every purpose while you have a multipurpose god."

"We are Jews," Akiba said with a glimmer of humor. "We like to economize."

I flung myself upright and paced the garden. "We shall never decide such a question," I said pettishly. "Talking this way clouds my head."

"Never is it decided together," Akiba replied. "Such depths of knowing come only to the alone with the Alone." He followed me as we went inside.

"Worshipping this Jesus as a god is a crime," I complained, "as you know. Only the emperor and the gods of Rome are to be worshipped."

"Then the Jews, as well, may be accused and tried and executed?"

"Not at all," I said hastily. "Your god is purely imaginary, a figment of thought. Whereas this Christ actually lived. Worshipping him is an act of the most hideous blasphemy."

"You believe God is imaginary?" inquired Akiba incredulously.

I raised my eyebrows and shrugged. "Everyone is entitled to his imagination," I said. "I have seen madmen who are convinced that the world is populated by nothing but red snakes from Mesopotamia and purple elephants from Egypt."

"We are mad?"

"Rome is generous," I said. "It allows you to be idiots as long as you keep the peace."

"But the Christians are peaceful," Akiba said.

"Religion makes men fools," I said aphoristically. "I predict that they will split into sects and be at each other's throats before many years are gone. This fellow Saul, himself a Roman citizen, too, wandered across the seas preaching this seditious doctrine and was condemned under the emperor."

"We have no concern with others," Akiba said testily. "We are concerned only with Jews, not with Gentiles."

"Even you, bound together by blood and ceremony, tear at each other's throats," I expostulated.

Akiba rose wearily, shaking his head. "You argue like a rabbi," he said. "Allow me, good Rufus, to depart. I am tired of such things tonight." A smile flickered. "Tomorrow I shall be better able to argue with you."

But we did not discuss it further. Akiba left before dawn on another of his mysterious missions to placate his people—I was satisfied it was only his pervading influence that had kept Judea peaceful up to this point—and, when I summoned Ficus to have Saccus brought to me, he shook his head sadly.

"What is wrong?" I demanded.

"He escaped last night," Ficus said.

"Escaped! A man who was nearly dead!"

Ficus hunched his shoulders like one ready to receive a blow. "He was one of us, an old Roman soldier," he explained. "What else could he do but escape?"

I opened my mouth and closed it again without uttering a word. Ficus was right to let Saccus go. Akiba was right: I was persecuting my own kind. Neither of us mentioned Saccus again. Nor did he ever appear before me. I have heard that he had his name changed (as Christians do) to Barnabas and went to Cyprus to preach. Being Roman, he was allowed to disembark, and vanished from history.

I had occasion to think long about his prophecy no more than three days later. Into the same square where he had been

221

stoned stormed a troop of cavalry. Their head and his escort clattered up the steps of the palace itself. I came to the door to order them disciplined—then restrained myself on seeing their leader.

It was Lusius Quietus. He strode into my residence like a conqueror. Even before he greeted me, he looked about him with the calculating air of a proprietor, pursing his lips and wagging his head as if satisfied by what he saw. Then he deigned to look at me.

"I heard that you had lost your arm," Quietus said. "But I had not believed it."

"You may," I said.

"I have come to relieve you," he said in his blunt way. "You are no longer governor of Judea. The great emperor Trajan has ordered me to take command."

"This small province within Syria is not worthy of your command," I protested.

"The emperor believes otherwise," Quietus said caustically. "Jews come from Judea. Here will be the heart of any future resistance."

"But there has been no revolt here!"

"I know your friend Akiba has been busy—and perhaps we owe much to him. But he will shift his allegiance from Rome. The Jews are notorious turncoats. Here: this is the order of supercession."

I bowed my head. When I raised it a moment later, I am positive that my face did not reveal the emptiness of my bowels and the fury that the words of Quietus had set raging. "I hear and obey," I said, accepting the scroll from the hand of Quietus. "One warning, good Quietus: the Jews are restive. They are dangerous. Pacify, do not provoke them."

Quietus rubbed his thumb across his nose, an insulting gesture. "Have no fear," he said. "I know these animals from long ago. I have dealt with them in Parthia, in Mesopotamia, even in Antioch. They understand a long spear and a short sword, a scourge and the cross. I shall have no trouble."

"Very well," I said and rose. Quietus watched me.

"I am of consular rank now," he said suddenly. "Even Hadrian has not risen so high. The emperor rewards those he loves."

"Vale," I said and stalked out. I was glad that my toga was full and well draped. Otherwise Quietus would have been able to see every hair on my back standing upright.

For days my head was full of dark and unspeakable chaos. I had no idea where to go or what I might do: cast away from imperial favor, stranded on the shoals of my own crippled condition. Not yet had I been forced to surrender my pleasant residence on the coast, but I knew this would come. I considered resigning my post as tribune and discarded it as a fool's strategy.

I refused social engagements, staying at home and eating pulse alone. My amusement, such as it was, consisted of sitting for long periods full of forebodings; afternoons spent on the portico staring out at the distant horizon; nights sleepless watching the dim clouds that covered the stars—unable to meditate or read philosophy, desolate alike of thought and action. Not even the remembrance of Sarra and my hopes to see Simeon again could relieve the depths of my self-pity.

For three weeks I was helpless to make a decision. Then abruptly I was notified by messenger that Quietus desired me to vacate my residence within a month. A spark stirred within me: the arrogance of the command stirred the ashes of my manhood and I swore blind vengeance.

But two weeks later all oaths were at usurer's discount. This drastic turnabout in my feelings was signaled by the return of Fiscus from Antioch. I had sent him there to request what I knew from the beginning would be hopeless: an audience with Trajan. It was a hot, still summer evening when, still travel-stained and weary, he came up on the portico to salute me. He approached with a strange stiff gait, almost as if he were drunk, recovering his balance each time he extended his foot. His eyes were glazed; his face fixed straight ahead. I watched him with annoyance.

"What's the matter with you?" I asked sharply.

Ficus gave me a mechanical obeisance. I began to think I might have to have him thrashed. "Noble Rufus," he began in a voice that threatened to strangle him, "noble Rufus." He stopped. To my amazement, I saw his eyes were bloodshot, full of tears. This bandy-legged tough of a soldier trembled like a child.

"What ails you?" I said in concern. "Do you have the ague from the swamps?"

Ficus shook his head from side to side, a man in agony, holding his arms rigidly to his sides. "No," he said thickly, "all that has happened is that the world is turned upside down."

"What do you mean, you madman?" I shouted in exasperation. "Have you been drinking and gambling and whoring?"

Again his queer shake of the head. "I heard the news at Antioch," he said.

"What news?"

"From Cilicia."

"Curse your news from Cilicia! What could possibly concern us from there?"

For the first time Ficus looked directly at me. His eyes overflowed. His tears dripped from his sagging cheeks. He spoke softly to me, as if to a brother in sorrow.

"The mighty emperor Trajan," he said, "has joined the gods."

CHAPTER 14

The Jews have a legend about a man named Lot. His wife, they say, looked over her shoulder at their doomed city of Sodom and was transformed into a pillar of salt. What they mean by this childish story, I suppose, is that anyone who looks back at the past is condemned to bitterness.

I take this warning for my own. But in writing such a personal history as this I cannot ignore the acrid taste of my recollections of those days. The assumption of the throne of the Roman empire by Publius Aelius Hadrian leaves too much unexplained. Too many signs daubed with blood point to mysterious darknesses.

Ficus had rightly said, the death of the golden emperor Trajan turned the world upside down. Not only for Romans but also for those they protected and for whom they had been given guardianship from the gods. The passing of Marcus Ulpius Nerva Trajanus Dacicus Parthicus Optimus was not unexpected—others beside Akiba had predicted it—but it was no less tragic. He left no indication of whom he wished to succeed him in the principate. In his death he committed the greatest mistake of his life.

Before leaving Syria, he assigned the most important post of Judea to Quietus. Next, he gave the command of the army in Syria to Hadrian. Turbo was still busy in Egypt, subduing the remnants of the Jewish uprisings. Satisfied with his division of power—and apparently not aware of black wings hovering about him—Trajan took ship for Rome in August. A week out, he suffered a relapse and paralysis. His vessel was ordered into the small port of Selintontum in Cilicia. Here he suffered a second fit. He died before the ides of the month. Clearly his time had come. It reminded me of the verses of Menecrates:

> *If one grows old and life be wanted*
> *Longer than the gods surmise;*
> *May one's foolish wish be granted*
> *By those cynics in the skies!*

Obedient to the orders of his uncle, Hadrian had remained in Antioch. But his schemes sailed with the emperor. Only Plotina and Attianus were with Trajan when he died—and one other person, the vile old slave Pontus, who had been my spymaster in Rome. Though Trajan was stricken to his couch and speechless, he is said to have adopted Hadrian two days before he died. On his deathbed, he is supposed to have spoken in a strange, ghostly tone to give Hadrian his blessing.

As if this were not wonderful enough, Hadrian was told of his succession two days later—on the same day that Pontus died by his own hand. Hadrian acted instantly to have the Syrian army acclaim him, giving thrice the usual donative to the soldiers. Interestingly enough, Attianus continued to Rome. On his arrival there, he was instantly reappointed prefect of the Praetorian Guard. A few years later, for an unknown offense, he was condemned to be executed. He demanded a private audience with Hadrian, and the sentence was commuted, but he retired wholly from public service thereafter. As for Plotina, Hadrian cherished her all her remaining days and erected a gorgeous monument above her tomb.

"Still, all this plotting is mere imagination on your part," Akiba said to me when we discussed it one evening in Antioch. "There is no proof at all of what you insinuate."

"None," I admitted. "Yet observe. Trajan, who always upheld the tradition of Augustus in duly appointing a successor, did nothing of the sort for Hadrian. Nor did he ever act to present his nephew as the 'best citizen' qualified for the office. Moreover, he allowed others, such as Quietus, the belief that they were higher in favor and appointed them to more responsible posts. And it is known that all who surrounded the emperor in his last moments favored Hadrian."

"What do you believe happened?"

"A dying man. Plotina, Attianus, the slave Pontus who must have been bribed away from the retinue of Quietus. The moment they had prepared for and swore to: the helpless emperor, Pontus with his gift of voices behind a curtain. And the decree of succession, mark you, signed not by Trajan but by Plotina herself!"

Akiba slowly got up to his extraordinary height and shrugged. "Whatever it is," he said, "Trajan is dead. We Jews shall have to make our peace with Hadrian. I trust it will be better than we could have made with Quietus."

I felt less charitable than Akiba toward Hadrian. The world I had known and helped make secure was trembling in the balance. In Britain, our forces were in retreat. In Germania, the wild tribes had broken the truces of Trajan. The newly organized provinces of Parthia seethed with revolt.

I had received the bronze tablets of my discharge. The diptych certified that my service was complete and satisfactory, missus honesta missione. It was a duly executed copy of the constitutio in the temple of Augustus with the seals of witnesses: "A veteran who has served in the legions, who deserved his pay and more, whose citizenship is confirmed." Reading that I was pia et fidelis gave me no pleasure. I told myself bitterly that I had been retired to the status of a private citizen evidently pro bono publico. Despite my savings and my excellent stipend and bonuses—which constituted a small personal fortune—I felt abandoned by Rome, merely because I had been crippled.

Sick at heart, if reasonably whole in flesh, I went to Antioch with permission for Ficus to accompany me. There I rented a small residence halfway to Daphne. It boasted a fountain-centered garden with walls slabbed with leaf-green marble, lined with cypresses. For weeks I nursed my grudge against the Army and then, at the urgings of Ficus, ventured out. Gradually I became fond of the diversions of the city and made occasional visits to Daphne. Antioch had largely recovered from the earthquake, regaining most of its gaiety. I confess I enjoyed my forced retirement, though chafing at the inaction. I kept my mind and body healthy through pride, resisting the temptations of wine and the company of women. Study, the theatre, and the baths, pleasant dinners and discussions in the evening occupied most of my time.

Many of these explorations of wisdom concerned themselves with the ancient race of Jews. My fate commenced to intertwine itself more closely with that of Akiba. The abortive revolts in the provinces had been systematically crushed, one by one. Slaughter had been great. Crucifixes lined the roads, burial parties plodded everywhere. Men in ashes and women in sackcloth sat weeping by their huts. The smell of hatred for Rome rose strongly in the air, like the smoke of burning. But Akiba and I remained friends, more to his cost, I discovered, than mine.

He visited me often from Lydda, though it was a long trip. Occasionally he brought friends, men of stony countenance who sat veiled and silent while we talked. His worries were about the sullen hostility of his people—glowing coals under the ashes of their repression. He begged me to do what I could to alleviate their suffering; he asked my advice and sought everywhere for peace with honor. In those days following Hadrian's accession, he was as troubled as I—for much different reasons—over what the forthcoming years would bring.

Hadrian showed no immediate inclination to return to Rome. He professed to be enchanted with the East—and thoroughly disenchanted with the imperial policies of his divine uncle. He showed not the slightest wish to continue on the course he had inherited from Trajan.

To the shame and rage—not to say astonishment—of the ones who had hoped for a greater empire, he entirely renounced Trajan's conquests. It was a great decision, one which reechoed in the world: Rome had retreated at last. It marked the beginning of the boldness of barbarians without and decay within.

There were mighty and powerful objections to his policy from all quarters. To each complaint, Hadrian blandly replied that he acted solely in accordance with secret instructions from Trajan which he alone knew. He was in no hurry to return to Rome. He took a leisurely nine-month trip through the eastern portion of the empire. He pointedly avoided Judea to humiliate Quietus; perhaps for the same reason he denied any of our officials (including myself) an audience. After spending much of his time in Greece and Egypt, Hadrian suddenly took ship in July and sailed directly from Alexandria for Rome.

I had not the slightest inkling of this unexpected departure —nor, it seemed, had anyone else. Rumors flew like pila in battle. I chafed for news: I even sent Ficus to call upon Quietus in my old residence in Caesarea to gain information.

He came back to report merely that the saturnine Moorish general had followed Hadrian to Egypt and had not yet returned.

It was during these days of uncertainty that I discerned the beginnings of the change in my ill fortune. I had spent several pleasant days in my villa discussing my favorite, Epictetus, with Akiba—and I must say that the old man got much the worst of the philosophic argument—when one afternoon he came to my door with two companions.

They were Jewish rabbis—evidently men of high learning by the black leather phylacteries they wore. Akiba introduced the one to me as Eliezer ben Hyrkanos—a thin-faced man with an arrogant expression—and Pappias ben Judah, a fat little fellow with a look of perpetual anxiety. I welcomed them —gazing with special interest at the one called Eliezer. I recalled that Akiba had spoken of him as his "enemy in thought." I wondered if I might slyly sow some seeds of Roman common sense in this rabbi. At any rate, I thought, it would do no harm to probe his sentiments. The fellow might be a useful counterpoise to the heavy weight against us in Judea. I led them into my garden and offered them seats. Then I looked inquiringly from one to the other, expressing my wonder at their visit.

"We have come to discuss with you the ancient troubles of Israel," Akiba announced. The others bowed their heads in assent.

"As long as you do not discuss present troubles," I said. "I am no longer in politics or even in the army. I am merely a Roman citizen, enjoying what remains to me of life."

"Which we trust may be many years," Eliezer said politely.

Akiba cleared his throat. "As you know," he began, "having studied many philosophies and religions, noble Rufus, the Jews were once the slaves of the Egyptian pharaohs."

"The Romans, I am sure, understand," Pappias put in, "for they, too, were once slaves."

"You are misinformed," I told him. "Romans have never been slaves and never shall be."

"I beg your pardon," Pappias said. "I was speaking of the reign of Tarquin the Proud, six hundred years ago. It was my understanding that he repealed all reforms and was a tyrant. That he slew senators and put priests to death. That he took the weapons from the common people and forced them to erect foreign temples."

228

Having vomited forth this nonsense, he waited for my reply, as expectant as a dog for a bone. "What you have said," I answered stiffly, "is merely a legend."

"I am sad," Pappias said, "for it must be also a legend that the Roman people rose in revolt and have hated foreign rulers ever thereafter."

"That is not a legend," I replied hastily. "It came about in a different way. We are not here to talk about Romans, but Jews, are we not?" I had conceived a hearty dislike for this rolypoly rabbi in the past few minutes. I determined to ignore him.

"The Romans believed in and fought for freedom," Pappias said argumentatively.

"You must know," Akiba broke in, "that this subject has been much talked of among the people. Eliezer represents the aristocrats among the Jews. Pappias speaks for the common people of the land. I, however unworthy, represent the people of the cities."

"Together we express the thoughts of all Jews," Eliezer interposed.

"We have told our people revolt is wrong, and it has brought curses upon us," Pappias said.

"Let them curse fire and sword, then," I said. "What the gods will, that is what occurs."

"Whatever God does, that is for the best," Akiba agreed. "I remember once in my travels that we came to a village and were turned away from the inn. My companions grumbled but I said it was for the best—though I did not see it clearly. With us was an ass, a cock, and we had our lamp. During the night the wind blew out the light, a cat killed the cock, and the ass died. My companions grumbled, but I was still assured of God's will. Before dawn a band of roving Arabs attacked the village and killed all the inhabitants. We alone escaped. Do you see the will of God? If we had been in the village, if the cock had crowed or the ass brayed or had they seen our light, we would not have survived."

"How did the villagers feel about the will of God?" I inquired. Akiba did not deign to answer.

"We do not think that war is the will of God," Eliezer said almost passionately. "We hope rebellion will never come. We hope for peace."

"It has already happened," I pointed out. "The Jews needed a lesson, and they have been taught."

"I myself have seen the need for many things," Akiba said

placidly. "Rufus here will bear me out. Every father owes it to his child, for example, to teach him how to swim—though we live on land."

"That is true," I said, remembering my experiences in the water with Ficus. "At least, one's orderly should know."

Pappias did not like these diversions of thought. "Akiba has great influence with our people," he said. "They listen to him and obey what he says."

"There must be those who disagree with his doctrines," I argued in high good temper.

"There are often such," admitted Pappias, "but their loud voices are lost when it is known that a whisper of Akiba opposes them."

"What do you think of this, Akiba?" I inquired.

"I know both humiliation and pride," Akiba said.

"Come, Akiba," Pappias said angrily. "Let us have no false modesty."

"I remember what Akabiah ben Mahalalel said long ago," Akiba said. "He was expelled from the order of Pharisees for stubbornness, yet his words are written in gold: 'Whence does man come? Out of darkness. Whither does he go? To the deepest darkness. What is he destined to become? Dust and worms. Yet who is his judge? The King of Kings.' "

"What is there left to judge?" I asked.

"The soul," Akiba said simply.

"I do not agree," Pappias said, puffing up. "I have kept the law, every jot and tittle. I have rendered obedience to God. I look about me for those destined for heaven. They are very few. If there be three, then my son and I are two; if there is one, it is I."

"You will die with a rock on your grave," Eliezer said sharply.

This seemed a favorable opening to discover his sentiments. "Perhaps you differ with your colleagues about Rome," I said suavely. Eliezer shot me a glance full of fear and hatred. If I had heard in words what his face expressed, I would have slain him on the spot. I turned away, a smoldering inside me rising against these recalcitrant Jews.

"It is best to be charitable," Akiba said mildly. "Charity is our duty. We are like men indebted to a king for far more than we are worth. We must pay something on what we owe, we must give gifts. We owe God, the King of all kings, our lives and whatever we have."

Enjoyable as it was to see these vain Jews at one another's

throats, I could not allow the digression to go further. I was curious to know more about the real object of their visit. "The Christians," I murmured, to introduce a provoking note, "have told those of their sect that believe upon Jesus that they should render unto Caesar what is his."

Eliezer gritted his teeth, and he said nothing. Pappias stared at the ground. It was Akiba who took up the subject, and he chose again to avoid direct reply. "If only Trajan's edict about our Temple might be fulfilled," he said gently.

Here was their purpose in coming, said I to myself. I restrained my tongue and the interval was filled by Eliezer. "The people still feel grief about Julianus and Pappus," he said.

"Madmen," I said curtly. "Both, madmen."

All three of my visitors commenced to speak at once, then they yielded deferentially to Akiba. "They were the wisest of of men," he said. "Perhaps they were misled in this single instance, but they are holy and blessed."

"What is a wise man?" I asked contemptuously. "One who loses his life in chasing a phantom?"

"A true wise man," responded Akiba, "is he who learns from every man, no matter how humble. Who is strong? He who controls his passions. Who is truly wealthy? He who is content with what God gives him. Who is honored in the highest? He who honors his fellowman."

"Whatever the opinion of Rome," Eliezer said quietly, "they were martyrs to our faith."

"All this is useless," I told them, cruelly putting an end to their dreams. "I have no authority in the smallest way. Even if I did, I would think long before pleading for the Jews after what has happened."

"As at Nehardea?" asked Akiba without expression.

"I owe much to your wife," I managed to mumble, taken sharply aback.

"Many more owe much more to her, even myself," Akiba averred. "She joins us in our plea."

"Go to Quietus. He is governor."

"He would lash us into dungeons and nail us to crucifixes," replied Pappias with conviction.

"We came here only because Akiba called you merciful and understanding," Eliezer added.

I felt a quick wave of frustration. I closed my single fist and looked at it. "I am not in Hadrian's favor," I told them. "If I were, something might be done. There is much to be said for the restoration of your Temple. Akiba knows I have said as much to the divine Trajan's face."

"What of Hadrian?" said Akiba. "He is another man, of another thought."

"He has not stayed in Judea," Pappias added.

"I have asked to see him," I explained, "but he has not responded."

There was a strained silence. Eliezer stood and bowed. "You have been courteous," he said, "but there is no help here either of advice or power. We build on walls of sand when we seek the aid of those who do not have the ear of the emperor. Come, Pappias."

I felt my muscles harden in resentment. But as Pappias arose and they began their stately exit, which was somehow an insult, Akiba smiled and said: "I shall remain."

"Does our failure amuse you, Akiba?" Eliezer asked sternly.

"Laughter protects the honor of all," Akiba returned.

Eliezer made no response. He and Pappias bid me farewell, ostentatiously ignoring Akiba. As they vanished from my sight, I said: "They are impudent dogs, my friend."

"If they are, they bark in a learned fashion," Akiba returned. "Do not forget that our whole lives are bound up in this, yea, the Life-to-Come. Your fretting is a thing apart from your existence."

"Do not speak so confidently," I said irritably. "Hadrian may yet send me to the block. Do not these fools know that?"

"Their foolishness is the wisdom of the Lord, blessed be He," Akiba said. "But do not fear the emperor."

"Why so?"

"I am not always without knowledge. I have had a vision which has told me you will be called of Hadrian for greater tasks."

My senses became alert. Whenever a Jew of Akiba's prominence spoke of a "vision," it really meant that their extraordinary intelligence system had received some information.

"When may I expect this miracle of favor?" I inquired cautiously. Akiba shrugged: "Of that I have no knowledge."

"He may call upon me to rise from the dead," I said ironically.

Akiba sighed. "When the words of prayer come easily to me for the sick," he said, "I know the patient will recover. But when I am interrupted and stumble, the hope is gone."

"What do you mean by that?"

"You and I, Rufus, must be as brothers. We have more

ties than either of us knows. On the one side, you are suspect to the Romans; on the other, I am hated by Jews as influential as Elisha ben Abuyah."

"Who is he?"

"He is a patrician who believes I am a hypocrite and an ignoramus. He claims I deceive them about the Torah, saying that such knowledge must be absorbed when one is young, taken into the blood—that it is useless for a man like myself to pretend to it. He thinks I began too late, spent too much time in working, to be truly a scholar. My opinions are often stricter in interpretation and more lenient in exposition than his—thus he mistrusts me."

I filed this in my memory: an enemy of Akiba might make a tool for the Romans. "And Gamaliel?" I asked shrewdly. I knew something whereof I spoke. Akiba sighed again. "He is a good man, but proud," he said, "and he rules the assembly with an iron rod. But he will change and become one of the truly revered ones of Israel."

"What of Pappias?" I asked. "He appeared to be the complete ass on this occasion."

"Pappias and I often argue," Akiba explained, "and his ideas need much work. He still thinks of God as some Old Man in the sky with a beard and bald like me. He worships an image in his head—but I shall soon win him over."

"I hope you will disabuse him of any ideas of revolt," I said warningly.

"When Israel obeys its judges, God gives them victory," Akiba declared. "When they disobey, God delivers them into the hands of their enemies." His voice had become sad and disconsolate. He rose and made his way out of the garden without a word more. I sat alone for a time afterward, wrapped in my own thoughts—more occupied, I admit, with Rome than Jerusalem. Only when the wind became cold, bringing the weird chanting of the priests from Daphne, did I shudder and go inside to the warmth of the braziers.

Perhaps it was persistence of the thought of Sarra safe far away to the south in Lydda. Or that of my own humiliation—discharged from the legions, dismissed my post—which kept me from summoning her to my side. Perhaps it was boredom or despair. Weeks had passed, and Akiba's prophecy was still barren. It is difficult to catalogue emotions that drive one to a decision. Most likely of all, it was simply a sudden emotional desire, without any reason at all, which set me defiantly

233

drinking wine as if I were the same young roisterer of many years ago.

But it was Sarra's image in my mind that I gave myself as an excuse. I dreaded her taking a lover. The jealousy I had no right to claim clouded my thoughts. In the words of the Greek poet Meleager:

> *Fill the cup and cry her name!*
> *Again, again! Again, the same!*
> *Pour me wine's untempered drop,*
> *Tainted with no other slop.*
> *And give me, too, the garland fair*
> *That round her neck our love did share.*
> *See! Its roses die in shame—*
> *She whispers now another's name.*

It was foolish and without sense. But I drowned myself in the wretched local vintages and staggered to bed each night without regard for the disapproving stares of Ficus (who had long since reformed and become an intolerable addict of temperance). It was more than a month after I commenced to indulge in these solitary drinking bouts that I experienced the strangest dream of my life.

I seemed to be asleep in those longest hours before dawn. Yet I was awake. I stared upward from my couch at the painted ceiling of my chamber where Jupiter struggled amorously with Ganymede. A shadow leaned over me. I recognized the face at once, though it had become thin and ascetic: it was that of Simeon, a ghost out of the past.

I tried to move. My body would not obey. It seemed that I lay paralyzed under the light coverlet as this shaggy-haired, muscular being, clad in skins, his eyes shining and fiery, bent over me. I looked up at him without surprise or fear: indeed, this was a moment I had long anticipated. My voice floated upward.

"Salve, Simeon," I said.

"Shalom, Rufus Teneius," he said in a voice grown deeper.

"What are you doing here?"

"Lie still," he said softly.

A face like one recalled from hell peered over his shoulder: twisted, leering, fringed with hair, the eyes cold and remote.

"Kill him now," it said. It was the face of Simeon's one-time slave-tutor, Glaucus, descended a thousand levels into cruelty and malice.

"Glaucus," I said.

234

His mouth gaped. "You know me," he said.

"Thinner, your face more evil, but still the slave."

Glaucus laughed noiselessly, horribly. "I shall tell you what will make you writhe," he whispered. "I am more than Glaucus."

"That is still less than excrement."

"Will you say that when I tell you I am Lucuas of Cyprus?"

"You!"

"Who else planned the riots there? Where else did their repulsive dialect name me anew?"

"Your life is forfeit," I said.

Glaucus bent closer. "And yours—is it sacred at this moment?"

"We have not come to kill," Simeon said sternly, thrusting him back.

"It is long overdue," mouthed Glaucus.

But Simeon stared in surprise, his eyes dilating, at my right side under the covering. "Until I discover the truth about myself, he lives," he said mechanically. "Rufus, you have only one arm!"

"You have been long away from cities," I told him, "hiding in the deserts of Goziba. All the rest of Judea knows I possess only a left arm. My right was lost on the banks of the Tigris."

"Who told you of Goziba?" hissed Glaucus.

I disregarded him. "Why have you come here, Simeon?" I demanded.

"What does Hadrian intend for the Jews?" the subdued Simeon said.

"I do not know."

"We hear rumors, gossip, murmurs, whispers—but nothing that is sure."

"I am as much concerned as you," I said. "But I am ignorant. I am no longer legate in Judea. Lusius Quietus is governor."

"I know," Simeon replied.

Glaucus sneered. "We paid his residence a visit and left some throats cut," he said, "but his honor was not at home."

I gazed upward at Simeon's immobile face. "Have you then become so low as to be one of the sicarii?" I asked.

Simeon shook his head. "But I am a Zealot," he replied.

"I do not know them."

"We shall do anything to free the Jews from the Romans," Glaucus said.

The room perceptibly lightened. Simeon looked about him

and took a deep breath. "We have stayed too long," he muttered. "Dawn is near." Glaucus nodded. Simeon bent over me once again.

"Who am I?" he asked tensely.

I hesitated and then decided to tell the truth. "My son," I replied.

"I cannot believe you," Simeon answered.

"If you did, you would be a Roman, not a Jew," Glaucus whispered.

"Just as a Greek has become a Jew," I said angrily.

"Impossible, impossible," Simeon said, thinking only of what I had said.

"He lies," Glaucus said roughly, "you are a Jew of Jews."

"Rufus also told me that once," Simeon said.

There was the sound of movement outside the door. The room was rapidly becoming light with sunrise. "Come!" Simeon exclaimed. They ran toward the window, dived through it, and vanished.

How long I remained in my dreamlike state, I have no idea. It was Ficus who roused me at last, as I drowsily quoted a verse from Palladas:

"Does life come to us as a dream?
Or does the dream receive us?
Do we realize what we seem—
Or does the real deceive us?"

"I beg your pardon?" Ficus asked inquiringly. I struggled back to life, glad that I could move my limbs again. I opened my eyes, slowly at first, then with a start. The dream was still vivid in my mind, but the early morning sun streamed into the room, giving it the lie. I sprang off my couch, then sank to a stool and moaned, holding my head. My unaccustomed use of wine, so long shunned, had wrought its vengeance. My mind clanged like a gong. Its booming echoes destroyed any coherent thought. With the utmost care, I stood up and staggered over to the fountain. Carefully, making sure my skull would not burst or fall off, I lowered my head into the icy water.

When I withdrew it a moment later, cursing and sputtering, it still ached. But it was tolerable. I tottered back to a stool and picked up my toga, throwing it around me. I paid no attention to the streams of water down my back and went to the fountain, to drink again and again: I had a thirst that seemed as unquenchable as that of the fabled Sisyphus.

A noise behind startled me into standing upright. I swung about despite the warning twinges in my neck: the fears of my dream were still with me. To my surprise, my bloodshot eyes—clearing as if by magic—saw towering behind the portly mass of Ficus the angular form of Akiba.

"What are you doing here?" I managed to ask feebly, sinking back, careless as to who might reply.

"I have a message from Alexandria," Ficus said promptly. "From the emperor."

"Why didn't you give it to me earlier, you idiot?" I snarled, snatching the roll from him.

"You were asleep," Ficus said with dignity.

"All sleep is holy," Akiba added.

"Why in the name of all the gods are you here at this hour of the morning?"

"I have been watching your gate for a week," Akiba said.

Suspicion chilled me. "Why?" I asked slowly. Perhaps this old Jew was in league with Simeon and Glaucus.

"I told you that a message would arrive," Akiba said. "It is in your hand."

I stared at him, then down at the missive. Shaking my head with the care I might have given a rare Myrrhenian vase, I sat down on the stool. There was more to this puzzle than I cared to decipher with my wits in such disorder. I slipped the thread of the scroll with trembling hand, making sure to keep the emperor's seal intact for my files. I read the few words it contained, and my heart contracted.

"Does it distress you?" Akiba asked gently.

"Your gift of prophecy or of spying does not fail you," I growled. "The emperor Hadrian commands me to come to Rome. Affairs of moment are afoot. He desires to speak to me on confidential matters."

"Ah!" Akiba said and was silent.

"I must go," I said.

"Yes," Akiba said. The old rabbi's eyes glowed as he said it. "You must go."

"But it is fifty days' journey! And I must go the quickest route, that by sea!"

"You are a philosopher, noble Rufus," Akiba said a little slyly. "You will endure it like a Stoic for the sake of Rome."

I was unable to reply. I glanced around me, at all that I must leave. I felt tortured. "To leave Antioch, all my possessions," I muttered.

"I will have them watched over while you are absent," Akiba said. "I am an honest man."

"You are a rascal," I replied.

"I shall get ready for our journey, sir," Ficus informed me briskly.

"No!" I cried. "I go alone! You will stay here and make sure that all remains as it is until I return!" I looked balefully at Akiba. *"Shall* I return, old man?" I asked, half-dreading his answer as Ficus disappointedly saluted and went out.

He nodded, and such was my faith in his divining powers that I actually felt comforted. I stood erect again despite the pains in my head. "I dreamed of Simeon last night," I said with difficulty. "Here in Antioch."

"It was only a dream, indeed," Akiba said.

I did not press him further. My thoughts were already winging toward the city of Rome, now so near.

"I am reminded of the remark of the great Marcus Porcius Cato," I said bitterly. "He declared that he regretted only three things in his life. That he told a woman a secret, that he passed a day without having made his will—and that he had gone by water when he might have gone by land."

Akiba made no answer, walking slowly toward the bright eastern window. I stretched and rose, my mind turning again to my dream. My head had hardened, my thoughts were sharp; I knew that what I had seen was nightmare. I began to laugh, but it choked off in my throat as I saw Akiba staring at the mosaic floor of turquoise and white. I came to his side, already envisioning what he saw. Before us, from my couch to the window, led a double row of muddy sandal-prints.

CHAPTER 15

It was my good fortune that en route to Rome, the ship hugging the coast of Greece, we put in at Nicopolis at Epirus. A contrary wind sprang up the next morning. It was impossible to proceed. We went ashore and, like a divine remembrance, I thought of Epictetus, the slave, my former teacher. He had been exiled to this very city and I, excited as a youth, hurried off to the marketplace where I knew I should find him.

He was there, leaning against a pillar of the portico, an assemblage of yokels about him, dropping golden words like coins at their uncomprehending feet. I thrust them away and greeted him, sinking to a seat at his side. He threw me a quick glance, composing the surprise and pleasure that crossed his face. We exchanged rather formal greetings and, after a time, I asked him why he did not return to Rome—since the decrees of Domitian had long since been annulled.

"I am old," he said in the dry irritated fashion I remembered and loved, "and here I must stay until I am summoned —although the baths are dreadful, the food atrocious, and the citizens stupid. Yet I have a certain love for wherever I am."

"How so?"

"Education is no more than learning to frame one's will in accordance with events. When I am alone, I call it peace and freedom, and I am equal to the gods. When others are around me, I pretend it is a high festival and conduct myself accordingly."

"You have been here many years, and still they do not seem to appreciate you."

"No great thing comes suddenly into being," returned Epictetus sardonically, "any more than a cluster of grapes or a fig. If you ask me for a fig now, I shall say it needs time. Let it flower, let it put forth its fruit, and then ripen. Would you gather the fruit of men so soon and so easily? I tell you, you cannot expect it!"

"You must be lonely," I protested.

"What else can a lame old man do, such as I am, but praise the gods and wait for my end? If I were a nightingale or a swan, I would do as they do; but as I am a man, this is my duty. I invite you to join me."

"I regret that I must obey the command of the emperor and proceed to Rome," I said sincerely. "But I shall return, old friend."

"The emperor? His command? You will find only sorrow at the court. Remember, it is among rich men and emperors that tragedies find room; no poor man fills a part in a tragedy except as part of the chorus. Beware!"

I said nothing. Epictetus, his hair gray and thin, his crippled body more wasted than I recalled, looked at me with his sparkling, inquisitive eyes. "Do you recollect when we spoke

239

to each other in the Forum of Augustus?" he asked me. "About things of life and death?"

"Yes."

"What did I say about prison and exile and bonds and death and dishonor?"

"That they were of no account."

"And you agreed?"

"Yes."

"Has your opinion changed?"

"No."

"Have you changed?"

"No."

"Repeat that old lesson. What things are of no account?"

"Those that are outside the will's control."

"Go on."

"These things concern me not at all."

"What things do concern you, then, dear Rufus?"

"A rightly directed will and the faculty of dealing justly with the impressions of the world."

"And what is the end which you seek?"

I choked and managed to stammer: "To follow you."

Epictetus nodded. His eyes veiled. He looked aside. "Do you still say that?" he asked gently.

"Yes, the same now as before!"

"Go on, then, to the emperor; go in confidence, and remember these things."

"But you, Epictetus," I exclaimed, "you cannot remain here. Come, take ship with me and return to Rome!"

"No," he said slowly, "I yearn to go, but I have not yet got my own principles by heart. I have not enough confidence in what I have learned and taught. I fear my own weaknesses. I would go, but I must show myself the sinews of a true philosopher first."

"You will die here, beloved teacher!"

Epictetus looked directly at me. He nodded. "That is true," he said calmly, "I feel it in my soul. But I know that all things are either good, bad, or of no account. All that lies between good and bad—such as wealth, health, life, death, pleasure, pain—these are not worth attention. I have refused to be evil, I have tried to be good; at all costs, I must not be indifferent."

"You talk nonsense," I said.

Epictetus roused himself angrily. "Man," he replied, "you, in your doubtless fine house in the East, have a boxing match with your servant Ficus! You turn the place upside down and disturb the neighbors who dare not complain—and you, a vulgar official, travel here and sit down with a solemn air like a wise man and criticize what I say! You try to disturb me, upset my thoughts—and expect me not to complain!"

"I am sorry," I managed to say.

Epictetus subsided. He stared off into the blue waters of the bay. "Rufus, I am a man who is returning to his own country. I stay at a wretched inn, but I cannot find gold enough to buy my way to another. But I am not traveling to this inn of Nicopolis—I travel through it. I shall return to my own country in a few years."

He closed his lips and, as was his stubborn custom, refused to say another word, even of farewell. At length I rose and left him. I sailed upon the next dawn—never to see him again. I was reassured by what I thought was a half-promise to come back to Rome, but now that I am old, I know too well what Epictetus meant as I approach my own eternal country.

Et haec quidem hactenus, enough on this score. My interview with Epictetus roused a vague melancholy in me for the rest of my trip. My feelings became intensified inside the gates of Rome. I knew that those beyond our borders thought it to be the mistress-city of the world; but I saw those within eating out her vitals as the fox did to the Spartan boy.

Its citizens no longer think of the wolf-mother who suckled them. They seem to have sunk into luxury, vice, and wantonness, rolling in their riches as dogs do in vomit. Boasting, it appears, is our national habit. Not satisfied with immense riches, the Romans spend hours talking to each other of vast crop yields, of the extent of their fields, of their houses in the country and city, counting a thousand of their slaves upon each finger. Families of the greatest names—which time has impoverished—wait eagerly upon the rich freedmen in expectation of favors. They submit to being counted up by the great man like a herd of cattle, puffing him up with flattery like a poisoned frog. But the chosen guests of such houses are professional gamblers, wild-talking astrologers, slaves who pretend to secret information, hired charioteers, actors, profligates of every sort.

How has this happened? The answer, of course, is that the days which used to be devoted to martial exercises, philosophy, deliberation upon the law, respect for custom and one's elders, have fallen off into the rattle of gambling, plinking of lyres,

241

and tootling of flutes; into the drunken shouts of feasting and orgies before foreign gods. The actor has fared better than the man of letters, the orator is replaced by the comic, the libraries are closed.

As for the rabble of the poor, their condition and their actions are equally revolting. Some spend their nights in wine-shops, others lurk beneath the street awnings ready to kill or maim anyone for a few sesterces; they quarrel or make love without the slightest shame. Their chief amusement is to spend all day in the circus—whether anything is going on or not—eating and sleeping and fornicating in their seats. Their greatest delight is to examine and comment upon the charioteers and their teams with hoots or applause.

I say all this with shame and regret. But I was not the only one of such an opinion. After a few days in Rome—having announced my arrival to the palace and being told to await the emperor's pleasure—I made it a point to seek out Annius Verus, my former comrade-in-arms and commander of my old century in the days of Trajan. I found his modest house, old but well furnished, near the Circus Maximus. He was delighted to welcome me. One afternoon at the sixth hour, when we had finished our collation, we sat drinking in sweet silence. When it was abruptly broken by the distant roar of the crowds at the weekly gladiatorial shows, I pushed back my cup in disgust.

"Annius," I said, "I have resolved at this moment never to return to this city. Yet once it was the center of the world for me."

"I understand," the retired old soldier said sadly.

"My contempt is so great, it sickens my soul. It is impossible for me to express my disdain of these people who dare call themselves Romans."

"I share your feelings," he said bitterly.

"Come back with me to the East, to the provinces."

He shook his head. "I have taken to writing history in the school of the eminent Tacitus," he said. "He knows little of military theory. I have agreed to explain it to him, in exchange for his tutoring."

I nodded. "I realize what you do is needed," I told him.

"If I do not, no one will ever be able to imagine what gave Rome the world."

"I agree. You must record what has happened, what truly made us great."

242

The balding, thoughtful man, with his ridiculous festal wreath on his head, sighed. "Valor and skill, yes," he said, "but also the rare, almost incredible, joining of goodness and luck."

"I am heartily in accord."

"For many years, as we know, Rome was the queen of the earth. But gradually the virtues of her sons declined. Now Rome is degraded by her noblest families."

"Vanity is the source," I said. "Today I actually met a man in the Forum who gave his name as Marcus Maecius Maemmius Furius Balburius Caecilianus Placidus."

"As soon as these people have bathed and had their hides scraped and perfumed, they put on, first of all, their rings as their ornaments of power; then they have the slaves bring them a whole wardrobe, such as a dozen senators might have, to choose one garment. They do all this without changing their loud tone of voice, their haughty expression, or their dignified pose."

"Imagine being dignified while naked!"

"It is difficult, but they do it—as proud as Marcellus never was, even after the conquest of Syracuse. I must admit that sometimes these heroes of the bath perform more difficult tasks."

"Indeed!"

"Yes: they visit their estates in the country. One of whom I know sat in Tuscany by a boar snare, studying a perfumed book, and was not interrupted once while his slaves captured three."

"He took the credit?"

"Certainly. What else did you expect? On hot days, of course, they sail in their painted galleys from the Lucrine lake to that of Avernus; or they post down the coasts of Puteoli and Cayeta to their elegant villas there."

"Comparing their trips to those of Caesar and Alexander!"

"Without jest, this is so. But they are far more careful. Abhorring sweat or blood, they also resent a fly settling on the silken folds of their parasols. They complain about hardship, if a single sunbeam lights upon their skin. They cry out that they wish they were born in Cimmerian darkness so as to protect the pearly substance of their flesh!"

"Nor do they go alone—as I observe, at least."

"Never. They advance like an army. Whole regiments of the household march with them. Just as cavalry and infantry, heavy and light-armed troops used to march with us, so are their slaves and eunuchs marshaled by their servants. The domestic officers bear a rod modeled after that of the fasces, as a mark of authority, and ride herd upon the people at the outskirts of the cloud of dust they raise. Not a trip is taken if the wind is not right, for fear dust should invade their master's carriage."

"I was a suitor to the wishes of such long ago. Once I served for money in such disgraceful circumstances, but the noble Trajan, bless his memory, set me free."

"Let us talk about more pleasant things," Annius said with a grimace. "Do you recall our days in Germania?"

I sighed again. "No worries, no cares, far from dancing attendance on the emperor," I said. I looked at the westering sun and reluctantly stood up. "Vale, Annius," I told him, gathering in my toga. "I am bid to a feast tonight. I must be off to the baths, dine, and see the great Hadrian after."

Annius rose with me. His face cracked into a grin. " 'Great Hadrian,' " he repeated softly. "We knew him when we called him other names, did we not?"

"Yes," I said.

There were giblets of geese, necks of wild boars, thighs of turtledoves. There was suave wine from the Ligurian rocks, smoky wine from the fields of Massilia. Mullet, capers and onions, bacon, pilchards and tunny, lettuces and sharp and smooth sauces; breast of sow, chine of pork, woodcocks, lampreys, whole pikes, chickens, and wood pigeons. There was ancient Falernian and snow to cool it. Robes of purple, silk cushions, servants with toothpicks and red feathers for vomiting, concubines waving huge white fans for coolness and youngsters to scare off the flies with a branch of myrtle—even slaves to massage our limbs while we ate.

I was halfway through the feast, not yet drunk enough to enjoy myself and shut out the sights of the debauch when I seemed to recognize a dimly familiar face. It was that of a woman of decayed beauty, lying opposite me on a richly broidered coach.

Her face shone, whitened with clay, raddled with rouge. Her body appeared so heavy that it almost escaped her control in quivering flesh. She smiled at me. I shuddered, but managed a smile in return. "You pretend you don't know me, Rufus Teneius," she said in a hoarse voice, thrusting upward at the monstrous peak of her red-dyed hair.

"I have not had the honor," I said.

244

"But you have," she tittered.

"My memory is not what it was," I stammered.

"It was such a long time ago, wasn't it?" Her face shifted, falling into deep lines, her faded eyes becoming intent. "Tell me, is he all right?" she said in a low tone.

Dumbfounded, I had no answer. Then, as I stared at her, I recognized, behind the caked paint, one I had known long before.

"Domitilla!" I cried. She nodded, smiled coquettishly, and ate a handful of olives with a flourish of a fat arm. "Yes," she said, simpering. "Do you still adore me, darling boy?" She spat out the pits, one by one.

My astounded expression answered for me. She did not wait for an answer but leaned forward once again. "Simeon," she said, "is he all right? Is he alive?"

"Yes," I managed to say. "He was taken to Judea by Akiba, and he is very well."

"Akiba?"

"You permitted it."

"Oh," she said vaguely, "the old Jew."

"But you are a Jewess yourself, Domitilla."

She shrugged. "So many religions, so many things to believe in," she replied. "It is easier to believe in nothing at all—nothing at all."

"He is a fine youth," I said with emphasis. Not seeming to hear me, she looked away with calculating appreciation at the jugglers. "A handsome boy," she said, indicating one with her heavily jeweled finger. "The one with the wonderful back muscles."

"Have you come to Rome to stay?" I asked her painfully.

"That adorable Trajan," she trilled, "he forgave us whatever we did. And Hadrian has approved all. Yes, in Rome to stay! All is forgiven, all is wonderful!"

"You will go to Judea to see Simeon?"

She glared at me, as if I had insulted her. "If he is doing well, that is enough, he has his life to live, I live my own."

Her face shifted in its expression; cunningly, she said: "Is he a handsome boy?"

For a moment I did not reply. Then I said slowly: "No, Domitilla, he is deformed, a very ugly child."

Her interest evaporated at my lie. "I always supposed so," she said. "It makes no difference. He must have resembled his father." She shook her glittering-ringed finger at me.

"Not you, not you, Rufus," she giggled. "We must renew

245

old acquaintanceship tonight, eh? Will you be my escort, ride with me in my litter?"

I rose so quickly that I nearly overturned my couch. "The lovely Domitilla will forgive me," I said rapidly, "but I have another engagement."

She sighed gustily, belching at the thought. "It makes no difference," she said. "You have lost much of your charm, you know. There are others, I suppose, for whom the niece of an emperor is good enough. And I am rich, Rufus," she added challengingly. "All my estates have been restored, including that famous villa you know so well outside Rome."

I bowed, making a sign of farewell. "You will forgive me, Domitilla," I said blindly, "I must take my leave."

I never saw Simeon's mother, my own lost love, again. I heard somewhere she had died of excesses: of young stallions from the street mounting her, of her gourmandizing, of drink and pleasure, sated unto death. That evening, as I escaped into the street, I felt as if I had avoided the embrace of a female horror, a Jezebel to the Jews, Poppaea without beauty to the Romans. Never did I think of the mother of Simeon again without shame to myself and honor to my son.

Late that night I was permitted to have my audience with Hadrian. He welcomed me in the same tablinium where I had bent the knee as a young soldier to Domitian; but this time the emperor himself descended and embraced me. He showed me to a seat below him on the dais and waved his hand. "Is this not better than before?" he demanded.

I gazed about me. The black statues had been removed, replaced by busts of soft white; the colors were not as garish, though the marbles were as polished. "Much better, Sire," I admitted.

"I am almost as newly arrived in Rome as yourself," Hadrian said to me. "I greet you as an old comrade. We shall have some pleasure together." He snapped his fingers and gave whispered instructions to the guard. "We shall have ordering of the court," he advised me. "Trajan has been gone for so long—and I on my tour of the East—that the members of the imperial household have become undisciplined. We know the cure for that, eh?"

I bowed my head in assent. As I did, a tall, thin man came hesitantly into the room. He bowed and fell to his knees. I was amazed at the richness of his attire, woven with gold and crusted with jewels. I turned to Hadrian in surprise. The

246

emperor gave me the wry enigmatic look I remembered so well.

"I sent for the court barber," he said.

"Surely this must be one of the great officers of the empire," I said.

The newcomer waddled forward on his knees—not without some difficulty in his armorlike metal-embroidered robe. "O great magnificence," he began. Hadrian held up his hand. "Merely call me 'emperor,' " he murmured ironically.

"O emperor," persisted the barber, "I am only a lowly shearer of hair."

"But you carry in your dress the veritable ransom of a king."

"One must dress properly before Your Highness," replied the barber with a tone of humble reproach. Hadrian set his chin on his fist and stared at the man. He made an abrupt gesture. "Rise," he said. The barber managed to stand erect.

"Tell me," Hadrian requested, "what does your profession gain you?"

"Twenty loaves of bread a day for myself and the same in stale loaves for my stable," the barber said hesitantly.

"Is that all?"

"There is also my salary."

"It is a good one, is it not?"

"Yes," said the barber in a low voice.

"It is as much as an ancient Roman might earn in a whole year?"

"I am not acquainted with history, mighty one."

"Tell me of the rich presents and rights of court that you possess and sell to others," Hadrian commanded him.

"It would take so long and the time of the throne is so precious," faltered the barber.

Hadrian's face hardened. The barber saw the change of expression. He sank again to his knees in fear.

"Get up, get up," Hadrian told him contemptuously, as if he were speaking to a horse that had fallen on its knees. "You shall not shear me tonight but I shall shear you and all others like you tomorrow and all days thereafter."

He waved his hand. The barber, his garments rustling and rattling about him, backed out of the room, his face a mask of gray fear. As the golden doors closed behind him, Hadrian turned to me. "Rufus," he said, "you will issue an order for all attendants of this sort, that minister to the vanity of men, to be dismissed. I shall sign it."

247

"All?"

"Every one of them. Cooks, valets, attendants, everyone. Their perquisites and salaries are stopped from this moment. They are free to go where they wish."

I hesitated; the emperor pounced on me. "What are your thoughts?" he demanded.

"Perhaps, Sire, this is not wise," I said humbly.

"What better way to convince these lackeys in the palace that they have a new master? How else break them to their knees but by hamstringing them? News of this will spread everywhere, and it will make them fear my power as nothing else might do. Rufus, you must strike nearest a man's heart, if you would wound him the sorest!"

I remonstrated as best I could with him but, as in all such cases, Hadrian's mind was made up. I pointed out that it was possibly not wise to cause the murmuring that would result; inferiors were expert at spreading gossip and malicious rumor. Their dismissal might result in all sorts of plots. But Hadrian would not discuss his order further with me. I transmitted instructions for a secretary to the tribune at the door.

To my surprise, the soldier broke into a wide grin. "Praise the gods," he muttered under his breath, "at last we have an emperor worthy to succeed the divine Trajan!" Then I realized that Hadrian's instinct for power had been right.

When I returned to the throne room, Hadrian lay sprawled out on a couch, sunk deep in thought. He beckoned me to him. "We have a problem, Rufus," he said, "and it is fitting that we should talk about it."

"Yes, Sire."

"Come, speak to me like a friend. I need advice, not compliments."

"What is it?"

"Good Rufus, I am a stranger in this supreme place. I feel as if I were a foreigner, that I have no right here, that my uncle Trajan has taken all the glory long ago. But as long as I am here, I am free to do what I wish."

"What is that?" I inquired cautiously.

Hadrian stood up. His eyes shone. "I shall bring back the true glory of Rome!"

"Without a doubt, Sire," I said respectfully. "But you must realize that such has been the dream of many before you."

"None have had my power or my will," Hadrian said. "Do you believe any would dare resist me?"

"None, Sire," I replied submissively. Hadrian rose from the

248

couch. He commenced to pace the marble floor nervously before the impassive guards. His normally pale face flushed with a vision I could not share. I was amazed at the change in this man that I thought I had known, obsessed as he was with a strange ideal.

"The others," he said intensely, "did not start at the root. The roots of a tree must be healthy before the fruit is good."

"But how will you cure the root?"

"By pruning. By giving it food and water."

"I do not understand, mighty Hadrian."

"By restoring the heritage of our forefathers! It is the ancient culture of the Greeks and Trojans that we must recapture! The arts, the sciences, the literature and philosophy! Rome should not depend on her armies alone but on her greatness of mind!"

I tried to speak to him with all deference, but he went on in an incoherent torrent of explanations and plans. My effort was like trying to stem a flood with a child's handful of mud.

Afterward, I grew to understand that, from the first days of his youth, this Spanish Roman had been inclined toward the worship of the oldest and most beautiful. He adored the charm and dignity of the rituals—not from piety but from his feeling for anything beautiful. The smoke of incense, the stately processions, the chantings, images and sacrifices were the breath of life for him—though they represented only one side of his strange personality which could be all things at any time to any man. His accession to the throne had made him flower like a bud in spring suddenly brought near the flame.

At the time I did not comprehend all this; I was only bewildered. I listened to him with growing confusion. "We must be bold!" he said passionately. "We must go back to our beginnings!"

"To the bold beginnings of the republic?" I inquired.

He shot me a suspicious look. "We shall be as bold as I please," he answered shortly. "There must be a source of power, and I, as emperor, must be the source."

"I agree, Sire," I said. I truly agreed with him. I began to see glimmerings of hope for the future of Rome. But the next instant he dashed all my imaginings. He smiled to himself, a small vicious smile that terrified me. "I have blocked up the Castalian spring at Daphne," he said. "I have no desire that others should use its powers. I have therefore filled it with stones and forbidden anyone to approach it."

"Is it such a dreadful place, Sire?" I asked. "It seemed pleasant enough when I viewed it."

Hadrian scowled. "I learned myself from its prophetic waters that I would rule," he informed me. "I have had mercy. If anyone else would believe the same, I should be forced to execute him."

Suddenly he smiled at me, the smile of an artful, mischievous child. "You are a scholar and philosopher, a lover of art and literature," he said. "I know this, Rufus, because I have often heard you recite verse to the divine Trajan, my uncle. Therefore, I have forgiven you all the plottings you have concocted with Quietus. I forgive you wholly—for that and another reason I shall make clear."

He continued to smile dreamily and, after a moment, beckoned. A slave approached, bowed, and set down a loose-lidded heavily gilded wood box. "Here is a gift for you," Hadrian said imperiously. "Open it. See the quality of my mercy for you." I stood stupidly, not knowing what to do. "Open it," Hadrian said again.

I pushed the lid aside; it clattered to the floor. I started, so much so that I nearly dropped the box.

"Well," Hadrian said, "what do you think of my gift?"

"I have no thoughts," I said in a low tone.

I gazed at the withered head of Lusius Quietus. It lay half buried in raw salt, withered and dark as that of a crone, the audacious eyes shut, the dark-curled hair gray at the temples, frosted with salt crystals. A bit of white vertebra shone from the neck.

"Such a gift is useful," Hadrian added. "It serves to notify you and me that Quietus is at last quiet. He will disturb us no more."

"Not unless his ghost walks, Sire," I murmured.

Hadrian laughed, a jarring mirthless sound. "The head that might have been where I am now," he replied. He paused then, said wryly: "Do you know who recommended his death to me? No less than Turbo, whom Quietus recommended to the governorship of Syria. Thus is true friendship rewarded." He looked strangely at me, and I said nothing. Hadrian, too, was silent. I pushed the box with the head of Quietus aside, not without a shudder.

Hadrian laughed again abruptly, a harsh overriding note. "I came back to Rome, not because I wanted to," he said. "I loathe this city. I shall spend as little of my time here as I may. The houses, the people, the nobles and rabble, the buildings overwhelm my spirit. I am of the East, of the delicate and wandering spirit myself. No: I came back here because of the Senate."

He paused. "Know then, Rufus," Hadrian said deliberately, "the conscript fathers are disturbed. I have imprisoned Servianus. I have also executed four men of consular rank—Quietus, Palma, Negrinius, Celsus. They conspired against me. They have suffered the penalty. A week after you sailed from Caesarea, another ship set forth carrying their four heads to me as evidence of punishment. That is why I have kept you waiting. But for you there is reserved a more dreadful retribution."

Instant visions of torture flashed through my brain. I felt as if I should sink to the floor before this inexplicable and menacing man, no longer human but a dark power. "Mercy, mercy," I muttered in a failing voice. "I had not joined them. They met a just punishment, but I am innocent."

"There shall be no mercy for you, Rufus Teneius," came the brittle voice of the emperor. "You must endure to the end. I condemn you to be governor of Judea at my pleasure."

His words brought me yet another stunning blow. I could scarcely believe what I had heard. I stood in my place, bracing my legs as if against the impact of battle. "Well," said the grim-faced Hadrian, "do you accept my mercy as punishment? Speak!"

"You overwhelm me," I stammered.

"It is an honor," he told me mockingly. "I do it to show my respect to you, both as a scholar and a soldier. It combines duty and power in the spot we both love best." His breath warmed my cheek as he spoke, so close had he come to me in his concentration. I drew back.

"You will be my servant in all things," Hadrian said in a whisper, "or I swear by the gods you shall go to the strangler this very night."

I did not immediately reply. Hadrian turned to pace away.

"Come, brave Teneius," he said softly over his shoulder. "Here is the power you have longed for. You replace the man that my divine uncle believed the most capable in the empire. You go as a soldier to the single greatest breach in the Roman wall. Think of the honor, think of the reward, think of—whatever you think of, in your grandest dreams!"

"Yes, Sire," I said stiffly.

"Do you accept?"

I straightened. My left hand went up in an awkward salute.

251

My veins flamed in defiance of the past and challenge of the future.

"Susceptio!" I cried. I used the old phrase I remembered from the dim forgotten days of Flavius Clemens. "If I may be bold, Sire," I said hesitatingly.

"Speak."

"The Jews have already come to me and declared their intentions of peace with Rome."

"Good."

"They have asked me to inquire with all possible submission if the pledge of the divine Trajan to rebuild their Temple will be confirmed."

Hadrian smiled. "Tell them," he said slowly, as if to make sure I missed no syllable, "that their new emperor has his own plans for their Temple." He paused, his fingers to his lips. "See to it, Rufus," he said, "that you examine the activities of one Simeon in Judea. My informers—whose ways, doubtless, you know—have warned me that he moves among the people to speak against the throne. With the speech of the Jews and the manners of a Roman: do not fail to mark him."

Hadrian waved me away with the gesture of dead Trajan. I bowed and left the tablinium.

But on my way to my hired quarters on the Via Janiculum, my head buzzed with conjecture and forebodings. Had Hadrian given me this office as an honor, to show his mercy and respect, as he said? Or had he given it to me out of the depths of some dark, secret, and subtle revenge?

CHAPTER 16

I rose at dawn after a night of dream-filled restless sleep. By daylight I was strolling the narrow streets of Rome. Past the entrance of the Suburra hung with the bloodstained whips of the torturers, making my way between the sheds of the cobblers and the barbers, I wandered to the Argiletum: there, opposite Caesar's Forum, I inspected the pillars covered with the titles of the books inside but found none I wanted to buy. I strayed by the temple of Castor, near that of ancient Vesta, and the majestic buildings on the sacred hill of the Palatine adorned with the great gilded statues of many emperors—thinking of Hadrian and his ambitions. I looked once again on the sun-rayed sculptures of the Colosseum, turning by the temple of Bacchus with its painted pictures of the wild Corybantes, hardly seeing what was in my way, jostled by the growing crowds.

A melancholy took me. Suddenly I longed for old sights and savors; I determined to find the places I had known in Rome. But I was disappointed. My old chambers by the Tiber had been torn down, a new wall of peperino concrete erected; the mansions of my friends along the fringe of the Capitoline were inhabited by strangers; even the house of Josephus was empty, "for rent to a noble tenant." I had an impulse to visit the old villa of Flavius Clemens in the hills, but I quelled it for fear of what I might find. By the end of that long afternoon, with my shadow at my feet in the Forum, I knew that it had been nearly twenty years since I stood here—and that part of my life had passed. In my soul I lifted a libation to what had gone and blessed it and abandoned it forever.

On my way back to the inn, I thought more of the rise of Hadrian, less of the duty he had assigned me. I wondered what his intentions were, what mask he wore that suited his purpose. Young—only forty-two years old—he had owed his whole career to Trajan, yet now he was about to turn his back upon his benefactor. I knew he had been educated by Greek tutors and that he had shared only Trajan's joy in the chase. Most significant was the fact that he had been made a high priest of the Greek colleges of mystery and an honorary archon of Athens—the only Roman of our time who enjoyed such distinction. I knew that the power to topple the Roman world was in the hands of Hadrian. I knew now that he would use it. I knew his lever would be Greek.

I have never had much use for the Greeks except perhaps for their remarkable language and literature. Whatever they may have been in the past, they are cowards in war, sharpers in the markets, snobs in society, disobedient as slaves, and thieves everywhere. They are a people with an eye neither for posterity nor for others. They are hopelessly aimless, always with an eye cocked for their own well-being.

We Romans have always had in view the greater glory of the state, of our race, of our law and possessions in the world that is. The Jews, at least, have a pious passion for their own

Law and their World-to-Come. But the Greeks are impossible.

What they care about are words, not actions; ideas, not facts; instead of common sense, the useless and impractical. Romans have always been in favor of what we can see and touch and feel; we would rather strike than refrain, die in action than live in peace. The Greeks are enamored of their "leisure" which, to them, is tossing ideas back and forth like balls of feathers. They regard it as a serious occupation, yet little is ever accomplished. I imagine it may leave a residue of conviction in the mind, but of this we know nothing. Their philosophies, such as that of Epictetus, are comforting because they balance thought so evenly, but this is a juggler's trick. I comprehend this as useful—like the game of cottabos, throwing lees of wine into a bronze bowl until it rings again—to rid one's self of heavy time. This is good, often necessary, to a man of cares and responsibility, but hardly essential to a Roman.

I hoped that the empire of the Romans would prosper during the rest of Hadrian's reign. I repeated the ancient wish aloud:

> *"Gods, give us good! Whether we pray*
> *With the worst or the best wit;*
> *And deliver us from the evil day—*
> *Even if we blessed it."*

There I dismissed such vaporings. I was anxious to leave Rome, even eager to get back to the shining cities and clear air of the East. Two days before me, I sent a tabellarius, a special speedy slave-messenger, to order Ficus to abandon the Antioch residence and to reoccupy our old house in Caesarea. I made my formal farewell call to Hadrian's palace and prepared my travel kit. The trip would be long and possibly arduous (despite my first-class transportation permit), but anything would be better than another sea voyage.

Taking a two-wheeled cisium that could make speed of more than six miles an hour—with changes of horses, of course—I fled southward by imperial post along the Via Appia back to Brindisium in less than eight days. We Romans have always loved the brisk routine of traveling, of seeing new places. I rejoiced in the sight of the golden campagna, the purpling mountains, and the white horses of the sea along the coast. I was not as happy to sail over to Apollonia on the shores of Macedonia, but to my surprise the crossing was smooth and easy. I took the route northward in a covered four-wheeled raedum, coming at last to the fork that turned eastward on the endless Via Egnatia which swung across the whole wild country to the sunrise. Heraclea, Pella, Thessalonica, I took with the rattle of hoofs and the rumble of iron tires, hiring fresh equipage outside the gates of the cities, sleeping in the upper chambers of the public inns above the snorting and thumping of the horses in the stables below. Most pleasant of all was the road to Amphipolis and on across the river Nestus, its magnificent scenery of mountains and forests bringing me happy memories of the days of my youth in Germany. I heaved many sighs at my thoughts; for now I was no longer a youth with fire in my veins and spring in my step. I was a middle-aged man of fifty-one. Yet I had achieved the eminence I had once dreamed of, despite my fading crown of hair and gray temples.

It remained only to cross the Strait and head southward to Antioch along the old familiar roads. But it was more than two months before I arrived at Caesarea from Rome. To my delight I discovered that the tabellarius had arrived two weeks before and that Ficus had renewed my residence as it had been. He welcomed me home with sniffles of joy. The honest fellow's blubbery face quivered and his eyes shone with tears to see me returned safely. For days he had been tramping back and forth through the city preparing all for my pleasure and direction; it was pleasant to realize that now both the troops and civic direction lay under my hand.

I embraced Ficus with my single arm and ordered my bath made ready. "Afterward," I said to him, "I wish to speak to Akiba. Have a messenger prepare to leave this very night for Lydda."

To my astonishment, Ficus replied: "Sir, that will not be necessary."

"It is my command!"

"Certainly, but it is unnecessary. The Jew is in Caesarea, waiting for your summons."

Taken aback, I considered. I frowned as I thought quickly, sorting out the reasons that Akiba might have for being in the city. "In that case," I said craftily, "let him wait until tomorrow morning."

"Yes, sir," Ficus said stolidly. "At what time shall you receive him?"

"Let the salutatio be at the second hour."

255

I had intended to inform him of my appointment as governor, but I sealed my lips. There would be time enough after I had told Akiba the news.

Refreshed and soothed by my return, I retired early, and before the sun had done more than redden the eastern mountains I stood to receive Akiba in the lamplight of the atrium. The old man in his queer dark robe bowed.

"Akiba," I said cheerfully, without preamble, "as the Christians say, you look upon a man reborn. As the Greeks say, *Evoe!*"

"I know," Akiba said.

I bent my stare upon him, my glow quenched. "Do you indeed?" I asked coldly.

"Yes."

"Then perhaps you can tell me what I refer to?"

"You are about to inform me of the good news," Akiba returned. "That the emperor Hadrian has appointed you governor of Judea."

I swallowed hard, striving to keep my face from revealing my amazement. "Has the news come to Caesarea so quickly?" I demanded.

"It has," replied the imperturbable Akiba, "but I had guessed it before."

"What?"

"I hoped it, rather."

"What is this riddle?" I inquired testily.

"When the great Hadrian was here last fall, he sent secret messengers to the Jewish leaders, requesting us to submit the names of those Romans who might be acceptable to the Jews as governor."

"He did?" I said stupidly.

"I suggested you and the others agreed. I am glad that the emperor agreed."

"So," I said angrily, "now you will claim that I owe my office to you!"

Akiba spread his hands placatingly. "Never, noble Rufus," he said emphatically. "I claim only that I brought your overlooked merits to the attention of the throne."

"However you may think," I interrupted, "I shall rule for the good of Rome, not for the benefit of the Jews."

"I ask no more," Akiba said.

Again he had outwitted me. "Why not?" I asked.

"Because the welfare of the Jews is one with the welfare of Rome, is it not?"

"Akiba," I said, surrendering, "enough of this kind of talk. I commanded you here to consult with you, on business of state."

"I am your servant, friend Rufus."

I bit my lip. "Then I want to talk to Simeon," I said abruptly.

Akiba lifted his head, his eyes guarded. "May I ask why?" he said with exquisite courtesy.

"Because the emperor has heard his name in faraway Rome. Because he believes Simeon may be dangerous to the state."

Akiba considered, his expressive features immobile. "I think, noble Rufus," he said, "that this rumor is false."

"So do I."

"But only false at this time," Akiba said slowly. "Eventually the emperor's information may be more correct than our belief in Simeon."

"What is our belief in him?" I asked sarcastically.

"That he is a rash boy, but not a madman."

"What do you mean?"

"The old embers from the ruin of the Temple have not cooled," Akiba said. "A new generation, not knowing the power and ruthlessness of Rome, has arisen. They burn for freedom and revenge."

"What greater freedom could the Jews have?"

"To be ruled by God alone," Akiba said simply.

I nodded, leading him on. "Is this your own opinion, Akiba?" I asked carelessly.

Akiba threw his head back. For the first time, I saw the pain in his eyes and the lines of suffering in his face. "No," he said, his voice trembling, "it is not my belief. And I have suffered because I have said so in the synagogues and on the streets. My friends have left me, one by one, with pity or with curses. Ben Zoma, Johanan ben Nuri, Ben Azzai, Simeon ben Nannos, Simeon ben Yohai—Meir, Jose, and Judah—my disciples and followers unto this moment, all have abandoned me. I alone stand as the mediator between Rome and the Jews because I stand for peace."

"I see," I said cautiously. "What, then, is your thought?"

"I say that there is no distress of a people, only of individuals—and that I look about me and see all prospering under the rule of Rome. There is no need for revenge or killing."

"But the others?"

"They dream of the days of David and Solomon. They say

257

that in times to come there may be a war of duty and that the bridegroom must leave his bride."

"And you?" I asked.

"They have listened to me for many years. Not because I am wise; there are many wiser. Not because of my wealth; there are many wealthier. Not because they know me; in the south, I have many friends but who knows me in fiery Galilee? No: they respect my age, my love of the Torah. And now they listen to me no more."

I strode about the chamber, deep in thought. "And your association with me does little to aid you," I said.

"Very little," assented Akiba.

"And mine with you does not aid me with the Romans," I pointed out. "But tell me, does Simeon join with these fools?"

"No," Akiba replied promptly. "He holds aloof from all, myself included. But he is high in their councils."

"I must see him," I said. "Bring him to me."

Akiba looked steadily at me. "You will not scourge or imprison him?" he asked.

"I make no promises," I said impatiently. "I am governor of this province and I pledge my justice to no one. But if you do not bring him, I shall send soldiers and seek him out."

Akiba bowed his head in understanding. "I shall bring him," he said, "but remember what lies between him and you, between you and myself. Do not dishonor your power."

He turned away, but I halted him with a malicious question. "Akiba," I said, "are you not considered a traitor to your people?"

"I stand with the commandments of Moses, blessed be he," Akiba said gravely. "No man who brings men together for the sake of peace is a traitor to God. He who prevents war prevents murder."

Before I could formulate an answer to this clear reproof, Akiba had left me.

Two days later he was ushered in again by Ficus. My orderly patted his companion on the shoulder and grinned as he went out. I sat before my two visitors and looked at them with all the sternness I could command. Simeon was taller than I remembered in my dream-memory: tanned, lean, his hair bleached by the sun. There was confidence in his bearing and an expression on his face I could not define: perhaps arrogance, perhaps nobility. He bowed his head to me with a solemn greeting. I addressed him directly.

258

"Simeon," I said, "I sit here today as a stranger. As no one but the governor of Judea, the voice of Rome."

"I understand," he said quietly.

"It has come to my ears that you intend to rise against Rome," I said. "The emperor himself has spoken of it to me."

Simeon considered me, a faint smile on his face. "When?" he said at last.

"Am I privy to your mad schemes?" I demanded irascibly.

"No," Simeon said. "But make your spirit easy. The Jews are quiet—and waiting."

"Then I have your pledge?"

"Noble Rufus," Simeon said courteously, "I can only swear that I am here and listening. God gives the pledge."

"Do you set yourself against Rome?" I said tightly.

"He sets himself against no one," Akiba said hastily.

"And I yield to no one," Simeon added. My admiration for him overcome my anger; I sank back against my seat. "You are young," I told him, "and you do not know that everyone must yield. The people to their governor, the governor to the throne—even the emperor to the gods."

"To God," Simeon said mysteriously. I went on, disregarding what he had said: "Simeon, the Jews are caught in Judea like a nut in a cracker. I have but to raise my hand and legions will come up from Egypt in the south and down from Dacia in the north."

Simeon shook his mane of hair slightly. "I have given up thoughts of war," he told me, "I meditate upon God."

"That is safest," I said with some relief.

Simeon's eyes flashed. He straightened and seemed to grow in size. A despairing gesture from Akiba had no effect.

"But if the Jews were so minded," he said loudly, "they would not disgrace themselves."

"But where is the mind?" I asked sardonically. "Where are the weapons?"

"It is possible they may appear."

"You may persuade each other and steal from still others," I said, "but who will organize your ambitions?"

"God will raise up a man."

"Yourself, perhaps?" I inquired.

"I have no ambitions," Simeon said colorlessly. I waited and determined to test him further to make sure in my own mind.

"Suppose I imprison you?" I said.

Simeon stiffened, and the muscles bulged in his shoulders as if he already resisted the hands of jailers. "I am in your power," he replied in a strained voice, "but I came here trusting to your word and that of Akiba."

"I gave no word," I said.

"But I did," Akiba broke in. His tone was almost defiant. I nodded irritably; Akiba had caught me out. The old man went on. "Josephus once led the Jews against Vespasian and Titus, yet became a friend of Rome."

"If he had remained with us, we would have conquered," Simeon broke in. "As it was, the whole of your empire tottered."

I sprang to my feet, impatient, trembling with an emotion I did not understand. "Why do you speak like a Jew?" I cried. "Why?"

"How else should I speak?" Simeon said tranquilly.

I closed my lips and turned away. There was, I thought, something noble and fearless about this youth—he was, as I knew very well, no more than twenty-six. I was on the point of acknowledging him for my love-child, this time publicly, cleansing him at once from his Jewishness. But I restrained myself and said in a gentler tone: "Then I may send a tabellarius to the emperor and tell him that his fears are groundless and that Judea will remain peaceful?"

"If you wish."

"Will I be writing truth?"

"At this moment, yes; but who knows what will come?"

"You conceal your thoughts from me," I said impatiently.

"Yes," Simeon said.

I contained myself. "Very well," I said, "think what you please but do nothing overt against Rome. See to it."

"There is a time for everything under the sun," he said, quoting a Jewish work.

"Is there a time to destroy yourselves?" I asked shrewdly. "Akiba does not think so."

"Akiba is old and wise," Simeon said, unperturbed. "I am young and foolish."

"A fool and victory are far apart."

Simeon spoke with a quick gust of passion. "War is a circle," he said, "and the farther apart the events are at the beginning, the nearer they come at the end."

"It is useless to argue this way," I said shortly. "I place you under probation. I shall keep watch upon your actions. If I hear news that is evil, I shall send for you again and I shall not be so lenient. Go."

Simeon wheeled and strode out. Ficus escorted him, and I

could swear, to my annoyance, he had a look of admiration on his frog-face for this youngster. I turned to Akiba.

"What do you make of this young man?" I demanded.

"The question is, what will God make of him?" Akiba responded.

I cried out and beat my forehead with my fist. "I come here as governor, I make a reasonable request, I expect to be obeyed!" I shouted. "What I get in return are stale quotations and the ferment from crackpots!"

Akiba shook his head and shook it again in a species of despair.

"What now?" I demanded in exasperation.

"If peace were as easy to wage as war," Akiba said in a muffled tone, "how pleasant a world this would be!"

Whatever the old man meant by that, I did not know or care. The next months, almost the next year, were consumed like papyrus in a blaze with the problems of administration. The disappearance and death of Quietus had left the civil bureaus in confusion, though the military establishment ground out its daily duties as usual. My attention was concentrated largely in the north, taking the form of almost monthly trips to Antioch to consult my superiors.

Yet despite all the press of my official business in Judea, I felt strangely isolated from the world. I had been used to the rough comradeship of the camps; now I desired a softer, gentler affection. A middle-aged, one-armed man, I had all the callow signs of a youth desiring his first love. I discovered in myself an unreasonable desire for perfumes, soft flesh, moonlight and warmth, sweet music, and dancing girls. Philosophy and meditation came to be abhorrent to me. And at each revel, disturbingly enough, I saw the face of Sarra in the darkness, hovering like a white moth above the flame of the dying lamp as I had last seen her in Lydda. Akiba, who had by now become my official advisor on things Jewish, must have sensed my loneliness, for it was he who brought about the next change in my life.

In the corner of my peristylium I had a tall screen, brought from Egypt. Its frame was of polished ebony, and the screen itself was of stretched crimson cotton interwoven with the mysterious symbols of their religion—men with the heads of dogs and hawks, triangular monuments, clumps of reed. It was, I thought when I purchased it at the marketplace in the city, an omen of good luck. Whether it was or not, you may be the judge.

One morning after a sleepless night, I came down from my upper chamber and halted, hearing the voices of a man and a woman inside the lower room. I recognized the deep tones of Akiba, and the light accents of the other were familiar, but they were speaking Hebrew. I slipped behind the screen (I had used it before for overhearing unknown visitors) and peeped through. I stifled an ejaculation: the visitor with Akiba was Sarra of whom I had dreamed only that night. She seemed taller and more lovely than I remembered her in my mind; her hands fluttered before her as she pleaded with the old man. I strained my ears, but I could understand only a phrase or two of the Jewish language.

Without warning, Akiba suddenly began to talk in Greek, and Sarra followed his example. "I would not be seen in this house," she said, "unless you had commanded me to come, Uncle."

"Why are you so recalcitrant?"

"Because I have escaped a great sin."

"What is this great sin, Sarra?" Akiba asked gently. "How have you escaped it?"

Sarra looked at him, her great eyes luminous with tears. "I cannot love the Roman," she said almost inaudibly.

A shudder ran down my body. I saw Akiba draw his white brows together. I could not see his expression, but his mouth was compressed. "Love is sacred in the eyes of God," he said. "It is no sin if love is given from the heart."

"But to love a Roman is a sin against my people," Sarra murmured.

"Who told you that?" Akiba's tone was suddenly sharp. He leaned toward her, his mood of complaisance entirely gone. "Who said that?"

"Why," Sarra faltered, "everyone says it."

"Do I? Does Rachel, blessed be she?"

"No."

"But there is a particular one? There must be one who has said it!"

Sarra was silent for a moment under the penetrating gaze of Akiba. Then she lifted her eyes to his. "Yes," she said simply, "Simeon tells me."

Akiba's brow became thunderous. "You have seen Simeon?" he demanded. I felt my muscles clenched and my body rigid in my hiding place. I wished I had never devised this plan;

yet I would not have been anywhere else in the world. Even more impatiently than Akiba, I waited for her answer.

"Yes," Sara said, "every night."

"He comes to you?"

"I don't know," Sarra returned. She commenced to weep silently. "I don't know if he comes to me or if I go to him. But every night when I fall asleep, he is there."

Akiba's gaunt figure relaxed measurably. "You dream of him, you mean?" he said in an almost kindly tone.

Sarra nodded, averting her face and dabbing at her tears.

"And Simeon tells you that it is a sin against the Jews to love this Roman?"

"Every night he says so."

"Well," Akiba said in a lightening tone, "I shall tell you every day that it is not a sin. True love is the image of God on earth. Of all His powers, praised be He, love is the greatest —as long as it is humble and selfless."

"But I am a Jewess and he is a Roman."

"Is this a gulf that is to be impassable forever?" asked Akiba in his old, kindly fashion. "Do you think our God is so selfish that He will not take Romans under his wing? The day comes, Sarra, when there shall be neither Jews nor Gentiles but one people, under the Law, across the world. The vision that Moses had on Sinai is clouded for others, but it will be clarified by time. You must explain much to Rufus about yourself and our people; more, I think, about himself."

"Forgive me," whispered Sarra. "You have so many other things to think of, Uncle."

Akiba nodded. "I have so many ideas, like bright new coins," he confessed, "but where shall I go to exchange them into the counters of common life? Be happy, my brother's daughter; you do nothing wrong and bring joy to Israel. Now go and ponder what I have said, and my blessing go with you."

Sarra rose and made an obeisance and ran off in the light, skimming way that I adored. Akiba rose slowly, his knees cracking from his long squat on the floor beside Sarra. To my surprise, he did not go; instead he yawned and flung his long arms upward. "You may come out now, Rufus," he said conversationally. "Have you heard what you wanted to hear?"

Flushed with anger at this unexpected revelation, I flung the screen down with a crash. Akiba and I confronted each other across its woven surface. "You knew I was there," I challenged him.

263

"Of course. Your bathing oil is perfumed with sandalwood, and my old nose is keen."

"You said nothing?"

"What should I have said?"

A dreadful suspicion struck me. "Perhaps all this was staged, you sly Jew," I muttered. "Perhaps Sarra scented me as well."

"No, no," Akiba said, preparing to leave. "She cannot smell. She has a gravedo, a stifling of the phlegm in the nose. If you were a sage skilled in medicine, you would have realized it from her voice." And he was gone.

I kicked the prostrate screen, then cursed, hopping on one sandaled foot and nursing my bruised toe. I shouted for Ficus to come and take the abhorred object away, to break it into bits for fuel for the baths.

Two days later, I sent Sarra a gift, a gown of curious shining stuff I had brought from Rome. Five days later, I commanded her to appear before me. I had decided to test her and myself in the crucible of common meeting.

"Come here," I said.

I saw no sign of obedience. I lazily repeated: "Come here. I command you in my official capacity as governor of Judea."

But Sarra showed no inclination to cross the peristylium to where I half-reclined on my couch. She refused even to look at me, her face downcast. She sat cross-legged on a crimson floor-cushion, her body faintly visible within the sheath of the seresian pink gown I had sent her.

I felt both amused and irritated. "Perhaps I have not given you your right name," I said. "Who is the Jewish female spirit that is surpassingly beautiful, that flies by night and drains the life out of men? I remember: it is Lilith."

Sarra turned half away from me. She gazed out of the window. She seemed intent upon the brightness of the full moon like a blown bladder on the horizon. I fell into thoughts, melancholy and soothing—of the Domitilla that had been, of the Simeon that was—gentle ghosts hovering in the clear night air but helpless to placate our emotions or change our wills.

"I saw no woman as beautiful as you in Rome," I ventured. Sarra did not reply.

"Did you see many one-armed men as handsome as I?" Again she was silent, gazing out the window.

"Come here, Lilith," I said softly, restraining myself.

She made no move. I repeated my command a fourth time. "You should not call me that," she said at last reproachfully.

"Never mind: come here."

"I am very comfortable on this cushion."

"Curse the cushion! Come here!"

Slowly she rose. She quivered as she stood. Her eyes were averted. Her feet drifted like petals across the floor, seeming to move without her will. I could not stand this slavelike acquiescence; I slapped my hand on the rest of my chair.

"No," I said quickly, "this is wrong, wrong! Return, rest where you were. One should not command such things."

"No," she said faintly. She mistook my meaning. I had meant only that such a girl could not be ordered about like a member of a legion.

"Would you always obey like that?" I asked.

"I should always obey the governor."

"Even if he were not I but another?" I cried.

She made no response, only lifting her sorrowful eyes to mine from where she sat. I bit my lip with vexation.

"You are obedient to the governor of Judea."

"Yes."

"And to the emperor over the governor?"

"I have not sworn to any of these what I have sworn in my heart to Rufus Teneius," she said in a faint voice. My own heart leaped in my bosom; I felt intoxicated.

"You would do nothing to displease the governor?" I said eagerly.

"Nothing," she said. I felt triumph, but I was baffled how to go further without commands.

"Lilith, Lilith!" I muttered. "Do you know why I call you that?"

"No. You should not; it is an evil name."

"It is because you suck out my soul."

I could have sworn a slight smile lifted her lips, but I could not be sure. She said nothing.

"If you thought," I said, "if you felt, that is, that you did not know whether or not it would displease the governor, what then?"

"I don't know," she said in a troubled voice.

O gods! With a maid from the stews, with a captive on the frontier, with a slave, with almost any other woman in the world, I should have known what to do. Stride to her, take her with my arm, bruise her against my chest, fling her on the couch and have my way with her, not forgetting a purse of

265

gold for the moment of release. Next day, such a one would come seeking to me, and I should be able to take or reject, choose or not. But with such a one as Sarra, how was a man to be known as a man and she as a woman?

"You must know something of it," I said.

She lifted that dark-haired glorious head and gazed seriously at me. "If there was any doubt in my mind, I would not do it."

"You mean if you thought it was wrong?"

"Yes."

"How do you know the difference between right and wrong? This is a philosophical question, Lilith, that has not been decided for thousands of years."

"It's only the way I feel," she said soberly, "that's all."

"Do you feel it's wrong for you to come to me?"

"Not if you command it."

There we were again at odds: the thing seemed a monstrous barrier, invisible but nonetheless towering. "You're an intolerable woman!" I shouted.

"Yes," she said, her eyes commencing to glisten.

"You are insufferable because you are a heroine, and men cannot love heroines."

"I don't understand."

I smacked my fist into my thigh, wishing that I were smacking her bottom like that of a child. "Heroines are so virtuous, so inhuman," I said fiercely, "that they only deserve to be statues of bronze or marble. They don't deserve to be loved."

"But you once told me," she said, her voice steady though a tear rolled down her cheek and another dripped from the tip of her nose, "that it was glorious to be remembered that way."

"For heroes, not heroines!"

"What about you?"

"I am a hero, yes!" I cried. "For enduring this, I deserve a statue!"

"Then everything is all right, isn't it?" she said, suddenly smiling.

I lay fast in my own snare, unable to struggle, unable to do anything but glare at her. "Is a statue better than warm flesh and blood?" I demanded.

"No, not at all," she replied, shocked.

"You're pretending you don't understand me."

"I'm stupid tonight," she said humbly, and I could see she meant it.

"No," I said after a moment in exasperation. "No, you twist

266

everything to your own purpose like Akiba. You Jews are devious and strange."

Sarra smiled. "But not so devious that we cannot be found out by a Roman," she said.

I managed to look down at my side. "Do you think me ridiculous, maimed like this?" I asked painfully.

Sarra shook her head. I was thankful she said nothing. I determined to put a more cheerful face on happenings: if I suffered, there was no reason she should suffer as well. At that moment she broke into my thought. "Tell me," she said, "about the campaign in Parthia. You must have seen many strange things."

"Nothing stranger than men and women," I returned. "I find their natures extend through all, even the vegetable creation."

"I cannot believe that," Sarra breathed, her eyes lighting with that curious illumination women have when they anticipate an untruth.

"You may believe it," I told her. "I have seen it myself. I made a singular discovery in that land. Have you heard of pearls?"

"No," she said.

"Well," I said tentatively, trying to remember what I had been told by a prisoner, "the Parthians like to adorn themselves with pearls, a certain gem grown in the sea."

"In the sea!"

"Listen. They are produced by fish with strong white shells which crawl laboriously up on the sand during nights of the full moon. They open their cold flesh to the moonlight and the drops of dew. These copulate, so to speak—forgive my plain talk, I speak as a soldier—and the shell closes. The fish then has stone children in the sea. They are round, of a milky color with a glow in certain lights and are highly valued—and the fish die when they are taken from them."

"This is wonderfully queer!"

"Strangest of all, the fish must avoid storms because it is well known, say the Parthians, that thunder frightens them so that their offspring are dissolved in their wombs. Thus pearls are so rare because thunderstorms are so common in that country."

Sarra's eyes sparkled. "And have you heard of palms?" she asked eagerly, almost mischievously.

"Palms?" I wondered. "There are a few in Rome."

"They are both male and female."

267

"You are deceiving me."

"You have eaten their children, fruit of their weddings, you must believe me. It is easy to distinguish the sexes because only the female produces honey and fruit. The she-tree needs only to be smeared with the semen of the male to have offspring. And if this does not happen, she droops her fronds and dies, and the fruit is aborted."

"But this makes them lovers," I said in amazement.

She nodded. "That they love each other is shown by the fact that the males and females lean toward each other, often interlocking their trunks, and not even gales of wind separate them. I have seen this myself. Sometimes, when the farmers do not know which tree is wed to which, they simply smear the female with her own perfumed blossoms."

"Why is that?"

"It attracts the nearest male."

"You are the wisest you have ever been, Lilith, the very wisest."

"But you wanted to talk to me about yourself," Sarra told me.

"Yes," I said. "I want to talk, but not about myself. You know that your uncle Akiba is in danger. He talks too much. He speaks for his religion, not against Rome, that I know. But there are many enemies even in his own people, high enemies. They will not hesitate to twist his words and condemn him out of his own mouth."

"What should he do?" she asked, alarmed.

"Simply keep quiet," I said.

"Never in his life has he done that," she replied. "He has always talked as much as he wanted to."

"It will be his torture and his death if he doesn't," I said.

She regarded me with horror. "You are such a powerful man," she told me, "but I do not believe you would use that power against my uncle."

"Of course not! But, you sweet young fool, I shan't be governor of Judea forever! Don't you understand that?"

"No."

"Think of it now, then," I said grumpily.

"With horror and despair."

"Your uncle, the holy rabbi Akiba, reaches for the stars. Well, he also reaches for prison."

"What can he do but what he is doing, what he loves to do, what he has taught himself to do?" she asked, the tears returning.

"Lilith," I said heavily, seating myself, "come here." The agony of temptation had been purged. I could speak to her like a child or a daughter. She came obediently, and I gestured her to sit on my knee; at the soft touch of her body, I gasped involuntarily. "Did I hurt you?" she asked solicitously, and I nodded. "It's nothing," I said, watching my hand with fascination as my mind forced it away from her, "stay where you are."

"What did you want to say?"

"The philosophers teach many things, all of them differently. I am man enough to admit I make mistakes, Hadrian is man enough to do the same. Any great man does it."

"Yes, that's right."

"But your uncle, the revered Akiba, will not admit that he might be mistaken about his so-called god!"

"How can he admit it," she said indignantly, "when he isn't mistaken? I don't want him to lie."

"I'm not saying he *is;* I say that he may be."

"But he couldn't be!"

I pushed her back and she stumbled slightly, almost falling on her way to return to her cushion. My heart beat violently as my knee lost its sweet pressure and the warmth of her thigh; but her youthful perfume remained.

"You talk like a Jewess," I said roughly.

"You talk like a Roman!" she flashed, coloring as she did.

I sighed. "We each talk the way we were born to talk," I said. "Reproaches are of little use. The Christians say that their prophet is god."

"He isn't!"

"You say that Moses is god!"

"We never said that!"

"One of you did," I replied cunningly, "and his name was Philo. You must read your philosophers more when you grow up, my dear."

"I am not a child," she said proudly. "I am a woman."

"Then prove it."

"Don't talk of love," she murmured blindly.

"Why not?"

"That is what the heterae talk of."

"It is a good word, an excellent word, abused," I said.

In a stifled voice, Sarra replied: "I am a free woman, as free as they. I may do what I wish."

"This makes no sense," I said despairingly. "Love is not words, it is deeds—like all else in the world."

269

"Must it not be told?"

"It must be expressed," I said vaguely, "like the wind, like the sea, like the moon on the hills. It is like that."

She made no response. I broke the silence roughly. "Do you want me to make love to you?"

"If you must ask," she said faintly, "you should not."

"Then I shall refrain," I said.

"I said we should not talk of love," she told me. "Let us forget either of us has spoken of it."

"That makes me a slave," I said bitterly.

Sarra smiled, her face lighting up. "How well you speak when you wish," she said.

I blinked at her. "What do you mean?"

"In saying that you are a slave to me."

"That was not at all what I meant," I told her. "I am a slave to thinking about love."

"You are contemptible!" she exclaimed.

Without another word I rose and went out of the room, despite the soft cry that followed me. My head felt as if it would burst. I could no longer endure talking to her in this mad fashion. What I wanted was—what was it indeed?

Early next morning I summoned Ficus. I ordered that Sarra should be hustled into a litter and sent on her way home south to Lydda and Akiba. It was intolerable to think of her in my house, to have undergone the frustration and longing I felt. It was worse to feel that there was no power in me to seize what I wanted; I knew that if I did it would vanish through my fingers like smoke.

The rest of that day was spent in a species of agony that nothing from books to music to business could assuage. I paced my rooms, called Ficus a dozen times to make sure Sarra had really gone and could not come to me; I could neither eat nor drink. I discovered her absence was more terrible than any punishment I could devise. At the middle of the afternoon I sent for my own litter and set out on the road to Lydda myself.

Late the next night I arrived in the city with my small escort. I saw them off to quarters and, unaccompanied even by Ficus, I went to the small synagogue near his tiny garden that I knew Akiba favored for meditation and argument. I had no sooner approached its doors than I saw him standing there to greet me, as if he expected my coming. But I had no time to

270

inquire the answer to this riddle nor to do more than exchange greetings.

"Why have you come to Lydda, noble Rufus?" Akiba asked.

I sank upon the threshold. "Dismiss the compliments," I said wearily. "I am sleepless and sick. I have come to you for advice."

"But I am not a physician."

"It is my soul that is sick."

"Ah," said Akiba and raised his expressive brows. "If it is something upon philosophy, let us talk."

"Nothing of the sort."

"If it is how to rule Judea, I have no knowledge."

"It is, as I told you, a matter of the spirit."

"I suspect," Akiba said with his annoyingly perceptive air, "that it has to do with Jews."

"In a way."

"I am glad," Akiba said with sudden seriousness, "because you said it was not a matter of the body."

I ground my teeth as Akiba went on: "It is possible that I understand my people, but never shall I understand women."

"Why do you say it is a woman?" I asked sharply.

"Because Sarra has already told me. You put her in great fear."

"No one would have known it," I grumbled.

"Why?"

"There was no need for fear," I told her uncle, "I gave her my word."

Akiba smiled slightly. "Your problem is that you have come to her uncle to ask him how to tame the spirit of his niece."

I stood up angrily. "I come to you," I sputtered, "as a friend, as a wise man, to offer me advice and nothing else."

"What else am I doing, friend Rufus?"

"I have no wish to tame her," I said, swinging away from Akiba in my restlessness, "but only to understand her. You have raised a wild, disobedient, strange girl."

"Would you have her any different?"

"No," I said, "no."

"No father raises a daughter," Akiba said gently. "He watches her in wonder. An uncle is much more helpless."

"That is no help."

"Would you make her your mistress?" Akiba asked flatly.

"Gladly," I replied. For no reason I could discern, I was on the defensive about the affair. It was ridiculous; I felt humiliated though there was nothing I could define that touched my honor.

"Romans have married the women of our people before," Akiba said quietly, "and have been proud and happy with their wives."

"Are you trying to make a good match for your niece, Akiba?" I demanded, ashamed of the blood that came to my cheeks.

"May God forbid such vanity," Akiba said. "Whatever there may be between you must be endured between you. Rachel and I have troubles of our own."

"There was none of what you call sin," I said.

"Do you not call it sin, also?"

"This is bandying words. It gives me no help."

"Then let me ask," Akiba said, "why you have not seized Sarra and taken her already?"

"What pleasure is there in forcing a woman?" I shouted.

Akiba shrugged. "It has been done by Roman soldiers occasionally before this," he said delicately. "But you are right. What pleasure is there in force of any kind?"

I planted myself before him. "Look at me, Akiba," I commanded, "I have known battle and toil and struggle since I was able to walk. I was the lowliest of the low in the empire. This head, this hand, this spirit gained me what I have today: these and the greatness of Rome. But love is different from all these. It is only pleasing when both give to each other, when both surrender to each other. In all other ways of life, there must be the victor and the vanquished. Only in love is there double victory and double defeat."

Akiba clapped his hands in wonder and joy. "If you know so much, why do you come to me?" he asked. "I am too old. I am no lover of men, as are your emperors. You cannot seduce me. Except by words, perhaps like those you have already spoken."

"Do you give me permission to seduce your niece?" I asked, my eyes bulging at the thought. "Are you so corrupt, Akiba?"

Akiba chortled. "Less loudly, if you please," he said. "I am a highly revered man, and I should not like to lose my reputation. I give you my full permission to treat Sarra as my daughter."

"You permit me? Do you use that word to me?"

"A moment ago you spoke like a lover, now you speak like a Roman. I spoke like a friend, now I shall speak like a

Jew. I permit you to do it only because you permit me to permit you."

"Forgive me, Akiba," I said. I sat down again and shook my rattling head from side to side. "I am not myself."

"I know," he said, his eyes dancing.

"I am not used to these things, the sweet emotions, the terrible emotions of love. I have read about them in the Greek, but I never before believed the verse of Sappho. I am shaken like an oak in the wind on the mountaintop. All I know are the rough, not the smooth; the things of march and war."

"You know much more. You are a man of sensitivity, of intelligence, of education—not as good as that of a rabbi, possibly, but still good."

I paid no attention to him, staring before me in utter misery. Akiba went on: "More than that, good Rufus, you are kindly and affectionate. I have long loved you. As a son, even as Simeon, my grandson. My own wife, dearest and most blessed Rachel, married me because I was kind. She took me when I was as dull and stupid as an ox. You see, women have the faculty of looking into the murky depths of the heart and finding them as clear as the springs of Jordan; we see only the shining surfaces of the mind and admire false gods."

"You are so eloquent," I mumbled sardonically. "Tell me what I am to do, what I am to say."

"Four things puzzle me, as they puzzled King Solomon," Akiba returned evasively. "The way of a snake on the ground, a ship on the sea, the way of an eagle in the air, the way of a woman with a man."

"Then all is hopeless," I said, exhausted by my own emotions.

"Not at all," Akiba said, exchanging his didactic tone for one of brisk energy. "Sarra told me herself what had happened. Why should she tell me since she knows that we are friends and that I would undoubtedly tell you?"

I stood up, staggering in the burst of illumination in my brain. It was a light I had never imagined. "She told you that because she knew you would tell me?" I stammered.

"What else?"

I grew rigid with suspicion. This meeting was going much too smoothly, as if it had been designed beforehand. I felt the jaws of a subtle Jewish trap closing about me. I glared at Akiba. "Your tongue is too glib," I accused him. "You are pretending to be what you are not. You cannot deceive me."

"I have never tried to do that," Akiba responded.

"Have you not? What of the doves and Trajan?"

"He was an emperor, and we are friends," Akiba said.

"Such words do not change the facts," I warned him. "I know that the laws of the Jews forbid such an easy acceptance of a woman—especially one who is as close to you by blood as Sarra—to be given away as a mistress."

"Have I said that?"

"What else?"

"Then you have indeed misunderstood me, and I am to blame for not making my meaning clear," Akiba answered. "No thought of that was in my mind."

This turnabout staggered me. "What else have we been talking about?" I cried.

"A woman may go with a man as a slave, a chattel, a bit of his property," Akiba said. "So much we know. She may also be attached by love. But there is a third way—which is law, love, and property together."

The light dawned upon me. "Do you mean that I should marry Sarra?" I demanded.

"Why not?"

I floundered. "A Roman marry a Jewess!"

"If she makes you happy, as she has; if you love her, as you say."

"Speak more clearly."

"She loves you as Mikal, the daughter of Saul, loved David —freely, of her own will."

"You Jews claim to be so proud. Do you not fear her marrying a Roman?"

"Why? Esau married two Hittite women; Joseph married an Egyptian; Moses himself married a Midianite. David had a Calebite and an Aramaean among his harem. You celebrate the power of Venus in your rites. We Jews have no magic against her."

I saw the chasm yawning before my feet. The thought sprang into speech. "I am not one like Marcus Curtius, the Roman of old, who sprang into the gulf of his own will," I said meaningfully.

Akiba shrugged. "You remember why he did it?" he asked. "It was to unite Rome—and, after he leaped, the chasm closed and became solid."

I narrowed my eyes speculatively. "It is as I thought," I remarked judicially. "You have something more in mind than merely uniting Sarra and myself in marriage."

274

"When you talk that way," Akiba said, "you are more than half married."

"Answer! Is that not true?"

"Of course," Akiba replied equably. "I have never pretended otherwise." His slight tone of raillery deepened into sincerity. "In this world, for me, there are two races: Jews and Romans. They now clutch at each other's throats. I am pledged in my heart to cease bloodshed, to maintain peace— and I have told the Jews this as often as I tell you, Rufus, as a Roman."

"Well?"

"What better way," asked Akiba guilelessly, "is there for our nations to be united than for the governor of Judea to take as his bride one of the most beautiful Jews?"

His reasoning dismayed me. "Then you hope to influence me toward the Jews through Sarra!"

"Of course. You will be influenced strongly enough toward the Romans by your own choice. Even as Mordecai the son of Jair, brought up his uncle's daughter Hadassah and she became Queen Esther and influenced her spouse Ahasuerus against the villain Haman. Who knows what good for God may come out of the love of man for woman?"

"Akiba," I said, "you are a fraud."

He touched my arm gently. "Rufus," he said, "the frauds of God are the wisdom of men."

"Impossible!" I cried. "I shall have Sarra, and I shall have her in my own way! Doubtless you have encouraged her in this!"

"Naturally," Akiba said in surprise. "She has asked my consent before this. But it is not my advice nor her infantile thoughts of the state of Judea that make her desire this marriage. It is you yourself, Rufus."

The sincerity of his words left me with nothing to reply. I still felt the turbulence of my bosom, but I could not doubt that Akiba believed what he said, though my own intelligence might deny it.

As I hesitated, Akiba touched my arm and spoke again. "Events come to a tryst," he said. "Much is in the wind and there will be no time later. Simeon has sent a messenger to me. He wishes to talk with you. Will you go?"

I laughed. "He summons me?" I replied scornfully.

"You are governor of Judea and he is prince of the Jews," Akiba said. "It is not a matter of honor or dignity but peace in the land. Is that not the duty of each of you?"

275

Twilight that same day and Akiba appeared with two mules. He nodded to me that all was ready.

"Do we go alone?" I asked.

Akiba nodded again. I felt a reluctance which was next to fear, but I summoned Ficus. I gave him instructions to wait until the first hour of the morning and then, if I had not returned, to organize a search. His eyes widened and he opened his mouth to question me, but I waved him away and Akiba and I mounted.

Before the light had died from the land, we were out of the town of Lydda, heading into the grim jagged darkness. It was the first time I had seen Akiba on a mule, and he did well, though his old knees flapped considerably. I kept furtive track of our direction by the stars. When Akiba gave the signal to halt hours later I knew we were somewhere near the foothills of the Valley of Jezreel. I had noted several ancient winepresses hewn out of the rock. "Here," Akiba said tonelessly, "our king Ahab of old had his palace."

"Is this the place appointed?" I asked, brushing off the mask of dew from my face.

"No," Akiba said. "From here I shall be your guide. But you must consent to a blindfold, my friend."

I had expected this. "Very well," I said, submitting to the herb-smelling scarf that he produced and wound around my eyes. "I am in your hands." We commenced a stumbling, winding walk upward, over boulders and prickling plants, weaving back and forth but always tending upward. Long before we arrived, I was as hopelessly confused as a child in a game. I gave up all efforts to decide where I was; somehow the fact that I was one-armed gave me a spurious courage, a confidence that such a half-man might escape an assassin.

After nearly another hour, I smelled wood smoke, pungent and fresh. Within a few minutes, we had mounted to a level spot and stopped. I felt the steady pressure of a sword-point in my ribs and remained where I was as Akiba stripped off the scarf and wound it again around his neck.

I blinked. I stood on a small shelf beneath an overhang of rock that blotted out the night sky. A fellow half clad in skins with ragged clots of hair upon his face held his weapon in my side. Behind him, silhouetting his figure, blazed a fire in the depths of a cave as dismal as the depths of Hades.

"Shalom, Roman," jeered my guard.

"Ave, Jew," I said and thrust aside his sword. I walked toward the fire and the motley crew that stood about it, faces

276

half-swathed, armed with short spears and knives. Two I recognized. One was Glaucus, his dark face twisted and suspicious. The other was the clear sharp face of Simeon sitting on what seemed to be a little throne of rock within the cave. My heart leaped as always to see him again. With Akiba beside me, I strode past the fire and confronted him.

His gaze was fearless. "I had not thought you would come, noble Rufus," he said calmly.

"The fates have not yet unwound the threads of our lives from each other," I said.

Simeon did not respond but looked at Akiba. "Welcome, my father," he said.

I felt a quick stab of resentment and shame at his words; I bit my lip to keep silent.

"I come with Rufus," Akiba said in his deep voice, "because I am the older, perhaps the wiser."

I saw the lips of Glaucus twist into a sardonic rictus at the words, but Simeon addressed me again. "Akiba has told you that I wished to speak to you," he said.

I nodded. "You visited me," I told him. "Tonight I repay that visit. These are troubled times, and I wish well to Jews as I do to Romans."

"We wish well to the Romans," Simeon answered, "but our hands are difficult to raise because of their chains."

"Rome desires to rule justly," I said.

"Then do so."

"Of what do you complain?" I demanded.

"Of life," Simeon said quietly.

"Do you not eat and drink and sleep well enough?"

"We eat tainted food, drink sour wine, and sleep on beds of flint," Simeon said shortly.

I shrugged. "The wheel of time turns," I said. "Once the Greeks defeated our fathers at Troy and made them flee the burning city. Now we have defeated and made slaves of them —all because we knew how to endure and take our revenge."

"Perhaps the wheel turns too slowly," Simeon replied.

"Our hands will make it spin faster," Glaucus spat. A growl of agreement rose among the group. Simeon raised his hand slightly. It subsided.

"I have no power to right what wrongs you may have suffered," I said, "but at the command of the emperor I may speak for you. What do you propose?"

"Freedom."

"Impossible!"

"Then death before submission."

"You bind yourself to the cross," I said.

"Better to hang on the cross than to cringe like beasts!" snarled Glaucus.

"Do you resist Rome?" I asked Simeon in growing amazement.

"If necessary," he said.

I made a gesture of disbelief. "You cannot be part of this rabble," I said. "You are a Roman."

Simeon smiled. "That is what I wish to know," he returned. He looked at Akiba. "Tell me," he said, "am I a Roman, Akiba?"

The old man did not hesitate; he must have had the answer long before. "Your mother was a Jewess," he told Simeon, "and the child of a Jewish woman is a Jew." I knew Akiba's thoughts: the conversion of Domitilla so long ago, her surrender of the child and my rejection of it, his own acceptance of the task. All of the past came together in this moment.

Simeon glanced at me. "So you lie, Rufus," he said softly. There was an inarticulate, threatening murmur from the others. I confronted Akiba. I could not deny the truth of what he said, but I could confound him.

"Do you advise Simeon and his friends to resist our armies, Akiba?" I asked harshly.

Akiba did not reply at once. He turned his face upward to the stars as if consulting friends for guidance. He gazed downward again and sighed.

"What is your advice?" Simeon inquired, his voice edged.

"Do not resist," Akiba said in a low tone.

Simeon half started upright; his tattered companions drew back their spears as if to impale the old man. Akiba lifted his head.

"Some," he said sonorously, "like Abraham ordered by God to sacrifice his son, submit in silence; others, like Job in his pains, cry violent protests; still others, like Hezekiah in his illness, plead for mercy; and a fourth group, like David punished for the sin of Bathsheba, kiss the rod that chastises. Each to his own way but the sin of murder is still a sin."

The men about the fire seemed to shrink back; the glitter on their blades was less. Simeon alone was still. "What do you advise?" he asked again in a different tone.

"Study of the Torah is more important than observing the

laws. If observing the laws leads to the destruction of the Torah, it is wrong. If you quarrel over the present, you may destroy the future."

"Is not our religion our life?" cried Glaucus.

"You are very zealous," observed Akiba to the Greek. "But our religion is not merely ceremony. It is knowledge of God."

"But the law," Simeon replied, "says that we should live by it."

"One may break all the commandments except those against unchastity, the one God—and murder," Akiba said clearly. "The proclaiming of the one God is holy, the home is holy—and life is holy."

For a moment there was silence as if stillness flowed out of the depths of the dark cave behind the men before us. Akiba's beard, escaping from his robe, glowed white in the dying light of the fire.

"The Romans have broken their promises to us," Simeon said, "not once but many times."

"We must prepare ourselves for suffering," Akiba said. He flung up his bare arm. "If happiness were destined to come in our time, how many of the martyrs would still be with us! But God, knowing what distress is in store for us, has taken them from our midst. It is written, 'The righteous is taken away from the evil to come!' "

Simeon sprang upright. "It is better to die for the right than to suffer for the right!" he exclaimed.

"How will you die?" I broke in. "In revolt and shame?"

"Rome tells us how to live, not how to die," Simeon responded, throwing back his young handsome head.

He looked at us with a proud contempt that was, to my surprise, more Roman than Jewish. "I spent many months in the deserts of Goziba," he said, "thinking upon these things. I had, perhaps, more visions than have ever been granted you, Akiba. They have come to me in darkness and at noonday; they do not tell me to yield to the Romans. Old men for dreams, young men for visions, Akiba!"

"What do they tell you?" Akiba asked dully.

Simeon looked away from Akiba, at me. "It is for the Romans to decide," he said. "If they try to keep us within their gates—it is no secret that we have men, that we will find weapons—"

"That you will revolt?" I interrupted. But Simeon was too clever for my ruse. He shrugged. "Why should we reveal our

279

plans?" he asked. "Perhaps we will submit." His tone hardened. "Take back that message to Rome."

I advanced a step, thrusting out my hand. "Simeon, Simeon," I pleaded, "you must not speak thus."

His eyes gleamed from the reflection of the fire. "I shall be told by other, better voices what I must do," he said in tones trembling with anger. "Go!"

Akiba's shoulders sagged. He turned away, and I followed him. Listlessly he put the bandage about my eyes once again and took my hand. As he did, another hand gripped my empty shoulder with its golden guard. "Listen to me," Simeon's voice hissed into my ear. "I know of Sarra's coming to your palace! I know the words you have spoken to her! If she suffers, if you touch her, I shall kill you!"

The hand released me, and we shuffled off down the path. Under the blindfold my spirit soared in the delight of defiance. If what Akiba had said was true—that Sarra desired me for myself—what a way it would be to take revenge on Simeon!

Three weeks later, with some privacy but no attempt to conceal what we did from either Romans or Jews, Sarra and I were married. It was an ancient ceremony on both sides, Roman and Jewish. We pledged each other in our own languages—I in faltering Hebrew, she in fluent Latin. It was simple enough in the act but complicated in the preparation, far more so on the Roman side. Sarra could not dedicate her bulla or virginal toga to the gods: she had neither. But her hair had been divided into the traditional six braids with a spearhead, bound around her waist and knotted, her head draped in a flame-colored veil. The omens were favorable, the ten witnesses (Ficus among them) were not wanting. We dispensed with the sacrifice to Jupiter and the procession around the altar, but we burned the blue-flamed cake of salt and spelt. And she told me: "Wherever you are Rufus, I am Sarra."

The Hebrew part was easier. I paid over the ten silver shekels of mohar to Akiba as her uncle (which he distributed to the poor). He gave his consent to the covenant between us, and we both signed the formal contract. I declared by rote: "Sarra is my wife and I, Rufus, am her husband now and forever." Thereafter I with my chaplet wreath and Sarra under her veil led the way with music and singing into the atrium where the feast was set.

Night fell and still the feasting went on and on. The drinking and eating seemed endless, the jokes both spurious and coarse. Sarra and I ate almost nothing; now and then we touched hands and looked at each other, longing to be alone. Once her lips quivered in a smile, and she seemed near tears. My heart was ravished. It was on the point of declaring that we must leave when my sleeve was pulled by Ficus. I hurriedly left the table and went outside with him.

"All is ready," he said portentously.

"What do you mean?"

"There are garlands in your bedroom."

"Of course."

"It has been dusted and sprinkled with perfumed water."

"Good."

"I have burned incense in the four corners, killed all cockroaches in sight, and have aired the bedding."

"You do very well for a soldier," I said.

"And," Ficus added triumphantly, "I have sprinkled roseleaves everywhere!"

"Did you bring me out here merely to recite these marvels to me?" I demanded.

Ficus regarded me reproachfully. "For your sake," he said, "on such a happy occasion, I have paid for a special sacrifice and I have taken to drinking wine once more."

"I can tell from your breath," I replied, "but thank you, thank you, Ficus the faithful." I slapped him on the back, hurting my hand. I turned to hurry back, throwing two pieces of gold over my shoulder. Ficus scooped them out of the air.

"An occasion of sentiment," he said, "and you will be very happy and lucky, according to the priest."

"I shall find out," I said.

"You'll find out, you'll find out!" he called after me.

When I reentered the room of the feast, I discovered that Sarra had vanished. My heart filled to overflowing: I knew where I would find her.

The doors of the inner chamber were barred behind me. The room shone with the moonlight and the single lamp by the bedside. The couch itself, high and piled with the richest cloths, was veiled as the bride had been. Through the window beyond I heard the sound of distant, drunken, epithalamial singing, floating and dying in the night as the guests made their way out of the palace and dispersed to their litters.

Unnerved, I looked at the bed with growing trepidation. I had no idea what to do. I felt trapped and frightened, as if

281

I were approaching an ambush. I half-turned toward the door, thinking vaguely that this was not the time, that my only security lay in flight. I was interrupted by the drowsy voice of Sarra from the bed, muffled by the curtains.

"Dear Rufus, my husband," she murmured, "shall we be tonight like the fish that creates the pearls? There is a full moon in the skies."

"And the dew?" I asked hoarsely. There was no answer from behind the hangings of striped linen. Almost without my volition, my hand commenced to strip off my garments in haste. I cursed the crippled condition that hindered me, but soon enough my toga and undertunic lay on the floor about my feet.

Naked, full of a lover's anticipations rising within me— emotions I had never experienced in the brothels of the city barracks—I moved toward the veiled couch. I nipped the wick of the lamp between my fingers. As I came closer, not daring to breathe, the curtains parted slightly. A white smooth hand emerged. It seized me gently by the rudder of love. I did not resist for I could not. I followed the urging through the curtains and then, suddenly, I plunged forward into bliss.

Thus Rufus Teneius, the mighty one-armed warrior, fought his best battle, though his weapon was captured at the outset. It was the only encounter of mine where the conqueror herself took my spear and plunged it into herself and died the silent death of love. Yet she, as the vanquished, rose to be invincible over me many times that night. At last I could hold the fortress no longer and surrendered all—and we slept in each other's arms.

CHAPTER 17

From the beginnings of time Judea has been a strife-torn area. It stands at the gates of all Roman trade with the east; it is the frontier against our deadly and persistent enemies, the Parthians. And it contains the most desperate and ill-assorted companies of people in the civilized world, among them the Jews.

The trouble with the Jews, of course, is that they are Jewish. I do not mean to say the problem of their rule is simple; rather the reverse. They have certain traits in common with one another, but they refuse to believe so. Even their features betray them and, as I think, indicate a certain ancient relationship to Rome. (At least, I told Akiba that his nose was Roman and he contended that mine was Jewish.) However that may be, I do not know to this hour if the Jews are a race, a religion, or a set of rites.

Their contentious nature—like that of the Greeks, to whom I think they must also be related—causes them to fall out with everyone, including one another. They are too quick in intelligence, too addicted to frenzied argument, to quarrels about tiny differences, to irreconcilable opinions, to agree even among themselves.

Yet—and here is the puzzle—though the Jews have been beaten and broken time and again by every nation on earth, they grow and flourish, as they claim, like the green bay tree. They become neither worse nor better but remain the same: they are an eternal people. Even the Romans have had their summits of power and their depths of degradation, as have the Egyptians and Babylonians of old. The Jews pass through the history of earth like a scarlet thread, shuttling back and forth over the centuries. Other nations conquer and die. The Jews succumb, survive, and go on.

However wondrous such survival may seem to me now, at that time it was of little concern to Rome. The enigma of Hadrian, the new emperor, occupied the minds and gossip of all Romans. The nature of his character was—and still is—a favorite charade at the feasts.

Here is a princeps of Spanish blood, feared and adored by Romans, who exalts the Greeks above all. Here is a leader who abhors war so much that he gave up Armenia, Assyria, and Mesopotamia, who paid tribute to the Sarmatians and Roxolani, who hid behind a wall from the Britons—yet who has made the army again the instrument of our might that it should be. He has renewed the exercitus Romanus for the troops, made the soldiers tougher and stronger than ever, kept impeccable discipline, and on occasions (as against the Jews) has fought like a lion himself. He has drawn the best of our youth from every part of the empire. So much so, that my friends in Rome complain he has filled the city with a motley crowd of soldiers, wild of aspect, dreadful in speech, and boorish in behavior. I myself do not complain, as they do, that this innovation has driven the native sons to banditry and gladiatorial careers. That is all they are good for.

But under his rule, for the first time in nine centuries, Rome has become an empire on the defensive. Forts, walls, ditches, palisades, towers are everywhere on our borders. Standing orders are to retreat, not to advance; to hold, not to reach out. The limes of Trajan are the limites of Hadrian. Yet from the first Hadrian has been plagued by wars and bold incursions by our enemies.

In the first year of his reign, he overcame the first rebellion of the Jews, as well as those of the Moors and Sarmatians, by arms, pacification, arbitration, and bribes. The next year, he drove back the savage Britons and commenced his famous wall across that lonely island. Then came a respite of three years (during which he claimed Quietus plotted against him in Africa). He put down a second rising of the Moors, only to have it followed by a threat from the Parthians. He visited Chosroes, gave him back his kingdom, and promised to return his golden throne (which, nonetheless, has never been delivered). Seven years later, by this time strong in his own self-regard, he set the stage for the one which neither gold nor flattering words could avert—and which came near over-turning the throne of Rome—the Jewish War.

As I write, Hadrian has been emperor for seventeen years. Of these he has spent nearly half in restless wanderings about the empire. Some say this is because he is pursued by the ghosts of those he has tortured and executed, but these are chiefly Jewish rumors. The fact is that he hates Rome and its empty luxuries, contemptuous of the tawdry display. He prefers to travel and see strange peoples and unusual sights, a self-made exile from his own race.

All this being true, it may be that the Jews are right and that Hadrian is pursued by the furies. The last dispatches which have come to me from Rome declare (on authority that I cannot disbelieve) that the emperor has returned there and is alone, diseased—and insane.

This is not the Hadrian that I remember. Next to the last time I saw him was in the year of Rome 881 upon his visit to Judea to observe the state of affairs. He was accompanied by his court and his favorite pathic, the beautiful Bithynian youth, Antinoüs. He took for his own the palace of Frontinus in Caesarea and summoned me to appear. As it was widely known that the emperor was in residence, and I was to report to him, Akiba begged for permission to go with me to the audience. I knew his purpose. In my heart, I hoped it would succeed: I could not deny his wish, and Hadrian was gracious enough to approve.

It was a hot day in early summer, with light winds from the turquoise-blue sea lifting the woven linen tapestries on the walls, when Akiba and I entered the tablinium. We found Hadrian seated on the marble tribunal with its dim brown stain reminding me of the spot where Frontinus had taken his life. I was surprised by the luxurious attire of the attendants about the emperor, since he had derided such display frankly to me years before in Rome. Hadrian himself wore a fresh white toga with its imperial purple striping. His head was more noble than I remembered it; his hair was faded but still thick. To conceal his receding chin, he wore a short curled beard, the first I had ever seen on a Roman ruler. His face and neck had thickened, ravaged by the lines of power: greed, cruelty, sadness, thought, pride, like the face of some sand-eaten god of the desert.

Below him, on the steps of the tribunal, sat a young man whose beauty astounded me. I knew instantly it must be young Antinoüs. His perfect profile was flawless, his flesh so clear that he seemed to glow with inward light; his eyes sparkled with blue. The fingers of Hadrian toyed idly in his curled blond hair.

"Greetings, good Rufus," Hadrian said genially. I was relieved to find him in equable temper—I had heard he often indulged in fits of black despair—and noted that his body, like that of Trajan, had become slippery with fat flesh. He had an air of ineffable confidence which I did not anticipate; he exuded overwhelming authority.

I bowed low. "Hail, most illustrious Hadrian," I said. I had no need to introduce Akiba; Hadrian recognized him immediately. He greeted him by name. "I see you keep your friends among the Jews," he said, turning to me. "That is well done. I have inquired among the officials in the province and have heard nothing but good reports of your administration."

I swelled with pride. "Many thanks, Sire," I returned. "You give your servant much pleasure."

"And you, Akiba ben Joseph?" Hadrian said banteringly. "You have asked to see me, and you are here. No Jew comes before the emperor except to ask for some concession. What is it?"

"Your famous uncle," Akiba said in his deep voice, "once

was enlightened enough to give permission to renew the sacrifices and rebuild the Temple at Jerusalem. I come here only to beg that you will verify his grant and once more give my people the pledge of Rome."

Hadrian did not cease to smile, but his lips grew thin. I knew Akiba had made a mistake in mentioning Trajan's name so prominently in his request. Hadrian did not care to make grants to oblige the dead, though he was generous enough on his own.

"Regardless of what the divine Trajan promised," I said quickly, "it may be possible that Hadrian himself will be generous."

Hadrian's expression became less stiff and, for a moment, I thought we had won the day. "It may be," he said carelessly, "it may be. The Jews have caused much destruction and death, but it is not my way to be vengeful. If there could be an end to these disturbances, it would be a blessing to Romans everywhere."

He leaned down and cupped the chin of Antinoüs, lifting his head upward. "What do you think?" he asked. Antinoüs twisted his head away petulantly and continued to play with two balls of ivory. "Come," Hadrian said playfully, "what do you think of this beanpole of a Jew?"

Antinoüs deigned to slip the balls into a blue deerskin pouch. He turned toward us, resting his flawless head on his hand and pretending to consider. "He is very ugly," he said at last.

"He is very wise," Hadrian smiled.

"Only the beautiful are wise," Antinoüs responded. Hadrian laughed. I had never before seen him so happy and light-hearted.

"Perhaps you are right," he agreed. "There is wisdom where there is beauty."

"Yet," demurred Antinoüs capriciously, "possibly I am wrong." He got up from his couch with a silky graceful motion and approached the rigid form of Akiba. The burning eyes of the old man gave me a shocking premonition of danger.

"He is so ugly he is almost beautiful," Antinoüs said. He put out his smooth hand and stroked Akiba's cheek.

The Jew jerked as if his body were thrust through. His tough calloused hand flew out. He knocked the perfumed palm of Antinoüs away. The youth's face turned fearful; he stepped back.

286

An indrawn hiss of amazement sounded from the courtiers surrounding Hadrian. Swords were drawn, a buzz of whispers rose and died almost instantly. Hadrian's face became swollen with fury, his eyes distending. The color changed to a deep flush, and drops of blood commenced to trickle from his nose. He reached out and took a cloth from an attendant, pressing it to his upper lip. But he never shifted his malevolent gaze from Akiba. His voice, harsh with anger, came muffled through the cloth.

"Vile Jew!" he said in a crackling tone. "Do you dare?" His voice rose almost to the pitch of madness. "Take him away!"

I fell to my knees and stretched out my hand in pleading. "Pardon, pardon, mighty Hadrian!" I cried. Akiba was not beside me; he stood erect and defiant, folding his arms.

The guards seized the old man from either side. They began to drag him off to what would have been inevitable mangling and death. As they did the mellifluous voice of Antinoüs interrupted them.

"Wait," he said, "wait."

They halted as readily at his command as at that of the emperor. "Publius," Antinoüs said, addressing Hadrian, "if you wish to please me, do not be cruel. I cannot bear cruelty."

Hadrian, his brow still lowering, shook his head. "Whoever strikes you," he said, "strikes me."

"But this is foolish," Antinoüs said gently. "He is a very old person. He is not in his right mind. It may be that he has spasms and could not help himself."

"You will die in your filth," Akiba said slowly and clearly.

Hadrian's face turned black. A rattling noise came from his throat. Before he could speak, Antinoüs had again intervened. "You see, sweet Hadrian," he said.

"I see, indeed," grated Hadrian, dashing down his blood-stained cloth.

"No, no! This one is cursed of the gods! If he were not, he would not dare to speak so before your majesty."

I began to breathe again. Hadrian's face changed slowly. He studied the placid, beautiful face of his favorite, calming himself. At length, he smiled a little. "Antinoüs, Antinoüs," he said, "you are so forgiving and kind. You are the only man in the world who has an emperor for a slave."

"Then I am the only master who would die for his slave," Antinoüs answered. "You do not believe that now, dear Hadrian, but I shall one day prove it."

Hadrian shook his head, his good nature beginning to return. "What do you wish me to do with this mad creature, then?" he asked.

Antinoüs shrugged negligently and resumed his seat. "Set him free to tell of the mercy of Hadrian," he said.

"And of the beauty and compassion of Antinoüs," Hadrian replied. He gave the familiar flip of his fingers. The guards dropped the bony arms of Akiba. I took my place at his side and urged him out, feeling his body still trembling with outrage and anger.

Halfway to the door, we were halted by Hadrian's voice. He spoke to Antinoüs but his tone was lifted so that we could not miss what he said.

"Delight-filled Antinoüs," Hadrian said carelessly, "you have given me a thought. Such a flourishing state as this deserves a city even greater than Caesarea. The divine Trajan, as I have been reminded, promised to restore the city and the Temple at Jerusalem for these animals of Jews. Truly, by tradition, it is the most favored spot."

He paused and looked at us from the other end of the hall. His face held a glinting contempt. Akiba's features lighted up. He halted and half-turned to listen. Hadrian went on.

"I shall fulfil what Trajan promised. The city shall be built again. The Temple shall be erected. The treasury of the throne shall pay the cost."

Akiba opened his mouth to shout hosannas, but he was forestalled by Hadrian speaking even more loudly.

"I have long wished to do this. Once I ordered the sanctuary of the Jews removed to another place, but the sanctified Trajan revoked my wish." His voice held a harsh sneer. "Now he is with the gods and I speak what shall be done." He smiled tightly. "The new city shall be dedicated to Jupiter and myself and shall be called Aelia Capitolina. On the site of the old Temple of the Jews shall rise instead a shining temple to Jupiter and there shall be within an altar dedicated to yourself, O Antinoüs! Only those Jews who sacrifice to you and adore you shall be admitted within its walls."

"Excellent, O Zeus Olympios!" crowed Antinoüs, clapping his slender hands. He had given Hadrian the supreme title which the people of Athens had bestowed upon him for his many favors.

"We shall endeavor to please all. As a just ruler, I shall be impartial in my favors. For the Christians, in the place where they claim their Messiah was crucified, we shall raise a statue of Venus unadorned. Where their Christ was supposed to have risen from the dead, a statue of naked Adonis. For the Jews, their temple shall be more glorious than ever—in worship of Jupiter, sweet Antinoüs, and myself. And every Jew who comes in to bewail his foregone splendor shall pay a fee of five sesterces and bow his head under a hog wrought in marble placed above the gate."

I clapped my hand, too—over Akiba's mouth. Thrusting my shoulder and leg against him, I propelled him out of the room before the astonished old man could formulate the curses that would have doomed him. Behind us floated the echo of silver peals of laughter from Antinoüs.

"You were wrong," I said.

Akiba shook his head. "I was mistaken," he said.

"What is the difference?"

"I was not wrong to thrust away the hand of that cursed pervert; but I was mistaken in doing so. It is hard to restrain an involuntary shudder when one is touched by the unclean."

I sighed. "Akiba," I said, "you lost your temper for the first time in all the years I have known you. In that single gesture you may have thrown away the hopes of the Jews."

Akiba rose agitatedly. He paced about my chamber where we had retired after the fateful interview with Hadrian. "No," he said at last. "Hadrian is more cunning than that. He could not have conjured up, like the witch of Endor for Saul, such a vision of horror at a moment's notice. This has been breeding in his mind a long time. What happened to his favorite was no more than an excuse."

I gestured silently, and Akiba continued pacing. After a time he turned to me again. "You saved my life, I know," he said.

"As you have saved mine."

"But I have lost my honor," Akiba said.

"I lost my arm," I returned impatiently. "Stop talking like a Roman. Being a Jew suits you better."

"I should have denounced that hideous youth and his seducer."

"It is difficult to denounce," I said dryly, "when one has a sword through his throat. As it was, you did more than any man has ever dared."

Akiba shook his head. "Trajan's nephew does not know what wrath he has let loose," he said sombrely.

"By tonight every Jew in the land will know about it," I admitted. "But what can they do?"

Akiba regarded me soberly. "Much," he replied. "Much. Do you think you know all there is to be known about my people? They will accept this, yield that. Then, like consuming flames, they will burst out."

"Then Rome shall have to extinguish them," I said.

Akiba sighed and turned toward the door of my chamber. "Rufus," he said unhappily, "today Hadrian has sowed the seeds of the extirpation of either the Romans or the Jews." He hesitated, and his expression shifted. "If Hadrian knew enough to take an infusion of the bark of olives," he murmured, "made from a tree as old as himself, it would cure his nosebleed." Before I could reply to this surprising statement, Akiba had gone, shuffling dispiritedly down the corridor.

What he had said, nevertheless, made a strong impression on my mind. I determined to reinforce the garrison of the city and to warn the command of the X Fretensis. For the next two days, until Hadrian departed for Alexandria, I watched the crowds closely, but I gained no evidence of rebellion—beyond the usual discontent—until a week later.

Lying half-asleep in the warm evening in my chair in the atrium alone, having just dismissed Sarra, I yawned. Not sure whether to cross the room to my couch and sleep or to continue with my rereading of the Platonics, I heard a rustle in the corner. Instantly alert, I turned in my chair—to confront Simeon once again—exactly as he had been in my dream but this time unaccompanied.

"Simeon," I said. "Is this another dream?"

"It was not a dream then, it is not a dream now." He brought one hand from behind his back. In it I saw gleaming what he had snatched from the side of my couch where I had it always ready: the knife I had picked up on the road to my post in Germania long ago and had kept by me ever since.

"Eternal peace, Rufus Teneius," Simeon whispered. He drew back his arm.

"Will you kill a man sitting?" I asked. "Did I not teach you more virtue than that?"

Simeon held back his thrust with an effort. "Stand," he said, struggling to control himself, "and I shall kill you."

"Will you grant me a weapon as well?"

"I shall kill you!"

"Very well," I said. I rose and held up my hand for a moment's respite. "Slay me if you will," I told Simeon. "I shall not cry out. But tell me, is this your revenge because the emperor has decreed a Roman city on Jewish sacred soil? Is this petty murder all you can imagine?"

Simeon's eyes blinked. He was bewildered. Slowly, as if the words were a confession drawn out by the hooks of torturers, he said: "You have betrayed Sarra!"

I began to laugh. I halted myself, the flood of my relief freezing in my veins. Simeon's brows knit in agony; his face convulsed. I could no longer hold him off or reach his mind with words. He lunged at me, the knife a streak in the lamplight. But what I had asked, what he had confessed, had shaken him so much that he was deflected from his aim for my bosom. I was able to twist aside and partially obstruct the thrust with my arm. The knife ripped along my left pap. I felt a sear of pain as the blood started. I retreated to the other side of the room, oversetting a bronze jug of water by my couch. It clamored like a gong on the marble floor.

Simeon hesitated. He began to creep toward me, intent on not missing a second time. I was being stalked like a wild beast.

Before I realized it, I laughed again, almost in hysteria. Hunted by my own son! "Once Orestes threatened his mother so!" I shouted. As I dodged about the room, the old anonymous Greek verses came to my tongue and I flung them, one by one, as if they were weapons, at the head of Simeon:

> *"Into my belly or my breast*
> *Will you thrust your manic knife?*
> *Into the breast that gave you breath?*
> *Into the gut that gave you life?"*

"Simeon!" It was the voice of Sarra: indignant, unbelieving, rejoicing. "Simeon!"

Simeon turned like a cat, rising to his toes in his sandals. His arm fell. I saw Sarra, half-naked in her nightdress, come through the door, running to Simeon to hug him. "I am so happy to see you again!"

"And I," Simeon said with sudden energy, "despise you!" He wrenched himself free from her embrace. She staggered back. "I am here to kill your lover," he cried, "and you shall join him!"

In the instant between his threat and its execution, Sarra's face changed. Very quietly, she said: "My lover? He is not my lover. Rufus Teneius is my husband, in both Jewish and Roman law. Will you kill my husband?"

291

Simeon gave a great inarticulate cry. "You lie!" he shouted. Sarra advanced fearlessly. "Do I?" she asked him. "Look at me, Simeon. His child stirs in my body. Touch me. Do I lie? You used to be able to tell."

He stared at her wildly for a moment, his throat working, his cheek pulsing. With a long groan, he flung the knife from him. It struck one of the painted pillars of my chamber and stuck quivering in the wood. Without another word, Simeon sprang toward the window and dived out headfirst. Running after, I saw him land on his hands, rolling over instantly and leaping to his feet. From a distance I heard the belated cries and hails in the alarm of the guards.

Behind me I heard a whimper, like a kitten in distress. I wheeled about from the window and saw Sarra had collapsed on the floor, huddling her arms about her waist. I ran to her, lifting her to my knee. She screamed, her face white, her eyes vacant with pain. "Sarra!" I cried.

As my voice broke on her name, Ficus ran in, half-clad. He jerked to attention.

"Quickly, quickly!" I exclaimed. "Send for Rachel, the wife of Akiba!"

It was two days later. The wound on my bosom throbbed, but I felt nothing. My brain was numb, my body walked like that of a wooden toy. I had no conscious thoughts, no knowledge: all that reckoned in my world without was that I had to do my duty as an official of the Roman empire. Rigidly I mounted the rostrum built at the side of the marketplace. I looked with loathing out upon the sunlit masses of people below me, upon the bright brass helmets of my guard. I heard the murmurs of the packed humanity below as if I stood on a high cliff and listened to the ebb of the sea.

I took a deep breath and held up my hand for silence. As I did, the murmuring ceased. The multitudinous heads, as if jerked by a common string, turned up toward me. The sun whitened the faces. It shone back from the eyes of this thousand-headed monster.

"People of Caesarea," I said lifelessly, "I have summoned you here because of riots and disturbances. Because of loose talk directed against the imperial majesty of Rome. Because of the slaughter at your hands of innocent people who did not happen to be Jews. I have summoned you here to issue a solemn warning.

"Many of you talk freely of war against Rome, of rebel-

292

lion and massacre. Rome does not endure threats lightly. Nor do we threaten in turn: we act." I stopped on the word.

"If all Jews were fixed on war with the Romans," I went on doggedly, "I would not stand here to speak to you. But I have talked with some of the best and most honest leaders among you, those who are old enough not to have forgotten the Jewish War of two generations ago. Some of you do not know what you do. Others have a vague hope of independence, still others have visions of enriching themselves in revolt. As one who has lived among you and perhaps has more understanding and sympathy with the Jews than most Romans, allow me to speak what I think to be your interest. As you know, I have a Jewish wife and married her in the Jewish ceremonies. Heed my words."

I took a long breath. The pale face of Sarra hovered somewhere before me in the shimmers of heat from the stones. I passed my hand over my eyes and abruptly continued:

"You have two reasons for your anger set in your minds. The first is that you believe you have suffered outrage and injustice in the news of the city to be built in your midst. Even granted this may be true, it does not follow that Augustus Hadrian and all other Romans are intolerably harsh or turned against you. It means merely that you have been misunderstood. Once properly known, your wrongs may be speedily put right. But war is an irrevocable step.

"As for fighting for your liberties, I say your passion comes late, too late." A murmur ran through the crowd below me. My guard tightened grips on their pila. I raised my hand again. A sullen silence fell. "You might have fought well and to the purpose when great Pompey first came here," I said, lifting my voice, "and your forefathers did their best. But they failed even against a small part of the Roman army. Will you, whose bent heads are hereditary, do better against the whole Roman army?"

An almost bestial growl of resentment rose from the white rank of robes, from the brown faces upturned toward me. I disregarded the sound and went on:

"If you wish to fight, where are the troops, what are the armor and arms, the engines, the supplies on which you must rely? Where is your fleet to carry the fight to Rome? Where is your treasury for the campaigns? Do you truly believe you are quarreling with Arabs or Egyptians? The Romans are powerful beyond your conception. We have not been satisfied with the world. We have gone beyond the Euphrates on the

293

east, the Danubis on the north, into the desert of the south, and in the east we have found a new nation called Britain, before unknown to history. Are you wealthier than the Gauls, stronger than the Germans, more intelligent than the Greeks, more numerous and brave than all the peoples of the world?

"We gain tribute from five hundred cities of Asia without a single Roman within their walls. The northern tribes put their necks under the yoke to twelve hundred Roman soldiers —though they have scores of cities equal to that number. Here, at your doorstep, is Egypt, with eight million souls, extending to Arabia Felix and Ethiopia, possessing a city in Alexandria thirty furlongs in length, not less than ten in breadth—and she takes pride in submission. She sends more tribute in a month than all Judea in a year. She supplies corn to Rome for four months and all Africa supplies it for the rest of the year. Yet two legions only hold her in leash.

"But, tell me, suppose you decide on war: where will you get the necessary allies? From the savage forests and deserts? From the depths of the sea? No: all in the civilized world are Romans. You have no hope, then, but in your god. I do not criticize this, but I ask you to consider if the Roman might could have reached such a perihelion without the aid even of your god. And how can you fight (for I know your holy writings) without going against the very precepts that you practice and the words you preach? In such a case, you anger your god and lose the war at one and the same time.

"When you can expect no assistance either from god or man in such a venture, you are doomed to defeat. He who has hope in the nature of things may be a hero; but he who has none is a fool in himself and a traitor to his country."

At this shouts went up, partly of anger and partly of approbation. Clubs were waved and fists brandished, but I could feel the hot temper of the crowd cooling, slowly changing shape under the hammering of my words.

"Perhaps you imagine such a war will be unusual enough to gain you special terms from the Romans. On the contrary, it has been the custom of the emperor to wipe out his enemy and to plow and salt the ground where their cities once stood. Even those who survive will find no help, no matter how far they flee; for as I have said, all the world is Roman. Thus your rebellion here will threaten the destruction of Jews everywhere.

"Take pity, then, on your children and wives, on your fellow Jews, on yourselves. Keep to yourselves the hope of a temple, preserve your holy city in another corner of the empire. Do not let destruction come upon you again from Roman arms: for me, even as a Roman, I have learned to love and respect you and yours. Whatever I have said, it has been for your good."

As I finished, I burst into tears. There were those who thought I was carried away by the emotion of my own rhetoric, but it was not so. What I wept for was real; but none of those present knew it. I was alone in my suffering.

As I flung the tears from my eyes and stepped down from the improvised rostrum, however, I saw a ragged, scarlet-sashed figure lifted on the shoulders of those before me. Murmurs of approbation for my speech were already rising as the newcomer flung out his arms, abruptly halting them.

"Friends! Fellow Jews! It is easy to reply to the noble Rufus. We do not need crocodile tears or bogey tales for children calculated to frighten us! We do not need the hypocritical words of a Roman, covering his own fright, to deceive us!

"We need to say only one thing: We will fight! We need to repeat it: We will fight!"

A vast roar burst upward from the crowd. It became a sea of flashes of hitherto-concealed weapons, brown arms, fluttering robes. Above it all, smiling and godlike in his composure and knowledge of leadership rode the man who was to lead them to their ruin.

It was Simeon, my own son. He had made his choice at last.

Beside him leaped and shouted his boon companion, Glaucus the slave and inciter to rebellion. I waited to make an answer, but the roar increased and became menacing.

"Bar Cocheba! Bar Cocheba! Son of the Star!"

They had christened him on the spot in memory of the old prophecy of Balaam. Into my head came the words of Akiba in the villa of Flavius Clemens that night long past as he held the child.

"Bar Cocheba! Bar Cocheba!"

The increasingly incensed crowd commenced to crawl forward against the helmeted line of guards. I heard the whiz of an arrow past me. I saw its flicker of flight and direction. It arched directly toward Simeon.

With unbelievable agility, he dodged aside, flinging himself from the shoulders of those who carried him. But the shaft did not altogether miss its mark. It sank into the throat of

Glaucus beside him, burying itself to the feathers. He dropped his sword; his shouting changed to a gurgle as he drank his own blood. His caperings continued a moment longer, like a death dance, then he collapsed face forward.

At the sight, the crowd drew back. It broke into fragments of flight, as we stood silent and waiting. There came the usual shower of clubs and stones. We bent our helmets to them and made no reply. I signaled. The legionaries broke ranks, pouring out in a charge, flailing with their iron fists and scabbards, urging the mob to greater flight.

That same afternoon I walked out of the gate of the city, following a tiny coffin. It held the body of my stillborn son, lost and unnamed. It was my duty facere justa according to the Twelve Tables, to put to rest this tiny shapeless thing from my flesh and Sarra's in the one-room house of the dead. I cast the earth on his grave and saw the leaden pipe inserted through which weekly libations of milk would be poured for his spirit. I gave orders for the tomb to be built and the days of casting violets and roses on the marble slab to be observed. But I could think of no suitable inscription or verse to be carved upon it—nor have I to this very day.

At the next dawning, I ordered two crosses erected outside the walls of Caesarea along the highway. On one I crucified the dead body of Glaucus, for all to see. On the other, I crucified the living body of the Roman archer who had loosed his shaft without orders.

As long as I was governor of Judea, justice was to be done and discipline maintained.

CHAPTER 18

"HADRIAN, EMPEROR, TO RUFUS TENEIUS: HEALTH. You recommended Alexandria to me. I have studied it. I know it thoroughly. I have discovered it is like a bag of wind—full of inconstancy, caprice, levity, wishing nothing more than novelty. There is not a chief of the Jews or the Christians here who is not at the same time an astrologer or a soothsayer or a false doctor. Only the priests of Serapis seem

296

devoted to their religion. Each of the discourteous and seditious citizens (however religious) acknowledges only one true god, that of his self-interest.

"I wish that this embroidered city—by grandeur and riches first in Egypt—could be swept clean and furnished with better inhabitants. Nothing equals their ingratitude. I have granted them everything they might desire: I have restored their ancient privileges; I have given them a hundred new ones. They are grateful to my face, but when I turn my back, they insult me and the majesty of Rome. Like the people of Judea, they need a strong governor such as yourself to control their impertinence."

I give so much of a letter written to me by the emperor from Alexandria a few months after he left Judea. It shows the extraordinary humor he displayed at this period of his life. The curt greeting, the sly reference to what Quietus had said long ago, the whim of mockery: I had never spoken to him of that great city or its people. But his mood of ironic gaiety did not last long. The death of his bosom companion, the Bithynian slave Antinoüs, plunged Hadrian into a fit of gloom which has darkened his life since.

The story is that the beautiful youth drowned in the Nile—either as a suicide in a fit of melancholy or in saving the emperor's life. The true reason, I think, was neither. It is my conviction that Antinoüs was a victim of the Mithra mysteries.

It is well known that the Mithra initiates celebrate eighty of these secret ceremonies. There are seven degrees—the ravens, the secrets, the fighters, the lions, the Persians, the sun-runners, and the fathers. The next-to-the-last consists of cutting the throat of a white bull while the initiate is nude, wearing only the coned Holy Cap. This mystic act confers upon the one who kills the animal not only the health and strength of the bull but also long life. The final and rarely performed mystery—highest of all—is to cut the throat of one's dearest friend for the sake of immortality—and the friend must willingly consent to the sacrifice.

This is especially longed for by those who are highly placed in orders such as those of Mithra and Eleusia—and Hadrian is master of all these dark rites. I am forced to believe that the emperor himself, in the depths of the Golden Crypt, took the life of Antinoüs (who undoubtedly offered it freely)—tangling his fingers in the curly yellow hair for the last time, pulling it back to stretch upward the perfect white throat for cutting—in the hope of living forever.

297

From this act the growing madness of Hadrian—which has of late appeared all too plainly—is supposed to have sprung. No lesser deed can wholly account for it. He has become a changed man. While his empire seemed at rest, the chief of the Romans wandered everywhere. A strange false peace fell upon the world as he passed from land to land, a gorgeous regal wraith. Even Judea, which had been on the verge of revolt, calmed itself for nearly two years. In accordance with the imperial orders, we had commenced to build the city of Aelia Capitolina directly atop the ruins of Jerusalem, next to the camp of the X Fretensis legion. I had anticipated riots and perhaps organized resistance, but there was nothing of the sort. The Jews avoided the place with superstitious dread. The Christians visited it with pleasure (their crucified prophet, they said, predicted such an event) and the soldiers eagerly anticipated a city for their own use. At the end of twenty months, the walls had been finished and the temple to Jupiter half erected.

All appeared peaceful and well in hand. Again I took up the pursuit of philosophy, and the hours fled before me. I spent my days in contemplation, my nights in dining with selected guests, hiring a visiting mime or company of players from Rome for entertainment, reading and reciting poetry and drama. Two shadows only lay across my mind. I did not know what had become of Simeon. And the visits from Akiba, once so frequent, had dwindled until it was a rare occasion when he came to my residence. Sarra, too, was a puzzle: she had recovered long before from the premature birth of her child, but she avoided my company and submitted to my caresses like a slave rather than a Roman wife.

Yet she, at least, was in my house. It might be, I thought, that she could help me solve at least part of the mysteries that plagued me. The determination grew in me that Sarra must supply the key to open a door I had hitherto not had the courage to approach. At last, one morning in the midst of my scrolls, I pushed them aside and went in search of her.

I found her alone, wandering in the garden in the sunshine, touching a flower now and then but plucking none, trailing the tips of her fingers in the fountain waters. She heard my footsteps on the path and whirled, like a deer ready to leap away from the hunter, her face fearful.

"Rufina," I said, using the Roman name I had given her, "what has come between us? Since the death of our child, we have been far apart."

"I am Sarra," she said dully. "I am not the wife of a Roman but the concubine of a conqueror."

Her reply startled me. "Had the child lived," I asked, clearing my throat, "would you have felt this way?"

"Who knows how I would have felt?" she said listlessly. "He is dead, and no one will ever know."

I examined her closely and was alarmed at the pallor of her face, the puffiness of her flesh; I had not known that her sorrow had struck so deep. Perhaps I had been blinded by my own grief, at the loss of a son who might have carried on my name. Inevitably my thought passed to Simeon, and a spasm of jealousy gripped me. His name rose to my lips, but I repressed it.

"You must realize that it is difficult for men to understand women," I said gently.

Her eyes glowed as she looked up at me, and a faint color came to her cheeks. "Is it more difficult than for a Roman to understand a Jew?" she said bitterly. "After all these years, you fail even to know Akiba."

"Thirty-five years," I said, amazed at the speed of time.

Sarra stood up, her tiny fists clenched at her sides. "Can you not see even what happens before your eyes?" she said fiercely. "Akiba is torn apart by wild horses and you stand ignorant."

"What do you tell me?" I cried.

"Listen," she said breathlessly. "All his long life, Akiba has desired to be blessed of God. He has wished for the vision of a prophet, to speak with the tongues of Isaiah and Elijah. But God has not given him this gift. He has had to do what he can with what he knows as a man. He has won only the contempt of those like yourself."

"Not mine," I replied, my anger beginning to rise.

"Perhaps you treat him as a friend but in your heart you despise him."

"Never!"

"He desires only that our faith, our knowledge of God shall survive. All else passes and withers like grass under the sun; only this is eternal in his eyes. But his appeals to Rome are spat upon, his hopes dried up. Everything has failed him—except one."

"What is that?" I demanded.

"Simeon."

My bitterness broke forth. "What has Simeon to do with this?"

Sarra wore a slight, pitying smile that heightened my temper. "You are a Roman and have conquered," she said slowly. "You know. What comes when entreaty, justice, compassion, and love fail?"

I was silent as Sarra paused. She went on, almost defying my tight lips. "Tell me, Rufus, what happens?"

"War," I said thickly.

"Ruin, death, destruction! Yes! What else can there be?"

"Do you tell me that Akiba would follow Simeon's madness?"

Sarra drew a deep breath. Her tears commenced to fall. "I say that he balances upon the edge of a great decision, thrust there by doubt of himself and failure of what he believes his mission. A small thing, like a pebble in an avalanche, can push him over the edge."

"So much the worse for him," I said grimly.

Sarra burst into a wild storm of weeping, hiding her face with her hands. I started forward to comfort her, but my pride kept me where I was; then I turned to leave. Her voice, broken with sobs, followed me: "Have you no pity—on me?"

If I had gone back to her, if I had taken her to my bosom, how much of the future would have been changed! But I did not; I left her to her weeping and her lonely thoughts. I went about my duties as governor, putting her frail grief-shaken form out of my mind.

But I was not to have rest. The issues of life and death, molten in my head, began to cast themselves into rigid, ugly forms. They were as ghastly as the images of native gods I had seen once in barbarian Thrace. Night after night I tried to escape from their stare, returning to winebibbing as I used to do, drinking solus and melancholy in my favorite nook in the garden. It was a foolish thing to do. Wine clouds the reason; it gives a man by himself the illusion that he may make godlike decisions, though he is only a man.

Thus it was a week later that I had my extraordinary meeting with Simeon and Sarra at twilight. The pair of them rose as silent and ominous before me as shades of the underworld. I recoiled, not steady on my legs, not sure whether I should summon my guard. Simeon stepped through a low hedge of flowering thorn, striping his legs with red weals. I fell back upon a bench as Sarra, more cautious, skirted about it and came to stand by his side.

"How—how did you come?" I demanded.

300

"I brought him," Sarra responded. It was the simplest reply imaginable. I could find no answer. Simeon stood unmoving in his rags, his face grave and expressionless, his eyes fixed upon me.

"Not as a warrior, not as anything more than a friend," Sarra added timidly.

"Once he tried to slay me," I muttered. Neither of them replied. I felt I had spoken like a child.

Simeon stirred; he sighed. "No, Sarra," he said. "There is no time left."

"Time?" I said roughly. "Who are you to speak of time? Chronos devours his sons." I laughed, feeling the wine in my head.

" 'There is a time for everything under the sun,' " Simeon said, quoting his Jewish prophets. "For the Jew today it is better to be feared than to be held in contempt."

"Do you speak of moving against the power of Rome?"

"No!" cried Sarra.

"Yes," Simeon said in a low voice, "I speak of that."

I did not answer at once: so astonished was I, so disarrayed were my senses from the fumes of what I had drunk. But I noted a new expression on the face of Sarra as she looked up at Simeon. Before, it had seemed to me—and this was my bulwark within her affections—she had looked down upon Simeon as no more than a boy. Big, wayward, more muscular than most perhaps, yet one who had not become a man. Now, with a quickening alarm, I saw this fortress of mine within her heart besieged by what she saw in Simeon. He was another person, a changeling, one whom she had begun to regard with awe. What he had said—his single word in defiance of Rome —had touched a chord in her heart so lofty I could never attain it.

The shock sobered me. "Have you come to hate the Romans?" I asked Simeon.

"All my life," he said slowly, "you have called me a good Jew." He paused, seeking what else to say. "A good Jew," he repeated. "I have followed the ways of peace that Akiba taught my people. But now it has changed. What Sarra brought me here to speak about, it is impossible."

"The Romans are the same. Akiba is the same."

Simeon shook his head, as if to get rid of his wonder. "No," he said, "it is the Romans who have changed, not we."

"I know what he means," Sarra said in a low voice.

"What does he mean?" I demanded.

"As if you wanted the Jews to revolt," Sarra said. "As if peace in our land was too much for Rome to bear. As if peace were slavery and war were freedom."

"Revolt?" I cried. "Desired by the Romans? What madness is this?"

"You think of the hilt in the face and the blade in the belly," Simeon said.

"Do you believe that of me?"

"When I think of Rome now," he answered steadily, "every Roman face seems the same. The arch of the nose, the tightness of the lips, the sunken cheeks, the cruel, glaring eyes. Your face, Rufus."

"Wait!" whispered Sarra. "Simeon, you came with me to talk of peace, not to quarrel!"

"I came because I hoped the face of Rufus might be different," Simeon said. "But it is the same as any Roman's. There is no hope, small Sarra."

It was my turn to remain silent. Simeon's expression twisted without humor. "You have been my friend, next to Akiba," he told me. "But that was a long time ago. Now our fates are fixed."

The voice of Sarra broke in. "Each of you," she said sadly, "wants the other to break, to give him some sort of excuse."

"It has been good to have an uncle," Simeon said, disregarding her. "I have been fond of you but only in your fashion. I have thought like you, obeyed you—to what end?"

"When have you obeyed me?" I asked sardonically.

"When have any commands been other than Roman commands?"

"Akiba," I said, my fury making the word indistinct, "what of your good rabbi Akiba? Do you reject what he says of peace between Romans and Jews?"

Simeon shrugged. "He believes what he says," he replied. "Possibly I believe a little of it, too. But he is old and I am young. He is patient, I am impatient. He looks for the Kingdom to come out of the sky and I want it to grow out of the earth. I want to share in its making. I do not want it to be created by a word out of the mouth of God. Do you understand, Rufus?"

Before I could reply, Sarra spoke passionately. "I understand!" she exclaimed. "I understand!"

Simeon looked at her sadly. "You?" he said. "You who are the wife of Rufus?"

Sarra drew herself up and proudly gave him look for look.

"I am not ashamed of that," she said clearly. "I forgive you, Simeon, because you do not comprehend, any more than Rufus does. If my body might have been the bridge between Romans and Jews, I was willing to give it. If men do not understand each other, how shall they understand women? It is always we who must come to you."

"Sarra," Simeon said, his voice breaking.

She did not hear the despair with which he uttered her name. She had already turned, running down the path, vanishing. A heavy weight slid into my soul; not of sorrow, not of pain, but a lethargy of the spirit.

"Let there be friendship between us," I said impulsively. I held out my hand.

Simeon disregarded it. "Friendship between the master and his dog?" he asked disdainfully. "Already you seek to leash me again. Does not the Jew know the Roman? Do I not know that I have come into a trap? Do I not know that you will never permit me to leave this place?"

An irresistible wave of anger washed over me. I had extended my hand to him as an equal and he had refused it! I felt the blood rise in my cheeks; then it receded. "You may go when you please," I said coldly. "You may go in peace."

For no more than a moment, Simeon hesitated. Then he made an abrupt gesture. "One day you will regret it," he said. With that he was gone as noiselessly as an animal. I remained where I was, my head sagging on my chest, with the numbing knowledge that I had indeed betrayed Rome. I had let go the one man who might successfully challenge her might. But I could not have kept him. Simeon had truly penetrated my mind. I had indeed intended to seize him, to cast him in chains—until the moment he had laid open my thoughts to my own shame.

I roused. My body prickled suddenly to have Sarra. I burned to seize her white body since I could not have the body of Simeon. "Ficus!" I shouted. He came running, and I issued my order. I waited, trembling, for him to return. In a moment, his frog-face grave, he came back.

"Sir, my mistress is in her room, and the door is bolted," he reported. "She does not answer. She is weeping. I can hear her sobs."

"Break down the door, and bring her here to me!" I exclaimed.

Ficus stood as still as stone. "Why do you stand there?" I shouted. "Do you not hear?"

303

Ficus saluted. "I am growing old," he replied solemnly, "and my ears have become deaf in your service. If your excellency will have the goodness to repeat his order, I will obey."

"Gods, gods!" I cried, flinging my arm upward. My desire for Sarra ebbed. "Let her weep," I muttered. "As for me, bring me another amphora." Ficus made a sign of assent and started off. "Wait," I said wearily. "Do not bring the good wine. Bring the newest and rawest in my cellars. I do not intend to enjoy myself. I wish only to drink myself senseless."

Ten days later, as I was attempting to put together some light verses in the manner of Meleager, I was interrupted by a visitor who proved what Sarra and Simeon had only intimated.

"I beg pardon," Ficus said, appearing at my left elbow, "but the Jew Akiba is here, requesting to see you."

"Yes," I said regretfully and laid down my stylus. I looked at what I had scribed on the wax and was seized by the premonition that I should not continue. Nor have I. The thoughts I had then are flown; I know not how to fit them together again. "Yes," I repeated, "where is he?"

"In the atrium, with his friends."

"With his friends?" I frowned, and Ficus shrugged. "I have never seen them before," he said.

"Very well," I told him, adjusting my toga with his clumsy help. I passed down the stairs and into the afternoon glow of the atrium. I stopped short.

Akiba confronted me, thinner than I had ever seen him, his face shrunken like an African mummy, his eyes burned black into his face. From time to time he passed his hand over his head or tugged at his beard. As he saw me, he became perfectly immobile.

I looked at his friends. They stared grimly back at me. One by one, I recognized them. They had never entered my gates before, but they had been pointed out to me as disturbers of the peace more than once. All were Pharisees, all were fiercely devoted to what they called "independence under the rule of God alone." Their obvious leader, a glowering middle-aged man with lines of force graved in his forehead, was Ishmael ben Elisha. For years Akiba had described him to me as his enemy in almost every aspect of Jewish life.

The half dozen others bowed as I entered and took my seat.

304

Ishmael barely nodded, and Akiba stared straight ahead. I felt a growing sense of confusion and anger.

"Rufus Teneius," Akiba said. His voice shook, and he steadied his tone. "Rufus Teneius," he repeated, "we have come to a parting of our roads."

"I did not know we traveled together," I said coldly.

"I have asked these friends here to witness my renunciation of all things Roman."

The words did not startle me as much as they might have done under other circumstances. Clearly Akiba was playing some sort of game for a selected audience. I decided to humor him.

"I am sure that the empire will collapse without your support," I said sardonically, "but I accept your renunciation."

Without a word, they bowed in unison, turned, and walked out of my presence. I watched them go in silence, my thoughts spinning. I had no idea of the purpose of this brief conclave. Speculation of every kind clattered in my head as I went into the gestatio, my path for exercise. Strolling back and forth in the twilight between the fragrant rows of burnet, wild thyme, and water mints, I thought about Akiba's visit with his fellow rabbis. It reminded me strongly of the secret message he had sent me from Rome to the camp at Colonia in my youth. I had the insuperable feeling that he wished to convey some momentous change in his life—and that I had failed to comprehend its meaning.

The more I pondered, the more bewildered I felt. Most of all, I was baffled as to the method of proceeding further. Obviously I must see Akiba soon and privately. Equally obvious was the fact that to do so would be to disturb some delicate balance set up in the community—or else he would not have brought solely hostile witnesses. I could not hope to confer with him secretly; the Jewish spies were quite as active and omnipresent as my own. Any show of friendship between us at this point would seem collusion.

I snapped my fingers and stopped my pacing. The solution was so simple it had escaped me; yet it had been before me all the time. I raised my voice in a shout for Ficus. Grown more than a little portly in my service, he came rolling down the path and halted.

"Reporting, sir," he droned. "What is your pleasure?"

"My pleasure," I said crisply, "is that you take four men and arrest the Jew Akiba."

Ficus goggled at me. "Arrest the good rabbi?" he gasped.

305

"You heard. I believe he is still in Caesarea but if necessary follow him to Lydda and bring him back."

"The magical rabbi of Nehardea?"

I ignored the veiled reference of my orderly to what Akiba had done for me in Parthia. "Exactly," I said. "I want him in prison as soon as possible. Hold him in the barracks cell farthest from the street."

Ficus gazed at me reproachfully. "Do you question my order, you rascal?" I demanded sharply.

Ficus jerked to attention and saluted. "Never, sir," he said mournfully. He moved off with reluctance, shaking his head.

I surveyed Akiba's cell and found it to my liking. One side faced an alley, but that could not be helped. It was large enough so that a private conversation might be carried on in a far corner. It was dry, light, warm, built of sandstone blocks and guarded with forged iron bars. I had ordered in a comfortable mat and provisions and wine—all ceremonially cleansed by the Jews. There was also a similarly purified jar of water, large and filled to the brim.

I turned to Akiba. "How do you like your lodging?" I asked him.

"I was not aware that I had committed a crime," he said. For a man as acute as Akiba—even at his age—I thought he was remarkably obtuse. "You are guilty of no offense," I explained. "This is no more than a ruse I devised so that we may talk further."

"A clumsy ruse," Akiba said. "Talk on what things?"

I began to grow irritated at his stupidity. "How long have we been friends?" I demanded.

"Nearly forty years."

"Very well. You cannot leave a friend—much less the governor of Judea—with such short shrift as was given at our last meeting. More needs to be said—or so much should never have been said."

"I was forced to come into your presence," Akiba said.

"So I thought."

"But what I said, I wanted to say."

I flung out my hand toward him. "Will you not speak clearly and simply?" I pleaded. "I cannot understand your barbarian subtleties." Akiba turned away from me and stared at the wall.

I walked about, peered out of the barred window and tested the bars. I turned back to Akiba. Since he had nettled me, it was only fair that I should be allowed to fling a dart of my own at him.

"You seem to have lost favor with your people," I said. "I had ordered an extra guard of soldiers about the prison but there is no disturbance outside."

"No," Akiba said.

"A few months ago there would have been riots in the streets," I said, settling myself on a stool.

"The Jew is a religious soul and a political beast."

"Then the reason for all this is politics?"

Akiba did not answer. His tone was strange and his appearance one of deep distraction. I determined to come to the point.

"What did that visit mean yesterday?" I demanded.

Akiba glanced at me. "Have you noticed that I have not been to your palace for months?" he asked obliquely.

"Yes," I said. I was, as usual, on the defensive with this man.

"I could not come," Akiba said, "nor did I want to."

"What has happened?"

"I don't know."

I felt astounded. "Akiba," I commanded, "I have come here to make inquiry on serious matters. Rome is not too patient, I warn you."

"Simeon," Akiba said. With that single word, he was silent.

"Simeon?"

"Simeon."

"What in the name of the gods has he to do with it?"

"You heard him in the marketplace," Akiba responded.

"I put a stop to that," I said.

Akiba shook his head. "You fanned the flames, scattered the coals."

"What about Simeon?" I asked. Evidently neither Simeon nor Sarra had told the old man of their last surreptitious visit to me.

Akiba waited a moment. "He has been preaching revolt against Rome," he answered.

I shook my head. "No," I said decisively. "There has been no evidence at all, and my spies are everywhere."

"Nor will you have evidence until the time comes. I say this not because I betray him but because—" Akiba stopped.

"Because?" I pressed him.

"Because I do not yet believe him."

"Yet?"

Akiba said nothing. "He is a young fool," I grumbled. "His antics mean nothing. You and I know him best."

"They believe in him," Akiba said.

"Who?"

"The people, my people, the Jews."

"Interesting," I said. "I have heard that Jews believe in nothing but their God. Why do they suddenly believe in Simeon?"

"Because they think he is the Messiah."

The words fell on my ears like a thunderbolt. I reared upward from my seat in anger. "Are all you Jews mad?" I cried.

"Perhaps they are, perhaps he is," Akiba said, unnaturally tranquil. "Perhaps I am. I may have spoken the words of God in the villa of Flavius Clemens many years ago, not knowing their Source."

"When you called him 'son of a star'?"

"You remember, too," Akiba said. "You see?"

"I see nothing," I said doggedly.

"God works through unworthy instruments."

"It does no good to insult me," I told him.

"I refer to myself."

"You are in your dotage, Akiba," I said fiercely.

He smiled for the first time, a benign expression. "We are all older, but some of us are wiser," he said sweetly.

I held back my retort: this led nowhere. What I needed was information which Akiba could supply. I threw out a crumb of my own. "I hear," I said cautiously, "that great numbers of Jews from other lands have been passing through Caesarea."

"There have been others going out," Akiba said.

"Why?"

"To spread the glad tidings of the return of the Messiah."

I struck the wall with my hand. "Curse the Messiah!" I exclaimed. "Both the Christians and the Jews! You have a messiah every year! You yourselves have proved all of them false! In Africa, Palestine, in Egypt! In Gaul, in Bithynia, in Cyrenaica! In Rome itself!"

"You are well informed," Akiba said. "It is true all these were impostors, but one day the real Messiah will come. Should we not be prepared?"

I calmed myself. "Akiba," I asked, "what does the Messiah promise the Jews?"

"For our sins, other sinners have risen up over us," Akiba

308

said with rising energy, "taking with force the kingdom which God did not promise to them, profaning the throne of David in their pride. The Lord will raise up to Him whom He appoints, to reign over Israel, with strength to crush unjust rulers, to cleanse Jerusalem, to cast out sinners, to break their pride and strength as potters' vessels with a rod of iron—to destroy the lawless nations with the word of His mouth—to gather the holy nation and lead it in righteousness."

"This is all very fine," I said patiently, "and I sympathize with your plight."

Akiba's eyes blazed at me from the shadows. "The Messiah will rebuild the Temple and gather in the dispersed! The laws of old shall be restored, the sacrifices renewed! As the prophet Micah says, 'in the end of days it shall come to pass, that the mountain of the house of the Lord shall be established at the top of the mountains'! He will be a great prophet and teacher, next to Moses, He will instruct all nations. He will prepare the whole world to serve the one God!"

"An altogether extraordinary fellow," I said.

"He will come in all His glory!"

I decided to try a shot in the dark. "Perhaps you believe Simeon to be this kind of heaven-sent person on earth?"

"I do not know. God has not spoken to me. I hope."

"If you do, you hope against Rome," I said darkly.

"All the world will be one kingdom under the Messiah."

I laughed shortly. "Romans and Jews one! This would be a savior indeed!"

Akiba shook his head vigorously. Marks of pain commenced to furrow his face. He wrung his hands slowly, in doubt, as he had when he appeared the day before. "I must think," he said in a low tone. "Good Rufus, allow me to remain in prison for a time, to meditate and pray."

"Granted," I said. "You may go when you like. Send me a message. Are you comfortable?"

"Yes."

"This is the best cell in the prison," I said unnecessarily. "Consider yourself my guest."

I started out but halted. "What of the peace you promised Trajan?" I inquired.

Akiba drooped. "I cannot control events now," he responded. "Simeon has taken them from my hands. But what of the restoration of the Temple that Trajan promised?"

"The emperor is not a Jew," I said roughly.

Akiba smiled tiredly. "His word is more sacred, perhaps?" he asked.

"Akiba," I said, changing my tone, "let this nonsense alone. Simeon will come around."

"He will not come," Akiba said steadily, "except with a sword."

"I shall greet him with a sword!" I cried, and banged my way out of the cell without a farewell.

They were foolish words to say and I regretted them as soon as I stepped into my litter. Halfway back to my residence, the way out of the dilemma came to me: I must visit Rachel in Lydda. I had some claim upon her regard, since she had saved my life. Of all people, not excepting Akiba, she had been closest to Simeon. He would listen to her most readily and, without a doubt, she was the only person alive outside the Sanhedrin who was able to influence Akiba's decisions. She had sold her hair to gain his food and had lived apart from him for years while he studied. He had honored her among all the wives of the rabbis with a stunning gift, a coronet of gold. Her reputation was such that when the mates of the other scholars complained, the invariable response was: "Had you done for me what Rachel did for Akiba, you too should have a headdress of gold."

The thought of seeing Rachel calmed my brain. Within the next three days, I decided, I should set out for Lydda.

It was not to be: fate had already decreed otherwise. As I came in the door, I found Sarra waiting for me—her lips trembling, her hands clasped whitely before her. As soon as I saw her tear-stained face, I knew the tidings were evil. Taking her hand in mine, I tried to pull her to me, but she resisted. "What has happened?" I asked.

Sarra looked up at me. Her eyes overflowed. "Rachel," she told me, choked with sobs, "Rachel is dead."

My heart swelled. "How?" I demanded. "When?"

"Two days ago, in Lydda. A soldier prodded her for not moving fast enough in the streets. She fell. She was very old."

With that Sarra turned and fled into her room on the opposite side of the atrium, bolting the door against me. I flattened myself against it, trying to find out what I must. "Does Akiba know?" I shouted again and again, but I got no answer.

I was being made ridiculous. A cold shudder ran through me. I stepped back. "Sarra," I said, loud enough for her to hear, "if you do not unbar this door and come to me, I shall tell you before witnesses that you have no property and that we stand divorced. You have borne me no children, you shall enjoy no more the privileges of a Roman wife. You shall be my slave. Do you hear?"

I waited. There was no sound but that of muffled, desperate weeping. "Do you hear?" I roared at the top of my voice.

"Did you call, sir?" asked Ficus' solicitous tones behind me.

I whirled, my hand clutching at my hair. "No!" I cried. "Get out! Get out!"

He saluted and turned. I tensed my muscles and fought for control of myself. There were other things more necessary and immediate to be done than pursue a quarrel with a recalcitrant wife. "Yes," I said quickly. "Hear these orders." I told Ficus to go at once to the prison and bring Akiba to me. As he ran out, I returned to my apartment to compose myself.

In less than an hour, Ficus returned. He was unaccompanied, his face grim. He reported to me that Akiba had disappeared. He had taken two of the guard to investigate; they had discovered how he had escaped. Someone unknown had stolen into the alleyway and lashed a rawhide halter to the bars. According to the hoofprints, they had used a team of four asses to tear them out of the prison masonry. Akiba had vanished into the night.

Such a small thing, to plunge the lives of so many others into misery and oblivion! The death of an old woman, far away, without office or fame, without power of any sort. Yet she was the light of Akiba's life, his adored wife, and when the thread of Rachel's existence was snapped, he passed over the gulf beyond my reach. I scoured Lydda to find the soldier who had caused Rachel's death, but he was never discovered. I am convinced it was an accident, one of those unforeseen, careless events that change the destinies of men and cannot, in the nature of the gods, be avoided. Blame, if blame there be, must be at the feet of mightier beings than we.

Nor did I have time to weep for her, she who had rescued me from Hades. Her own death shattered the last hope of Rome keeping peace in Judea. Two nights later, the reports from my agents came in. Each one had the same ominous message: Akiba had joined the forces of Simeon. In a secret massing of the Jews in the southwest wilderness of the hills of Jezreel, the old sage had acclaimed Simeon as the Messiah— as the last and best hope for the freedom of his people. It was no less than a declaration of war against Rome.

I sent urgent couriers to Antioch and to Egypt, asking for

311

reinforcements. The X Fretensis was put upon a campaign footing. I doubled the guards at the city gates and began a systematic expulsion of the Jews within Caesarea, even including those who had sworn fidelity to Rome. But, in regard to the strategy of battle, I did not trust myself. Such measures needed a practiced mind. I had been removed from the field for such a long time that it was with a good deal of relief I welcomed a surprise arrival four anxious days later.

He came unannounced behind a beaming Ficus, spreading his arms wide to embrace me. "Ave!" he exclaimed.

"Ave!" I cried, springing from my couch. He flung his arms about me, and I responded in kind, as best I could. He thrust me back and surveyed me with wonder.

"By the gods," he said, "I had heard that you had been hurt, but I had no idea it was this."

"One can use only one sword at a time," I assured him, "and at my age one's skin is so tough, it serves as a shield in itself. But being one-armed has the disadvantage of not being able to embrace an old comrade as one should."

"I refuse to offer any further sympathy," said Julius Severus. I recognized in him the same spirit of the young centurion who had given me the corona cerialis when I had rescued him in Germania, fighting together under Trajan. "But what are you doing here?" I asked the tall, rosy-cheeked man with the scar on his face that marked him from those days. "I heard you commanded the legions in Britain."

Severus nodded and took the cup of wine Ficus held for him. "So I did," he admitted, "until two months ago. I am ordered here to take charge of the legions."

I slapped my hand on his knee. "I have never been so glad to see you before," I said sincerely. "As you know, I think highly enough of my own ability—but with one arm, I cannot inspire valor in the legionaries who follow me. We have need of you."

I explained rapidly what the situation was, as best I could. Severus was not overly impressed. "When one has spent years repulsing the wild blue-painted Britons," he said, "these Jews in this hot enervating climate will be only a military exercise."

"Do not be sure," I warned him. "These are a fanatic set of tribes and priests."

"So are the Druids."

"Well," I said comfortably, "at least you came swiftly, as if the wings of Mercury were tied to your heels."

"At the highest priority," Severus replied. "Behind me come two legions—the II Augusta and the VI Victrix, both of which you know very well."

"Both!" I exclaimed.

Severus nodded. "The orders for the movement were put in my hands three months ago by Hadrian himself," he added.

I meditated. Evidently Hadrian had not forgotten his interview with Akiba. I bowed my head to the incomparable military foresight of the emperor. Whatever his own grief or madness, he did not neglect a tittle of his duties as the supreme ruler.

Severus roused me by finishing his wine and speaking a note of caution: "You know it will take a long time to move such a body of men from one end of the empire to another. If the danger is as imminent as you believe, we shall have to depend on what troops are here."

"The Jews are rousing themselves to a fever," I assented gloomily. "We shall have to fight soon."

"What legions have you?"

"The X Fretensis, of course. They may be depended upon. Antioch may send me the IV Scythica or the VI Ferrata, but what others I do not know. Within the week, the XXII Deiotariana from Egypt will be here, but in my opinion it is totally worthless."

"Why is that?" Severus asked sharply.

"Even during the riots of a dozen years ago in Alexandria, they proved unreliable. My information is they have become slothful through a long period of peace. They grumble at camp duties and have never fought a war. There are veterans among them who have never been on guard—who look upon the rampart and trench as strange and fearsome things. Many possess no helmets or breastplates. They are sleek and fat and rich from bribery. From what I hear, their service has been passed in strolling through the towns, intimidating the natives with the name of Rome, taking their exercitus in chasing the wives and daughters of their neighbors."

"Oho," Severus said and was silent. He roused himself and declared: "We shall have to use what we have. There is no time to vinestock these habits out of them. Let us begin our plans now: where do you think these criminal Jews will gather?"

I reached for the shelf behind me and spread out a parchment map on the bench. Severus held it wide, and I placed my finger on the Valley of Jezreel. No sooner had I done so than a clatter of hooves resounded in the court outside, the

313

sound of a messenger in desperate haste. Severus and I looked at each other in dark speculation without a word.

It was Ficus who came in with the messenger, a dusty squat little man, wounded in the shoulder. I recognized him as one of the X Fretensis, Second Cohort.

"Honored Rufus Teneius," he said, "I have wretched tidings."

"Speak," I said.

"The Jews have risen. They have seized the city of Aelia Capitolina."

Severus and I said nothing. The man hesitated, then went on: "They have also taken our camp and scattered the legion. We have been ordered to take refuge in this city."

"Ficus," I said, "take this man away and see to his wound. We shall want to speak to him later. Have the sentinels at the gates ordered to admit all fugitives from the X Fretensis and place them in barracks under guard."

"Noble governor," protested the messenger, "we fought as long and as well as we were able."

"Take him away," I said brusquely. "Imprison him with the rest."

He said no more. Head hanging, with Ficus in close attendance, he passed out of the peristylium. I looked inquiringly at Severus. He nodded solemnly.

"Well?" I said.

"We shall have to do the best we can with what we have," he repeated. He smiled. "If the Jews seek open battle," he said softly, "perhaps we may accommodate them when the X Fretensis is regrouped and the XXII Deiotariana arrives." He leaned forward and took up the pitcher of wine. "Meanwhile, old comrade, let us have another glass. Let us talk of those glorious days in Germania."

Severus was right. A battle in the open was precisely what the Jews desired, as events proved. They had no desire to storm or besiege Caesarea—it would have been futile since it was a well-defended port. They spent their time, insofar as we could ascertain, by sending out exploratores, in throwing down the partially built temple of Jupiter and improving the defenses of Aelia Capitolina. Meanwhile, Severus and I reorganized the X Fretensis, instituted constant training in arms and waited for the arrival of the XXII Deiotariana.

Ten days after the capture of Hadrian's city by the Jews, the legion from Egypt arrived. I swear by all the gods that I have never seen such an undisciplined and hangdog lot in my career as a Roman soldier. They marched unopposed into Caesarea and presented the spectacle of an imperial legion exhausted by a mere forced march. The work of conditioning and training began immediately with centurions and tribunes selected from the X Fretensis, with plentiful use of beatings and one or two executions in the barracks square as example to the laggards.

It was three weeks before a semblance of military fitness appeared in their ranks. Severus showed a growing impatience, and I knew the reason: the Jews as well as ourselves were improving their forces. We were warned that Simeon bar Cocheba's countrymen, excited by the news that he was the true Messiah and reincarnated the tradition of the Maccabees, were pouring into his camp. Arms appeared overnight in their midst. Siege machines were being constructed. Plainly it was no time to delay a test of strength.

At length Severus expressed some satisfaction with the status of his legions. Shortly afterward, we gained intelligence that the Jews were gathering in force in the Jezreel. It appeared that the moment was at hand. At dawn, the day before the nones of July, Severus marched out of the gates of the city at the head of his army, bound for the battleground where he hoped to crush the Jewish revolt for all time.

I remained behind, chafing at the inaction but mindful that the rear of the legions had to be protected and a refuge maintained in the unlikely event of a defeat. All day long I paced the walls, looking toward the southeast and hoping for some courier to bring news of our victory. At sunset I spied a cloud of dust on the road and sent a lookout to the highest tower in the city. Before he could descend, it was plain that the arrivals were racing at full speed for the gates, their shadows streaming behind them. I went down to greet them.

To my amazement, the riders were Severus himself and two of his staff. My heart sank at the expression of my friend: his face was black and fixed, his armor dusty and battered, his head bare. He spoke not a word, dismissing his escort with a wave. He galloped onward as I snatched the reins of a mount and threw myself into the saddle, riding recklessly after him through a throng of dazed and silent citizens.

I found Severus in my atrium, slumped in a chair, staring straight ahead. He thrust away Ficus and the wine; nor did he seem to notice my entrance. I sat opposite him and waited until the terrible fixity of his face commenced to dissolve into

315

sheer lassitude. For the first time, Severus recognized me. He smiled without mirth.

"Send orders to the barracks," he said hoarsely. "All of the XXII Deiotariana who manage to struggle through the gates shall be held for decimation. Their standards are to be taken from them and broken."

"What happened?" I asked in terror.

Severus did not reply. "I shall recommend to the emperor that the legion be disbanded," he said slowly. Then, with a fierce shout: "Did you not hear my orders?"

I stiffened in resentment, then nodded to Ficus who had been eavesdropping at the door. Severus stared at me with eyes glazed by his weariness.

"I was at fault," he said abruptly. "You were right about the Jews, about the legion from Egypt."

I did not utter a word. After a moment more, Severus began to talk in a dull droning tone:

"We came to the head of the valley before noon. We rested under the hot sun and pushed on to the place where we had been told the enemy was gathering." He did not use the contemptuous term of "Jews" but the honorable epithet of "enemy," I noticed. I knew his recital was one of defeat, but somehow my heart twisted in pride at the thought it was Simeon, my own flesh and blood, who had humbled the sword of Rome. Inwardly, I reproved myself.

"At the eighth hour," Severus went on, "as our scouts had reported, we confronted their army. They had troops in regular order before a barricade of a huge circle of carts. We spread out in battle array and, to give our soldiers a rest, I ordered forward the right wing of our cavalry. At the same time we harassed the Jews with shoutings and clamor, blowing trumpets and clashing our shields, sending clouds of arrows and javelins into their midst. But they did not break and flee as I had anticipated. It was an evil omen."

"They stood firm?"

"As a rock. And our left wing of cavalry had not yet arrived on the plain. I did not intend to join the fight until they had come up to the main body—and at that time, to my surprise, the Jews sent envoys to ask for a truce."

"You agreed?"

"I refused, thinking it only a trick. I was right. The enemy had done so purposely, I believe, hoping that our soldiers might be dismayed by the sight of their numbers—nearly triple our own forces. Or perhaps they thought that the legions might yield to their thirst or the fiery summer heat."

"But they did not?"

"They tricked us," Severus said harshly. "They had built great fires all across the plain—and with the wind at their backs, the smoke and fumes and heat blew directly into our faces."

"We must remember that," I said.

"Both armies waited, the Jews impatiently with shouts and curses of defiance; our own, in silence. I have never trusted silence in a soldier. Suddenly, without orders, the archers and light-armed soldiers of the XXII Deiotariana rushed forward on the flank and were easily thrown back by the Jews. The sight inflamed the rest of our army. Regardless of our efforts to hold them back, the whole front moved forward to join battle."

" 'And Bellona blew her lamentable trumpets,' " I quoted softly.

Severus glanced irritably at me and continued:

"You have seen battles but none like this. Almost instantly the field became covered with bodies of dead and wounded. Over this pavement of heaving flesh, the living in a frenzy extended their swords and spears, slipping and falling, trying to reach the foe. The marksmanship of the Jews was remarkable. They impaled many of our soldiers with their homemade spears and a rain of arrows."

"You pushed the Jews back to their wagons?"

Severus shook his head. "The left wing of our Roman cavalry," he said sombrely, "was crushed as it came hastily into line. It managed to cut its way into the Jews almost as far as their carts, but it had lost the support of the foot soldiers. It was surrounded. Those that tried to run to its aid were encompassed by so many Jews that their shields were thrust back against them. The pressure kept them from moving, even from pulling out their swords. Whole sections of men, like pieces of a rampart, fell helpless in the slaughter."

"But you did not despair."

"There was no hope in this battle. Hordes of Jews overwhelmed everything before their ferocity. Our soldiers could not retreat. So monstrous was the press of men from the other side that they trampled over both horse and man."

"But you killed many Jews yourselves?"

Severus shook his head.

"They would not retreat?"

317

"Both sides gave up the idea of returning alive. It seemed to me that all pressed forward to destruction. But the nature of the battle and the fortune of it slowly changed the boldness of our men to fear. The Jews were like madmen who had no regard for any fate hereafter."

"Yes," I said.

"Finally, our men lost spirit in the right wing. The infection spread to all ranks. Careless of our officers—who struck at their own men—they turned and commenced to run. Panic replaced courage; fear took the place of boldness. The Romans ran pellmell for their lives before the fierce Jews who shouted in ecstatic victory. I was swept away in the rout. The Jews pursued us mercilessly. Our retreat became a massacre as we were blocked by those who lay mortally wounded, impeding our progress with mounds of horses and corpses. It was only when dusk came, dusk without a moon, that we were able to escape, to put an end to a battle so costly to the Roman people."

"All this does not sound like cowards," I said.

Severus flushed, and his face stiffened. "The right wing was that of the XXII Deiotariana," he said, spurning the name. "It was from thence that the cowardly spirit came. Rufus, they dropped their eagle on the field of battle," he whispered, as if it were sacrilege to say it.

I covered my face with my hand, hardly believing. I took a deep breath and rose. "Noble Julius," I told him, "you shall have wine and a bath and sup with me, and we shall talk of this hereafter. My own wife shall attend you."

His face expressed his surprise. I bent my head. "She is a Jewess," I said bitterly.

I heard Severus rise painfully from his chair. "I understand," he said. "Send her to me."

He left the room for his chamber. My heart burning within me at the disgrace to Roman arms, the desire for revenge on the Jews running in my veins like molten metal in the veins of the giant Talus, I shouted for Ficus. He came on the run.

"Bring Sarra to me instantly!" I exclaimed.

"Your wife," Ficus said, "is not here," omitting his usual expressions of respect in his perturbation.

"You are wrong," I said, "because she must be here."

"Yes, sir."

"Gone?"

"Yes, sir."

318

I glared at him. "If she is gone, where did she go?" I asked him. Ficus shook his head and looked at the floor.

My wrath went out of me like air from a pricked bladder. The stiffening of revenge inside me melted and left me sick and weak. I sank to the couch, knowing it was true—that nothing else could be true. "You are right, Ficus," I said slowly. He did not reply. I found no more words to say. There was no moon in the sky over our heads. The imagined smell of flowers and herbs was strong from the desolation around me that had been my garden. There was no sound except for the trickling of a distant fountain, the quick sniffles of Ficus. I roused myself.

"What has happened," I said, steeling my voice, "is the ending to my last campaign of love. Rome was destined to conquer, as always. But the prisoner escaped and we, merciful to those we have crushed, will not pursue."

"I know where she has gone, sir," Ficus told me.

"So do I," I said, rising unsteadily, "so do I. Good night, good night."

After that, I stood over the fountain of my atrium pensively. I took a corner of my tunic and stuffed it into the mouth of the bronze pipe, stifling the flow. When the water quieted, I stared down at the reflection of my face in the pool of the black marble basin. I saw the thinning hair, the lined face, the puffy chin—above all, the wretched lack of an arm. "A pretty fellow for anyone to love," I said aloud, echoing my thoughts. With a wrench, I freed the mouth of the pipe, and next moment the image was shattered.

CHAPTER 19

Ad residua narranda pergamus—let us go on to relate the rest of the story which leads to the fate of Akiba and Simeon. The blinding-white sunrise over the hills of rugged Judea next morning found Severus and myself in the already hot shadow of the terrace fronting the wind-stroked sea. We were busy reviewing the battle and rout of the day before.

"It should be considered not a defeat but a warning," I said.

"It is no more than the flogging by a pedagogus in the school of war."

"What lessons is it possible to learn?" asked Severus. His sober face shifted into an expression of quick interest.

"Lessons from both sides that will bring us victory another time."

"You have plans for the battle?"

"I do not think there should be another battle," I said flatly. Severus studied me, smiling incredulously. "You are not the daring tribune Rufus Teneius of old," he said.

I ruefully matched his smile. "No," I admitted, "I am merely the aged politician, Rufus Teneius, who has learned that a battle is not a campaign—and that the Jews are different from the barbarian Britons and Germans."

"I have learned that at great cost," confessed Severus. "There is much to be explained, I see."

I set myself to my scheme. "This country, except for the seacoast," I told Severus, "is a maze of hills and wilderness. It has as many holes as a warren of conies. There are a few broad plains but they must be avoided by the skillful tactician. In my opinion the only ways in which a war may be won in this land are by siege or ambush. The terrain is not hospitable to outright battle. The inhabitants are too clever to risk all— unless the odds, like yesterday's, are heavily in their favor."

"What do you suggest?"

"I suggest both siege and ambush."

Severus looked at me with dismay. "But that means months of war!"

"It will be a long war."

"It means thousands of men!"

"We shall have to secure them."

Severus shook his head doubtfully as I went on. "I believe it is the only way to victory," I said, "but there may be more to be anticipated, if they become so rash as to venture another battle. Tell me, when did you fling the pila?"

"As usual—when they came within range."

"And the Jews?"

"They waited until they heard the trumpet; then the first two ranks rushed forward at full speed and halted. Most of the pila went over their heads and struck harmlessly into the ground behind."

"I see," I said thoughtfully.

"At the second discharge, the same maneuver was repeated and at the third our supply of pila was exhausted."

"Clever Jews," I said. Simeon's talent for war inspired me with respect. "Continue."

"They advanced in a tumultuous shouting mass as fast as they could run. There was no proper order, I saw no leaders. But they kept their ranks in the mass and leaped upon our first line of shields with such weight that our finest soldiers were driven half a dozen paces backward. This trapped the rest, holding them in a human snare of their fellows. They could neither fight nor flee—and, as you know, it was then that the XXII Deiotariana panicked and broke."

"Notice the use of axes against our armor," I said. "There is more to be considered."

"Still more?"

"The condition of our soldiers," I said simply. "They are not accustomed to this climate. We must have more time to train them."

Severus said nothing; I could sense the struggle of his pride against his professional instincts as an officer, but at length the latter won. "What, then, is the remedy for Romans arms?" he asked almost humbly.

"I have these suggestions. First, to recruit and strengthen the troops by drill and exercise against simulated tactics of the enemy. Second, to incite them by the desire for revenge and glory. They feel enough humiliation at being worsted by the despised Jews."

"Thirdly?"

"The pila should be discharged without command or trumpet, immediately after the Jews have come to their first halt. In any case, they must be thrown low, never high. Even if they miss, they will form a palisade of sorts."

"I observed the second rank of Jews pulling up the pila and using them against us," said Severus.

"We might resist the final charge by a ruse. Merely prop up our shields in the front ranks and withdraw three paces. Double the space of the open order and use light targets for defense."

"We might also bring timbers capable of being fitted together as a barrier," Severus added. I nodded: I had done my work. The martial imagination, so necessary to a soldier and congealed in his brain by defeat, had commenced to flow again. He would be able to invent enough of his own tactics from this moment on. As it came about, we never used this stratagem because there was never another pitched battle in

321

the open against the Jews. But our discussion served a vital purpose.

As Severus rose, I could not forbear asking: "Had the Jews a leader?"

Severus gave me a curious glance. "Yes," he said. "I thought you knew."

"No," I said.

"A youth of flowing dark hair, clad in rags with a scarlet sash, of the most consummate energy. He led every sally of the Jews. He was the man who broke our ranks, the one they followed like mad dogs despite wounds and death."

I bowed my head. The guess of my heart had been correct. "Why should I have known?" I muttered.

"I heard his name as Simeon," Severus responded. "I was also informed that he had visited you here. That is nothing, of course, but it interested me."

"Yes," I murmured, "that is true. He had been welcome here—what Jew has not? But he violated my hospitality and is now a renegade,"

"It is unfortunate that he was not born a Roman," Severus said casually. "He might have made a great general, even an emperor."

I nodded briefly. I gestured politely for my guest to precede me out of the room. But Severus hesitated at the door.

"They have a curious war cry," he said, almost apologetically.

"What is that?"

"Something like 'Bar Cocheba, Bar Cocheba!' "

"Yes. That is it."

"You have heard it before?"

"Yes," I said, "but not as a war cry."

Severus considered me. "What does it mean?" he asked.

"In the Jewish language, 'son of a star.' "

"What does *that* mean?"

"By the gods, I have no idea!" I said explosively. "We have more to do, good Severus, than to follow these fancies. Let us get on with our work."

The legions commenced to pour into Caesarea. Swinging ranks of soldiers became an almost daily occurrence, cohort after cohort forming on the docks or at the gates to march through the cheering streets to the barracks. The III Gallica and the IV Scythica came down from the north. The VI Ferrata was called in from the south with the II Traiana. The III

322

Cyrenaica and the XII Fulminata arrived together. Last of all, weary of the overlong voyage, arrived the tough seasoned troops of Severus, the II Augusta and the VI Victrix, from Britain. The X Fretensis was reconstituted and brought up to full complement by new recruits. But the XXII Deiotariana, forever disgraced, vanished from the army rolls with the assent of Hadrian. Its insignia were broken, cursed in due form, burned, and buried in an unknown spot. Those of its members left after the official decimation were distributed among other legions to live a life of misery under the contempt and derision of their fellows until they should redeem their honor upon the battlefield.

During these days of hurry and preparation, the news came that Epictetus had died in Nicopolis, without ever returning to Rome. A pang of regret seized me, but it passed: if I had not kept my promise to return, it had been fate that had intervened. This the ghost of my old tutor would find acceptable.

Reports trickled in to our headquarters from the field. Most of our agents, at the triumph of the Jews, had deserted our service. A few remained, however: these informed us that the Jews were using Roman weapons manufactured by themselves. They had been secured by a shrewd device invented by Simeon. As a subject people, of course, they had been forbidden any arms at all. Nevertheless, they were allowed to manufacture weapons for the legions. It seemed they had deliberately forged defective pila and untempered swords. Our unsuspecting armorers had rejected them as below standard. The Jews promptly reworked them into usefulness and concealed them in caches about the country.

During the past two years—when we Romans had flattered ourselves on peace—the Jews had been busy preparing for the war to come. They fortified scores of hilltop strong points. They made hundreds of villages into hotbeds of resistance. They burrowed underground and constructed miles of tunnels useful for bushments and communication and hiding. Food and water, wine and oil, had been buried secretly at numerous places in anticipation of the very campaign we planned to wage.

Indeed, I never altogether believed that Simeon—not only hailed as the so-called Messiah but also the acknowledged general of the Jews—really wanted the battle of Jezreel. I suspect to this day that his untrained masses broke the leash of his command and conquered by sheer weight of numbers and intensity of fury. Whether it was deliberate or accidental was never discovered. Certainly Simeon's maneuvers from that time forward exhibited the skill of a veteran.

One of his first moves was to evacuate the city of Aelia Capitolina. It might have been defended, but it was not provisioned against a siege. Its inevitable capture would have meant a breakdown of the enthusiasm of the Jews, which was their chief asset. Simeon gave as his excuse that the soil of the sacred city had been defiled by the Romans. As such, he reportedly said, it was better to abandon the spot until it could be cleansed. Instead he concentrated on provisioning and fortifying a smaller but much more strategically defensible spot above Jerusalem called Bethseba. It was here, I guessed early, that the final phase of the war must be fought, near the old "new city" of Agrippa.

Owing to the sheer number of our legions, it took long months for their guerrilla training to be concluded. Almost a quarter of the total force of the empire was committed in Judea. Severus possessed an army of nearly 65,000 men. It was far more than either he or myself had requested: the mass of troops was assigned by command of Hadrian himself, evidently alarmed by the growing restiveness of the diaspora of the Jews spread across the empire. It was apparent they believed that the true Messiah was at hand in Simeon bar Cocheba. Money and recruits came over the borders of Judea from every direction. Orders had to be issued and strictly observed about emigration from other provinces. Even in faraway Rome the Suburra was placed under close watch and walled in to make it easier to detect and suppress any signs of insurrection.

One of our first acts in the disaffected province itself was to seal off the borders. Even with this accomplished, no life was safe outside the walled cities. Travelers, except under the strongest hired escort, went at their own risk. Trade ceased; communications languished. It was easier to receive a message and supplies from Gaul than it was from Palmyra. Our own reconnaissance squads were often waylaid and found with their throats cut next day. Zealots and sicarii were everywhere, sometimes in open companies but more often in disguise. Throughout Syria, towns and cities commenced a systematic expulsion of the Jews for their own safety, not knowing whom to trust. Those who did not take the side of Simeon were handed over to his forces by default. The Christian Jews were especially persecuted both by Romans and the partisans because they insisted on remaining neutral.

324

There were ominous signs against all Jews. Not only in the array of power which we were amassing but also in signs of the gods. Wolves and hyenas in larger packs than had ever been seen before, attracted by the unburied corpses and abandoned villages, invaded the countryside and terrified the inhabitants. The tomb of Solomon, a Jewish relic of the most ancient and venerable kind, collapsed into dust. Every day our scouting parties brought in copies of the Jewish sacred books which were publicly torn up and burned. Captives were dragged about the city in chains, then executed. Captured mules were deemed much more valuable than prisoners.

No less merciless were the acts of the Jews against our own legions. Simeon showed himself in every way as ruthless as the war demanded. Roman soldiers were tortured and slain daily. One cohort experienced a disastrous ambush in the pass leading to Beth-horon where the Jew Joshua had once defeated five Canaanite kings. Blocked by parties before and behind, our cavalry unable to skirmish because of the defile, half our men perished under darts and arrows and stones before they could escape.

For a time Galilee, the old fester-spot of the Jews, threatened to revolt, and the forces of Simeon held Mount Asamon facing Sepphoris. We advanced against them and, after suffering some two hundred casualties, turned their flank and cut them down with mounted troops. In Alexandria, the Jews attempted to arise again, but the governor instantly loosed the legionaries upon them. They marched to the Beta and Delta quarters of the city with permission not only to kill and disperse but also loot. The Jews resisted for a short while, but when they at length gave way they were slaughtered or driven into the houses where they perished in flames. There alone, without distinction for age or sex, some fifty thousand died. The soldiers carried away immense piles of spoils.

Our own campaign began at the end of the year. It was a systematic sweeping-up of the countryside. Separate armies advanced from Peraea, Galilee, and Judea, proceeding northward, then following the coast and turning inland. Such cities as Philadelphia, Heshbon, Gerasa, Pella, and Scythopolis were devastated. So too were Gadara, Hippos, Gaulanitis. Kedasa, Ptolemais, and Gaba were spared but occupied. Other cities such as Sebaste and Ascalon, Athenion and Gaza were cleansed and garrisoned.

Meantime, Simeon trained his men—evidently in the Roman fashion—for a similar war of attrition against us. He erected walls in caves, put forts around the cities, increased the number of officers, improved his system of signals and messages, and—inflamed undoubtedly by the aid of Akiba—kept alive the faith of the Jews in him as Messiah. He instituted a severe system of discipline: he cut off the right hands of those who disobeyed him and sent them into our lines as traitors.

In a real sense, his strictness proved his downfall. As time went on, his own people commenced to fear him and his undying hatred of things Roman. They saw no end for the war except utter destruction for themselves. The only hope Simeon possessed, after six months of our campaign, was to raise his forces to the number, disciplining, and weaponing of the Romans. This, we knew, we must prevent at all costs.

Therefore we redoubled our guards along the frontiers to prevent succor from reaching the Jews. Our plan became simple and effective. The cohorts, broken down into small, flexible units with supplies which rendered them independent of the main body for months, acted as hounds on the trail of the Jews. When they at last turned at bay, we simply tore them to pieces. War forced upon us its own inhuman necessity, as it did upon Simeon. Village after village was taken, the few dwellers enslaved or killed, the buildings sacked and burned. Underground burrows were smoked out or countermined and collapsed. One by one the fortified places were put under siege.

The slow inevitable process gradually increased the area of scorched earth under the caligae of the Romans. Simeon made desperate efforts to gain food and weapons and recruits from other countries. We intercepted most of his messengers and, even when they achieved their task, they found none willing to aid in view of the concentration of legions in Judea and the threat of reprisal. Even a small Roman fleet, dispatched by Hadrian, cruised along the eastern coast of Nostrum Mare, making sure no ports accepted contraband goods.

Once the campaign was fairly launched, Severus and I felt satisfied with its progress. It seemed to us that the end, however costly and delayed, was inevitable. But we had not reckoned with the impatience of the emperor. He was not happy with reading the constant reports which we forwarded to him via Rome. In the eighth month of the second year of the war, Hadrian himself came to Judea.

"Why has this war taken so long?" he demanded. "Do you choose to disgrace Roman arms?"

Despite his fierce words, as he sat in the atrium of my

residence—I had, of course, surrendered it to him and his pleasure immediately upon his arrival—Hadrian appeared haggard. He had lost flesh and fire. His spirit seemed damped, even to his low, rasping voice. The ardor for living, which had induced him to follow so many activities for which he was not fitted, appeared to have cooled. A certain deep burning in his eyes made me shudder. Such hidden malignity, such wild gleams I remembered only from the eyes of battle-maddened German barbarians. It lurked as an assailant in ambush and thought nothing of hazard or reason, only of its own mad whims.

"Speak!" cried Hadrian, curling his fingers like talons.

"Glorious Hadrian," I said rapidly, "it is not a war that can be ended quickly." Speaking alternately, Severus and I explained what we had planned and how it was progressing.

"So," Hadrian said in a dead voice. "So." He stared into space before him. The feral flicker in his eyes became more apparent.

He had arrived in Caesarea without warning. His enormous retinue swelled the already overburdened facilities of the city. But when Severus and I were summoned for an immediate conference, we found him alone—as he was ever in private, now that Antinoüs was dead.

We watched him rise and pace up and down, still with that unearthly look on his face. We dared not speak. His appearance made us shiver: the unmistakable pale tinge of his frenzy, the saliva leaking from the corners of his mouth, his disjointed walk. At last he turned to confront us. His words struck us with fear.

"If you are cowards," he said, "your emperor is not." He assumed a pose. "In the old times, such wars as these were decided by the commander of each army meeting in single combat on the field of honor."

"I implore you, great Hadrian!" I said involuntarily.

"Did not Cornelius Cossus slay the Tyrrhenian Tolumnius, did not Claudius Marcellus kill Britomart, king of the Gauls? Did not Romulus himself slay Acron, king of the Ceninetes?"

"Yes, mighty Hadrian," Severus murmured. He would have continued if the emperor had not interrupted him.

"Is not the spolia opima reserved for the general who has himself slain the general of the enemy?"

The chill in my veins increased. Hopeless insanity, to destroy our work, to venture the whole majesty and power of Rome upon a single gage of battle! "Sire," I begged him, "if I interpret what is in your mind correctly, consider it well, I implore you."

Hadrian turned and surveyed me with wide, colorless eyes. He laughed until spittle ran down into his graying beard.

"Who will deny me the pleasure?" Hadrian asked. "If this Bar Cocheba is king of the Jews, I am emperor of the Romans. One must not disdain the rank of a man, however humble a tribe it may represent. Do you think I am too weak? I, who swam the Danubis in full armor with my Batavians? I, who disarmed the slave at Tarragona who tried to kill me with my own sword? I, who march twenty miles in a day under a soldier's pack? I, who hunt with the first and return with the last—who has fought the gladiators themselves with their own weapons?"

He paused. His words rang in our ears, dinning out the sense we had. Hadrian had indeed done all he said; he was famous for his endurance and skill in every camp in the empire. But what he had done was years ago. Now he was old, more than sixty. He did not know that his assertions were supported only by memory, not by sinews and strength.

One could not reply in these words to the emperor. With such a man, who would tell him that he was in error, that his youth had passed? No one dared. As Favorinus, the orator, had said after Hadrian had disagreed with him over a question of rhetoric: "Who will win an argument with a man who has thirty legions on his side?" Apollodorus, the great architect of Trajan, had criticized the emperor's designs for a building and had suffered death for it.

"No one will deny you the right or the pleasure, and the gods will give you the victory, great Hadrian," I said humbly. "Our only wish was that you might remain with the legions to inspire their bravery and bring them good fortune."

Deliberately Hadrian reached out. He took me by the nose, gripping it by pincer fingers and lifting me toward him. My eyes spurted tears. My mouth opened in a series of gasping breaths.

"You have a large nose, Rufus," Hadrian said. "It makes such a convenient handle." He dropped his hand and spoke coldly, incisively, in one of his customary changes of mood. "This Simeon bar Cocheba is a bandit and impostor, making his way with the Jews by false charms. I have heard that, like the pillars of Moses, he vomits flame by night and smoke by day."

328

"I do not know, mighty emperor," I stammered, not daring to touch my aching nose in his presence.

"He is said to be a child of your old friend, the Jew Akiba," Hadrian murmured. He stared at me. At that moment, I confess, I felt the wedge of the executioner's sword at the nape of my neck.

"It may be," I muttered desperately. "Akiba himself has turned against the Romans, thinking Simeon the Messiah."

Hadrian flushed, the first touch of color to come to his face. "Traitor, traitor," he muttered.

"He expected many things from the Romans," I said apologetically.

"He may expect no more than death," Hadrian said. "It is you who are to blame for nursing this old crocodile in the bosom of the divine Trajan for such a long time," he added. He gazed out of the window. "We shall see how this fellow is when he finds that the emperor leads the soldiers."

"Do you still intend to challenge the upstart?" asked Severus. "I only inquire, noble Hadrian."

His brows lifted disdainfully. "Why should I honor him?" he said shortly.

Hadrian beat his hands together, and a slave entered. He gave instructions for his litter to be brought to take him for an inspection of the barracks. He did not invite our company, but Severus and myself trailed him obsequiously outside with the usual compliments—"glory of Rome, dear to the hearts of the ancients, most powerful and worshipful Hadrian." He vouchsafed us only a nod as he got inside and pulled the curtains. From the foot of the steps Severus and I watched him depart.

"He has changed," Severus said decisively. "It is hard to believe that this man once marched bareheaded and jesting with his troops, that he disliked flattery."

"All of us have changed," I said.

Severus regarded me with a touch of contempt. "Had he done to me what he did to you," he said, "emperor or no emperor, I should have stabbed him to the heart."

"He is the emperor," I replied with controlled anger. "But if you think so little of my courage, good Julius, my nose is within your grasp. Do you take the same liberty. I promise you my response will not be the same."

Severus sucked in a deep breath and touched my shoulder. "Forgive me, Rufus," he said apologetically. "We must endure where we cannot cure."

Hadrian was right. His presence seemed to inspirit the troops. Not only did he personally investigate weapons, engines, trenches, ramparts, and palisades but also the private affairs of the men and officers—their lives, quarters, and daily habits. He oversaw many of the drills, giving honors and reproofs with an equal hand—all without the imperial trappings, which he never used outside Rome. But he was cruel and arbitrary in his punishments. For the first time, I saw a growing resentment among the officers and men of the legions against the throne.

Nevertheless the war went better. In less than three months, we cleared the Jews from most of the country about Jerusalem. We were ready to deal with Simeon and his city of Bethseba.

This stroke of strategy was not part of the design of our original plans of campaign. We had scheduled its reduction, certainly—but as one of the final operations. Hadrian, viewing our advances with impatience, ordered an immediate assault to be prepared. He declared that the taking of such a citadel was worth the cost, inasmuch as it would deal the cause of the Jews a mortal blow. More specifically, he chose such a course because one of the deserters from that city told him of Simeon himself being immured within the walls. This report was given further substance by the capture of a courier from the beleaguered city, bearing an urgent request for supplies. It was signed by Simeon bar Cocheba himself.

In order to comprehend the difficulties that confronted the Roman forces, it is necessary to describe the situation of Bethseba. It had a peculiar advantage in its location which rendered it both weak and powerful, depending on the case. Nestling at the foot of a spur of rocky hills, it was double-walled and well-defended. But just above it loomed the village of Caathas, beetling over its mother-city like a hornet's nest. The Jews held both in force. It was reckoned that if Bethseba were lost, they might recover it from the vantage of Caathas.

Their belief was justified by the difficulty of capturing such a fort, defended as it was by nature. It was surrounded on all sides but one by wide and deep ravines of rock. On the fourth side, the inhabitants had laboriously cut a deep trench to be crossed only by a drawbridge. On the spur itself, they had erected their village that hung above Bethseba. The houses, huddled together, one against the next, on a steeply ascending slope, gave the village the air of being suspended in the air, about to tumble on the city. A spring within the walls gave it water. It was well stored with provisions. Caathas

330

was famous for its resistance to sieges, crowded with refugees from other cities in Judea—so many, in truth, that the place refused to admit any more. It had been a key post in the previous war against Vespasian and Titus. Then it had held out for seven months. Now it was, the Jews boasted, provisioned for as many years.

The capture of Caathas would determine the fate of Bethseba. From such an eminence, a constant hail of missiles and darts might be hurled down into the city. Vespasian had captured it only just before the fall of Masada, the last fortress to yield in the first Jewish War. Since then, it had been immeasurably strengthened. Its fame gave it an aura of invincibility—and I was disquieted because I was sure Simeon must have taken into his calculations the possibility of its being attacked. I feared what I already knew of his genius for war.

As was customary with him, Hadrian determined to attempt the reduction of Bethseba and Caathas first by peaceful means. Following the belief of Vespasian—who had always declared "the victories won while sitting down are the cheapest"—a display of Roman might was ordered. It was arranged on the days set aside for the payment of wages to the legionaries.

The paymasters set up their tables and tablets just beyond the range of the farthest-ranging Jewish weaponry. The legions turned out in full force, armor and swords burnished like mirrors, marching in long ranks with eagles and pennons like the legendary bright-scaled dragon of the Persians. For four days, the sounds of war were suspended and the clink of coins took their place. The martial exercises with uncased weapons, the richly caparisoned horses of the cavalry, the gleams of armor and shouts in rhythm with marching feet—as I saw it from my post—was like the recurrent roar of a gold-and-silver sea. Awe-inspiring and thrilling as it was to us, however, the spectacle was jeered and ridiculed by the Jews. They thronged the walls of Bethseba to watch. The wind brought us only abuse and curses and laughter from the city and the village above. Our soldiers, their spirits enlivened by the liberal pay and issues of free wine, filled with confidence in themselves and their fellows, swore to return each malediction into the throat of its giver, edged with steel.

On the fifth day, no indications of yielding had appeared. Therefore, secretly that night, Hadrian ordered the assault to be feigned at the gates of Bethseba, screening a massive drive directed at the citadel of Caathas.

Soon after sunset the night thickened, as if it were black

331

flour cooking in a sooted pot. No stars could be seen. Then, without warning a tremendous storm swept over the Roman camp. A hurricane of wind, torrents of rain, drove against us. Every tent had to be restaked, every man found it difficult even to advance a step into the teeth of the wind. Pack animals and horses had to be double-tethered to keep from being blown off into the abysses below. Though torches could not be lit because of the wind (nor could they stay alight because of the rain), illumination was no difficulty. Lightning was almost continuous, streaking down to earth, gnawing at the rocks, splintering them off in crashing falls. The thunder-claps were fearful in their long, deafening rolls. Even below us the earth shook and trembled as if it were afraid. I was reminded of what Akiba had once told me of his holy sayings: " 'Hell is moved to meet thee at thy coming.' "

These portents, far from daunting Hadrian, actually encouraged him. He ordered the advance upon Caathas without delay. It is doubtful whether the soldiers would have obeyed their officers in such turmoil except for the fact that the gods themselves briefly seemed to favor the Roman cause. Just after midnight, the storm ceased. It was succeeded by an absolute calm. This was hailed by cheers; the spirits of the soldiers rose in proportion. All became convinced that heaven favored the emperor, that the war would be speedily brought to a close.

The night remained thick and sultry. Black clouds roiled overhead, hiding the stars. Masses of men advanced, silent in darkness, toward the gates of Caathas. Behind us, throughout the camp, thousands of yellow torches glowed. The diversionary attack went forward against the gates of Bethseba. Shouts and cries came up to us, toiling in multitude, as we ascended the slope toward the ditch before the village. The engineers threw across timbers muffled by hemp pads, quickly cross-laying the planks. The first men sprang across. Their feet thundered on the boards, the first sounds we had made. Three battering rams commenced to boom against the gates.

I looked at Severus in alarm. He returned my question with an equally perturbed shake of his head. The forces within Caathas could not be asleep. "Ah!" I said involuntarily. The walls became bright with torches and fires. From within came the whistle and thump of stone-throwers, the hurtling murmur of great stones, the phlut of arrows flying and fleshing. Burning oil draped the walls in great luminous yellow wreaths. For a moment, our attack was blunted: the bridge was burning.

The engineers flocked in to repair it. Testudos went up to cover the attackers.

"But this silence!" I whispered to Severus.

He shook his head, not understanding any more than I. Our soldiers had been instructed not to make a sound—but what had happened to the fierce cries from the Jews within?

Suddenly, surprisingly, the leaves of the great gates yielded, parted, swung back and sagged on their hinges.

The crash of the gates tumbling from their wooden pivots onto the pavement within was followed by the brief pause that always comes after such a noise. Trumpets resounded, echoing deafeningly. With exultant yells, centurions leading, ranks of our soldiers leaped inside: victory!

No: never was it farther away than at that moment. Clash of arms, hoarse battle cries, loud and more loudly; groans and shriekings, echoed by thunder grumbling in the sky, coming nearer. Severus and I struggled with the flood of men across the bridge, into Caathas. Pouring against nature upward; through the gates, up the narrow cobbled street that led to the top of the town.

Everything happened at once. Shrill trumpets. Screams, shouts, defiances from every side: Jews everywhere, upon the housetops, lining the road, leaning from the windows of the houses: arrows, stones, javelins, pila, incessant deadly rain. Most terrible of all, brilliant pitiless lightings of fires and torches everywhere and—at the top of the street—a monstrous sight. Here stood a cluster of Jews, streaming shadows of fire, enormous to us in perspective. I recognized Simeon as their leader. Before them lay piled massive round boulders. One by one, they thrust them down the steep incline, down the chute of the street.

The stones rolled slowly, then faster, faster, at last bounding into the air, as if with delight, coming to meet us with irresistible force. Our men turned to flee. Their own mass, the wall-to-wall masonry of the buildings, trapped them. In a moment the stones sprang upon them like live beasts. In seconds the whole of our best troops were mangled, pounded flesh and blood and bone, smeared against the stones of the wall and pavement. Again and again the deadly missiles rolled down.

"To the roofs, to the roofs!" I cried in a ringing shout.

Severus took up my cry. It spread. Our soldiers leaped from one side to another, clawing their way upward despite the Jews that lined the housetops. They suffered calamities of casualties but gained and held positions that mounted in number and width every moment. The tide of battle held perfectly equal, as if the gods weighed it in their own balances.

To my astonishment, I saw the unmistakable figure of Hadrian, sword in hand, darting upward toward the top of the blood-drenched incline, his face ghastly and set; hiding in doorways, slipping in and out again, agile far beyond his years. I flung myself down from a roof at the same moment as Severus. We raced after him, determined to save him at the cost of our own lives.

Behind us the street still served as a trap for our oncoming, unwarned soldiers. The stones struck sparks and extinguished them in blood, still coming in endless streams from above. From every side, missiles and arrows poured in.

Far ahead I could spy Hadrian. He was fighting like a madman, sword rising and falling like a flail upon the enemy, even turning its edge upon some of our own soldiers. Beside him, a torch caught the thatch of one of the huts. Fire commenced to spread, to sprinkle blazing sprays. Soon the street would be a blazing holocaust. We must make our decision whether to hold it or flee.

Far behind and below us, from the gates of Bethseba, came a vast shouting. Tubens sounded the signal to retreat and regroup. My heart sank. I realized what had happened: Simeon's consummate strategy had caught us in a fool's trap. We had attacked Caathas for a vantage point. Simeon had designed it as a snare. He was about to attack us from the rear. Our only hope was that the well-garrisoned camp and the special troops set to guard it—enjoined not to leave their posts under threat of instant execution—would be able to hold off the Jews from the city. Here, in flaming Caathas, we would be forced to fight for our own victory, to depend upon no reinforcements whatever.

At this moment, the Jews fronting us commenced to give way. They fought back and up the street in sullen clusters, leaving death behind at every stroke. Our own warriors could not seem to fight as well as usual in such difficult and extraordinary circumstances. Unable to repel the Jews fast enough to escape the fires at their rear or to retreat—in view of their own comrades pressing from behind—they were sheep for slaughter unless they sprang upward (with their comrade's help) onto the roofs beside them. Most of them had succeeded in doing this, but the roofs, unaccustomed to such weight and weakened by the increasing conflagration, began to collapse. The coverings of the stone houses, in most cases no more than mud and straw, smothered many of the fires in the night but also left our men gasping, unable to breathe. Worse, one fall often caused the next house to begin to collapse and more were buried in the thickening ruins.

The Jews raised a cry of savage rejoicing at our predicament. Now they pressed their attack forward, regardless of their own losses. From protected positions they leaped out to hurl stones from the debris onto the unprotected heads of the legions below. Torches and arrows supplied more death. Some daring Jews even leaped down and wrenched the swords from the fingers of bewildered Romans, thrusting them through with their own weapons.

Our duty was to reach Hadrian. Keeping abreast of the centurions, fighting with wonderful vigor for such a man, the emperor had inspired and kept together the vanguard of our forces. Slowly—perhaps without realizing it—he had come to the highest part of the village of Caathas. Here the danger was immense, surrounded as he was by Jews eager for imperial blood. Hadrian knew it: he ordered those around him to link together their shields, one around another, protecting themselves and him against the tide of war.

Here was the highest point, the roof of the highest house, built entirely of stone and virtually immune to flame. Here occurred the most extraordinary sight of all, one that for the brief moment of encounter, held both Jews and Romans from strife. Upon the roof sprang a tall figure in the full light of the flames and torches. I could not help recognize the man. It was Simeon, in full armor, sword in hand. Directly behind him clambered the figure of a gaunt tall old man. It could be no other than Akiba.

I had heard Akiba had become Simeon's armor-bearer. All the same, it surprised me. More of an Eastern than a Roman office, it meant that the chosen one was the intimate of the leader, both on and off the battlefield. Such a one was either protector (at the risk of his life) or comrade, according to orders. In spite of Akiba's age, I knew his amazing strength, agility, and endurance. But his selection by Simeon could never have been because of his fighting ability: the old man was little more than a symbol, an inspiration to the Jewish hosts—who saw in them both their god and their might fighting side by side.

Propelled from below by a burly centurion—who fell, arrow in his back—Hadrian sprang from the roof to confront

Simeon. Simeon's face grew into a distortion of fierce pleasure. Next moment their swords clashed and glittered. Again they came together in a jarring series of blows that I seemed to feel on my own corselet.

Simeon staggered, slipped, dropped to one knee. Akiba sprang forward, placing his body between Simeon and Hadrian. The emperor raised his sword in a tremendous sweep. At its height, in mid-air, he reeled. The weapon fell from his hands. He fell prostrate, seeming to slide down his own body and collapse.

The Romans gasped. The Jews roared where they had gasped a moment before. Simeon, his face glaring-red with fire and ferocity, raised his sword with both hands over the fallen man. Next instant, he would have impaled him to the heart.

It was Akiba again who threw his own body between, deflecting the stroke by the shield of Simeon that he held.

The spell shattered. Severus and I sprang upward to the roof. We shouted together. Simeon saw us. He sprang back. Next moment, he and Akiba had vanished over the edge. We vaulted after them. Severus stumbled, uttering a moan of agony. His leg had twisted under him; I felt it hastily and found the bone jutting out. It was broken.

A shadow fell over me from above. A figure dropping from the burning roof next door. It came to attention and saluted. "You—you—you Ficus!" I yelled.

Together, we burst around the corner of the house. We plunged into the melee at the very top of the steep street, just as Simeon disposed of his second Roman soldier with Akiba, gaunt and openly distraught, beside him.

There was no one else about, as I recall, though this seems impossible. Only Ficus and I, only Simeon and Akiba, crouching and stalking each other. All of us felt afire, even more than Caathas, with the hatred and violence we held against each other. All of us—except Akiba. He wept.

What happened after this, I cannot exactly describe. Memory has been merciful. It has blurred the details of that last chaotic struggle. Imagine, as I do, the field of battle. A place of rasping darkness and fire, of slippery blood and shorn limbs and bodies, disemboweled and stripped, of the red half-glitters of armor and weapons in motion, of hoarse cries both angry and fearstricken, shouts of pain and pleas for mercy. Figures in the night advancing irresolutely or plunging madly, fleeing or recoiling from pursuit, shadows long and darkly crossed, all forgotten in the moment of total energy. Inhuman stinks of entrails disgorged and salty gore, hot sweat of fury and cold sweat of fright and death.

And, over it all, clamped down with calm, the dispassionate black clouds of the night sky. Remembering it now, it seems no more than a cluster of shining beetles quarreling under a child's overturned dish—but the dish of an ogre's child all the same.

In the midst of this desolation of death, Ficus and I fought Simeon and Akiba. We stood, four alone, to determine the issue between us. If Simeon triumphed, he might well rally the Jews again, and the war would continue; if he died, all would end. None to rally, none to see; none to rescue, none to succor. At last we faced our naked fates. It seemed to me that time itself waited on the outcome, as the Jews claim the sun once did for their tribal hero Joshua.

Nor did I have much hope for the outcome. I had learned to wield a sword, clumsily enough, with my left arm, but I had no shield. Simeon, lunging at me, had none of his own; but Akiba, always practical rather than gallant, carried it next to him, keeping Ficus and his spear at bay and striking out at him with wonderful dexterity. Yet I must say he was almost ignored. Ficus did not want to bring down the ancient rabbi; puffing and blowing with exertion, his eye was fixed upon Simeon—even as Simeon's was upon me.

We must have fought only a short time, but the end of it all seems long in my recollection. Simeon, it seemed, recoiled from my first parry and sighed. He raised his sword in a fierce sweep. I ducked under it and thrust. Akiba interposed the shield so that my sword glanced off. Simeon thrust. I dodged. Ficus aimed a spear-thrust which Akiba's weapon parried. Then I thrust again, and Akiba, ever watchful, put the shield between my blade and Simeon. It was the most foolish act of his life. It left Simeon's left side open—not to me but to Ficus.

Instantly, Ficus drove his spear into the gap—not thrusting but cutting deep. The blade went out of sight. I saw it, in a horrified instant, sink into the exposed body of Simeon as he raised his sword for another blow at me. He tottered and swung about with a terrible stroke on the helm of Ficus. Akiba thrust at him in the same moment and his weapon pierced under the cuirass.

Ficus sank slowly to his knees, toppling to his side. His

eyes were vacant, the pupils vanished. His nerveless hand dropped his spear. The swooning Simeon fell back into Akiba's arms. The old man dropped the shield as I stayed my stroke. He looked wildly about him, staring for help; he passed a trembling palm over the face of Simeon, and his features contracted with a spasm. He allowed Simeon to slip to the ground and stood erect, his arms widespread, a dreadful figure on the heights of the flame-lit top of the town. His sword clattered from his hand to the street. From his lungs came an inhuman cry of grief and wretchedness that resounded over the clash of arms. It was the death-cry of a hope and a faith that came to the ears of every Jew.

Instantly, all faces turned toward that towering weird figure above them. As if by magic, the Jews—who had enjoyed equal if not better fortune than the Romans thus far—commenced to fall back. From that moment their fierce spirits evaporated. Their cause was lost.

A shivering cry, like that of a creature from the underworld, wavered along the Jews. Those who had been bravest a moment before turned and dug their way into the ranks behind, striking their own comrades with their swords. Like a pestilence, the panic spread. Shrieks and shouts of dismay arose on all sides: the firm outlines of the Jewish front shook and dissolved like powder in water. The next instant, it seemed, the whole of their host was in flight out of Caathas, seeking safety once more within the gates of Bethseba. The fugitives were crushed to death between the portals and our guards. They fled in every direction, stumbling and falling, careening off the heights in flurries of robes and sparkles of swords, screaming for help or mercy. On their heels, closing in for the kill, harried the Roman legionaries. They struck and slew and struck again, point and blade. Methodically they stabbed the wounded and stripped them of plunder, beheading all who seemed to be officers. They spared nothing stirring.

Akiba had vanished, I did not know where or how. As for me, I stayed where I was, not recking of death in my double sorrow. Gently I laid Simeon aside and bent over the unconscious Ficus, spitting on his face in the heat and crackle of flames, rubbing him to revive him. He opened his eyes slowly and recognized me.

"This is the wrong time for being killed," he grumbled.

"Yes," I said.

"Wrong time, wrong place, against these lousy Jews."

"Yes."

338

"You all right, sir?"

"Yes."

For an instant, his head lolled back. I thought he was gone but he regained control of his neck muscles. "All the same, a good fight," he said. "I would have beat them both, but my foot slipped."

"Yes," I said.

His eyes began to film, but he looked steadily up. "Toughest cock in the whole army," he said. His body went limp. I bowed my head. His mouth gaped and his soul fled.

How long I remained with the mound of his cold flesh I do not know. I was roused by the approaching jangle of soldiers. I looked up. Two of the first cohort of the II Augusta were escorting Akiba. "He wants to talk to you," said one roughly. "Maybe he has a treasure some place."

"I do indeed," Akiba whispered. "Rufus, Simeon beside you is dying. I knew it when I touched him."

I indicated the corpse of Ficus. "Take him up," I commanded the soldiers. "I wish him buried with honors." I stared at Akiba. "Stanch the wounds of Simeon," I told him.

He began his task, and I looked down at the scene below. Rome held the field: Bethseba had not been taken, but the sally of the Jews from the city had been repulsed and the pursuit was in full cry by the flickering lights across the plain. As I watched, the thunder grumbled more loudly than ever overhead. There was no lightning, but slow heavy drops of rain, like tears, commenced to fall.

I turned to the kneeling Akiba. My mind clouded. Not with rage or revenge but grief. Not for Rome or for Judea. But for Akiba, for Simeon and Ficus—for myself.

"It is cold in spite of the fire," Akiba whispered as his fingers busied themselves. "I am lonely."

"I shall be lonely the rest of my days," I said.

CHAPTER 20

Triumphantly, smiling his old gay smile, Simeon said, "I am dying." The expression of supreme fierceness, which had marked his face during the battle, had vanished. He looked up at us surrounding his couch in my tent in the old X Fretensis camp.

"I think, as my ancestor Vespasian said when he was dying, that the Jews will make me a god when I am gone," he murmured. It was my first intimation that Akiba must have broken our pact of silence about his birth. Startled, I looked at the old man across the dark-stained couch. The gaunt Jew nodded briefly, sadly. Beside me, my personal physician, Harpocras, knelt beside Simeon. He adjusted the brown-linen bandages beneath his ribs.

Simeon sighed. Harpocras wiped a trickle of blood from the left corner of his mouth. Simeon stirred restlessly, his thin features contracting.

"I am young," he said painfully, "but I am fortunate. The time has come for me to leave this life, since both the gods of the Romans and the God of the Jews summon me. I rejoice, as did the good Cicero and the sage Abraham, that I shall return to nature what it gave me and to heaven what I owe."

"Do not speak," Harpocras muttered. "You weaken yourself."

"You and I have learned, dear fathers both," Simeon said, looking from Akiba to myself, "how much happier is a soul than a body."

"Do not speak," I said. I caught my voice breaking. The grief-struck Akiba wagged his head wretchedly.

Simeon coughed. He stared up at me almost angrily. "You are too sad."

"Sir, sir," whispered Harpocras impulsively, "do not tax yourself or your wound will flow again." Inwardly I blessed the Egyptian-Greek. He was a warmhearted fellow for a medico: his tears shone on his cheeks.

"The gods, whoever they are—or God, whoever He is—or fate," Simeon said softly. His voice became slower, more measured, deep as the Ionian music of Greece. "I do not say that I am such a one, either good or evil. But I shall share in what rewards there are. I have never sought greatness for myself. You know that, Rufus; you know that, Akiba."

"I know it," I said, my mouth dry. Akiba nodded opposite me.

After he had said so much, Simeon seemed to rest more easily. Harpocras busied himself with pads and bandages, Akiba bowed his head in prayer. The cool of the long night had lessened with the darkness at dawn. I heard the sound of rising winds outside, once more the rumble of distant thunder; lightning played faintly through the thin-bellied cloth of the tent. Sand like rain beat against the linen. The dangling, brown-blooded spears at the door made a melancholy sound against the shields.

"Simeon, you shall not die," I said strongly. The blood from his side seemed to have ceased oozing. I began to believe myself, to entertain the wild hope that what I said was true. The weeping Harpocras applied herbs and unguents and renewed the soaked bandages. He crushed a handful of pungent leaves and held them to Simeon's nostrils to revive his senses, but his patient did not seem to notice the piercing fragrance.

"Much have I thought about dying," Simeon said. "I do not regret any deed of mine in my life."

He stopped. His eyes shifted in his head, rolling upward. I thought the last moment was at hand. My heart caught. But Simeon recovered himself and spoke more firmly than ever. "I am not ashamed to admit," he said, "that at the last I allowed many of mine to become Christians, though I think it a fool's belief." His eyes rested fondly on Akiba. "I am not the Messiah," he said gently, "nor should you think me so any longer. He is not yet come: wait a little."

For the first time Akiba's eyes swelled with tears. Simeon paused. "I learned long ago that I should die by the sword," he said. He paused again. "But I die by the spear," he said querulously. He shook his head, a man entangled by the cobwebs of last thoughts. He looked at me. "Have I ever desired to die when I should not?"

"No," I said.

"Have I ever sought to avoid death?"

"You have your wounds in front," I said.

"Thank you, good Rufus," Simeon replied. He sighed, and his voice weakened. He put his fingers to his side, pushing away the hands of Harpocras. He looked at his palms. "My strength runs out with the red drops," he said. "What a fine color blood is!"

"Simeon, Simeon," said Akiba, suddenly falling to his knees, his old bones rattling. He clasped the cold hand tightly. "Who shall take your place?"

Simeon made a quick impatient gesture. Harpocras raised his head in alarm at the increased flow of blood. "I do not know nor shall I choose one," Simeon said. "I may err through ignorance; I may choose someone who ought not to undergo the dangers."

"Have you no wishes in the matter? Does not God speak to you?"

"God and I have never spoken," Simeon enunciated. "Perhaps He does not know I exist. I wish only, as a good Jew, that someone worthy be found to succeed me." He looked around him once more and said: "Where is Jonathan?" I did not know at the time to whom he referred, but I knew it must be one of the subordinate leaders of the Jewish revolt. Akiba bowed his head. "He is happy," he said in a low tone. I realized the man must be dead or else within the city of Bethseba.

Simeon's eyes filled with tears. He sank back, struggling feebly, his left hand on his right arm. He removed his armlet of a golden asp and placed it in my hand. He had returned my gift of long ago. I knelt to take it: I knew Simeon had made his last choice.

In that instant, longest of my life, the dying man and myself saw each other clearly. I seemed to vision what was in his brain. The slender dark-haired figure of Sarra, the undulations of her slight body, the sparkle of her face, beside him. I saw again the sight of Simeon running to meet me at the doorway of Akiba's hut and of his bright-haloed form defying Rome in the marketplace. Then I saw no more, blinded by tears, rising unsteadily to my feet.

Simeon looked up at me. He attempted to smile, but his lips would not obey his will. Nevertheless he spoke for the last time—a mystic repetition of that which we both remembered and which had no meaning for anyone else on earth—that which would never be repeated again by either of us, the ancient riddle of the Greek Cleobulus.

"No one sees me when he sees," Simeon said, laboriously and painfully, "but he sees me when he sees not; he who speaks in me speaks not, he who runs in me runs not; but though I am untruthful, I know all truth."

The words of the riddle were quite distinct. It was an enormous effort of will that Simeon had spoken so long. He glanced at Akiba with an expression of adoration and love. Then, last of all, he looked at me with a strange grimace I could not identify: respect, perhaps, hatred, or it might have been affection.

Next moment, despite Harpocras, Simeon tore away the bandage from his wound. The blood gushed out. In less than seconds, he was dead, stiffening as his blood cooled on the couch.

I bowed my head and plunged out of the tent. A half hour

afterward, I was still there before it, pacing back and forth on the sand, biting my fist to stifle my sighs and trying to control my thoughts. Akiba emerged solemnly and stopped before me. It seemed to me that his face, for the first time I had known him, was soaked with tears, though it bore marks of clear transfiguration. His garments were rent. There was dust upon his head.

"You weep for Simeon," I said in wonder and pity.

"I weep for Israel," he answered.

"Akiba," I said unsteadily, "you are a prisoner." I motioned and the guards came forward to take him away.

"There was much blood lost three days ago," Severus said. He patted his leg under its splints and bandages.

"Yes," I admitted. We were sitting in the peristylium of the residence of Severus in Caesarea, warmed by the sun through the roof, cooled by the fountain's flowing.

"There will be more before Bethseba is reduced."

"I believe it."

"The emperor has sent notice of the conquest of the Jews to the Senate in Rome. You know how it has always begun."

" 'If you and your children are in health, it is well; and I and the legions are in health,' " I quoted. "It is the oldest salutation of victory."

"But the emperor did not use it," Severus said meaningfully. I sat upright. "I do not understand," I said tightly. "Perhaps it is because the fortress has not yet been reduced."

Severus shook his head. "The war is over," he declared. "It is no more than a matter of weeks before Bethseba is starved out and the countryside cleared of Jews. We have merely to sit and keep guard, to keep patrols and local actions in motion—and their leader is dead. No: such an omission by Hadrian means only that much more Roman blood has been shed than we know about. I have sounded the soldiers."

"What do you mean?"

"I mean," Severus said bluntly, "that the emperor has lost the trust of the troops."

"I cannot believe it."

"Did you know that he sailed yesterday from this very port without ceremony—secretly, and at night?"

"No," I said, amazed, "not at all. I should have been notified. It is not usual."

"He knows the legions no longer have faith in him."

"He fought well," I said. "He led them well."

"He fought like a man demented," Severus replied, "not like a man in his senses or one who held the empire in his palm. He led them not like a sensible commander but like a maniac, a man given to such despair that he will bring down the world with his own death. The soldiers fear him. They seek a new emperor."

"Hadrian is good enough," I said, slumping wearily on my couch. "Let them endure him a little longer; he will soon be divine."

Severus surveyed me sternly. "If you were to step forth at this moment," he said, "the troops would acclaim you."

I sucked in my breath at this maiestas. "I shall stay here, and they shall be silent," I responded, an ache of wonder in my head.

"I claim the right to announce you emperor," Severus said flatly. "I know that once Trajan himself had such thoughts. Perhaps I do no more than his will long-delayed."

"With a single arm?" I said, shrugging my maimed shoulder.

"That is superstition," Severus said sharply. "There is always a first time for something to be done. This is the time. Not only the legions but also the people in the east will be with you. Remember the old formula: elected by the consent of the soldiers and the authority of the senate."

"Has the senate agreed already?" I asked ironically.

"They will—once the soldiers have affirmed it."

To my surprise, I found myself not at all tempted but rather amused. "No, good friend Severus," I told him. "I cannot accept. Only twice has such a thing happened. Scribonianus tried such a revolt, and his troops stayed with him only five days, I have heard. I know myself of the revolt of Saturninus in Germany against Domitian and how it was crushed by loyal commanders. No: I cannot accept, and you put yourself in danger by suggesting it. I am not destined to be emperor, as Trajan himself once told me."

"You will not accept an empire?" Severus demanded incredulously.

"It is no more than a throw of knucklebones," I assured him. "In any case, I am not worthy."

"What would you do if there were no emperor?" asked Severus heatedly. "What if he had been killed in battle? Would you not put aside all scruples and take the leadership and save the soldiers from their dangers and provide victory?"

"Yes," I said.

"This is such a moment."

344

"No," I said.

"I myself will throw the purple rag upon your back and lift you on my shield in the barracks!"

I hesitated. I saw a dim vision of Trajan in Colonia, elevated on the shields of the legionaries; I heard the shouts and saw the fires glinting on the weapons thrown upward; I saw the tight strained expression of the newly crowned princeps. The image shifted. I saw the faraway look in Trajan's eyes on that dawn when we had stood together in the amphitheatre of Antioch with the earthquake ruins about us. I shook my head to pull my wits together.

"If you need an emperor, there are others, noble Severus," I said gently. "I am ill, I am old. You must have youth and strength and ambition to be emperor. I have none of these."

"By the gods, the united vote of the armies of the east and west shall decide!"

"No!" I cried loudly. I sprang to my feet, confronting Severus in anger. "Not against my will!"

Severus recognized the irrevocable decision in my voice. His face changed uncertainly. He paused, then made a curt nod. He said stiffly: "You know, of course, good Rufus, that you hold my life in your hands."

My feeling dissolved in his words. I stepped forward and put my arm across his shoulders. "Severus, Severus," I said affectionately, "you have spoken as you have for the good of the empire. I am only sorry that I cannot oblige you. If I hold your life, as you say, I hereby give it back to you and swear, by the most holy altars, that my lips shall be forever sealed upon this matter."

From that moment to this—when the dust of the generous Severus has long been lying in his family tomb along the Appian Way—I have never told of this singular incident. If Trajan's offer perhaps were pure mockery, certainly that of Severus was in earnest. It is something to have an empire offered you and something more to accept it—and even possibly something yet more to have refused it. In the years since, I have tried to explain to myself why I refused a venture that might well have succeeded and made me the most powerful man on earth. Others (such as Nerva) have been older and sat the throne; still others (such as Claudius) have been more ill and are recalled with veneration.

But I was sick and weak of another disease, old before my time of another plague. Sick of blood and conquest, old from wandering across the face of the earth, I wanted only to find

345

peace and happiness in a land far from turmoil and war and death and torture. If the ghosts of those I had loved and condemned were to follow me, at least they should gibber at me in my own private chamber.

I no longer had the strong stomach which is needed for power. Truly, I was not the man to be emperor.

The siege of Bethseba went on for three weeks. The city had two barricades of stone and, after thoroughly investing the outside with three walls of shields, we sat about heaping up mounds against the outer ramparts, bringing up and mounting the siege engines, repulsing the sallies from the gates, covering the walls with the missiles of our slingers and archers. It was a routine operation of siege and harry, one destined to arrive at an inevitable conclusion. The Jews within undermined our sixty-cubit towers, set fire to our engines despite the covering of green bullhides, emerged from tunnels in night raids and fended off our battering-rams with mats of straw and planks, looping and pulling up the lighter engines (and sometimes our soldiers) by ropes and hooks cast from the top of the wall. We captured the first fortification and were content to wait outside the next—for the signs of famine and thirst were plain to be seen in the occasional prisoners captured.

What made the siege extraordinary, however, was the fact that not a single deserter found his way to our camp. As a matter of fact, when Bethseba surrendered, it was by silence, and this was the way of it. Their leader, a fanatic Pharisee called Jonathan (the same man Simeon had asked about), perceived that resistance was useless.

Outside the city that evening, the legions heard frenzied cheering and the silence which came after it. We were full of wonder.

At dawn, our soldiers formed columns of assault to take Bethseba and cautiously advanced. But they saw none of the enemy, they heard none of the customary cries of alarm. On all sides of our scouts, an awful solitude prevailed. Within, rising in pillars, the army saw smoke and flame. Our soldiers burst in the gates without opposition. They rushed into the streets—only to find them heaped with corpses. They shouted and searched, but they discovered only one person alive, a young woman babbling in hysteria, who told us the whole story. Those Jews with wives and children had cut the throats of their families as they embraced them. Then the survivors

346

had gathered together all their stores and flammables and ignited them. Quickly choosing by lot a dozen executioners, the rest flung away their weapons and lay down beside the bodies of their dear ones. The chosen dozen had unswervingly killed all the rest, then chosen one to slay the other eleven. The last man, after making sure none survived and that all was aflame, drove his sword through his body and fell in his tracks. Only the woman—who had fled and burrowed under a pile of bodies, scarcely daring to breathe—emerged alive to be sold into slavery. Among the slain was Ishmael ben Elisha, with his proud, uncompromising look sealed upon his face.

As for Sarra: I searched myself in the dead laid out in Bethseba before they were thrown into the ravines and covered with rocks and earth. I found her. The body I had loved, that I had held, was crushed; but her face was untouched and calm in death. I sent all away and studied it for a long time, at last pressing my lips to her cold face without a shudder. I ordered her to be cast first and deepest into the pit.

So Bethseba fell. With it collapsed all the hopes of the Jews and their allies of lifting the yoke of Rome. From that moment onward—for more than a year later—the legions roamed the countryside, cutting down all who could not identify themselves as Romans, camping by caves or suspicious redoubts in the hills until they were satisfied they were without denizens. Within six months the country was desolate, yet these bands still roved to extirpate the Jews. If any still exist —beyond those that espoused the Roman cause from the beginning or fled to other lands—they are certainly immortal.

I took no part in this. It was the task of Severus to see to the completion of the military duties, mine to supervise the restoration of the province itself. The Greeks and Egyptians, naturally, rejoiced at the destruction of the Jews whom they had always hated. I repressed their mass demonstrations of joy with an iron hand. I knew—and it proved to be so—that they would turn against each other in due time.

The Jews kept as captives were all sold into slavery, most of them to be transported to hard labor in the mines of Dacia and Germania. As for Judea, it became a consular province, with the X Fretensis remaining with the addition of the VI Ferrata stationed at Caparcotna.

What had happened at Caathas to the emperor, I never discovered, but I suspect it was the hereditary disease of his family that struck him down—as it had his uncle—at the most critical point of his career. Whatever it was, Hadrian has never marched since with his legions.

Meanwhile, just as Titus had granted Josephus the privilege of freeing a certain number of prisoners, this privilege was also given Simeon ben Yohai, who had always upheld the Roman cause. Ben Yohai ransomed as many as five hundred, most of them teachers and scholars, among them such fools as Pappias. But he did not request the freedom of Akiba. Even if he had, I would not have been able to surrender such a notable captive. In my own way, however, I was determined ultimately to set the broken old man free, to send him back to his home in Lydda. It would take time; emotions would have to cool; much would have to be forgotten. But in the end it would be possible to do the deed covertly without too much public notice.

As a preliminary step to this eventual release, I gave Akiba permission to be taken from his cell for daily walks under guard along the shore of the sea. This liberty was managed a month or two after the fall of Bethseba. I congratulated myself on the lack of any general curiosity about the affair. But in less than a week disturbing rumors commenced to come to my ear. I decided to pay Akiba my first visit since his capture.

As I entered his cell past the guard, he looked up. His eyes brightened. Then his countenance became impassive, and he fixed his gaze on the floor between his squatted legs, taking up a cockroach to examine it minutely. The door clanged to.

"Akiba," I said sternly. I took his stool for my own seat.

"I am pleased to see you again," he said calmly. I noted that he was much thinner, his frame more wasted than it had been. Little remained of this man except the flame within and the skin and bone that encompassed it.

"I hear you have been teaching the Torah and its interpretation to those who follow you on the seashore," I said abruptly.

"Perhaps my interpretations are wrong," Akiba murmured.

"Akiba," I said sternly, "I represent the Roman government. The emperor Hadrian long ago promulgated an edict that the Torah shall not be taught by anyone."

"I was merely explaining it."

"It shall not be explained."

"Let us say that I was telling them about it. There is no law against that."

348

"You are evading the fact, Akiba," I told him. "You know you were doing wrong."

"Not wrong," Akiba said, "but right. Perhaps you are doing wrong."

"I am not breaking the law, as you are."

"Is the law the only right? Are there not other rights? To speak and to gather, to teach and learn?"

I pinched my cheek, pulling it in vexation. "I do not wish to punish you," I said to Akiba, "but neither do I wish to argue with you, as you do with Pappias and your fellow Jews. What are you going to decide? Silence as a free man or silence as a prisoner?"

Akiba hunched his shoulders. He spread his fingers in the immemorial and expressive gesture of his race. "Shall I say what the business of this disagreement is like? A fox once walked along the bank of the stream and, looking into the water, he saw a school of fish preparing to flee. He said to them (for you know foxes understand all languages): 'From what do you flee?' The fish replied: 'From the nets with which men assault us.' The fox then advised: 'Let it be your pleasure to come up on the dry land and you shall take shelter with me.'

"But the fish were wiser and chorused: 'Are you the cleverest of animals? You cannot be a fox, you are a fool! For if we are afraid in a place which is our life element, how much more shall we be afraid in the air, our death element!' "

"What does this mean?" I demanded crossly. I was weary of Akiba's habit of telling his little homemade parables.

"In the Torah it says that its study is 'thy life and the length of thy days,' " Akiba responded. "If we are in such a plight when we study it, how much more so are we if we neglect it."

"Now you are breaking the law again," I declared. "You are trying to teach *me* the Torah."

"What better instruction can there be?"

"For a prisoner, none, perhaps," I said, "but for me it is rank sedition. I must warn you, as well, Akiba, that I know of these pretended peddlers that appear to chant their verses outside this cell. They are none other than disguised rabbis asking you for opinions. This must stop."

"Will you cut their throats?"

"Perhaps," I told him grimly. "And you must use the water brought you—however much—for drinking rather than washing."

349

"Impure drinkers are worse than poisonous water," Akiba murmured.

"Your superstitions are none of my business," I replied. "Keeping you alive is my business." Akiba said nothing. I rose and strolled about the cell, noting that it was the same one in which I had imprisoned him during the mock-arrest. It gave me the sudden hope that I might set him free if I could get him to confess his error about the Messiah and recant his mistakes.

"Did you hate Simeon because of Sarra?" asked Akiba suddenly.

"Did you hate Rome because of Rachel?" I flared. Akiba's spirit retreated within him, and he did not answer.

"I am sorry, old Jew," I said repentantly.

"If a man could live without loving anything," Akiba said in a muffled tone, "he could escape being unhappy. But he would never be happy, either."

"Akiba," I said, "confess you were deceived."

"Deceived?"

"By thinking Simeon was your Messiah."

Akiba's eyes burned. "Isaiah, blessed be he, has said: 'The Lord doth cut off from Israel head and tail, palm-branch and rush, in one day. The ancient and the honorable, he is the head; and the prophet that teacheth lies, he is the tail. For they that lead this people cause them to err; and they that are led of them are destroyed.' "

"I don't understand."

"Good Rufus, am I the ancient and honorable? Is Simeon the prophet that taught lies? Even now they call him Bar Goziba, the son of lies, and denounce me in whispers."

I shook my head. "Simeon was never the Messiah. He himself denied it."

"He was the stone not cut by human hands, not knowing it himself."

"In the eyes of the Romans, he was a criminal," I said. "In the eyes of the Jews, he is worse."

Akiba stared at me, and I knew his thoughts. He had told Simeon of his Roman blood as well as of his mother converted to the Jews. The old man had hoped for Simeon's divine destiny so strongly that perhaps it had affected his brain; perhaps he had convinced himself that Simeon was his own son. He had striven for peace in the world of Romans and Jews and had failed; he had turned to the sword and lost; now he was indomitably resigning himself to a new

350

faith—an exaltation of belief—in his god. Whatever the way out of his dilemma, Akiba was content to wait for his fate to be decided by other forces.

"Simeon belonged to neither of us," Akiba murmured in a curiously tranquil voice. "Neither to the Romans nor the Jews. He belonged to God."

What I so dearly desired—to be rid of this nettle under my flesh, this friend I abhorred—was not to be through his cooperation. So much, at least, was irrefutable. But I could allow him visitors and close my official ears to what was spoken in his cell.

One of the first to request a visit was Pappias, the pompous little rabbi with whom, for some obscure reason, Akiba dearly loved to argue. I was happy to give him clearance into the prison. But after a time I became struck with curiosity as to what the topics of their conversations might be. Certainly they might be those of plotting how to set Akiba free or how to subvert the Roman rule once more.

One afternoon, therefore, I strolled down the corridor to Akiba's cell. I waved away the impassive guard and put my ear to the door. I stiffened in astonishment. The pair were wrangling in high tones about points of doctrine!

"But a suicide is the worst of men!" exclaimed Pappias. "He must be buried with the chant, 'Alas for the fool, alas for the fool!' "

"God is merciful," Akiba returned. "Do not praise such a one but do not blame him either."

"He will go to Gehinnom!"

"But even in Gehinnom he will only suffer twelve months," Akiba said. "God is merciful and will annihilate rather than torture."

I heard Pappias gasp and gently shot back the bolt and opened the door. The rolypoly rabbi was gesticulating at Akiba, his face puffed with rage. "It is all very well for you to maintain this," he said, "but God thinks differently." Akiba did not reply, seeing me. Pappias, unaware, went on.

"It is written by Job, blessed be he, that God is One and who can turn Him?" continued Pappias impatiently. "This means He may do with you as He wishes."

"Be quiet, Pappias," said Akiba tiredly. "What you say is true, but you must add that He does what He does in justice. The heavenly courts have their laws as do the earthly courts.

351

Mercy and justice stand with the Judge, side by side. God knows every creature and every thought in our minds."

"But then are mercy and justice superior to God?" demanded Pappias in horrified tones.

"Nonsense!" said Akiba with asperity. "God is at one with all virtues. There is judgment above as there is below."

"And the judgment below is Roman," I said, breaking in. Pappias jumped and turned; he bowed deeply to me.

"We speak of things divine, not human," Akiba said in rebuke to my remark.

"Argue about your Messiah," I said, setting them at each other.

"There is no dispute," Akiba said. Pappias sprang at his words and commenced to worry them like a puppy with a rag. "At least we know it was not Simeon of Goziba," he said meaningfully.

"Perhaps it was," Akiba answered.

"How can this be?" demanded Pappias. "According to the words of Isaiah, 'he shall not fail nor be crushed, till he have set the right in the earth; and the isles shall wait for his teaching.' "

" 'He is despised and forsaken of men; a man of pains and acquainted with disease; and as one from whom men hide their faces: he was despised, and we esteemed him not.' "

"Perhaps he was the 'king of fierce countenance, and understanding stratagems,' " said Pappias. "He is one who is 'mighty but not by his own power' who 'shall destroy wonderfully,' according to Daniel, blessed be he. 'He shall . . . stand up against the prince of princes . . . and shall destroy them that are mighty and the people of the saints.' "

"It is Daniel who has said that 'he shall plant the tents of his palace between the seas in the beauteous holy mountain,' " Akiba said deliberately, "yet he shall come to his end, and none shall help him.' "

"Nothing of the sort happened!"

"Pappias, Pappias," Akiba murmured, "when will you come to know that there are things not to be touched with the hand or seen by the eye that are far more glorious and real than those you believe in? The Temple will rise in the spirit, if not on the mountain. Enter in, then, and make your sacrifices of a contrite and humble heart."

Pappias became pale and darted a second look at me. He bowed stiffly. "I cannot remain," he said. "Forgive me if I leave you both." I nodded amused permission, and he went strutting out as if he were a cock on parade. I shut the door behind him and looked at Akiba for an explanation. He gave me back a look as sly and meek as a child.

"I have been arguing with Pappias," Akiba said.

"In these days," I said severely, "when you Jews need so much that must be held on to, what can you find to disagree about?"

Akiba's smile illuminated his face. "The only thing that two Jews can agree upon," he said, "is how much a third Jew should give to charity."

"And that will take a fourth Jew to judge," I added.

"Pappias needs so much teaching," Akiba sighed.

"You need a few lessons yourself," I reprimanded him. "Else you would not be here."

"It is very comfortable here."

"That is not the point. The point is that you *are* here."

"What difference does it make where I am?"

I grew indignant. "I come to you to try to save your life," I said. "Instead of offering me an answer, you talk gibberish. You ought to be scourged."

Akiba appeared to recover himself. "I have been whipped before," he said, recovering his old ironic way of speaking. "Rabbi Johanan ben Nuri complained to Gamaliel about me. I was whipped five times for my impudence, as they called it. But he came to me afterward and kissed me and begged forgiveness, saying that I was wiser than he because I had accepted the rebuke."

"Did he whip you until your skin fell into shreds?" I demanded. "For such is in my power. I assure you I shall not comfort you with kisses for endangering my post as governor."

"Nay," Akiba said, "it is I who rebuke you, Rufus."

"Very well, then," I said, furious on the instant, feeling each word puff my lips like frozen spittle. "If you will not swear by your god to cease your teaching, Akiba, you must die."

He bent his bald, capped head in submission, his beard into the dust. He raised his face. He looked into my eyes with the dark, peculiarly hypnotic gaze that I had known for forty years.

"But you, Rufus," he said mildly, "you must live."

Into my head, as if scribed instantly upon the wax of my brain, there flashed a long-dormant memory. It was of the words of Epictetus, spoken to me when I complained about his being exiled to Nicopolis. "Remember," the Greek teacher said in his reedy voice, "that the door is always open to everyone. If the smoke is moderate, stay; if it is excessive, go out. I am exiled to Nicopolis, very well. If Rome is not for me, I go. If I am forbidden Athens, too, very well."

"What if you are ordered to dwell in Gyara?"

"Barbarous Gyara seems a smoky room indeed, and I shall depart where none shall hinder me from dwelling. Beyond the last inner tunic, which is this poor body of mine, no one has any authority over me at all."

I stared at Akiba. "Do you find this prison intolerably smoky?" I asked abruptly.

He stared back at me in astonishment. "Are you exiled to Gyara?" I persisted. He said nothing, not taking his eyes from mine. It was the only occasion of my life, I think, when Akiba failed to recognize my inmost thoughts.

I tightened my jaw and turned, grinding my sandals angrily on the sandstone of his cell floor. I heard the soft hiss and jar as the copper door turned on its pivots to close behind me. I walked down the prison corridor, abstractedly holding my toga over my left shoulder, spoiling the drape of the fine linen.

Tomorrow, I thought, I shall discuss all this with Akiba once again. I shall prove to him beyond doubt what a fool he is to argue with the might of Rome. Only a night to clear my head of its fuddling aches, then I can set him straight about his idiot obstinacy. Surely, for old times' sake and friendship, I can persuade him to say enough in extenuation so that I may set him free to go back to his small, white, pleasant house in Lydda. Or I could let him "escape" as Ficus had let Saccus escape.

I was wrong. As I got out of my litter and entered the hall, the heel-slam and outthrust arm of a Roman messenger greeted me. He had come from Hadrian in Rome, a Praetorian courier, dusty and sleepless, on an urgent imperial errand. I ordered him the usual bath and proper quarters, with food and wine. Then I took up with slow dread the papyrus scroll with the personal seal of the emperor—the profiled face of his dead Antinoüs, exquisitely wrought. I slipped the threads and read the clear characters of the secretary's writing and the scrawled signature. I read again and again.

Brief and terrible it was. Akiba was condemned.

Within three days, he was to be executed in full sight of the garrison and populace of Caesarea, an example to all of the punishment for resisting Roman arms and law. Because of our known friendship, there was a special clause. If Akiba was not certified dead in the prescribed manner, within the time limit—or if, meanwhile, he escaped my custody—I was to be punished in the same fashion in the same place. Hadrian had remembered all, forgotten nothing.

The penalty was expressly stated. He was to be flayed alive, publicly, in the amphitheatre at dawn.

I was to confirm personally his punishment to the emperor. I was to be the official witness to the death of Akiba ben Joseph, the Jew.

CHAPTER 21

The strangeness of fate is not that it spins its threads. It is the artful source and the unpredictable way in which they are woven. Not merely as an image did the Greeks see Arachne, the spider, as fate drawing the lines of her webs from her inmost being and entangling all of us.

What might have happened if I had not been the lover of Domitilla, an informer for Domitian, and had not gone to Upper Germania and met Trajan? What if Quietus rather than Hadrian had won the race to Colonia? What of my more-than-chance meetings with Akiba, again and again across the whole breadth of the Roman empire? What of the mystery of Trajan's sudden death? What of Saccus, of Sarra, of Glaucus, of Mercellus and Frontinus, of all the others? What of Simeon and his dying? Indeed, what of a thousand events that make up a life like mine? And, at the last, what was the meaning of the hideous fortune which made me executioner and, most awful of all, witness of Akiba's death?

These, and many more, of the threads of chance will not be unraveled in my lifetime. Nor will their direction and meaning be revealed, leading—as I verily believe—into the future as far as man is allowed to conjecture. All events of the present have a mystic influence on what will happen, drawing the substance of their portents from that which has happened. We are old when we are born, young when we die: why else did Simeon die when he did and Akiba as he did?

"I ask you," Epictetus said to me once on Agrippa's hundred-columned portico in Rome, "where are you to escape death? Point me out the place, point me out the people, on which it does not light; point me out the charm against it. You and I cannot escape death; but can we not escape the fear of it?"

That is all very well, my old teacher, whose voice still wakes in my ears. For myself it is enough. But for others, innocent and sacred in the eyes of the gods themselves, it is not enough. I am not satisfied.

We have wisdom unutterable in our souls if only we can discover it. We are the heirs of worlds which have died intestate, like so many wealthy Roman knights and freedmen whose holdings have been seized by the emperor. We may find the good and true only if we supplicate it always as clients and have the courage to thrust ourselves forward and make our claims before the Emperor's agents. Our fault must lie in the stars, not ourselves—else so many that I have known, like the noble Akiba, would have never perished.

Enough: I must write what happened. Like the Macedonians of King Philip, I decided what must be done when I was drunk and reconsidered it when I was sober—and the results were the same. The edict of Hadrian stared me down even in the visions of the night. At last my feelings about the affair became remote and strange. A mood of cold sternness came over me and persisted. I took the decision which had already been made for me.

I visited Akiba in his cell. I found him sitting on his stool beside his mat of dirty straw, sipping his morning gruel. He looked up as I came in, and beamed.

"Blessed be God!" he ejaculated, wiping his beard.

"What in the name of the gods does that mean?" I demanded.

"He has created so many to be my servants. How much work had Adam to perform before he could taste a bit of food! Plowing, finding seed, sowing, waiting, reaping, gathering, threshing, winnowing, grinding, sifting, kneading and baking his bread—while I awake and find everything prepared. How many must arise at dawn, in how many places, to supply my needs!"

"Thank your god for what you can while you may," I said.

"He who eats but a little herb must recite the full grace," he replied.

"Have you been comfortable as the guest of Rome?" I inquired ironically.

"I have lived like this or worse, all my life," Akiba declared. "When I used to gather wood to stay alive, my neighbors were annoyed by the smoke. I told them it gave me a four-fold benefit: I studied by its light, was warmed by its heat, used it as a couch—and sold it for charcoal."

I restrained my wrath at this sort of talk in the face of execution. I determined to make Akiba confess his error in resisting Rome.

"I have listened to you speak of the Messiah in the synagogues," I said, "and it seems there are many different opinions, now that Simeon is dead."

"True," Akiba said. "Out of many thoughts comes the One Truth."

"None of you agrees on the identity of the Messiah."

"No."

"Simeon did not free your people, he did not set up his kingdom, he did not bring mercy and justice, the nations did not throng to fall at his feet. He died—a noble death, true, but he is dead and has left only destruction behind. Akiba, do you realize how many Romans have died?"

"Nor can I care."

"No matter, then. But you will care when I say that Simeon's beliefs killed nearly six hundred thousand Jews and laid waste more than a thousand cities."

Akiba groaned involuntarily. I kept silent and, after a moment, in an agonizedly small voice, Akiba said: "Perhaps it is not in the flesh but in the spirit that his kingdom will come."

"That is what the Christians claimed. You know what happened to their Messiah."

Slowly the pain in Akiba's face lessened and the lines of torture smoothed themselves. When he spoke again, he was almost radiant. "The life is in the Torah and the Torah is the Life," he said. "Faith is what we do not know but what we trust, what we see only in visions and believe to be."

"So said the Christian, Saul of Tarsus," I reminded him cruelly.

But Akiba's face did not dim. "Many men go with God," he replied with a vestige of his deep resonance. "The dream is not that of mine alone nor of the sages and prophets but of all who have worshipped truly and believed unto the end.

If you were one of us, Rufus, you would know this in your soul."

"But Simeon himself proved he was not the Messiah," I persisted.

Tormented beyond endurance, Akiba turned on me. "He lived and he died, poor boy!" he cried. "He was born a child, grew into a man, found his path to what he believed, and did his best to make it be true! Shall you or I or anyone else say as much when we come to our last moment?" He subsided, almost as if he were ashamed of his outburst. Then, in a calmer, more subdued tone, Akiba went on: "What do we mean by the Messiah? We Jews have always thought of him as divinely sent, with all-conquering powers, come to rule the earth and turn its heart toward God. But there is nothing so precise and exact in the sacred Scriptures. What if the Messiah is like us, only a man struggling and sinning and still yearning for purity and the light? Is his suffering not to count toward his holiness? What are suffering and despair and failure but the blackest sin; what is rising beyond and above it to the place Simeon has already achieved but being a Messiah to show us the way to eternal bliss?"

Stunned at this outpouring of words, I found nothing to say. Akiba addressed me almost reproachfully: "He was your son, Rufus, and mine as well. We share in his good or evil. In some part we are responsible for him and what he did before heaven and earth. Do you deny this?"

"No," I said slowly, "no, I cannot."

Akiba nodded. "Then judge the Messiah to be yourself," he said, "even as I beat my breast to let loose the spirit that will carry on what Simeon attempted."

"Why did you spare Hadrian?"

"For the same reason I tried to spare Simeon."

"But Simeon was a Jew."

"Was he?"

"I mean," I said, confused, "he had chosen to be a Jew."

"No man chooses to be a man by birth," Akiba said, "but that is all he is, neither Roman nor Jew. I spared him not because he was worthy but because he was human."

This was an impregnable old man, residing in a fortress I could not dream of storming no matter what hordes were at my command. "I am not one of your Messiahs, Akiba," I said, "and I thank the gods for it. I am a practical man." I waited for a reply but he merely continued to look steadily up into my face as if he wanted me to speak further.

"Quit this idiocy!" I shouted. I beat my knuckles against the damp stones of the cell wall. A guard came running. I waved him away. I leaned against the door, covering the peephole with my back.

"Has your god warned you of this, Akiba?" I said heavily, in a tightly controlled voice. "Tomorrow is the day of your death."

Akiba raised his head yet higher. His sunken eyes held mine. "Everything is foreseen, yet freedom of choice is given," he said mildly. "The world is judged by grace offered to each man but all judgment is according to good works. You must know, Rufus, that everything one does in this life is given in pledge. A net is spread for all living."

"This is Jewish foolishness," I said irritably. "It makes no sense."

"Not to you, possibly," Akiba returned equably, "but to those who share in the World-to-Come, there is meaning. Have you seen the shops of the merchants in the market-place?"

"Of course," I replied.

"The shop of the universe is open," Akiba said, his voice becoming rich and full. His face shaped itself into an expression of exaltation. "The Dealer gives credit. The ledger lies open, the Hand writes. Whosoever wishes to borrow may come and borrow, but the Collector regularly makes his round and exacts payment from each man, whether it pleases him or not."

I smiled. "Do you threaten me?" I asked.

Akiba paid not attention. "The judgment is a judgment of the truth," he said, "and everything is prepared for the feast."

"The feast?" I inquired bitterly. "Am I invited to your couch?"

"Dear friend," Akiba said softly. "I hope you will be my guest."

I straightened upright. "Why do you choose to do this to me?" I cried.

"God puts before us the two ways, the way of life and the way of death," Akiba said humbly. "The moment comes when no man can resist the summons."

"Then you have no choice!" I said angrily.

"My choice is His choice," Akiba murmured. His head sank upon his bosom. I stood over him for a moment, not knowing if he prayed or if he slept from exhaustion. Irresolute, I went out of his cell to my palace in the city. His words

359

resounded in my ears as those of Epictetus had once rung in the silence of my thoughts.

After a night of misery, I summoned up enough will to pronounce sentence upon Akiba. The charge was maiestas, treason against the emperor. It was the old catchall of criminals, first instituted in my youth by Domitian and now revived by Hadrian.

According to the law, Akiba was stripped of his shift in the prison. The troops were turned to and ranked according to regulations. The guards brought Akiba out, naked and shivering, into the midst of them in the parade ground in the great amphitheatre of Caesarea before sunrise. His wrists were lashed together. He was suspended, like an ox for slaughter, his withered feet dangling a cubit from the ground, in the midst of a tripod of stout poles.

The trumpets sounded. The drums rolled and stopped. I stood rigid and cold in the dress of my office, to the left of the tripod. To the right, licking their lips, stood the executioners. The pair were two soldiers condemned for the rape of a loose townswoman. They were mandated to mercy if they performed this act of torture and death which none other would touch.

In the eyes of the VI Ferrata and X Fretensis garrison drawn up in quadratum around us, there shone a cold glitter. They were interested but not absorbed. The spectacle involved duty but not their professional instincts. This, after all, was not the famous Bar Cocheba. Simeon had died months before on the battlefield. This was merely an old man, one of his numerous followers, brought to a dreadful penance.

But to the tiers of townspeople, ranged row on row like perching vultures—many of them Jews who had recanted their faith, the rest visitors to Judea or campfollowers of the legions—this wretched man symbolized the desolation and distress that had descended upon the country. Not a single true Jew had appeared to see the spectacle of their spiritual leader in ridicule and death. He was the scapegoat to be sacrificed for the dire fate that pursued them. Perhaps Hadrian, in his uncanny wisdom, had foreseen such a reaction. To them all this figure, no longer hidden under the coarse robe —ribs showing and belly sunken—represented the epitome of their wasted land.

Akiba dangled, turning slowly, silent, eyes closed. His skin rose, lumped with cold in the predawn. He hung there, pitiful before their pitilessness. I raised my trembling baton in the required signal. The executioners commenced.

Taking curved whetted knives, they drew the blades deeply, quickly, from neck to shoulder, down the thighs. They pried the flesh wide. Akiba gave a long hoarse cry. It shivered upward, the first and last he uttered.

To my stupefaction, the crowd about us, ranged beyond the silent troops, began to bay to drown out the sound. Then it burst into a storm of raucous laughter. The executioners hesitated, conferring for a moment. They concluded that the old man might struggle and prevent them from performing their task efficiently. They took strips of hide and bound his feet apart, spreadeagling them to the base of the widest part of the tripod.

They began with delicate strokes of the sharp-edged, hard-leather whips of rhinoceros hide from Africa, seasoned until they were stiff as iron. As the blood soaked and softened the edges, they exchanged these for whips of reed. These hissed more loudly and cut cleaner and deeper. The two had diabolical skill: they stripped the skin from Akiba's back as if it had been a suit of yellowed, wrinkled clothes, despite the way it clung to his old bones. So neatly did they do it that there was little blood after the first two knife-cuts. Only the oozing from that which lay beneath. Indeed, Akiba did not have too much blood in his whole body.

Behind the glimmer of the golden-helmeted lines of immobile soldiers, the crowd stopped its wild laughter. It commenced to shout in rage. It flung curses and abuse in a growing shower. It became a mass of spitting fury, drunken at the sight of what was happening before it. The people howled their madness in the vilest manner. They screamed the foulest epithets, not only against the victim but also against Roman justice. There were some who jeeringly shouted false encouragement to Akiba, bidding him hold out, that his god would rescue him from this punishment and that then they would themselves become Jews because of the miracle. Others loudly cried that much worse than a mere flaying should come to a Jew. Still others merely howled inarticulately. The whole made a terrifying discordant noise—as if the watchers were a tremendous pack of hounds on the trail of a kill. Again and again, a deep insistent growl sounded or a universal chant was repeated for minutes. The whole marble amphitheatre seemed to shake. It produced an effect on my ears as if I were pillowed on some obscene, intolerably soft flesh. The people rose and surged back and forth restlessly. I think that only the ranks of soldiers prevented them from rushing and tearing the thin frame of Akiba limb from limb by themselves. Only my own self-control kept me from ordering the legionaries to turn and massacre the crowd.

The flaying went on. Careful not to disturb any vital organs or to sever any large blood vessels, the two executioners hung small lead weights to the edge of the skin to pull it downward. They used the knives again, delicately. They cut beneath the growing flap to make sure of the direction in which it should go.

As they did, attendants stepped forth and waved palm branches above them to fend off the flies which appeared in hordes from nowhere. Despite this, clouds of the insects settled on the raw carcass of Akiba, masses of shimmering blue-black. The sawing buzz of their carrion search penetrated even the ululations of the mob behind my screen of soldiers.

Down the thighs, down the legs. Cut off at the ankles, it was flung down as it was torn off, a nauseous blanket. Before me lay a bloody similitude of skin of the man who sagged limply between the tripod poles.

Nothing could be heard above the roar of the spectators. Even the faces of the legion showed emotion. Two men in full armor pitched forward in a faint. I made a mental note, reserving them for discipline later. Other than that the lines of soldiers remained solid and unmoving; rushing down from the seats, almost upon their backs, the people stopped inches short, held back by the visible authority of Rome.

I gazed at Akiba with a feeling I had never before experienced. He was a stranger, a creature never seen in the world or even in dreams. A bolster of slowly-dripping red, forked like a gigantic root. He had no resemblance at all to a man, except for the skin of his face and his closed eyes. The tendons of his body—muscles, nerves, all his organs—lay bare to the pale light of morning. The flies settled everywhere to their feast, even into the black orifice that was his sagging mouth. Only his beard waggled in the rising breeze, a foul dangling thing.

I extended my baton firmly. The task was done. The flayers, well pleased with themselves, retreated grinning into the ranks. The crowd sent up roar after roar into the gray skies. Of relief, of applause, of frenzy—I did not know nor care. I motioned to the centurions.

"Drive them out!" I shouted, barely knowing what I com-

362

manded. Next moment the legion had broken ranks. The troops fell upon the people, striking shrewdly with clubs and scabbarded swords, with scientific preciseness at groin or armpit, at belly or face. They drove them, shrieking and dismayed, to the other end of the amphitheatre, struggling for the narrow exists, crushing each other heedlessly. I showed my teeth after them. The cruel show was over.

With dragging, slow steps, terrified of myself, of my audacity in approaching such a being, I went alone toward Akiba. I did not regard him any longer as a friend, as a human being. Any more than I thought of him as having been attached to the simulacrum of skin that lay on the sand behind the spattered tripod. I scarcely knew what I did there. Curiosity, shame, what was it that brought me? With a sweep of disgust, I knew I was no better than the lowest in the crowd which I had dispersed.

With weak fingers, I doffed my helmet. I waved off the flies with its plume. The insects angrily surrendered their prey for a moment. The eyes in the untouched face opened to look directly into mine. I felt the shock of recognition return: this was a man, a friend.

"Does a Jew like you truly have magic that he can suffer what you have suffered?" I whispered hoarsely.

Akiba made no reply. Only his sightless eyes probed into mine. The hair rose on the back of my neck. I felt frightened of nothing at all, a feeling alien to my nature. It angered me.

"Speak!" I said.

The great eyes widened, darkened with pain. But he seemed to perceive something behind me. I twisted my head. Nothing but the red streaks of the rising sun in the sky. I turned again to Akiba. I saw he had thrown back his head until the cords of his neck stood out raw and bloody, his beard soaked in his life-stuff.

I could not believe what I saw. This miserable man, from what depths had he summoned the strength and fortitude to resist the agony of the moment? He was not answering me, he was reciting the creed of his people, the condemned Shema: "Hear, O Israel, the Lord is our God, the Lord is One. And thou shalt love the Lord thy God with all thine heart, and with all thy soul, and with all thy might."

His voice died away. His ghastly racked body hung from the tripod, a shambles of blood and entrails and sinews, horrible beyond belief.

"Die, Akiba!" I cried frantically. I drew my own sword,

regardless of law, to put him out of his torture. As I did, the bleeding mass which had been Akiba seemed to increase in weight. So much so that the poles of the tripod swayed. His feet touched the drenched sand.

The sky whirled dizzily about me as I fell into the blackness and madness which afflicted me justly—but not before I had heard the last words of Akiba.

From a great distance I heard him shout. "Our God is one God!" he cried. Then all was blotted out.

I had done that which no Roman witness nor officer may do without disgrace. I had fainted in my tracks.

Six weeks later, I found myself barely alive upon my couch in my sleeping chamber at Caesarea. I could remember nothing of what had passed in that time. Physicians, summoned by the sublegate, had not agreed upon my malady, but they had allowed my slaves to force food and drink down my throat while avoiding my staring crazed eyes. From time to time I had fallen into fits of raving. Slaves had been employed to hold me down for hours, an ivory rod in my mouth to prevent me from biting off my tongue.

Nevertheless, despite everything they knew, I grew weaker and weaker. At the end, I became so emaciated as to be at the point of dissolution. What summoned me back to life, I do not know. I seem to recall a voice speaking soothingly in my ear: "It is not yet time for you to leave your post; wait, as a soldier, for the signal of dismissal."

When I regained consciousness and knew where I was, I had a high fever. For this I underwent sweatings and light purgatives. But they feared for my life for many more days. Those who had heard my ravings reported to me that my gibberings were more Hebrew than Latin. I did not credit them. As soon as I was on my feet and could write, I applied for retirement. In spite of my disgrace, the illustrious emperor Hadrian was gracious enough to grant it without penalty of fortune or rank.

Sometimes still, at night, against the thin flesh of my eyelids, the spectre of Akiba's death will visit me. I have no recourse except to rise and light the lamps and pace my chamber until the nightmare passes. Not for me is the sword of Frontinus jammed into the chink of the wall, pointed at my own breast, nor the easy ways of poison or opened veins in the bath. Akiba would not want me to take revenge upon myself in this fashion. But then, he is a Jew and he can afford to be forgiving. I am a Roman.

Philosophy is my only staff to help me through what remains to me of the pilgrimage of existence. The end of Akiba, my friend, was in the fullness of time in his own land. Unlike myself and those who follow the rootless legions of Rome—in spite of his agony—he died happy. Happy where he was born, his long life accomplished, his faith blinding in the light of its certainty. Such will not be my fate. Exiled by age and circumstance, I must find comfort in thought.

Since each of us must answer the great riddle propounded to us, as young Simeon used to answer me—the riddle of his life—I often ask myself why Akiba died when I have lived on. Strangely enough, I find answers in the doctrines of Epictetus. Even more strangely, these agree with the conclusions of the Jews and Christians.

In the case of the Christians, they claim that their Jesus came to save the world from its sins. When he was crucified as a common criminal, this—though it shocked his followers—created the conviction that his mission had been only delayed. He would save the world later. Naturally, now, they talk about their Jesus saving the world of the spirit rather than that of substance. What else can they do?

The Jews, on the other hand, flatly reject this Jesus as their Messiah. For the Christians, such a one has already come and gone; for the Jews, he is merely around the corner of the millennium. But while the Jews wait and maintain the status quo in hopes of a conqueror of all, the Christians have sense enough to attempt to arrange the world-as-it-is to their satisfaction. Even now they are making efforts to organize on the pattern of the hierarchy we Romans established. It is more than a little amusing to reflect that the command chart of their religion is exactly that of our empire—and that their tolerance of others, which they have always preached, is far less than ours, though we have never preached it.

I believe that, in the end, neither the Christians nor the Jews shall prevail. Rather, I hope for a world of sanity, common sense, and justice. I return to Epictetus and a last conversation I had with him the year previous to the execution of Flavius. I had bemoaned my disreputable post and tried to excuse myself. "In days like these," I said gloomily, "it is necessary to yield to the most powerful."

"To make yourself like the many, do you mean?" demanded Epictetus.

"What else? How can one avoid it?"

"Priscus Helvidius avoided it. When Vespasian himself told him not to come into the Senate, he replied: 'You can forbid me to be a senator, but as long as I am, I must come in.'"

"But Vespasian did not yield."

"He said: 'Come in, then, but remain silent.'"

"But what came of it?" I queried.

"Priscus said: 'Question me not and I will be silent.' Vespasian, irritated in his majesty, replied: 'But I am bound as emperor to ask your opinion.' Priscus responded: 'As a man, I am bound to say what I think is right.'"

"An excellent answer!" I said enthusiastically.

"Perhaps," Epictetus replied, "but Vespasian said: 'If you say what displeases me, I shall kill you.' To this, Priscus calmly answered: 'When did I ever say I was immortal? Each of us must do his part; it is yours to kill, mine to die without fear.'"

"What good then did it all do, Priscus being but one man?" I asked plaintively.

"The same good that purple does for a garment: it makes it outstanding, an example that noble men may follow."

I became sunk in thought as my teacher waited, scribbling in the dust with his stick. I roused myself. "How, good Epictetus," I asked him, "may a man discover what suits his character?"

"When power comes to you, consciousness also of its nobility will come to you. Recognize this. Learn to beware of the price at which you sell your will. If you do nothing else, do not sell yourself cheaply."

Well, perhaps I have sold my life cheaply. It may be that I have been like one of those cuts of flyblown meat on the counters of the Suburra that I held my nose at and passed by. But who put me up for sale, and who set the price? I see behind me the causes flow one into another. I am unable to distinguish the effects, not even the last effect. Things happened, that is all. I have existed and, like every man—even Epictetus—I have sold myself for a price. Whether I was cheap or dear, let someone else answer.

When one is old, the doubts of the past flagellate the memory. Were events really what they seemed, or was a power moving behind the scenes of life, shaking and prompting, the way that Pontus used to do for the mimes of Domitian? Do we really take part in what happens or are we pawns in a game of the gods? Or is it the work of humans who have no pity either on themselves or others and therefore become gods themselves, as immobile and detached as stone or brass?

I say this only because, when I reflect, I wonder if Hadrian assigned me to the post of governor of Judea as a punishment rather than as a reward. He said nothing of my association with Quietus, though he knew; he has no illusions about my opinion of him. Did he know of Simeon (perhaps Domitilla in one of her wild orgies of the flesh told him) and set me to be his assassin? Certainly he knew of Akiba. Even while I pleaded the case of the Jews before Trajan, his subtle mind may have been plotting in the future.

Such speculations are useless. They belie the nature I have cultivated: the will to be and to be nothing else. One small item is important to such a man who prides himself on what he is. Out of all this rubbish of philosophy—Greek, Jewish, Christian—what is left for a Roman? We disdain to be otherwise than patient in power, biding our time to act, enduring the results for good or evil or whatever else the scales weigh out. We deal only with the world that is, not that which might be; we respect what gods we know and are cautious about the others. Is there not an ancient altar on the Palatine Hill dedicated to the Unknown God?

Akiba, on the contrary, wanted to save the world of things unseen, to restore the Jews not only in this world but in the next—and I believe he was the only one who might have done it. Like the Christus, he was slain by the necessities of Rome; unlike the followers of the Nazarene, I cannot be confident that he will rise again to lead his people to greater glories and bend the neck of all peoples under a more beneficent yoke than that of Rome. Both died at the hands of others than their own race; both were persecuted and despised in their day; both were adored and misunderstood and reviled. And both sold their lives to the future very dearly because they recognized the nobility of their power.

All these represent symbols which I am too tired to unravel or understand. The difference for Akiba, I suppose, is that he had no cure for the ills of the world. He did not require people to believe in him as a god and, as a matter of fact, derided those who did. Epictetus did not care either way what others thought, and there he and I are one.

That part of my life is gone like a season of the year. I sit here in Gaul and summon slaves, dismiss visitors, eat and drink and observe, spend my daily hours with tablets and stylus. I watch the leaves changing color this autumn with a strange new sensation. It is one I have never had before, one not entirely unpleasant. I sit suddenly transfixed, as if by a sword, by the conviction that I shall not see the next autumn.

Here I sit at the end of life, drinking bitter lees. I am lonely. Not for the vanished Sarra, not even for the brash boy Simeon whom I loved, nor for such friends as Ficus, nor for all the noble souls I have known. No: I sit and am lonely for a lanky, gaunt, bald old Jew to come to me and whisper his assurances of eternity and compassion to come. This is a queer mood for a Roman veteran who has sworn by so many other gods. I am sometimes ashamed of myself for it; but, will it or not, it comes back to me unbidden.

The wind passes through the golden shade of twilight. The shadows gather and murmur. The moon rises and shines just above the bluff like a light in a tower. Voices whisper to me, but they do not answer when I speak. Delectable visions pass, but they do not pause at my side. The wine cup stands empty. The warmth of the days is gone, and the fire no longer heats my hide as it used to do.

Akiba, Akiba! Beckon to me but once, white shade in the darkness of the woods across the lake as you did in the wilds of Germania! I will gladly come with you, as an old comrade, to whatever curious land in which your soul dwells. I have traveled so far and seen so many strange sights that new ones, whatsoever they be, will be welcome with you as a guide.

No sign is given. Slowly the tide of moonlight rises in my chamber as I lie upon my couch; slowly my heart sinks to peace. It may be that I shall stay here on the next incursion of the barbarians, dismissing my slaves to go south. I shall welcome the wild Germans, a ridiculous figure that they will honor, in superstition, as a priest or guardian spirit of my villa. But they will find that I have no powers of magic or divination and, at last, when they are tired of my babblings, they will kill me as children destroy a bauble of which they weary—as Simeon, laughing, used to crush a toy.

In my memory is a mingling of teachings. Of Epictetus: "Suppose the judge says, 'I will judge you to be a wrong-doer'; you reply, 'May all go well with you! I did my part, and it is for you to see that you do yours: for the judge's part, no less than mine, do not forget, has its own danger.'" Of the Christians: "'Forgive them, for they know not what they do.'" And there is, too, the memory of the unspoken, of the last tender look from the eyes of Akiba, watching me as his spirit fled.

Old friend, old friend: I have done my duty in this life as best I know how, as a pledged Roman and as a man. If it was evil, judge and condemn me; if it was what was fated for my life, judge and forgive me. I lie here in darkness with the many gods aloof. You lie there in far-off Judea, in the growing dawn, the time (as you told me so often) of the recitation of your Shema, which says your god is one.

Whichever is true, putting all the gods aside, it is enough for me to say we were friends. That we were men who met by chance in this vast desert of existence called life and who were fated to be bodies apart and souls together. That is all that can be said, and it is enough for us both, is it not?

THE END

NOTE

Two easily traced but not often recognized events in the history of the first century after Christ marked it as a historical watershed.

The first was the remarkable crystallization of pure genius in the government of the Roman Empire. It assumed its most definite form under Trajan and its superb, if more corrupt, faceting under Hadrian. The second was the beginning of the revised expression of the Judaic faith. While the Jews held to their identical beliefs, they exhibited an extraordinary series of liberal practices in order to preserve their essence.

Working both for and against these, of course, a most powerful influence, was the more-publicized Christianity. This amalgam of spiritual and secular power achieved its eminence by the fact that it shared the most popular and adaptable characteristics of both the Empire command and the Mosaic credo. It adopted the political hierarchy of the Empire; it arrogated to itself the most attractive features of Judaism, as interpreted by Jesus Christ. Its rituals even came to include many features adapted from such pagan religions as the worship of Mithra and Isis.

In sum, Christianity gradually and inevitably grew to be the synthesis of religious apologia that we know today. Constructed on a largely utilitarian foundation with a sincerely idealistic facade—one of the most appealing structures known to man—it attacked directly the psychological underpinnings of the world. It persevered with a sure instinct for the spiritual jugular. It did not fret too much about the facts: the literally exact translation of the word *propaganda* as "church nonsense" hits very near the truth.

Nevertheless, Christianity supplied an essential spiritual and organizational need. As the confluence of these two flows of thought, Roman and Jewish, it was also swelled by a series of masterful reworkings of Greek philosophy, grand military strategy, and pagan ceremonies. Its two major religious elements were reconciled by the genius of time. The soul of the Judaic faith was inflexible, exclusive, detailed in observance, exact in reward and punishment; the Christian belief was flexible, sociable, and all-inclusive. The Roman psyche was unrelievedly worldly, practical, and pessimistic; that of the Christians was ecstatic, spiritually attuned, and infinitely optimistic.

It is no wonder, then, that the meld known as Christianity triumphed. In the ironic phrase of the eighteenth-century historian Edward Gibbon: "It has been remarked (by Hegisippus) with more ingenuity than truth, that the virgin purity of the church was never violated by schism or heresy before the reign of Trajan or Hadrian, about one hundred years after the death of Christ. We may observe with much more propriety that, during that period, the disciples of the Messiah were indulged in a freer latitude both of faith and practice, than has ever been allowed in succeeding ages." Gibbon observes pointedly (repeating Eusebius, an early Christian bishop of Greek extraction) that while the heads of other Christian churches throughout the Roman world were converts from all religions and races, the first fifteen bishops of Jerusalem—the fountainhead of Christian authority—were all circumcised Jews.

The millstones of the Romans and Jews, grinding against each other for a century, produced the exceedingly fine grain of organized Christianity: adulterated by the grit of either side, perhaps, but highly acceptable to the masses of despairing people that looked upon the world as chaos after the collapse of the Empire. The Jews, whose own world had largely collapsed with the destruction of their second temple in A.D. 70, looked grimly in another direction.

But in this century of seemingly destructive conflict there were a number of non-Christian men of great good will who refused either to deny or despair. Instead they worked on toward goals in an unseen but hoped-for future. Akiba ben Joseph was one of them, on the Jewish side; on the other, the Roman Sextus Rufus Teneius.

The story of Teneius must be largely apocryphal. He certainly existed. It is known that he was the friend and executioner of Akiba. He was the governor of Judea who did his distasteful duty and thereafter fades from record. There is relatively little more known about Akiba. Born just before the middle of the first century, he died A.D. 134. He married a wife, Rachel, who bore him at least two children. Peasant until forty, he went to school and became the foremost expounder of the "new" version of Judaism. He was a lanky, earthy man of great perception who espoused the cause of the city plebeians and loved hairsplitting arguments. His appearance was tall, bald, and bearded. He visited Rome in 95, with three other rabbis, to plead for the Jews; but he also advocated submission to the Empire. He took an active part in the rebellion of Simeon bar Cocheba, A.D. 132, and was imprisoned afterward for continuing to teach his faith. He probably died in prison, though legend has him flayed alive by Teneius.

Akiba and his story have escaped the facts. His thought and leadership were to become the very heart of Judaism for more than a thousand years (he is quoted in the Talmud 261 times, more than any other Jewish sage). His interpretations, with the force of tradition behind them, still dominate the synagogue as much as his arguments used to convince the majority at Jabneh. More than any single man, Akiba established the reputation of the rabbinate, as well as the worth of the Talmud, as next to the Torah itself.

He admired Rome. He was quick to adopt many of its tenets to his own faith. He did not see the destruction of the second Temple as the end of his religion but rather as the judgment of his God which commanded a fresh start to be made. He admired order and abhorred confusion. Still, in the end, he turned away from Rome and became the aged armor-bearer of the revolutionary leader, Simeon bar Cocheba himself.

The reasons for this turnabout cannot be sought in his history but only in the imagination. As "the Jew of Rome," as he was occasionally and contemptuously called by his enemies, Akiba never deserted for a moment his conviction that his faith and its perpetuation were all that mattered. Any means toward this end, as long as the means did not contravene the whole, was his to employ. It is worth noting that Josephus, the eminent Jewish general and historian, felt exactly the same way—in an activist rather than a philosophic fashion. And, in the long view of nineteen centuries, both have been justified of their works.

One theme dominates *The Soldier and the Sage*. It is as old as man, as fresh as his hopes. It is, simply: How shall a good man live in an evil world?

This question, pertinent as it is now, was even more relevant to the age comprised in the first century after Christ. It is fitting that the Christ-figure should center it; it is equally significant that the temporal rulers of that age included one of the worst (Domitian) and one of the best (Trajan). The era represents the golden heights of imperial Rome—already admired by the Greeks, Jews, and—to a lesser degree—the Christians. The substantive mass gods were being replaced by the subjective personal god: the twilight of the gods and the dawn of God. Neither was to make his triumph unconditional. The rigid laws of the Jews were relaxed; the pagan customs were assimilated by the Christians; and both became organized in the light of the impressive common sense of the Romans.

In a real way, Akiba was the great man of this period. He was never a doctrinaire; in fact, he destroyed more than he created. He sensed his mission as the maintenance of the Jewish faith—adjusted as it was to conditions after the fall of the second Temple. He was an exponent of individual religion expressed in the smallest feasible groups, rather than celebration in the mass. This he would, and did, give his life for.

In all else, Akiba was a compromiser and appeaser. He believed in cooperating with the civil elements; he preached obedience to Rome. He was willing to yield everything but the quintessential core of his religion; able to endure anything as long as that core was preserved intact. He was often wise, sometimes foolish; using his own peculiar logic with an intent far beyond the nonsense of ceremony. He was a man of the people—the farm people by birth, the city people by adoption. He was an enemy of sham, a friend of the new wedded to the old. He was, in a word, a visionary moderate.

Though his phrases run through the Talmud, picturing a kindly, humorous, quizzical person, his works—if he wrote at all—have perished. There are almost no direct quotations in spite of the hundreds of attributions. Akiba survives in the minds and tongues of his friends and disciples. Like most abiding religious teachers, he proposed to talk rather than transcribe his thoughts. In this he was right: conviction requires the witness of a personality.

Anyone who cares may read the Talmud and discover that Akiba was a prophet and a seer. But what is important here is Akiba in the flesh. Those who seek him out in human fact will find he was holy and profane, intelligent and stupid, joyous and sad, comic and tragic. Revelation was never vouchsafed him. His evidence of the World-to-Come was pure faith, so clear and hard that it scored other, softer faiths like a diamond.

Akiba was never a saint. By his own confession, he sinned. But he was always capable of passion and pity; of comprehending the souls of the lowest and the highest. It is too bad that Christ died before Akiba was born: what pure delight a debate between the two would have been for both! But it is entirely possible that Paul and Akiba met and exchanged opinions in some obscure synagogue, most possibly (chronologically) in Rome. They were both orthodox Jews until their martyr-deaths; the difference between them was only that Paul believed Christ to be the Messiah for Jew and Gentile while Akiba deferred his conviction until the coming of Bar Cocheba. As it turned out, Akiba was wrong. The evidence on the side of Paul is not yet complete.

At any rate, he who seeks Akiba as the spokesman for the new Jew will not find him here. Instead, it is hoped that he will find Akiba himself. As commanding as a Roman, as shrewd as a Greek, as inquisitive as himself, he partakes of all their characteristics. If any man remains in the historical memories of that period as typical of the age it is not Hadrian, nor Epictetus, nor Paul—it is the indefatigable Akiba on his endless journeys, in his unfinished disputations, with his eternal doubts and hopes, clinging to what was—for him—the one Truth.

Akiba was that proud and wretched thing which is the same in every age of earth—an honest man.

—RICHARD G. HUBLER

Ojai, California
September, 1965